THE ASSASSIN

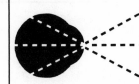 This Large Print Book carries the
Seal of Approval of N.A.V.H.

THE ASSASSIN

STEPHEN COONTS

THORNDIKE PRESS
A part of Gale, Cengage Learning

GALE
CENGAGE Learning

Detroit • New York • San Francisco • New Haven, Conn • Waterville, Maine • London

GALE
CENGAGE Learning™

Copyright © 2008 by Stephen Coonts.
Thorndike Press, a part of Gale, Cengage Learning.

ALL RIGHTS RESERVED
This is a work of fiction. All of the characters, organizations, and events portrayed in this novel are either products of the author's imagination or are used fictitiously.
Thorndike Press® Large Print Core.
The text of this Large Print edition is unabridged.
Other aspects of the book may vary from the original edition.
Set in 16 pt. Plantin.
Printed on permanent paper.

LIBRARY OF CONGRESS CATALOGING-IN-PUBLICATION DATA

Coonts, Stephen, 1946–
    The assassin / by Stephen Coonts.
     p. cm.
    ISBN-13: 978-0-7862-9491-6 (hardcover : alk. paper)
    ISBN-10: 0-7862-9491-4 (hardcover : alk. paper)
    1. Carmellini, Tommy (Fictitious character)—Fiction.
2. Grafton, Jake (Fictitious character)--Fiction. 3. Qaida
(Organization)—Fiction. 4. Intelligence officers—Fiction.
5. Undercover operations—Fiction. 6. Large type books. I. Title.
PS3553.O5796A93 2008b
813'.54—dc22   2008020103

Published in 2008 in arrangement with St. Martin's Press, LLC.

Printed in the United States of America
1 2 3 4 5 6 7 12 11 10 09 08

This book is dedicated to all the men and women around the world who are fighting the war on terror.

ACKNOWLEDGMENTS

While the author was working on the manuscript for this novel, Chase Brandon of the CIA arranged a tour of the agency's Langley facilities for a handful of writers, including this one. Seeing the physical layout of the facilities and having short chats with various CIA employees, including Mr. Brandon, was helpful to the creative process. The look of the buildings is described at various places in the tale. Still, it needs to be said again that Jake Grafton, Tommy Carmellini and the numerous CIA employees whom you will meet in the author's tales are pure fiction, and that the words the author puts in their mouths are viewpoints necessary to tell this tale.

As usual, the author is deeply indebted to his wife, Deborah Coonts, for her assistance in plotting this novel, and for her patience.

PROLOGUE

October — Iraq

"Ragheads dragged the driver out of the vehicle and took him away," the sergeant told the lieutenant, who was sitting in a Humvee. "They shot the woman in the car. She's still in it. Iraqi grunt says she's alive but the assholes put a bomb in the car. They're using her as cheese in the trap."

"Shit," said the lieutenant and rubbed the stubble on his chin.

The day was hot, and the chatter of automatic weapons firing bursts was the musical background. The column of vehicles had ground to a halt in a cloud of dust, and since there was no wind, the dust sifted softly down, blanketing equipment and men and making breathing difficult.

U.S. Navy Petty Officer Third Class Owen Winchester moved closer to the lead vehicle so that he could hear the lieutenant and sergeant better.

He could see the back end of an old sedan with faded, peeling paint sitting motionless alongside the road about fifty yards ahead. Three Marines and three Iraqi soldiers were huddled in an irrigation ditch fifty feet to the right of the road. On the left was a block of houses.

"Let me go take a look," Winchester said to the lieutenant.

"Listen, doc," the sergeant said, glancing at Winchester. "The ragheads would love to do you same as they would us."

"I want to take a look," Winchester insisted. "If she can be saved . . ." He left it hanging there as distant small-arms fire rattled randomly.

The place was a sun-baked hellhole; it made Juarez look like Paris on the Rio Bravo. The tragedy was that real humans tried to live here . . . and were murdered here by rats with guns who wanted to rule the dungheap in the name of a vengeful, merciless god, one who demanded human sacrifice as a ticket to Paradise.

The lieutenant had been in Iraq for six months and was approaching burnout. The wanton, savage cruelty of the true believers no longer appalled him — he accepted it, just as he did the heat and dirt and human misery he saw everywhere he looked. He forced himself to think about the situation. A woman. Shot. She would probably die unless something was done. So what? *No, no, don't think like that,* he thought. *That's the way they think, which is why the Devil lives here.* After a few seconds, he said, "Okay. Take a look. And watch your ass."

The sergeant didn't say another word, merely began trotting ahead in that bent-over combat trot of soldiers the world over. With his first-aid bag over his shoulder, Winchester followed.

They flopped into the irrigation ditch directly opposite the car, where they could see into the passenger compartment. There was a woman in there, all right, slumped over. She wasn't wearing a head scarf. They could see her dark hair.

Fifteen feet from them was the rotting carcass of a dog. In this heat, the stench was awe-inspiring.

An Iraqi soldier joined them. "She has been shot," he said in heavily accented English. "Stomach. I get close, see her and bomb."

"How are they going to detonate it, you think?" Winchester asked, looking around, trying to spot the triggerman. He saw no one but the Iraqi soldiers and Marines lying on their stomachs in the irrigation ditch, away from the dog. The mud-walled and brick buildings across the way looked empty, abandoned, their windows blank and dark.

"Cell phone, most likely," the sergeant said sourly. "From somewhere over there, in one of those apartments. Or a garage door opener."

"Saving lives is my job," the corpsman said. "I want to take a look."

"You're an idiot."

"Probably." Winchester grinned. He had a good grin.

"Jesus! Don't do nothin' stupid."

With that admonition ringing in his ears, Winchester ditched the first-aid bag and trotted toward the car. From ten feet away he could see the woman's head slumped over, see that the door was ajar. He closed to five feet.

She wasn't wearing a seat belt, and a bomb was lying on the driver's seat. Looked like four sticks of dynamite, fused, with a black box taped to the bundle. The woman moved her head slightly, and he heard a low moan.

Winchester ran back to the ditch, holding his helmet in place, and flopped down beside the sergeant.

"There's a bomb on the driver's seat," he told the sergeant, whose name was Joe Martinez. "And she's still alive. I think I can get her out of there before they blow it. Takes time to dial a phone, time for the network to make the phone you called ring. Might be enough time."

"Might be just enough to kill you, you silly son of a bitch."

"The door is ajar and she isn't wearing a seat belt. I can do this. Open the door and grab her and run like hell."

"You're an idiot," Sergeant Martinez repeated.

"Would you try it if she was your sister?"

"She ain't my sister," the sergeant said with feeling as he scanned the buildings across the road. "What do they say? No good deed goes unpunished?"

"I will go," the Iraqi soldier said. He laid his weapon on the edge of the ditch, began taking off his web belt. "Two men, one on each arm."

"She's *my* sister, Joe," Owen Winchester said to Martinez. He grinned again, broadly.

The sergeant watched as Winchester and the Iraqi soldier took off all their gear and their helmets, so they could run faster.

"You fuckin' swabbie! You got balls as big as pumpkins. How do you carry them around?" Martinez laid down his rifle, took off his web belt and tossed his helmet beside

the rifle. "I'll get the door. You two get her."
He took a deep breath and exhaled explosively. "Okay, on three. One, two, threeeee!"

They vaulted from the ditch and sprinted toward the car. The sergeant jerked the door open. The other two men reached in, Winchester grabbing one arm and the Iraqi the other, and pulled the wounded woman from the car, then hooked an arm under each armpit. Joe Martinez picked up her feet, and they began to run.

They were ten feet from the car when the bomb exploded.

CHAPTER ONE

Washington, D.C.

The limo pulled up to the front door of the Hay-Adams Hotel after a short jaunt across Lafayette Park. A Secret Service agent standing there opened the passenger door. The president got out and walked into the hotel, accompanied by two agents. He didn't look right or left, just walked straight across the lobby to the elevators and went into the first one. One agent joined him. Together they rode in silence to the fourth floor. Another Secret Service man was standing there by the elevators when the door opened.

At the end of the hallway, the agent with the president rapped on the door. When it opened, the president went in. The agent stayed outside in the hallway.

"Thanks for coming," the man who greeted the president said. He was in his early fifties, with graying hair and a square chin, still trim and fit and apparently as vigorous as he had been when he played cornerback for Boston College.

"Sorry about your son, Hunt," the president said. He held on to the other man's hand, grasping it with both of his own. The president had had plenty of practice at this and knew damn well how to do it.

Huntington Winchester nodded, extracted his hand from the president's grasp, and led the way to a portable bar. "I know you don't drink, but I'm having one. You want a Coke or something?"

"Club soda with a twist."

With the drinks in hand, the two men sat in easy chairs near the window. The White House was visible through the bare treetops of Lafayette Park.

Winchester took a sip of whiskey, then spoke: "The Marines tell me Owen, a sergeant named Martinez, and an Iraqi soldier named Abdul Something tried to pull a wounded Iraqi woman from a car with a bomb in it. They knew it was there and tried to rescue her anyway. Martinez said it was Owen's idea, and I believe it. That was Owen; that was the way he thought. If there was a way, he would have tried it.

"The bomb exploded when they were only

a few feet from the car. Killed Owen instantly, mangled Martinez's arm. The Iraqi soldier escaped with only a concussion. The woman they were trying to rescue died in the helicopter that took her and Martinez to the hospital."

The president didn't say anything. Sometimes there isn't anything to say.

Winchester took another pull on his drink, which looked like Scotch or bourbon. Then he said, "They're trying to save Martinez's arm. He may lose it."

After a while, Winchester added, "You know the amazing thing? I don't personally know anybody else who has a son or daughter in the military. None of the people on my staff, none of my executives, none of our friends, none of the people at my clubs, no one."

The president sipped at his club soda.

"Kids from our socioeconomic group aren't supposed to join the military," Winchester continued. "They never think of it, and if they do, their parents demand that they change their minds. And having a draft wouldn't change that. I was too young for Vietnam, but all the older men I know managed to avoid the draft back then some way or other, or if they did get drafted, they wound up on a general's staff in Europe or

Tokyo. Caught the clap three or four times and had a marvelous time. Not one of them actually went to Vietnam and risked his precious ass."

The president shifted uncomfortably in his chair. He was old enough for Vietnam, yet somehow ended up in the National Guard, which in those days rarely got called up for active service overseas. Today, in the absence of the tens of thousands of young men a military draft would bring in, the National Guard and reserves were getting called up for extended active duty in Iraq and Afghanistan.

Just how he managed to land that Guard billet when the waiting list had hundreds of names on it was a question that he had asked his father, who merely shrugged. "I didn't call anyone," his father the senator had said, and the president had believed him. The truth was the senator didn't have to call — his influential friends would take it upon themselves to ensure that the senator's son didn't have to join the common herd in the Army and risk life and limb in combat. And no doubt that is what happened. That's the way it has always worked in America for the scions of wealth and privilege.

Of course, the president had known all

that even then. The question to his father was the sop to his conscience. He didn't want to go to Vietnam — no one he knew did — and since he was his father's son, he didn't have to. Being mortal clay, he had let it go at that. Still, the memory of that little compromise with fate wasn't anything to be proud of.

"Owen enlisted in the Naval Reserve three years ago," Winchester continued, "after his sophomore year in college. He was in premed, knew he wanted to be a doctor, help people. Signed up to be a corpsman. Took all the training, did the drills on weekends, all of it, and then four months ago his unit was called up and sent to Iraq. He was in his first year of Harvard Medical School.

"His mother didn't want him to join the military three years ago, and she threw a fit when his unit was called up. Demanded that I pull strings — call you and our senators and Admiral Adams." Adams was the chief of naval operations. "Yeah, I know Adams, too. We've bird hunted in South Dakota together."

He sighed and took another slug of his liquor. "I refused. Told her this was Owen's choice, and I was proud of him. The truth was that if I had pulled strings and denied

19

him his opportunity to serve, an opportunity he sought, he would have felt betrayed. I couldn't do that to him." He took a deep breath, exhaled slowly.

"When the news came last week that he was dead, Ellen told me she was divorcing me. She's moved out, hired a lawyer. The process servers are probably looking for me right now."

"I'm sorry, Hunt," the president said. He put the club soda on the stand beside the chair; he didn't want any more of it.

"Owen was our only child. God fucking damn!" Winchester finished his drink. "So here I sit, dumping all this shit on you, as if you weren't carrying enough of a load as it is."

"You're my friend, Hunt. Have been for twenty years."

"You have a lot of friends," Huntington Winchester said. He went to the bar and poured himself another, came back and resumed his seat. He eyed the president carefully.

"The real problem is that people in my class view the war on terror as a nuisance, something that doesn't really affect us. Blue-collar kids join the military and risk their lives and limbs; not *our* kids, who are getting first-class educations and going to med school, or law school, or getting a finance degree and joining some Wall Street firm. We sit in our big houses with maids and chauffeurs and modern art collections and all the rest of it, reading in the newspapers about suicide bombers murdering people and watching the mayhem on television. We think it is someone else's fight. It isn't. That's what Owen understood. It's *our* fight."

"We are fighting the terrorists, Hunt," the president said. "The best way we know how. Is it going well? Depends on whom you ask. But we're doing our best. I assure you of that."

Winchester wasn't buying. "Our enemies are not the thugs who kidnapped that man from that car in Iraq, murdered Owen and that woman. Our real enemies are the people who put them up to it — the imams who preach hate, who are defending a fossilized religion that has been unable to come to grips with thirteen centuries of change, and the people who are financing terrorism, the scum who enjoy seeing other people suffer or who want to buy peace for themselves. *Those* people are the enemy."

He picked up the daily paper, which was lying on the couch. "Look at this — another ignorant, illiterate holy man hiding in

21

Pakistan has exhorted the faithful to attack Americans, anywhere they can be found." He tossed the paper across the room. "Car bombs in London, shaped charges in Iraq, nuclear threats from Iran . . . 'Death to America!' "

"Trying to silence individual voices won't do much good, Owen. The war will be won when Muslims classify these people as lunatics and ignore them."

"By God, those bastards want a fight," Winchester snarled. "We should give them one. How many innocent people have to die to satisfy these fanatics' thirst for blood before that wonderful day comes?"

The president didn't reply. He glanced at Winchester's drink, wishing he could have a sip of it.

"*I* have some friends," Winchester continued, staring at the president's face, "some of them Americans, the rest Europeans. We've talked about this for years, about the fact that we owe civilization more than paying taxes and tut-tutting at the fucking golf club."

"You've given your only son, Hunt. Sounds to me as if you've put more than your share into the collection plate."

"My friends and I are businessmen, bankers and shippers. The thought occurred to us that locked somewhere in the records of our daily businesses are the money trails that terrorists leave behind whenever they move money or material across borders. We do business worldwide. We can help find the people who are moving the money, and behind them, the people who are financing the terrorists. From there we can work backward to the preachers of hate who are firing up the fools."

"Who are your friends?" the president asked.

Winchester gave him names and companies.

"And after you identify these people?" the president asked.

"We'll put up the money to finance assassination squads to kill them."

The president didn't say a word. He didn't really want to hear this. Any of it.

"I want your help," Winchester continued, his eyes holding the president's. "We have money, enough to fund an army, and we're willing to spend it. But we need some help data-mining our records. It's all there if we can just dig it out. And we need some hard men who can pull the trigger and thrust in the knife. I want you to find the people who can help us."

"If this ever comes out," the president said

frankly, "the least that can happen is your companies get a black eye for violating privacy statutes. Customers may sue —"

"Damn them!" Winchester exclaimed. "Terrorists have no privacy rights, and everybody else can just go hang."

"Oh, there's more," the president added. "If you do anything beyond giving information to the government, you'll probably go to prison. Conspiracy to commit murder, murder for hire, money laundering — maybe they'll even throw in a terrorism charge."

Huntington Winchester didn't say a word.

The president rose and went to the window. He stood there with his arms crossed looking at the war protesters in Lafayette Park, at the trees, at the top of the White House and the Washington Monument beyond. He thought about the last few years, about the politicians and promises and coffins and kids brought back on gurneys, maimed for life.

Finally he turned and faced Winchester. "I'll think about it."

Winchester wanted more of a commitment than that, but he held his tongue.

"If this blows up in your face, Hunt, I'll make sad noises. Nothing else. There will be no presidential pardon, so don't even entertain that possibility in the back of your mind. You and your friends want to play a very dangerous game, and your lives and your fortunes and your freedom are the stakes."

" 'We pledge our lives, our fortunes, and our sacred honor.' Wasn't that the way the phrasing went?" Huntington Winchester asked softly.

The president wouldn't let it rest. He walked forward until he was three feet from Winchester and scrutinized his face. "You aren't proposing business as usual, Hunt. This isn't doing market research for a Wall Street tender offer, buying an oil concession from some impoverished dictatorship or launching a new brand of toothpaste. I want to make sure you understand precisely how big the pile is that you and your 'friends' are shoving out onto the table."

"I *do* understand. Goddamnit, man, Owen was my only son! What do you think he gave to his country? *What the hell do you think Ellen and I gave?*"

"Owen was wearing a United States Navy uniform. You aren't. There's a huge difference."

"I understand. I'll not ask you for anything else. Ever."

The president made a gesture with his

right hand, one hundreds of millions of people had seen him make countless times. "Who knows, if you help us find a few of those bastards, it might actually do some good."

He stuck out his hand. Winchester rose from his chair and took it.

One firm shake, then the president headed for the door. "I'll think about it," he said, almost to himself. He opened the door and passed through and closed it behind him.

A week later Huntington Winchester received a call from the president. He was at home, in his empty house. The cook left after dinner, and the maid and butler had the evening off. He answered the ringing telephone. There were no social preliminaries. "The Java Hut in Marblehead. A man will meet you there tomorrow morning at ten. He knows what you look like."

"Thank you," Winchester said.

"Good luck," the president muttered and broke the connection.

Downtown Marblehead was a cutesy tourist town, and this late-autumn morning the tourists were out in force, filling every parking place, cramming the sidewalks and shops. Huntington Winchester was ten minutes early when he walked into the Java Hut. The place was packed, with every seat taken. He glanced at the faces, saw no one he recognized and got in line. When he made it to the counter, he ordered a medium-sized cup of gourmet coffee. After he paid, he went to the stand where thermos bottles of cream, skim milk and 2 percent were located. He poured in a little skim milk.

As he turned around with coffee in hand, a man said, "Come with me. Let's get outta here."

Winchester followed the man, who was a little over six feet and lean, with thinning hair going gray.

Out on the sidewalk, Winchester got a better look at the man who had spoken to him. His short hair was combed straight back, his nose was a trifle large, and he had the coldest set of gray eyes Huntington Winchester had ever seen. He was wearing jeans and a dark blue jacket. Under the open jacket he wore a golf shirt. The skin on his face, neck and arms was weathered — at some time in the past, probably a lot of times, he had been exposed to too much sun.

"Name's Grafton," the man said. "I think there's a boardwalk just up the way where we can talk."

Winchester walked along, his coffee in his hand. When they were both leaning on a rail looking at the bay, the man named Grafton said, "I hear you have a proposition."

Winchester glanced around to ensure there was no one in earshot and repeated the plan he had told the president. "I asked our mutual friend to find someone who could pull it off," he said. "Apparently he thinks you are the man."

During Winchester's explanation, he examined Grafton, who had his hands folded, his forearms on the rail. He was wearing a wedding ring and a cheap watch on a flexible band — no other jewelry. He looked, Winchester thought, like a truck driver, one close to retirement.

Grafton said nothing, just looked at the bay and the boats and the people strolling on the boardwalk. "Mr. Winchester," he said after a while. "I came today to size you up. I am not committed to anything, and you aren't. Right now we're just doing a little preliminary shuffling to determine if we really want to dance."

"What do you want to know about me? Ask away."

"There's nothing to ask. I did a little research. You were born in 1955 to Robert and Harriet Peabody Winchester. You were the second of three sons. Your older brother is a banker with Merrill Lynch and your younger brother is a thoracic surgeon. You were educated as an engineer at Boston College, worked for several oil firms for the first five years after you got out of school, then founded a company that made oil field equipment. You sold that company ten years later for cash and stock, about six hundred million dollars' worth. You bought another company, grew it, bought out a couple of competitors, and are now supplying oil field equipment to major producers all over the world. You have a net worth in excess of two billion dollars."

Grafton's lips moved into a smile. The gray eyes crinkled, but they had no warmth.

Winchester wasn't impressed. "You could have gotten that information off the Internet."

"As of the close of business last night, you had a checking account balance of six hundred thirty-two thousand, three hundred and twelve dollars at the Bank of Boston. Your wife, Ellen Stalnaker Anderson Winchester, filed for a divorce on the nineteenth of October, but this isn't the first time. Eleven years ago you had an affair with your secretary. Ellen found out about it and filed for a divorce then, but you reconciled. You gave the secretary a hundred thousand in return for a release of liability, fired her and haven't ever seen her again."

"Okay, okay. I'm impressed. Just who are you, anyway?"

"Name's Jake Grafton."

"Were you in the Army?"

"Navy."

"Retired Navy?"

"That's right."

"Do you work for the government now?"

"CIA."

"Got some ID on you?"

Grafton removed his CIA building pass and handed it to Winchester, who inspected both sides of it. It was about the size of a credit card, but heavier, and had Grafton's photo on it. Under the plastic, out of sight, were magnetic strips that could be read by turnstiles, door locks, and scanners hidden in ceilings.

"Jacob L. Grafton," Winchester said, reading the name on the card. He handed the card back and sucked at his coffee, which was getting cold. "You aren't what I was expecting."

"You thought your friend would send you a snake-eater?"

"Something like that."

"As I understand it, Mr. Winchester, your company does business in every oil patch in the world."

"That's correct."

"Our problem, Mr. Winchester, is not finding men and women to fight terrorists, it's finding the terrorists. That is the most pressing problem facing the Western world today. We are looking for violent criminals who hide among the innocent, look just like them, behave just like them, except for that few seconds when they become soldiers for the Devil.

"To hunt these men and women, there are things we can do and things that we can't do . . . legally. On the other hand, private industry doesn't suffer from some of the restrictions that government employees must deal with on a daily basis. As you mentioned to the president, moving money is one of the things terrorists must do. The holy warriors must pay their bills, buy food and transportation and shelter and weapons and bomb materials and everything else they need. Someone must provide that money."

"Two of my friends are bankers," Winchester said.

Grafton nodded and kept talking. "Currently the terrorists are washing money by

31

buying and shipping commodities, such as food or medicine . . . any unrestricted commodity. For example, vegetable oil is used in cooking worldwide. A terrorist might buy a quantity in one place and ship it to another, where the consignee sells it and gives part or all of the money to local terrorists or a terror organization. Drug smugglers have been using this technique for years to wash money, and now the terrorists are using it. We need access to shipping records to find the transactions that look suspicious. To identify the people involved, we have to trace the money at both ends of the transaction, which brings us back to banks."

"Wolfgang Zetsche is the chairman and chief executive officer of one of the largest shipping firms in Europe and the Middle East," Winchester said. "He has offered to help."

"Is he trustworthy?" Grafton asked innocently. He had already gotten that name from the president and done some research on Herr Zetsche, but wanted Winchester's opinion.

"If I had a daughter I wouldn't let her in the same building with Wolfgang, but I'd trust him with every dime I own."

"Better tell me all of their names and what

banks or companies they are with."

Winchester did so. One of the names he threw out was Jerry Hay Smith. When he had finished, Grafton said, "Why Smith? He's a journalist — writes syndicated columns for newspapers."

"Jerry Hay is an old friend. We went to school together. He called me immediately after the news of Owen's death was in the newspapers. I talked to him, asked him how I could personally get involved in the fight against terrorism. He suggested I talk to the president, and he knows I did."

"Hmm," Grafton said. "Since he doesn't have access to anything we need, can't we leave him off the invitation list?"

"We could, I guess, but he'll be mighty curious."

Jake Grafton flexed his hands, then glanced at Winchester's face. "Security is always a problem. Through my agency, I can put people in the banks and shipping companies, and they'll look and act like all other employees, yet they are our people and working for us. We'll have cover stories, such as they are working with auditors or bank examiners or gathering data for some government entity. The fewer people who know their real identity and what they are doing, the better — and those people must keep the secret."

"Security in business is always a problem, too," Winchester said. "We trust people until they get greedy and betray us. Then we fire them or turn them over to the prosecutors, or both. What else can I say?"

Grafton turned around, leaned back against the railing and casually scanned the crowd.

"What are you going to do when you find terrorists?" Winchester asked.

A smile crept across Jake Grafton's face. "Why, we're going to prosecute them, of course, if all the governments involved decide to cooperate."

Winchester made a rude sound. "Why don't we hunt them down and kill them?"

"Assassination squads are hard to justify, get approved and manage through a bureaucracy. Then there are the lawyers. And congressional oversight. And people talk . . . to writers like your friend Jerry Hay Smith. Journalists need scoops, and that would be a big one."

"Sure as hell," Winchester agreed. "But could it be done?"

"Perhaps."

"As I told our mutual friend, my friends and I have the money to finance a private army."

Grafton smiled again, and this time his eyes had warmth. "I think we might be able to do some business. You envision me recruiting the people and pointing out the targets, and your group will fund the adventure. All that's well and good. But we need to have an understanding here and now: I will be running the show and you will be taking orders from me. You will do precisely what I say, when I say to do it, precisely the way I say to do it. If you follow orders diligently, thoroughly, without question — and maintain ironclad security — we might just be able to pop off some of these bastards and get away with it."

"I see."

"There's one more thing. I don't want you telling a single living soul that I work for the CIA. If the others suspect it, you must tell them you don't know. I'll tell them myself. Can you do that?"

"I *can* keep a secret."

"I hope so."

"How about these soldiers? Who will you get?"

"I'll be able to find some good people. That is the least of my problems."

"Pay them anything you want."

Grafton looked at Winchester, capturing his eyes. "You're entering a world where money doesn't mean much, Mr. Winchester. The men I want will work for the pay they would have gotten in the military. Everyone has bills to pay, but money isn't what motivates them. That said, you and your pals are going to get stuck with the expenses, and there will be a lot of those. Weapons, equipment, transportation, bribes — you're going to be amazed at how fast the money disappears."

"How about you? How much do you want?"

"The government pays me. The extracurricular activities I'd do for free."

"Why?"

Grafton's brows knitted, as if he were thinking about this question for the first time. He started to say something, obviously thought better of it and simply said, "This is what I do."

"That's a popular, trite phrase that explains nothing."

"Perhaps," said Grafton, eyeing the billionaire. "Let's put it this way: This is what I know how to do."

Winchester sighed. "Well, it's new ground for me."

"Even with the leads from the various companies, finding the bad guys will take a lot of doing. It'd be nice if they wore distinctive uniforms, but they don't. Still, I kinda think this might be worth a try. We might get some bad actors that deserve to be sent on their way."

Winchester's face brightened. "I hope so," he whispered.

Grafton turned back around and again put his forearms on the rail. "Personal revenge is hard to come by in this day and age. It takes a team to sail a ship or catch terrorists. Every member of that team is responsible for its success or failure." Grafton rubbed his chin, then said, "I might as well tell you the rest of it. Sooner or later the bad guys are going to figure out what is going down. That's if some government entity hasn't gotten wind of it first and tried to prosecute you for violating bank secrecy and privacy laws, money laundering, conspiracy to commit murder and a dozen or two other crimes. Your stock prices will go to hell and you'll be up to your ass in lawyers, trying to stay out of prison. You will also be in line to make some real enemies."

"Terrorists," Winchester whispered.

"They'll put your name on the bullet."

"I can live with that."

"The question is, Can your friends live with it? Why don't you invite them to your house, perhaps a week from today, and let me talk to them, too?"

"I don't know anything about you," Winchester said. "I'm in the dark here, and I don't like the feeling."

"Better get used to it. It'll get dark as a coal mine at midnight if I agree to get involved with you people."

"Tell me about yourself."

"I'm a retired naval officer, retired as a two-star. If you want to check me out, do it discreetly. If I hear you're asking questions, or anyone is, you failed the test."

Winchester was silent for a while, apparently lost in thought. Finally he said, "Next week."

"See you there," Jake Grafton said. With a wave of his hand, he walked away.

Huntington Winchester watched him go. After Grafton was lost in the crowd, he jammed his hands in his pockets and headed for his car, thinking about his son, Owen.

CHAPTER TWO

Washington insiders said that the most influential man in town was the president's aide Sal Molina, a Hispanic lawyer who had been with him throughout his political career. Just what his title and official position at the White House were no one seemed to know. Or care. Molina was the man who got things done. The fact that he didn't attend social events or make speeches or shake hands at fund-raisers only added to his legend.

The evening after Grafton's meeting in Marblehead, he offered Jake Grafton a beer. "So, how'd it go?" They were sitting in the basement rec room of Molina's house in Bethesda.

Grafton popped the top and took a sip before he answered. "There are seven of them, three of whom are Americans: Winchester, Simon Cairnes, a World War II veteran who runs the biggest bank in the

United States, and Jerry Hay Smith."

"Jerry Hay Smith, the syndicated columnist?"

"Yep. He's the guy who said that AIDS is the last, best hope of African wildlife. Remember that crack? It lit a firestorm in the black community and the Hollywood raise-money-for-AIDS crowd. They tried to get him fired."

Molina nodded.

"Have you seen his column today?" Grafton continued.

"No."

Jake removed a torn piece of newspaper from his pocket, put on his reading glasses and read, "Any religion that advocates the murder of anyone who isn't a believer isn't worshipping God — it's worshipping the Devil."

"Mr. Gasoline Mouth," Molina muttered. "He's a master of saying the unpleasant truth in a way calculated to piss people off."

Grafton folded up the clipping and tossed it onto Molina's table. "Winchester talked to him, and Smith suggested Winchester talk to the president. I suggested we leave him out. The problem is Smith already knows way too much."

"Some of these reporters can keep their mouths shut."

"If this little party explodes in their faces and Smith gets hauled in for questioning," Grafton continued, "you, me, the president and every literate person in the country are going to read all about it every day."

Molina sighed audibly.

"In addition to our American heroes, the group includes a Russian that Winchester does business with on a regular basis, Oleg Tchernychenko. He left Russia after he had a falling-out with Putin over oil deals. Winchester says he has ears in the Russian intelligence community, for which he pays dearly."

"I've read about him in the intel summaries," Sal Molina said.

"There's also a German named Wolfgang Zetsche. He's a socially committed, politically active businessman. Runs the largest shipping company in Europe and the Middle East. If it gets hauled to, from or through the Arab world, Zetsche hauls it. He's big with the Green Party in Germany. Nobody hates polluters like Wolfgang Zetsche. Apparently he also has a powerful dislike for Islamic terrorists."

"The sixth person?"

"A Swiss banker, Rolf Gnadinger. He's chairman and CEO of one of the biggest banks in Zurich. Reputedly he has connections at banks all over Europe."

"Number seven?"

"Isolde Petrou."

"I've heard that name before."

"She is the chief executive officer and chairman of the Petrou family of banks, which are the largest and most profitable banks in France. Her husband built the banks, but when he died a couple of years ago she took over. The word is she's got a better head on her shoulders than he had, and is a better banker."

"But isn't there something —"

"Her daughter-in-law is Marisa Petrou."

"Oh, yeah."

"Seven people, seven different motives for getting involved in a conspiracy to wage a private war."

"We know Winchester's motive."

"Do we?"

"You are the most pessimistic bastard I know," Sal Molina grumped.

"I doubt that. Even talking about this to you shows that I'm the biggest idiot you know — I'll give you that."

"Do you ever take anybody at face value?"

Grafton ignored the question. "Security will be impossible," he said pointedly. "Even if Jerry Hay Smith doesn't write a column about how he and his friends are fighting the good fight that the government is too incompetent to handle, that little cabal will leak like a sieve."

"So?"

Grafton chuckled. "The amazing thing is that Winchester assumes that the United States government is not hunting very hard for the terrorist leaders. Even the president's friends have lost faith. I'm supposed to use my contacts — unspecified contacts — to find key terrorists using the information our data-miners can glean from their computers and contacts, and send some hard-asses after them. Winchester et al will pay all expenses and salaries."

"You told him you're CIA?"

"Yes. I doubt that that impressed him, however. I'm a man his friend the president trusts, and right now that's enough."

"So what's your recommendation?"

"I can tell you right now that the director" — he was referring to the director of the CIA, William S. Wilkins — "wouldn't touch this with a ten-foot pole. When the leaks start, everyone will assume this is a CIA operation, a poorly planned, incompetent, idiotic one, and if PR or legal pressure builds on these companies, they may decide that this whole operation was the government's idea after all. Won't be pretty."

"Can you get information with their help that you can't get now?"

"Maybe," Grafton said. He sipped beer, looked at the baseball game on television, a league championship game, watched the pitcher shake off a couple of signs, then wind up and throw. "I don't know. The kicker is that these people will all know what the agency is up to. I'd almost rather hack into their computers — and we're doing some of that — so they don't know anything to tell. The private army thing — I don't know. I really don't."

"Winchester wants to help. He can make noise if he's brushed off."

Grafton ignored that remark. "The reason I think we must go forward with Winchester is that somehow, for some reason, Winchester included Isolde Petrou in his circle of conspirators. I know it's a small world and all that, but still . . ."

"The daughter-in-law, Marisa," Molina said. "I haven't forgotten. You think she's Abu Qasim's daughter." Qasim just happened to be the most wanted terrorist alive.

"She might be," Grafton said, weighing his words. "Maybe it's coincidence, maybe it's our good luck, maybe it's a dangle, but I think we have to go forward, get into this, see what we can get and where this

44

thing goes."

"You smell Qasim, don't you?"

"I'm getting a little whiff of evil," Grafton agreed. "And if he's really hidden in there somewhere, some of those seven people are probably going to get killed. Maybe all of them. If we put bodyguards around them, we'll never see the tiger."

"Presumably Winchester and the others know what's on the line."

"I doubt it," Grafton said sourly. "They think getting arrested is the big risk. They've all got tons of money, armies of lawyers, gilt-edged reputations. They know they can beat the charges or plead them out and get some minimum sentence. Here and abroad. They're all filthy rich, so they don't really care about money or bad publicity. The Americans will think a pardon is a possibility when the president leaves office. The last thing on their minds is winding up in a coffin."

Sal Molina was not squeamish. "Innocent people get murdered every day by terrorists. Casualties are inevitable."

Jake Grafton only grunted. He worked on his beer and idly watched the ball game on television.

Sal Molina took a long pull of beer, then said, "Car bombs alone kill dozens of people around the globe every day. True, Abu Qasim and his minions aren't responsible for all of them, or even most of them, but they do their share. And they are the people capable of pulling off big, complex operations, such as shooting down airliners, blowing up trains, sinking ships, assassinating heads of state . . . How many casualties are you willing to take to get Qasim?"

Abu Qasim was the most dangerous terrorist alive, in the opinion of most of the people in the upper echelons of the intelligence community. Grafton had crossed swords with him once before, and Qasim escaped alive. And Marisa Petrou had been close by.

Sal Molina, the lawyer, bored in. "One . . . ten . . . a hundred . . . a thousand?"

"That *is* the question, isn't it?" Grafton murmured. "Winchester and his buddies better update their wills and get right with the man upstairs."

"You'll give it a try, then?"

Grafton finished his beer and crushed the can in his fist. "I don't think that using this cabal creates more risk for my people. In the final analysis, the job is fighting terrorism, one way or the other."

"Winchester and his friends are all volunteers," Molina said, "for whatever reasons

46

they think are good enough. Your clandestine operators are also volunteers."

"Don't give me that shit, Sal. We don't send people to commit suicide. Not for God, or Allah, or the holy flag, or any other reason under the sun. We send people to take calculated risks to achieve results that we hope will benefit all the citizens of this republic. And I'm the idiot who calculates the risks and has to live with the outcome, good or bad."

The silence that followed that comment was broken when Molina murmured, "Sorry."

"All things considered," Jake Grafton finally said, "I think we should give it a try."

Winchester's estate in eastern Connecticut comprised almost fifty acres. His wife owned thoroughbreds, and although she was gone, the horses weren't. They sported in pastures doing horsey things behind carefully painted white board fences. The barn was recognizably a barn, painted white and trimmed in red and blue. It had paved floors and stalls and mechanized hay-bale-moving equipment. I thought it needed a CHEW MAIL POUCH sign on the side, but there wasn't one.

I stood in the middle of the barn looking

at the horses, some of whom were in their stalls looking at me. They looked a lot smarter than some of the people I spend my time with.

"It doesn't even smell like a barn," I said to Jake Grafton, who was standing beside me looking around in silent amazement. "Look up there." I pointed. "Aren't those odorizers of some type? I thought I smelled lavender."

Grafton looked, shook his head and walked out of the barn without saying good-bye to the horses. I trailed along behind him.

I should probably introduce myself. My name is Tommy Carmellini, and I work for Jake Grafton, sort of. Officially I'm a tech-support guy, but Grafton, who is the agency's head of European Operations, wants me to do nontech chores for him from time to time, so when I'm not bugging embassies in Bulgaria or tapping phones in Buenos Aires, I trail around with him doing whatever he tells me.

Today he led me across the paved parking lot behind Winchester's mansion and past the row of limousines and their chauffeurs, who were standing around visiting and smoking and wiping invisible road grime from their chariots with white linen towels. As we went by the manicured flower beds, I nodded at the gardener, a lady in a wide-brimmed straw hat kneeling in the dirt, digging up the dying fall flowers, and followed my boss into the mansion.

The place was stunning. The back of the building held the living quarters, kitchen, dining room and guest rooms, while the front was one huge room. The second-story living quarters had a balcony in the room, the ceiling of which was at least three stories high. The largest white marble fireplace I have ever seen was on the left wall; the other two walls consisted solely of soaring glass windows — the entire walls. Sunlight streamed in. The ceiling pitched down away from the fireplace, and through the windows to the right, where it was lowest, I could see a patio, a pool and a cabana of some sort.

The floor of the room was broken up into seating areas, one around the fireplace, one around a wet bar and piano and one around a library collection housed in bookcases under the balcony. Several nice bronze sculptures sat on coffee tables, and a large stone one stood in one corner. It was an Indian chief, I think, or perhaps a wood sprite.

I decided the architect either was a really far-out, avant-garde genius or had a serious drug problem.

The house sat on a low hill, so there was a view. Looking between the mature trees in the lawn, way out there I could see Long Island Sound.

I would have liked more time to gawk, but it wasn't in the program. Huntington Winchester, whom I recognized from his pictures, shook Grafton's hand and introduced him to the people standing around the fireplace area. Being the hired help, I hung back; no one tried to introduce me.

A dog came over to check me out. She was a collie, reasonably well groomed, dressed in a nice collar. She did her sniffs and moved on. I didn't try to make a friend. It's not that I don't like dogs, but I can never bring myself to pet strange dogs. Been bit too many times, I suppose.

Grafton had given me the names of the people, so it was easy to put faces to them. Simon Cairnes, the American banker, was a tall, erect, elderly man with an enviable mane of white hair. He walked with the help of a cane.

Near him was Oleg Tchernychenko, the Russian who lived in England. He was a medium-sized guy, lean, in his fifties, dressed in a Scottish golfing outfit. Amazingly, even in duds like that, he fit right into this eclectic crowd.

Next Grafton shook hands with Wolfgang Zetsche, the German shipping magnate. He was a skinny, feisty fellow, full of nervous energy. This guy, Grafton had told me, was a lady-killer of some renown, but you wouldn't know it by looking at him. Well, maybe the ladies would, but his charm escaped me.

Jerry Hay Smith, the American journalist, was also a little shrimp of a guy. He was in his early forties, I thought, whippet thin, a Boston Marathon type. I thought he was also probably one of those guys who go through life with something to prove and wearing a perpetual chip on their shoulder. He almost elbowed Zetsche out of the way so he could pump Grafton's hand. He was wearing a cheap sports coat that he might have stolen from a used-car salesman.

The Swiss banker, Rolf Gnadinger, was wearing an Italian silk suit that must have set him back a couple of thousand euros. Unfortunately he had a paunch that was a little too big and round shoulders, so he didn't cut quite the figure he was striving for. On the other hand, that was a heck of a nice suit. A nice watch, too — I got just a glimpse, but it looked like a platinum Rolex accented with diamonds.

Last but not least, Winchester introduced

the admiral to Isolde Petrou, the French widow who was running the biggest banking operation in Europe. She was in her early seventies, I think, dressed in the latest French fashion; even so, she looked as tough as shoe leather. She was wearing small diamond earrings and a little blue stone on a necklace that complemented her tailored knit dress. (I don't mean to bore you, but being a former jewel thief, I notice these things.)

Grafton asked them all to take a seat. He stood with his back to the white marble fireplace. "Tommy, check that we are indeed alone."

I checked the doors, even went upstairs to ensure no maids were listening just inside the doors to the balcony. I gave Grafton the Hi sign.

"Mr. Winchester tells me you are friends of his," Grafton began. "He also tells me you have agreed to allow my agency, the CIA, access to the records of your businesses for the purpose of finding money-laundering transactions that we can use to find terrorists. Except for Mr. Smith, of course, who doesn't have a business. Is that correct?"

They all murmured assent. Then Jerry Hay Smith said loudly, "He didn't tell us you are CIA."

"An oversight on his part, no doubt," Grafton said with a straight face, then motored on. "He also tells me you are each ready, willing and able to fund a small private army to hunt these terrorists, wherever on earth they may be . . . and kill them."

Silence followed that remark. He looked from face to face. As he did so he called the roll, beginning with Huntington Winchester.

"Yes. I am on board," Winchester said.

Each of the others murmured assent.

Satisfied, Grafton discussed the malignancy of the people who directed and funded terrorism. "Terrorism is cold-blooded murder of the innocent," he said. He went on, not mincing words: These people were dangerous, and they might come hunting those who were hunting them. Not to mention the fact that prominent, wealthy businessmen and -women were prime kidnapping and terror targets in their own right.

My attention wandered to Jerry Hay Smith. Big writer . . . it seemed like he should be taking notes. Maybe he was.

I also watched Isolde Petrou while Grafton was talking, and wondered about her. Last year her daughter-in-law, Marisa, was up to her gorgeous eyeballs in Abu Qasim's scheme to assassinate the leaders of the G-8 nations. Which side of the street was Isolde really on?

Grafton also talked about security, the need to keep secret the fact that the records were being mined by restricting its circulation to those in their employ with a need to know — and those people were very few.

"Who will you get to mine the records?" the Swiss banker asked.

"I can find some competent tech-savvy people for the job. If I couldn't, I'd be the wrong man for this job."

"How do you know they'll keep the secrets?"

"I only hire people I trust. You see, the world you are entering runs on trust, on faith in your fellow man. In the end, that is the only value that really counts."

"Of course, if terrorists who dealt with your institution are arrested or killed," Jerry Hay Smith pointed out, half turning so he could see Gnadinger's face, "they or their friends will know who they dealt with."

Isolde Petrou fixed a cold stare on the journalist. "If we are afraid to search for and apprehend these people, we are already defeated."

"Well put," Winchester said, nodding.

"Heck, every bank in this country has

systems in place to identify money laundering," Simon Cairnes said roughly. "It's required by law. Our systems will just get improved. I don't see what the big deal is. A bank is just a big corporate box."

Grafton talked about a few specifics, such as how each person there would be told who to hire, and how the undercover data-mining experts would actually proceed. Then he opened the floor for questions.

"You know who we are, but we don't know you," Simon Cairnes pointed out. "Tell us about yourself."

"My name is Jake Grafton. I retired as a two-star admiral from the Navy."

"Weren't you involved in that revolution in Hong Kong a few years back?"

"I was."

"And the turmoil in Cuba after Castro died?"

"Yes."

"And didn't you testify before Congress about the loss of USS *America* a couple of years ago?"

"You've done your homework, I see."

"Will you tell us the results you achieve?" Jerry Hay Smith demanded. "In other words, what will we get for our money?"

"Blood," said Jake Grafton.

No one spoke. Or coughed. Or breathed.

Jake Grafton broke the silence.

"It is my hope that with the information we get from your companies, and with the valor and skills of the men and women I will recruit to help us, we will achieve significant results. How significant remains to be seen. But I will tell you this — we are hunting the most virulent vermin alive today, and when they find out they are being hunted, they will strike back. I want you to think about that. Perhaps you already have. If you want out, don't want to help us search your records, don't want to contribute money to Winchester's enterprise, now is the moment to withdraw. Once we begin, it will be too late. Let there be no mistake, none whatsoever: You are putting your lives, your families' lives, your businesses and your employees at risk."

None of his listeners twitched. They sat like graven statues. I wondered if any would chicken out.

Isolde Petrou spoke first. "So our choice is to actively take a stand and lead the fight, or to hide in the crowd and share its fate."

Grafton nodded. I thought I could see a trace of a smile on his face.

"Well put again," Huntington Winchester told her. He stood and looked at the others. "Civilization has treated us well. We have built institutions that provide employment for tens of thousands of people, allowing them to support and educate their families. We enable other people and other businesses to do the same. And we have earned enormous fortunes. The real question is, Are we going to allow these fanatics, these xenophobes, these religious zealots, these *madmen* to destroy civilization and drag us back into the seventh century, or are we going to fight back? *Are we going to take a stand?*" Winchester faced Jake Grafton. "Admiral, I am with you, even if you and I stand alone."

"You're not alone," Oleg Tchernychenko said. There was iron in his voice. The others murmured their assent.

"I suggest we all have a glass of wine and a snack," Winchester said, trying to lighten the moment. He went off toward the kitchen to summon the staff.

Later I heard him say softly to Grafton, "It went well, I think. They'll all cooperate."

While Grafton mixed and mingled with the zillionaires over caviar and wine, I zeroed in on Mr. Smith. As fate would have it, I managed to spill a glass of good chardonnay on Mr. Smith's atrocious sports coat.

"Oh, my heavens," I said. I got busy trying to clean him up with a couple of the waiter's napkins.

"Take your hands off me," he said loudly, trying to push me away.

"I'm so sorry, but that stuff will ruin your coat if we don't get it off," I said. I held him and dabbed and swabbed vigorously.

"Who are you, anyway?" he demanded as he searched my face.

"Security."

"Well, stay away from me." He pushed me with both hands.

"You bet." I gave the napkins back to the waiter.

The other folks were watching, so I beat a judicious retreat.

Later, when we were in the rental car on the way to the airport, I gave Jake Grafton the little digital recorder I had snagged from Jerry Hay's pocket and told him where I got it.

"I didn't know you could pick pockets," he remarked.

"One of my many talents," I replied humbly.

Grafton glanced at the recorder, then tossed it over his shoulder onto the back seat.

"You know," I said conversationally, "if the activities of this little group become public, it's going to be bad. Really bad. A private war, with the unofficial aid and encouragement of the president and the agency — it'll be a first-class firestorm."

Grafton merely grunted.

"How did this operation get approved?" Proposed covert ops had to go before layers and layers of lawyers and committees. This is the new CIA we're talking about, one that the worthies in Congress don't think could spy a bomb on the Capitol steps.

"Well," he said with raised eyebrows, "I don't think it was approved. I'm sort of doing what the White House ordered me to do, and if it goes bad, heads will roll, mine, Sal Molina's, Bill Wilkins' . . ."

"The president's," I suggested.

Grafton eyed me. "I sorta think so," he said softly.

I searched for something to say and couldn't dredge up a thing.

"Of course," Grafton mused, "I don't think the big dog and Molina thought they were putting their dicks on the chopping block when they sent me to talk to Mr. Winchester. They thought they could send me to keep him happy, let him spend some money and think he and his friends were doing some good, and, who knows, maybe it would. That was the upside. If it went bad and started to stink, I would take the fall; they would tell Congress that they were trying to fight the good fight and I botched it." He shrugged. "This terror war has got them twitchy. They must be seen to be fighting the good fight, giving it their all. Their mistake, they would explain, was trusting an incompetent — that Grafton fool. But, by God, they tried."

"Why are you telling me all this? I kinda wish you hadn't." I silently promised myself that I would never, ever again complain about Grafton not telling me things.

"I need your help," Grafton said, his eyes pinning me again. "If we can kill Abu Qasim, this whole mess will have been worth whatever it costs, including a prosecution and trip to the pen for me."

"The terrorists have lots of soldiers," I pointed out.

"And damn few really good generals. Qasim is unique. He speaks five or six languages, has a network all over Europe and the Middle East — maybe even in America — and he thinks big. Most of these guys think small. They *are* small. Qasim is a great white shark with brains."

I watched his face, which mesmerized me. The years had left crow's-feet around his eyes and weathered his skin. Still, behind those gray eyes I could see the fire. Jake Grafton was a warrior to the last drop of blood. Sitting there beside him, I could feel the heat of that flame.

Maybe I'm a fool, but I would have followed the man through the gates of hell to shoot it out with the Devil — and it looked to me as if that was precisely where he intended to go.

"The key is Marisa Petrou," he said. "She knows this bastard better than anyone alive, and I've got a hunch she knows what he's planning."

His eyes were focused on infinity. I had seen him like that before when he was trying to see what other men could not.

The admiral was silent for a while. Then he said, "The Islamic jihadists want to destroy civilization. They reject religious freedom and the right of others to live as they choose. They want to deprive us of our right to think. In the name of a bloodthirsty, vengeful, merciless god, they are trying to drag the people of the earth back into a new dark age."

He thought for a bit as he drove along. When he spoke again, Jake Grafton said, "Those people in Winchester's living room are willing to make a stand. They're willing to risk everything they have — their reputations, their fortunes, their freedom and their lives. *So am I.* I'm going to help them if it's the very last thing I do. And, God willing, I'm going to lay hands on Abu Qasim."

CHAPTER THREE

November

Even in late autumn Paris is full of tourists, most of whom speak some variant of English. With digital cameras dangling on straps around their necks and wearing backpacks stuffed with snacks and guidebooks, they lead their wives and children through the endless crowds and stand restlessly in the eternal queues. They are white, ubiquitous and unmistakable. From London, the Midlands, Boston, California and everyplace in between, they crowd the Metro platforms and mill around the maps of the system. They pack the cafés, restaurants, and hotels and bitch endlessly about the prices. They also congregate in the public restrooms, where they complain loudly about the coin-operated stalls.

Jean Petrou tried to ignore the foreigners as he strode purposefully along the sidewalk and joined the line leading to the stairs into the Metro station. Just before he went down into the station he looked around, trying to spot anyone he knew. He saw no familiar faces or figures. The swarm of sightseers was the perfect place to lose oneself, he thought, as he went through the turnstile and joined the throng on the platform.

The truth was that he didn't blend into the casually dressed crowd. He was wearing a dark blue silk Armani suit, accented by a white shirt and light blue tie. Over this he wore a tailor-made black coat that reached to his knees. His shoes were rich black leather, highly polished. When he shot his cuffs, as he did while he waited for the train, his diamond-encrusted Rolex sparkled and gleamed under the lights.

The train roared in and ground to a halt. After another look around, Jean Petrou entered the nearest car and found a handle to hold. Tourists surrounded him, jostled against him, and the children eyed him without curiosity. He ignored them all.

Petrou changed trains at Les Halles station and rode the 4 train to the Cité station, where he got off and walked toward the stairs. He glanced back over his shoulder, checking the other people who were also getting off. No one he knew.

A short walk led to the narrow streets of

the restored old town. The streets were packed. Tourists strolled and read the menus posted in front of the restaurants, snapped endless pictures and paused in family knots to refer to maps and guide-books. Petrou angled through them and entered one of the restaurants. He paused in the doorway and looked around. Ah yes, in the far left corner. He waved off the maître d' and walked over to the table. He nodded at the man sitting there facing the door and, without removing his coat, seated himself.

His tablemate wore a goatee streaked with gray, long black hair, which was also gray-ing, and horn-rim glasses. His dark suit was not as fashionable as Petrou's, but it was cleaned and pressed. On the table before him sat a glass of water and a menu.

Petrou looked around, ensuring that he was seated among strangers. He was. Tour-ists filled every other table. A knot of students on holiday sat at the large table behind him. To his right a family from America, somewhere in the South judging from their accent, were oohing and aahing over the menu prices.

"Did you bring it?" Petrou asked softly in French.

His companion glanced down, under the

table. Petrou leaned left and looked. He saw a brown leather attaché case sitting on the floor by the wall.

Before he could speak, the waitress brought him a menu and a glass of water. He ordered a glass of white wine. The man with the goatee said water would be enough for him.

After the waitress departed, Petrou said, "I want to count it."

The expression on the face of the man across the table didn't change. "You earn it and you can count it in the men's room," he said.

Petrou looked around again. He was plainly nervous. "I don't trust you," he said.

"It is difficult to believe that you are actually in the diplomatic corps."

Petrou glanced around again without moving his head. He hesitated, then apparently reached a decision. From an inside coat pocket he removed a folded piece of paper and passed it across the table.

His companion slowly unfolded the paper and held it in both hands as he read. "Your mother?" he said.

"Yes."

The man folded the paper along its original lines and put it in an inside jacket pocket.

"It's yours," he said.

Petrou reached for the case, then saw the waitress bringing his wine. He withdrew his hand.

After thanking her, he took a sip. Cool, tart and delicious.

The man across the table consulted his menu. "I am thinking of having the fish," he said pleasantly. "I hear it is acceptable here."

Petrou didn't pick up the menu. He took another drink of wine, a healthy swig. "I remind you that you promised nothing was going to happen to Mother."

The man glanced up from the menu, met his eyes and said, "So I did."

Petrou drained the wineglass, then reached for the case under the table. As he rose from his chair he caught the waitress' eye. "He'll pay," he said, nodding at his companion. Then he walked out, carrying the attaché case.

Abu Qasim took his time over his meal. Petrou had told him last week that a small group of wealthy Europeans and Americans was funding a private army to search for and kill key members of the Islamic Jihad movement with information mined from the records of some major international financial and shipping concerns. Now he had supplied him with a list of the people and institutions involved . . . in return for money, of course.

As he ate, Qasim weighed the information he had received. His networks were going to have to be more careful, avoid the companies on the list if possible. Sometimes it was not possible. Zetsche's shipping concern was really the only major shipper in much of the Arab world. Still, the data-miners would get little information if all parties to the transactions took the proper precautions. As for the private army . . . the holy warriors could and would deal with them, if they should become a nuisance.

He had made a good bargain with Petrou, receiving very valuable information for a relatively modest sum. As he dined, Qasim marveled again at what a low price most people put on their honor, and their souls.

December

Abdul-Zahra Mohammed drank the last of his tea as he stood looking through the dirty, fly-specked window at the crowds in the narrow street below. Two- and three-story flat-roofed buildings lined the street in the Old Quarter, which had stood essentially unchanged on the flanks of the hill under the mosque for almost five hundred years.

The crowds in the street . . . they, too, looked as they had for generations, with only a few changes. Many of the men and all of the women wore robes, and the women were veiled, yet here and there a man, usually young, usually a common laborer, wore trousers and a loose shirt. The street was too narrow for vehicles; instead of the mules, donkeys and camels that had hauled food and merchandise through the Old Quarter since the dawn of time, most haulers used a bicycle, a motor scooter or even a motorcycle.

The window was open a few inches, admitting the smells and sounds of the quarter. Spices, unwashed humans, leather, animal dung, smoke from cooking fires, spoiling meat and fruit — it was a heady aroma, one Mohammed rarely noticed anymore. He was used to the sounds, too, a cacophony of voices, power tools, small gasoline motors, and whirring fans.

Abdul-Zahra Mohammed had spent his life in this quarter. Born in the back of his father's shop, educated in the mosque, he left the quarter only when he needed to meet with people in the movement who could not or did not want to come here.

The quarter was watched — Mohammed knew that. Everyone did. The entrances

69

to the narrow streets of the Old Quarter were under constant government surveillance.

The followers of Abdul-Zahra Mohammed also watched the entrances, but from the other side. Keeping the quarter safe for the faithful and as a base for holy warriors to rest, equip and train was an essential task.

Still, today Abdul-Zahra Mohammed was uneasy. It wasn't the crowds — the people looked like they always did. The rug merchant, the boy on his bicycle carrying fruit, the man who made "genuine" leather souvenirs for sale to infidel tourists — who used to come to the quarter but were no longer welcome — the butcher, the imam and his students . . . Mohammed knew or recognized most of them.

The air smelled the same, the noise was the same . . .

And yet . . . something was wrong! What, he didn't know.

Ah, he was getting old. The government didn't molest him because he and his organization didn't cause trouble in-country. Their efforts were directed against infidels abroad.

Someday, someday soon, the government's turn would come. The generals and faithless would be unable to resist the power of the organization, the might of the faithful focused in holy zeal. Someday soon.

Abdul-Zahra Mohammed finished his tea and left a coin on the table. The proprietor nodded at him, as he always did. They had known each other since Mohammed was a boy and his father brought him here. Mohammed descended the narrow stairs and paused in the hallway, which was empty. There was a gentle breeze here, just the laden air in steady motion, coming through the open door. He stood listening to the voices, the shouting, cajoling, earnest conversations, some light, some serious, some haggling over prices.

The merchants had been haggling for as long as Mohammed could remember. Mohammed's father had been good at it, and loud, and hearing his voice rise and fall, ridiculing ridiculous offers and pleading for justice, was among Mohammed's first memories.

So what was troubling him?

He stood in the hallway, just out of sight of people on the street, as he weighed his feeling of unease.

Abdul-Zahra Mohammed took a deep breath, exhaled and stepped through the door into the crowd. He went to the corner, avoided a bicycle loaded impossibly high with copper pots and strode along by the leather merchants and their customers, who were fingering the merchandise and haggling.

Something — or someone — was behind him.

He could feel the danger, the evil.

Mohammed glanced behind him and saw the cloth on the head of a man at least three inches taller than the people surrounding him. A strange face, a tall man . . .

Mohammed pushed his way into the crowd, galvanized by a sense of urgency and fear. Yes, he could feel the fear. It surged through him and stimulated him and made him breathe in short, quick gasps.

He glanced over his shoulder again, and the tall stranger was still there, only a few steps behind. It was an evil face, the face of the Devil, the face of the enemy of God.

He tried to run, but the crowd was too thick. Too many people! *Get out of the way! Let me pass. Don't you understand, let me through!*

Now he felt panic, a muscle-paralyzing terror that made him lose his balance and stumble and grab at the people around him like a drowning man. He was drowning — drowning in his own fear and terror.

He sucked in a deep breath to scream and

opened his mouth, just as an unbelievably sharp pain shot through his chest. A hand roughly grabbed his upper arm.

He had been stabbed! The realization came as he felt the knife being jerked from his body with a strong, steady stroke.

He staggered, felt his legs wobbling, felt dizzy . . . then the knife was rammed into him again. He looked at his chest and saw the shiny steel tip of the knife protruding from his robe. Blood . . . there was blood!

The pain! He felt the knife being twisted by a savage hand. The pain was beyond description! He couldn't draw breath to cry out.

The world turned gray as his blood pressure dropped. Then the light faded and he passed out.

Abdul-Zahra Mohammed didn't feel the hand on his arm release him, nor did he feel himself fall to the stones of the street. Nor did he feel his heart stop when his chest filled up with blood.

The man who had killed Mohammed walked on in the crowd, his brown eyes roving ceaselessly, taking in everything and everyone. He was in no hurry, merely moved with the crowd.

He did hear the excited exclamations and

shouts behind him as the crowd became aware of the body of Abdul-Zahra Mohammed lying in the street. He kept going.

Five minutes after he knifed Mohammed, Ricky Stroud, former master sergeant, U.S. Army Special Forces, now just plain Mr. Stroud, walked out of the Old Quarter. He hailed a taxi and told the driver in perfect Arabic to take him to the bus terminal.

Sitting in the taxi, he realized the sleeves of his robe were spotted with blood. A spray of red droplets, hardly noticeable . . . yet the cab-driver was looking, glancing in his rearview mirror.

He shouldn't have pulled the knife out for a second thrust. That had been a mistake; he realized that now as he looked at the tiny red stains on the dirty white robe. Ricky Stroud hadn't been sure of the placement of the first thrust, so he had surrendered to temptation and tried to improve his chances of killing Abdul-Zahra Mohammed. He and his three comrades had worked for two months to set up that fleeting opportunity in the street, and he wasn't willing to take the chance that Mohammed would survive. So he jerked the knife free and put the second thrust dead center in Mohammed's back, just to the right of the backbone, between the ribs, and gave the blade a savage twist to cut and tear tissue, speeding the loss of blood.

"You pays your money and takes your chances," he said silently to himself, and forgot about it.

At the bus terminal he paid the cabbie and disappeared into the crowd, went into the station and out a side entrance and kept going. He walked for a mile, hailed another cab, then another, and finally arrived at the safe house where he was staying.

There was another man there, also former Special Forces. His name was Nate Allen.

"Get him?"

"Yep. And I got photos of the two guys who left the tea joint before he did. I think I recognized one of them." He held out his digital camera.

"Oh, yeah," Allen said when he looked at the shots. "I recognize this second dude. He's a bomb maker."

"Got some blood on me," Ricky Stroud said. He sighed and pulled off the robe.

"How'd you do that?"

"Pulled it out and stabbed him again, just to be sure."

"Get another robe and let's clear this joint," Nate Allen said. He picked up his pistol, checked the safety and rammed it between his belt and his belly.

"I wasn't followed. I'm sure."

"People saw you. Get a new robe on and let's get the hell outta Dodge."

Both men pulled on robes, made sure their headpieces were properly in place and took a last glance around the room. There were fingerprints, but nothing else. The place was as spotless as careful men could keep it.

Allen jerked his head toward the door, so Ricky Stroud put his ear against it and listened intently. His eyes went to Allen, who had his hand on the pistol under his robe. He shook his head, then pulled the door open.

As the door opened, a man in the hallway rammed a knife into Ricky's belly, doubling him up.

Nate Allen didn't hesitate. He jerked the pistol free, grabbed it with both hands and opened up across the doubled-over Ricky Stroud, who was sinking toward the floor. He kept his shots low, waist high, gunning the figure coming through the door and moving the muzzle right and left, firing through the thin wall in a deafening fusillade. The .45 slugs weren't full-metal-jacket hardball military slugs; they were made of hardened lead so they expanded when they struck flesh. Nate fired the whole magazine, eight shots, as fast as he could pull the trigger.

He ejected the empty magazine and reached in his pocket for another as a high-pitched, keening wail came from the other side of the wall. Someone was thumping the wall, kicking it, it sounded like.

He got the second magazine in and was thumbing off the slide release when a shot came through the wall, tugging at his sleeve. Before he could get the gun leveled, Ricky Stroud's weapon began hammering. Stroud fired four times, spacing his shots along the wall. A cry and a thud followed when he stopped shooting.

Stroud struggled to rise on one knee, his belly and crotch covered in blood.

"Get out," he whispered hoarsely. "I'm finished. Won't be long. Get!"

Nate Allen didn't hesitate. He stepped over Ricky, glanced right and left. There were four men lying in the hallway. He stepped around them. One of them was struggling to rise. Nate shot him in the head.

As he exited the building he heard a shot behind him. Ricky Stroud had shot himself.

There were people in the street, all facing the building from which the shots had come. Ignoring them, Nate Allen walked through the crowd and kept going.

■ ■ ■ ■

"Abdul-Zahra Mohammed is dead. The killer used a knife and got blood on his sleeves and chest. He was seen. There were two of them. The brothers killed one, and the other escaped after killing all four of the brothers."

Abu Qasim's face was impassive as he heard the news.

The man who delivered the bad tidings shifted uncomfortably. He started in on Allah and his mercy, but Qasim lifted a hand, stopping the sermon.

"How did they find Mohammed?"

"He was dead in the street —"

"No, fool. How did the infidels find him?"

"He rarely left the Old Quarter. Everyone knows that." The truth was that with no education, limited life experience and a xenophobic outlook, Abdul-Zahra Mohammed hadn't felt comfortable outside the tiny circle in which he had been raised. This mind-set was so common in the Arab world that it was unremarkable.

"More to the point, how did the infidels learn he was in the movement?"

The messenger had no answer and, wisely, said nothing.

"So, this man who escaped — where is he now?"

"Rome. We have him under surveillance."

Rome was Nate Allen's favorite city, the one place on earth he loved above all others. It was modern, stylish, very Italian and literally built on top of ancient Rome, which cropped up in ruins and walls and columns when one least expected it. In Rome one got a sense that one's life was merely an eye-blink in the cosmic experience, and yet one sensed the Italian urgency to enjoy, to savor, each and every moment. There was a woman, too, a dark-eyed slender woman who loved life and Nate Allen. So Rome was . . . special.

On pleasant afternoons Nate liked to sit on a patch of grass with other men, most of whom were older, most of whom wore laborers' clothes, and listen to the Italian language being spoken around him. Some of the men brought wine, and as they smoked they passed the bottle around. Behind them, in the center of this little urban paradise, young men kicked soccer balls around, shouted and laughed and strutted for the girls who paused to eat lunch and watch. It was very pleasant, a world away from North Africa.

Ricky Stroud had screwed up that hit . . . and paid for it with his life. Damn, that was hard.

Of course, Ricky knew the odds and the risks and signed on anyway, as Nate had. Sitting in the grass in Rome listening to the laughter and watching the girls and boys, the smells and heat and palpable religious frenzy of the Arabs seemed like something from a nightmare, some horrifying thing that had grown in the corner of your mind yet wasn't real.

But it had been real. Ricky Stroud was really dead. Real damn dead. Of course, so was that murderous asshole Abdul-Zahra Mohammed. Blowing up airliners was his chosen quest. He had never actually been on an airliner — had never been more than four miles from the Old Quarter in which he was born — but the idea of destroying two to three hundred infidels in one stupendous, spectacular, fiery blast appealed to his sense of righteousness. The nonbelievers lived so well, flaunted their sin at the sons of Islam, tempted them with sins of the flesh and spirit — they deserved to die in a horrible, public way. Mohammed knew God wanted it that way, so he did everything in his power to recruit the people and provide the money to make it happen.

Well, he used to. Now he was just plain dead.

Nate Allen took a deep breath of Rome and tried to forget Abdul-Zahra Mohammed and Ricky Stroud, who had given his life to rid the world of a great evil. A man has to make a stand somewhere. Nate had learned that in the U.S. Army as a very young man, and it was the guiding star in his life.

He glanced at his watch. Sophia would be home from work now and cooking dinner. Lord, could that woman cook!

Nate eased himself erect and picked up the sports coat and the backpack that contained his pistol. He draped the backpack over his shoulder and the coat over his arm.

With a last look around the square, he set off for Sophia's flat. On the way he bought a bottle of wine and a loaf of bread. They didn't need either one, but it was a private joke.

Humming, he climbed the outside stairs to her apartment, the entrance to which was on the roof of an old building that stood on the side of a hill. This flat had been the building superintendent's home on the roof here by the water tank until developers condo-ized it.

He paused at the door, the old instinct of caution very much with him. No one in sight was paying any attention to him. He opened the door. Halfway through the opening something slammed him in the head and he felt himself falling. Hitting the floor, trying to move.

A kick in the head, stunning him.

The backpack was ripped from him. Rough hands hauled him erect. His legs didn't work very well and he almost fell.

As his vision cleared Nate Allen saw her, her mouth taped shut, fear in her eyes, her dress ripped half off. Sophia! Blood covered her torso. The men who held her had knives and had been cutting on her breasts.

There were four of them — two beside her and two beside him.

"Nathaniel Allen," the man beside Sophia said. He was middle-aged, of medium height, clean-shaven, with short dark hair. In his hand was a pistol, an automatic with a silencer on the barrel. The muzzle was pointed at him. "You need to answer some questions for us," he said in English. The accent was so faint it was barely there.

Allen said nothing. The horror of the moment had him in its grasp. He could see the fear and terror in Sophia's eyes, and the guilt hit him like a hammer. *He* had brought these animals here, to harm her.

The pistol moved a hair, and he saw the muzzle flash as something rammed him in the stomach. A bullet! The shock doubled him over.

The man smiled. "We have many questions. You can answer them truthfully and completely, or we will butcher this woman before your eyes. When she is dead, we will butcher you." He leaned forward. "You are both going to die. Do you understand? You can die slowly, horribly, or you can answer my questions and have a clean, quick death. Those are your choices."

Nate Allen felt the pain as the shock to his abdomen wore off. He found he couldn't stand. As he sank to his knees, he whispered, "Who are you?"

"I am known by several names. You don't need to hear them. God knows who I am, and that is enough. Now tell me, who hired you to assassinate holy warriors?"

"I don't know."

The man on the left side of Sophia slid a knife into her breast. She writhed, thrashed; the veins and tendons in her neck stood out like cords as she tried to scream against the tape.

"Perhaps, perhaps not. We will explore that. Let me ask another question. Who is your contact, the man who gives you your target and pays you?"

There was no hope — none! All they could hope for was a quick end. "He is a Russian," Nate Allen said as he stared at Sophia, writhing with the knife in her.

"You're lying. You work for the CIA."

The man on the couch shoved his knife slowly into Sophia, who groaned against the tape.

"No," Nate Allen hissed.

"Who, then?"

"Jake Grafton."

When he heard the name, Abu Qasim knew he was hearing the truth. Yet he wanted more, a lot more.

The torture and questions went on until Sophia passed out from loss of blood. Her blood was all over her, the floor and the man beside her, who was obviously enjoying torturing her. When she fainted, Nate Allen spit in Qasim's face.

The man wiped the spittle from his face and, with a glance at Sophia, nodded. The knifeman pointed a silenced pistol at her head and pulled the trigger. Her head slammed back. The knifeman let her corpse fall to the floor.

His interrogator put the muzzle of the silencer on his pistol against Nate Allen's forehead. "Tell the Devil that Abu Qasim sent you," he said, and pulled the trigger.

A week later Abu Qasim attended a meeting in Karachi. Eight men were there. After they prayed, the man on Qasim's right, an Egyptian, said, "Abdul-Zahra Mohammed was the fourth brother of the inner circle to die in the last six months."

"The CIA is sending these killers," another man said. "Two of them are Russians, I am told, and one is thought to be a German. Some are Americans. They have killed four of us and we have now killed two of them." He didn't bother to mention the four holy warriors that Nate Allen and Ricky Stroud had gunned down in the space of seven seconds. After all, the sons of Islam were on their way to Paradise, and there were plenty more believers to take their place. Every devout brother wanted to go forth to meet the Prophet with the blood of infidels on his hands.

"The American CIA is getting information from the banks and shipping companies that our brothers dealt with," Abu Qasim said. "The owners and officers who control these companies are cooperating with the American CIA. The CIA spies discreetly investigate, look for patterns and report to an officer of the CIA named Jake Grafton. He recruited these killers, names their victims and pays them. When I learned of this, I thought that if we took precautions, were careful, avoiding these companies as much as possible, Jake Grafton would have little success. I was wrong. He is a clever man and his men are competent."

The others nodded. Allah's enemies had the help of the Devil, so of course they were clever, which made the glory of defeating them so much greater.

"The infidels who run these companies fancy themselves the new Crusaders," Qasim continued, "and like the Crusaders of old will be utterly consumed by the fury of Allah."

"Who are they?" one of his listeners demanded.

Abu Qasim gave him a name. "There are others," he said, "but that name I know." Actually he knew all the names — he had gotten them from Jean Petrou — but he didn't want these men knowing and discussing those names. Even the walls have ears.

Inshallah, several said forcefully. God willing.

"Stated simply," Abu Qasim continued, "the problem is to kill them before they kill us. And, of course, to do it in such a way that the power of Allah is on full display to the nonbelievers."

"Allah akbar," his listeners muttered. Yes, indeed, God is great!

CHAPTER FOUR

January

Her name was Kerry Pocock, she was as English as tea and toast, she had a gorgeous head of long, curly, dark brown hair, a good figure and a smile to die for, and she was an MI-5 — British counterintelligence — op. Oh, yes, she was married to a guy who ran a pub and had two kids. She hadn't shown me their photos yet, for which I was grateful. Tonight she was wearing a lovely dress and a simple necklace of real pearls.

We were sitting in a really nice restaurant in Mayfair, the hip and trendy section of London. The place had white tablecloths, real silverware, bustling uniformed waiters and soft light. Since we were in the British Isles, I ordered a single-malt Scotch whiskey. She ordered a bottle of French wine.

"A whole bottle?"

"You can help me with it, if you like."

The waiter presented us with menus in

bound leather, and we opened them. I heard her sharp intake of breath — she had seen the prices. I scrutinized them. They looked in line, I thought, for a high-toned beanery in New York or Washington, if the prices had been in dollars. They weren't. They were in pounds, so if you doubled the numbers you got roughly the price in U.S. dollars, which is the currency Uncle Sugar pays my salary with.

My name is Tommy Carmellini — I think I introduced myself before — and I work for the CIA, the Central Intelligence Agency, or, as it's referred to in some profane quarters, Christians In Action. Not that we are all Christians, because we aren't, nor is there a lot of action. Most of what we do involves ruining perfectly good paper with ink squiggles and symbols. Entire forests have their existence violently terminated so we can have paper to ruin. But on this wet, chilly winter's night I wasn't destroying paper; I was out on old London town with a beautiful woman.

"Bit expensive cutting a dash in here," she remarked, not looking up from the menu.

"Good thing this dinner is being paid for by loyal American taxpayers," I muttered.

"Those colonials have their uses."

Kerry was pondering her dinner choices

when the man we were here to observe, one Alexander Surkov, a Russian expatriate, came in with two other men. They sat at a table near the window, Surkov with his back to me, which was fine. He didn't know me, had never actually seen me, and I didn't want him getting a good gander at my face since I was going to be following him for some weeks. I didn't want to make eye contact, so I, too, concentrated upon the menu.

"What's good?" I asked Kerry.

"When I got this assignment yesterday," she said, "my officemates said the beef is excellent. All these French dishes . . . one never knows what one is getting. I'm a toad-in-the-hole or fish-and-chips girl myself."

Yesterday after I learned that Surkov had made this reservation, I asked MI-5 if they had a female staffer who might like an expense-account meal in a good cause. The ladies of the CIA London office somewhere near my age all pleaded prior commitments or jealous spouses. Kerry was my volunteer.

Mayfair was the heart and soul of the Russian community in the U.K. Here the refugees could spend money like drunken sailors, soak up vodka, talk Russian as loudly as they wished and hang out with other people just like them, all the while pining for the good old days when Mother Russia was a worker's paradise and they were in the driver's seat.

Surkov had been a KGB man, then, when Communism imploded and the bureaucrats reshuffled, a foreign intelligence service officer. Six years ago he left the agency and got into the private security business in Moscow, which meant he guarded old Communists who were emerging from the closet as new capitalists by buying up government assets on the cheap and selling them dearly, getting filthy rich in the process. Then, a couple of years ago, he decamped from Russia and moved his wife and daughter to London, where he set up a consulting business, supposedly helping Western companies that wanted to do business in Russia learn what permits they needed, who to talk to, who to bribe, which taxes to pay and which to ignore, that kind of thing. These days he was Oleg Tchernychenko's right-hand man.

Grafton had me keeping an eye on Alexander Surkov. "I want to know where he goes and who he talks to," the admiral had said. "We're monitoring his cell phone and telephone calls, so don't worry about that. Your job is to keep track of him."

"This guy is Tchernychenko's chief lieutenant," I said. "Don't you trust ol' Oleg?"

Grafton merely smiled.

So here I was, eating high on the hog with a beautiful woman across the table, pretending I was spending the money I had just made selling a truckload of AK-47s to some Pakistani businessmen who needed them for hunting in the Hindu Kush. It was nice work.

After we ordered — Kerry ordered for both of us — I set forth for the men's room, the "loo" as it was known in these parts. I photographed both of Surkov's tablemates with the Dick Tracy camera hidden in my watch as I went to and from. I had never seen either of them before. They were speaking Russian as I passed their table.

In the men's room I hid a small microphone and recorder that would store every sound made in there for the next four hours. I put it on top of the paper towel dispenser in plain sight, held in place by brackets that contained magnets.

As I sat back down at our table I got a shock. I recognized the woman standing with the maître d' and a man at the door, waiting to be seated. In her late twenties, with high cheekbones and eyes set far apart, she carried herself erect, her back absolutely straight, and wore her long, dark brown hair brushed over to one side, exposing her right ear, from which hung a large diamond earring.

Marisa Petrou!

She nodded toward the window, and the maître d' led the way. She paused for a moment to speak with Surkov, who introduced her and her escort to the other two men. Then, with nods and smiles, they continued to the empty table where the maître d' was waiting, holding a chair. She sat with her back to me.

Well, her mom-in-law knew Oleg, and so it figured that she might know Oleg's segundo.

"You haven't been listening to a word I've said," my lady friend said, with a tiny hint of mind-your-manners.

"Sorry."

So what was Marisa Petrou doing here? In London? Here at this restaurant tonight? And who was the man? Her husband? She and he had separated, last I heard.

Unlike some people, I am a big believer in coincidence; random chance rules our lives. Meeting a certain person, a car wreck, being squashed by a falling piano — all those things happen by chance, and they change lives. On the other hand, since I am not a bigot, I will admit that cause and effect is also fairly important in human affairs.

Marisa Petrou was the daughter — maybe — of Abu Qasim, the most wanted terrorist alive. Grafton and I ran into her in Paris when Abu and his pals were trying to assassinate the G-8 heads of government in the Palace of Versailles. She and I had met the previous June, in Washington, when she picked me up at a party. That was no coincidence, either — I was trying to get picked up.

The problem was that Jake Grafton never tells me a thing more than he has to. He'd been after Qasim on and off since Paris, and madly plotting since Winchester and his friends joined the war, but would he tell me how things stood? Nope. Go here, go there, do this, do that, use your best judgment. Aye aye, sir. Fair winds and following seas, anchors aweigh, and so on.

I scrutinized the other diners, trying not to obviously stare — I should have done that sooner — looking for anyone I might recognize. One man, on the opposite side of the room, near Marisa, was being accosted by his fellow diners, smiling and shaking hands.

"Who's that?" I asked Kerry, nodding discreetly in his direction.

"Telly star. Very funny."

"Oh."

Kerry was rattling on about American politics and I was trying to pay attention while nursing a second Scotch when two waiters delivered our dinner with a flourish. Marisa and her man engaged in quiet conversation, no smiles or laughter, and Alexander Surkov and his friends had a serious discussion. The telly actor was polishing off drinks and having a jolly good time with his companions.

I looked at my plate. Three little piles of something. Thank heavens there wasn't much of it.

I toyed with the idea of stepping outside and calling Grafton on my cell phone to deliver the happy news about Marisa, then decided to wait. God only knew who might overhear my side of the conversation.

"So, Mr. Smooth, are you married or divorced or shacked up?"

She had one eyebrow raised. Fortunately I was taking her home to her husband in about an hour. "Dear Mrs. Pocock, my deepest apologies. If I seem preoccupied tonight, it's because I am. I'm thinking of my three little waifs at home with their mother, desperately awaiting my return. I humbly beg your pardon, gracious lady."

"You are the biggest American bullshitter I've had the misfortune to meet, Carmellini. The things I do for a free restaurant meal!"

"My sincere condolences."

"How's your dinner?"

"What is this yellow gooey stuff?"

"I'm not really sure."

"Now that we have become better acquainted, I can diagnose your problem, dear Kerry. You're a bum magnet."

She smiled at me. "I love you, too," she said and poured herself another glass of wine.

The dinner proceeded without incident. Surkov and friends were served, no one else approached their table, and they didn't go to the men's until they had finished eating, when they went one at a time. Kerry and I lingered over coffee and dessert and, since Surkov and friends were still in earnest conversation, ordered an after-dinner cognac. She still had about a quarter of a bottle of wine left, but with my fellow taxpayers footing the bill, I wasn't counting pennies.

Marisa and her man finished their dinner and left. She gave me no hint that she saw me — not that she would recognize me instantly, but she might. If she glanced my way I didn't see her do it.

When Surkov and company departed, I went to the men's, retrieved my recorder, then came back and settled up.

I drove Kerry home and said good-bye in the car.

"What, no kiss on the doorstep?"

"The neighbors might talk. Say hello to your husband for me."

"Trot on home to your three little waifs." She opened the door and climbed out. With the door open, she paused and said in a high-pitched, old-woman's voice, "See you tomorrow, dearie." She slammed the door and headed for her stoop.

"Right," I said. I waited until she was inside her row house, then put the car in motion.

As I drove I called Jake Grafton on my cell phone. This was a hazardous undertaking — driving on the wrong side of the road and talking on a cell phone took every brain cell I have. I told him about the evening, and about Marisa.

"She see you?" he asked conversationally.

"Don't think so."

"We'll listen to the recorder tomorrow. See you at the office."

He didn't seem surprised that I had run across Marisa. Did he expect me to see her there?

I went home to my flat, which I shared with a guy from Detroit who worked for General Motors, and crashed.

The next morning I was up bright and early at nine o'clock. My roommate was long gone, off to do some capitalism. After I drank my two cups of real American coffee — I had brought the Mr. Coffee with me from the States — I dined on toast and jam and got dressed. Read the morning paper, checked the e-mails on my computer, then went to the garage for my car, an agency sedan, small. Actually, very small. When in Rome . . . After wending my perilous way through London's narrow streets I parked at a public garage and took a subway downtown.

At eleven I was strolling by Harrod's department store in the beating heart of London, watching pedestrians and generally hanging out. I went inside one of the shops across the street that sold high-end ladies' wear and did some shopping near the front window, where I was behind a display and could watch the street. Sure enough, right on the dot I saw an elderly British woman in a nice dress get out of a taxi, cross the sidewalk and go inside.

As I was sorting through dresses and

checking pedestrians on the street, the clerk came over and asked if she could help. I was tempted to ask her if she had anything in my size, but didn't. "My wife is a four," I said, "and we've been invited to a party."

Ten minutes later, without making a purchase, I was back out on the sidewalk. I strolled to the corner and waited.

Seventeen minutes after she entered the store, the elderly lady emerged carrying a shopping bag over one arm. She turned my way and headed for the subway. I waited until she passed, then strolled that way myself.

There were only two other passengers on the platform, both schoolgirls wearing short skirts, long cotton stockings and jackets and carrying backpacks. Both were smoking. Ditching school, I suspected.

When the train pulled in, they tossed their butts and climbed aboard. So did the old lady. Apparently undecided, I loitered until the last moment, as the door was starting to close, then stepped aboard. The train was about half full.

People got on and off at every stop. I recognized none of them. Four stops from Harrod's, the girls left the train. The old lady and I got off at the next stop. She disappeared in the direction of the parking garage.

I waited at the entrance to the subway, watching the crowd.

Finally I set off for the parking garage.

The old lady was sitting in my car with her bag on the floor between her feet. Kerry Pocock had the wig off, revealing that mane of curly brown hair.

"You look lovely this morning," I said after I was behind the wheel and buckled in.

"You are so sweet," she said in her old lady voice. Then she dropped it and said normally, "Here it is." She handed me a plastic film container. "He hid it in the chicken." As I pocketed the container, she said, "The bird looks good — better than that last one he gave me. It must have been an old rooster."

"Young roosters are the best," I remarked.

She snorted.

I took her home, so she could get out of her makeup and go to work.

Our agent was a guy named Eide Masmoudi, an American Muslim who was worshipping at the biggest mosque in London, one run by a controversial cleric named Sheikh Mahmoud al-Taji. When he wasn't hanging out down at the mosque, Eide worked as a clerk in Harrod's food section. The store employed over a dozen English Muslims, some of whom were members of his mosque, so Eide had to be careful. Kerry was his courier. Jake Grafton was personally running him, and I was the help that made sure she wasn't followed. If someone started to check on her, Eide and his pal Radwan Ali, another American Muslim, were under suspicion and would have to be jerked out of the mosque PDQ.

The CIA's London office is in a big old house in Kensington. The sign out front tells the world that we are in the import-export business, but that's just another tiny lie on a huge big pile. When I arrived, Jake Grafton was in his office in the classified spaces in the basement reading a newspaper. He swiveled and latched on to the film container like a dog who had been given a bone. He opened it and took out the paper that had been folded and rolled tightly and stuffed in there.

"She was clean," I said. "No one took the slightest interest in her."

He merely grunted. After he had unrolled and unfolded the sheet of paper, which was densely covered with tiny script, he took his time reading it. Then he read it again. Finally he slipped it inside a folder and put it in his desk.

At last he fastened his eyes on me, on the other side of the desk. "Tell me about last night. All of it."

I tossed the recorder on the table and ran through it. There wasn't much to tell, since I didn't think he wanted to hear a rehash of Kerry's and my repartee.

While I was talking, Grafton punched a button and a tech guy came in. Grafton handed him the recorder.

When I ran dry, he pulled out his lower drawer and propped his feet up on it. "I got a call this morning from MI-5, Kerry Pocock's boss. Seems Alexander Surkov was taken to the hospital last night by his wife. Food poisoning, they think. They'll know more this evening."

"Food poisoning?" I remembered that gooey yellow stuff. "Montezuma's revenge, at those prices? That's gotta be a new record. Wait until you see my expense account."

It wasn't food poisoning, as it turned out. Late that afternoon Pocock's boss called again. Alexander Surkov was suffering from radiation poisoning.

The story came out that evening. Surkov had eaten nothing after he returned home from the restaurant the previous evening, and that night he began vomiting. His wife took him to the hospital when the usual over-the-counter remedies had no effect. He was showing all the classic signs of radiation poisoning.

Jake Grafton got this from a guy he knew in New Scotland Yard, who called him.

"Come on," he said, grabbing his coat. "Let's go to Mayfair."

It was eight in the evening when we arrived. The restaurant was lit up, all right, but all the customers were police. I tagged along as Grafton introduced himself to an inspector Connery. We shook hands all around, and the inspector took us inside.

A team of soldiers was working with a Geiger counter, going over every inch of the place. "It was cleaned last night, of course, but not to the point of decontamination. Mr. Grafton said you were here, at this table, Mr. Carmellini?"

I nodded.

"And Surkov was at the table over there, with the yellow tape around it?"

"That's correct."

"That table is radioactive."

Inadvertently my eyes went to the table in the corner where Marisa Petrou and her escort had eaten. I saw yellow tape there, too. "That table?"

"It's warm, too. Not as hot at Surkov's table, but warm."

I looked down at the table where Kerry and I had gobbled our goo. Nothing.

"Any other hot spots?"

"One in the kitchen, all over the dishwashing area, very slight but detectable. Perhaps it was contaminated when the dishes were washed."

"Perhaps," Grafton echoed, looking around. He turned back to the inspector. "You are interviewing the staff, I assume."

"Of course. Those that can be found."

Grafton waited, and finally the inspector said, "We are having difficulty finding one of the waiters. He lived in a rooming house, and didn't go there after work last night. Visiting a friend, perhaps."

I couldn't think of a thing to ask. On the way back to Kensington, I was going over every moment of the evening I could remember, when Grafton asked, "What do you think?"

"Marisa paused at their table, talked and shook hands. Could she have salted something on the appetizer or the drinks? Of course. Everyone looked at her — she was well turned out, nice dress, a few jewels, delightful face and figure — so her hands could have been busy. Same for her escort.

Marisa's table was the one in the corner that was also contaminated.

"On the other hand, maybe the missing waiter poisoned Surkov and salted Marisa's table. More likely, one of Surkov's companions slipped something into his grub. After all, they had all evening. Or he could have been poisoned by his wife. Or someone could have dosed him that afternoon, before he got to the restaurant."

"That about sums it up, I think," Grafton said sourly.

The next morning the newspapers had it. A big splash on the front page of every London paper. Alexander Surkov had been poisoned with polonium 210, a radioactive isotope. The story didn't stay local, either. Within another day it was all over every newspaper and television in Europe and America. Still, an exotic poisoning would have been merely a brief sensation without something more . . . and Surkov gave that something to the press. He held a hospital bed interview and accused the president of Russia of ordering his murder.

The Russians hotly denied the accusation, of course. Regardless, two days later, four days after he was poisoned, Alexander Surkov was dead. When the photographers took his photo in his hospital bed, his hair had already started to come out. His ghastly countenance was the photo of the year.

If that weren't enough, British and German investigators had found a radioactive trail from Moscow to Germany to London. Apparently another man who had been at the dinner where Surkov was poisoned, now labeled as one of the suspected killers, had dribbled radioactivity everywhere he went. This man was hospitalized, according to the television, in Moscow due to radiation poisoning. A third man, in London, claimed he, too, was ill, but he wasn't in the hospital. British, German and Russian politicians were in a tizzy.

Meanwhile, Grafton and I flew back to the States. He wanted to confer with his bosses, and I wanted to find out if any of my female acquaintances still remembered me.

The day after Surkov died, I was in Grafton's office watching some of the latest on this story on television. When the talking head went on to another story, Grafton used the remote to kill the idiot beast.

"Pretty amazing," I muttered.

"A novelist would have rejected a scenario like that," Grafton mused, "as too far-fetched. A deathbed accusation, the president of Russia, an alpha-radiation source

emitting isotopes of helium nuclei . . ."
Obviously, Grafton knew a little more about
nuclear radiation than the average Joe. And
he knew more than I did.

"What I don't understand," I said, "is why
the Russians used a radioactive isotope to
pop this dude when the chemists have a
cornucopia of undetectable poisons."

"There is no such thing as undetectable,"
Grafton said, sighing, "if you have the time
and equipment to run enough experiments.
Still, the Brits claim they wouldn't have
tested for plutonium poisoning if it weren't
for a medical-student prodigy working the
intake desk, who suggested it as a possibility." He glanced at his watch and stood. "I
have a five o'clock meet downtown. I would
appreciate it if you would come along."

"Sure," I said. Although Grafton phrased
his order like a request, it was indubitably
an order, and I was smart enough to know
it.

As he checked his safe and burn-basket
and made sure his desk was locked, I asked
who we were meeting.

"A Russian."

"Oleg Tchernychenko?"

"No. I talked to him a while ago on the
telephone. He is stunned and devastated, he
said. He also claims that the Russian govern-

ment killed Surkov."

"Why?"

"He had a dozen reasons." Grafton made a gesture with his hands.

"This guy we're meeting — what's he want to talk about?"

"My guess is a murder in London. Want to lay a little wager?"

I didn't. Betting against Jake Grafton was a sure way to lose money.

Washington, D.C., in winter is a miserable place. It's too warm to snow and too cold to be pleasant. The wet, chilly wind that blows most days cuts like a knife. I trudged along beside Grafton after the guy driving the agency heap let us off on the Mall near the Washington Monument. The only people out there were hard-core runners in Lycra and spandex, drug addicts in the various stages of euphoria or withdrawal, winos and a few screwballs from Iowa, snapping away with cameras. The people from Iowa actually thought the weather was warm, but being from California, I knew different.

"So how are you and Sarah getting along these days?" Grafton asked, for want of anything better to talk about. Sarah Houston lived with me for a while after our adventure in Paris.

"We broke up again. She moved out."

"Ahh," he said, as if my revelation explained the state of the world. He asked no more questions.

A wino mining a trash can glanced at us as we walked by but said nothing. Probably figured the chances of wheedling change out of us were too slim to be worth the air. We passed the Smithsonian castle and were nearing the Hirshhorn when we passed another wino sitting against a tree. He made eye contact with Grafton and nodded.

We went into the Hirshhorn, Grafton leading and me following like a good dance partner, and headed for the Sculpture Garden. A uniformed guard standing at the entrance told the couple in front of us that the garden was closed, then let Grafton walk on by with me in tow. The woman started to get nasty — another unhappy taxpayer — but I heard the guard tell her we were employees of the gallery.

The man sitting in front of a huge sculpture looking it over stood as we approached. He was tall and spare, wearing a dark suit and muted tie. "Good morning, Jake," the man said.

Grafton gestured to me. "Tommy Carmellini, Janos Ilin." He sat down as Ilin and I shook hands. Ilin seated himself on the bench beside Grafton, and I took a seat on a nearby bench.

"You're clean," Grafton said. The winos on the Mall, the guards in the gallery — all these people were making sure neither Ilin nor Grafton was followed to this meet. If there had been any problem, someone would have called Grafton on his cell phone. In the old days they would have put a chalk mark on a wall, but technological man was marching right along to the Happy Ever After.

"Very good." Ilin nodded once. He was still eyeing me. "I have heard of you, Mr. Carmellini." He didn't have much of an accent, so perhaps that nuance I heard was irony.

"And I've heard of you," I said brightly, as if he had just released a new album of highbrow jazz. "A mutual acquaintance mentioned your name once, a couple of years ago."

"Anna Modin."

I nodded. I wasn't going to mention her name, but if he wished to, that was his business. Ilin was, I knew, a senior officer in the Russian foreign intelligence service, the SVR — Sluzhba Vneshnei Razvedki — the bureaucratic successor to the First Chief Directorate of the KGB. His rank, as I recall, was the equivalent of a lieutenant general.

Ilin turned to Grafton, giving him all his attention. "Thank you for coming, Admiral. This Surkov killing — we have to talk."

So Grafton was right, as usual.

"The timing couldn't have been worse," Ilin remarked.

"People never die when you want them to," Grafton said.

If you're like me, you know how true that is. Through the years there'd been a few of my bosses that I fervently wished would wake up dead, but they came to the office regardless.

"We didn't have him killed," Ilin said flatly.

"Who is 'we'?"

"Putin, the service, the Russian government."

Grafton made a rude noise. "Years ago I warned you about taking blanket oaths. You're still doing it. I know you are not naive enough to believe everything you are told by the people in Moscow. Neither am I."

Ilin lowered his head in acknowledgment of the point. "Let me rephrase my remark. I do not believe anyone in Moscow ordered or arranged or participated in the murder of Alexander Surkov. I believe the evidence was planted so that it would look as if someone in Moscow were guilty. Surkov, I believe, was picked for assassination because he had a history of conflict with powerful people, and it would be easy for the British, the Germans and the Americans to believe that he had been murdered for revenge. Indeed, his death has cast a pall over Russia's relations with all three of those nations, and others besides. That is, I believe, precisely why he was murdered. He was sacrificed."

"By whom?" Jake Grafton said. I was watching his face, and I couldn't tell if he believed Ilin or not.

"That I don't know," Ilin countered. "I have my theories, but no facts. You can form your own."

"I see."

"We need your help on this, Admiral. My service has its resources, and I have a few of my own, but they are not enough. We are tainted. We need you to use your resources to investigate this crime and find the identity of the culprit."

"Don't tell me you want me to send Carmellini to question Russian officials."

"That would do no good. They know nothing. The answer is elsewhere in Europe. Someone at that table in Mayfair, or one of the kitchen staff, doctored Surkov's food or drink with polonium. Someone supplied it to the killer. Someone probably paid the killer. That is the trail you must follow."

"Why polonium?"

"Indeed," Ilin muttered. "Why?"

They talked for another ten minutes about how America might help investigate this crime, but I didn't pay a lot of attention. I didn't believe a word Ilin had said. The Russians were a slimy lot. The murder of one little man who pissed off someone powerful wouldn't even make the back pages of the Russian newspapers. Heck, Stalin had ordered the murder of Leon Trotsky, who was half the world away in Mexico City. Stalin also murdered tens of millions of Russians he thought might make trouble someday, just in case, and the KGB had diligently kept that happy tradition alive. The Communist habit of tracking down disloyal exiles and immigrants to execute them was a well-known commonplace. Murder for hire — assassination — was as Russian as vodka and ballet.

Grafton made Ilin no promises, nor did Ilin expect any. Grafton had a legion of bosses, all of whom had opinions and turf. They would decide what, if anything, the United States was going to do to unearth the killer of Alexander Surkov. If they wanted the killer's identity brought to light. After all, Russia's discomfiture played well in some circles. If it were up to me, I would let the bastards sweat.

With a last glance at me, Ilin rose, shook Grafton's hand and left the garden. I sat there looking at something big made of metal. Grafton seemed lost in thought. He glanced at his watch from time to time, then pulled out his cell phone and frowned at it. He put it back in his pocket, stood and stretched, then shrugged at me.

"What do you think?" I asked.

"I think I could use a beer."

That also struck me as a good idea. We went wandering off to find a place that served those marvelous elixirs.

We burrowed into one of those terrific business-account lunch and after-work drinks places on Pennsylvania Avenue. Standing at the bar sucking suds and looking over the hot women, I saw a couple of senators and a congressman or two. Then I spotted a television news correspondent chatting up a cute dolly. Sitting two tables away was a corporate CEO who was in serious trouble with the SEC and, according to the newspapers, was in town to tell Congress all about it. With him were two prominent lawyers, the dung beetles of our age.

I got this center-of-the-universe feeling. This city was the axis upon which the earth turned, and, amazingly, this bar was smack dead center in the center of the axis. From this vantage point you could see the gears and springs that drove the whole damned thing. The revelation was almost too much for me. To be here, be a part of it, was the reason why almost every nincompoop between the Atlantic and Pacific was running for Congress or president. I quaffed half a pint of Guinness and began thinking about throwing my own hat in the ring.

Grafton brought me back to reality.

We were standing in a corner, leaning on the bar, and he began talking about Russia, probably trying to bring me up to speed. I had to lean toward him to hear his voice, which was almost drowned out by the hubbub of conversation swirling around me.

"After the collapse of Communism, everybody in Russia began grabbing for the gold in a no-holds-barred, hair-pulling, eye-gouging, backstabbing brawl that is still going on. State assets were sold off, or more often given away in return for massive bribes in one form or another. In less time than it takes to tell, the folks at the top jettisoned social justice and adopted a perverted form of capitalism, a cancerous capitalism, virulent and malignant. A few people, the oligarchs, got filthy rich, and the former Communists who ran the place got dusty rich. In this new Russia, status is what you need, and money is the yardstick that measures it. Russians are snapping up luxury goods, watches, jewels, clothes, cars, yachts, mansions in tourist resorts, trying like hell to see if happiness can be bought. It's astounding, really. They've become the world's most conspicuous consumers —"

"The blingsheviks!" I said, interrupting. "I've heard about them."

"Of course, most of the people in Russia are still desperately poor. In the last few years the people in power decided that the oligarchs were too rich. They began using all the levers at their command to jail the oligarchs, cut up their empires, do whatever it took to once again become the absolute masters of Russia. Vladimir Putin is the driving force. He is consolidating his power, becoming the new czar of Russia.

"The old KGB was the state organ that maintained the Communists in power, doing whatever was required to destroy those the Communists perceived as a threat. After the fall, the KGB was broken up, but the men and women who were in it became the soldiers in the brawl that followed. They had connections, they knew who to bribe, they kept their mouths shut, they were willing to do whatever it took to get the job done as long as the pay was right. They own houses in Mayfair, eat at London's finest restaurants, wear the best clothes, the flashiest watches, drive the best cars and bed the skinniest, hottest women. Alexander Surkov, who was murdered in Mayfair, was one of these men. So were the men who are the prime suspects in his murder.

"The oligarchs and the new rich have their money and toys only at Vladimir Putin's pleasure, and they all know it. So when Surkov whispered his name on his deathbed, the Russians trembled. Very neat, eh?"

I heard the question and scrutinized Grafton's face. He had used the pause to sip beer. "Do you think Putin ordered Surkov killed?" I asked.

"Killed in England with an exotic poison that left a trail of radioactivity all the way to Moscow? And chilled Russia's relations with Britain and Germany and the rest of Europe?"

"But no one was supposed to know Surkov was poisoned," I objected.

"It's true that the test for polonium

117

poisoning is rarely given, but any competent physician who examined Surkov would suspect poison of some kind. After he died, medical experts would have sliced and diced the corpse until they came up with the answer even if it took weeks, and the trail would still be there, pointing straight at Moscow."

"A bullet would have been just as fatal," I mused, "and the assassin could have easily walked away — but there would be no trail."

Grafton locked eyes with me. "To find the people who ordered this killing, we must have a satisfactory explanation for the choice of polonium as the deadly weapon. It's an alpha-radiation emitter, easily shielded by something as simple as aluminum foil or a sheet or two of paper, easily washed off, and shouldn't hurt anyone as long as it stays off their skin and outside their body. To use it as a weapon, you must somehow get someone to ingest or inhale it, which presents a whole host of problems. The best explanation for its use is that it left a radioactive trail."

"Did it?"

Grafton smiled. "That's another question."

"So Putin was delivering a radioactive message to every Russian alive?"

"Or someone chose this method of chilling relations between all the European countries and Russia," Grafton suggested. "And, incidentally, terminating Surkov."

"So you think there is a possibility that Putin and company are being set up? That Ilin is telling the truth?"

Grafton attracted the barman's attention and signaled for two more beers.

"Somehow we must explain what Marisa Petrou, the daughter of Abu Qasim, was doing at that restaurant. The man you saw her with was her husband, by the way; apparently he and she are back together."

"It could be coincidence," I said.

Grafton's eyebrows twitched. "Maybe. Maybe not."

"And Abu Qasim?"

"He's burrowed in someplace. No one seems to know where."

"Is she his daughter or isn't she?"

"I don't know."

I sighed. One of the things about intelligence work that will drive the average person crazy is that there are no absolute answers. It's a world of mirrors and mirages, where perceptions rule and reality is often unknowable. I had never gotten used to that.

"So what are the powers that be going to say about helping Ilin and the Russians?"

"Darned if I know," Grafton said with a sigh. "I just work here."

Now, I'm not the swiftest guy you ever met, but I was beginning to see daylight. Jake Grafton was professionally interested in Surkov before today's meeting with Janos Ilin. I had thought it was because he didn't trust Huntington Winchester's pal, Oleg Tchernychenko, or his guy Friday. Then he took me with him to see and hear what Ilin had to say. I thought I knew the next move.

"Do you think it's time for me to chase down Marisa?"

"Wouldn't hurt. I've been waiting for Qasim to surface and make a move before we moved in on her. This might have been it."

I stared into my beer. Polonium! Oh, boy.

"Marisa may be aces with the French government, but her reputation in intelligence circles is not the best. I asked the Brits if they could send someone over to surveil with you. I promised that you wouldn't cause any trouble or get in their way."

"Have I ever?"

"Of course not."

CHAPTER FIVE

Jake Grafton's cell phone rang as he walked the two blocks from the Rosslyn subway stop to his condo. He checked the number, then answered it.

"Hello, Robin."

"Good evening, Admiral." Robin Cloyd was a data-mining expert who had been working for NSA. She had been temporarily transferred to the CIA and assigned as Jake's office assistant. One of the many things she did for the admiral was hack her way around the Internet, which was, of course, illegal. Robin worried about that, but she did it anyway because Jake Grafton asked her to.

Robin was a technical genius, a tall, gawky young woman who lived in jeans and sweatshirts because the rooms where she spent her working life were filled with computers and heavily air-conditioned. She also wore glasses, large, thick ones, because she didn't trust the doctors who did eye surgery. "After all," she remarked to Jake when she interviewed for the job, "I only have two eyes, and why take a chance?" Why, indeed? Jake hired her on the spot. That was four months ago.

"I'm into three of their computers now," Robin said, "Winchester, Smith, and Wolfgang Zetsche — so I see all the e-mails they send back and forth to each other. They're using a fairly sophisticated encryption code, one that —"

"Right."

"You don't care about the code."

"Not really."

Robin sighed audibly. Nontechnical people have no appreciation for logical beauty. "Anyway," she said, "Jerry Hay Smith is the most interesting. He's writing a book about the conspiracy and incorporating the unencrypted e-mails."

Grafton snorted in derision. "How much has he written?"

"About forty thousand words."

"Oh, Lord!"

"It's interesting reading. I don't think there's much truth in it, but it is certainly exciting."

"Send it along with all the e-mails and your analysis. I need some bedtime reading."

"Yes, sir."

When he got home, he found the morning paper on the kitchen counter, where his wife, Callie, had left it. He took it with him to the den and dropped into a chair. The trial of Sheikh Mahmoud al-Taji in London was the lead story on the front page. The British were trying to deport him for giving incendiary sermons in his London mosque about the duty of Muslims everywhere to serve Allah by battling infidels. His defense was that he was not a terrorist but was merely exercising his religious and free-speech rights. He had not, according to the press, actually advocated mayhem or murder. The British government argued that his speech went too far and was the equivalent of shouting fire in a crowded theater. British Muslims were demonstrating outside the courthouse.

A verdict was expected in a few days, and if it went against the sheikh, his lawyer promised an appeal. "The government has the right to prosecute terrorists," he said, "not legal immigrants commenting on the issues of the day, even if they use a pulpit to state their views."

Grafton read the entire article, then leafed on through the newspaper.

■ ■ ■ ■

After my conversation with Grafton, I rode the Washington subway — the Metro — back to my stop on the edge of Metropolis, where I parked my car every morning. I couldn't stop thinking about Marisa Petrou and her father, Abu Qasim.

When Qasim and the head of the French intelligence agency, Henri Rodet, had plotted to murder the G-8 heads of government at the Palace of Versailles, Marisa Petrou had posed as Rodet's mistress. She was nominally the daughter of one Georges Lamoureux, a high officer in the French diplomatic service. Grafton thought she was really the daughter of Abu Qasim and had been taken in, or adopted, by Lamoureux, a friend of Rodet's, when she was ten. We didn't have any proof of that, naturally, but when Grafton voiced an opinion it was usually a fact. He sometimes got these insights, and — but I digress.

One of our difficulties was that we didn't know what Qasim really looked like. Sure, I had seen him a couple of times, and so had Grafton, while he was disguised as an old man. I even got a photo that the wizards at the FBI enhanced so we could see what he might look like without the makeup and wig. Wasn't any help. Oh, we searched, followed every lead, rumor and lukewarm tip we could squeeze out of anyone, as did every other police and intelligence agency in the civilized world, but Qasim had disappeared as completely as if he had dissolved in the human solution.

One of the things Qasim did to hide Rodet's role in the plot was stage a fake kidnapping and slice up Marisa's face. I had seen her, unconscious, bleeding and tied to a chair, moments after he finished the job. She was a hell of a mess; it took a plastic surgeon a couple of months to put her back together again as best he could.

I know Grafton is Grafton and I'm just a grunt in the spy wars, but still . . . a father doing that to his daughter? What kind of animal was Abu Qasim? Or was Grafton wrong? Maybe she wasn't his daughter but was a female holy warrior determined to get to Paradise on virtue, or fanaticism if virtue didn't work.

The people on the subway, the pedestrians on the sidewalks — I watched them walk along, looked at their faces, wondering . . . Oh, we read about twisted, drugged-out freaks in the newspaper every so often, the refuse of humanity, who murder wife and kids for reasons that only the Devil could understand. But slice them up?

Maybe I have a low tolerance, but I can only visit a sewer for a few minutes before I need fresh air. To get some, on the way home I stopped by the lock shop I own with a guy named Willie Varner. Our ten-year-old van was parked out front and the light was on, so I unlocked the door and went in.

"Hey, it's me."

"Back here."

I went into the workshop in the rear of our space. Willie was a dapper black man twenty years my senior, slender and trim. What he didn't know about locks wasn't worth knowing.

"Wanta see something cool?" he asked as I examined the project he had on the bench. "This little thing will open any card-reader lock I've ever played with," he said with a touch of pride in his voice. "Gonna call it the Varner mechanism and get me a patent."

He demonstrated his creation on a hotel-room lock he had mounted on a board held by a vise. Normally this lock opened when a properly programmed plastic card was inserted in the reader slot. He inserted a card-sized probe that was wired up to a PalmPilot and stood watching. In about five seconds the green light on the lock came on and there was a click. Willie pulled the probe from the slot and turned the door handle, which opened. It was that easy.

"Whaddaya think of that?"

"I didn't know you knew anything about computers."

"Don't." He waved the PalmPilot. "I had a local lady geek program this for me."

"I see."

"Gonna put her and my name on the patent app. Both of us gonna make some money outta this."

He opened a small refrigerator that he had plugged in under the bench and pulled out two beers, one of which he passed to me. When he was seated and sipping, I said, "Willie, I wish you'd asked me about that thing before you started working on it. The agency's got gizmos that do the same thing."

He stared. "You're jivin' me, right?"

"Honest."

He swore a little. Drank some beer and swore some more. After a while he smacked the workbench with the flat of his hand and said, "I *knew* it was too good to be true! Invent something, make some money." Then he glowered at me. Sooner or later he'd decide his misfortune was my fault, and it turned out to be sooner. "You're like a little black cloud, Carmellini. When the sun starts shinin', you show up and rain on ever'thin'."

"Uh-huh."

"You come around a little more often, we could talk about stuff, partner to partner, but you're off alla time sneakin' into this or that, peepin' through keyholes, spyin' on folks who don't want to be spied on. Someday somebody's gonna stomp your sorry ass."

On that happy note, I went home. I had ruined a friend's day, and that was enough. Hi-de-ho.

The next morning at the office I asked for Marisa's file. It was sorta thick. While I was there I also checked out her husband Jean Petrou's file, which was not thick.

I took them to the cubbyhole the government euphemistically refers to as my office. With my door locked, I opened Marisa's classified file and perused it. About half of the contents were newspaper clippings. It had grown some since I saw it last.

According to the file, Marisa was the daughter of Lamoureux and his second wife, a woman named Grisella. She attended private schools until college, dabbled a year or two at the Sorbonne and a couple of Ivy League joints in the States and married the son of a wealthy financier, Jean Petrou. They lived together a year or two, she split, did some more American college, never graduated, had a fling with a French heart surgeon and wound up as the mistress of Henri Rodet, the director of the French intelligence service. That's where she came into my life.

Grafton insisted then that Marisa was a co-conspirator with Rodet and his buddy Abu Qasim. His assertion that she might be the natural daughter of Qasim, and Rodet had arranged for his good friend Lamoureux to adopt her when she was about ten years of age, was in the file. Our agents had checked the public records in Switzerland and France and had come up dry. Which only proved that if there had ever been adoption papers filed on the child, they weren't in the records now. The French and Swiss police had also made inquiries, they said, and their negative reports were also in the pile.

Being smarter than the average bug, we wanted to interview the people who knew the truth about Marisa's parentage, Georges Lamoureux and wife number two, Grisella. Unfortunately they were dead. Grisella succumbed to cancer in a Paris hospital five years ago, and Georges died in a single-car crash in the Swiss Alps a couple of months before the Paris G-8 summit.

I flipped through page after page of this stuff until I came to something interesting. After the flap in Paris, Marisa and Jean Petrou had buried the hatchet, patched up their differences while Marisa convalesced and once again taken up housekeeping as husband and wife. Then, a couple of months ago, Jean accepted a posting in the French diplomatic service. He was currently attached to the French embassy in London, but he also spent a lot of time in Paris at the ministry.

Apparently the French government wasn't nursing any grudges against Marisa, or her hubby would never have gotten his political post. Of course, French politics being what it is, the French government had never officially admitted that there was ever a plot to assassinate the G-8 leaders, nor that the late Henri Rodet was anything other than a recently deceased civil servant who had done his bit for *la belle France.* Jean and Marisa were apparently aristocrats in good standing.

I was happy for them.

There was more info in the file, lots of details, addresses and so on. I took some notes.

Finally I closed the file and arranged it

squarely on my desk and sat staring at it. I had a ruler in my desk, so I took it out and checked. The file was precisely one and three-eighths inches thick, counting the stiff folder that contained it.

I also measured Jean's file. It held an inch less paper.

I opened the husband's folder and began reading. There was a photo in there, a snapshot. No place or date. The guy was of average size and weight and looked smarmy. A fop, I decided.

The info in the file sorta went along with that assessment, making ol' M. Petrou sound like your average rich young Frenchman. He was the only son of a seriously rich financier, so he had expectations. Private schools in his youth, a few regrettable incidents with young women, an expensive car wreck — a Ferrari, no less — flunked out of one school and was thrown out of another, some dabbling in recreational drugs. What else? Enjoyed pornography and erotic art. Collected some of both. Didn't drink to excess and wore expensive suits and jewelry. He had worked in various capacities for his father's banks before he entered the French foreign service, and apparently got a nice allowance, because he lived well above his salary. Had a mistress, whom he saw a lot when he was separated from Marisa. No info about whether he and the mistress still had a thing going since he had reconciled with his wife. His pop had died two years ago, and his mom was running the banks.

That raised my eyebrows. Most European aristocrats of old man Petrou's generation married cute, curvy, clotheshorses from the right families who looked good at society parties, had their kids by them, then began a long series of dalliances with younger and younger mistresses. Maybe old Petrou had done that, but his wife, Isolde, was still a natural force. Someone had clipped an article about her and stuck it in the file: The banks were more profitable last year under Isolde's stewardship than they were under her late husband's. He'd be whirling in his grave if he knew.

All this dross was background, of course, to help intelligence evaluators weigh the worth of any tidbit an agent might glean from young M. Petrou at a cocktail party or other venue. He was not a regular intelligence source. Still, an agent had noted a comment of his about French foreign policy in Iraq made during a business luncheon in Paris six months ago. That tidbit was also in the file. It looked like a blog comment to me, but what do I know?

That was the crop. Ho hum. I took the files back to the library and headed for the Starbucks on the ground floor to get a cup of coffee. Ah, the fast, hot life of an international spy.

Of course, Marisa was in my future. I wondered if she had really taken up poisoning people, an ancient and dishonorable trade. Even if she hadn't, she wasn't ordinary, not by any stretch of the imagination. Amazingly, I was actually looking forward to seeing her again.

I took my cup of cappuccino into the cafeteria, where there were tables, and was sitting there musing about poison when Robin Cloyd, Grafton's new assistant, came striding over and dropped into the chair across from me. She had coffee in her hand and a little cup of yogurt.

"Good morning, Tommy," she said brightly. She had long hair that she wore frizzy, which hid most of her face. What you saw was the mountain of hair above the sweatshirt — today she was advertising New York University — and, peeking out of the hair, the big glasses, which magnified her green eyes. The glasses dwarfed her nose, which was working overtime holding those things up.

"That your breakfast?" I asked, glancing at the yogurt.

She flourished a plastic spoon. "Oh, yes. I'm so healthy that sometimes I can't stand myself."

"A common affliction among certain classes," I replied politely. I slurped at my coffee, which was still warm.

"We haven't really had a chance to get to know each other," Robin said as she tore off the foil from her yogurt.

"Hmm."

"Mr. Grafton said you're single."

"He did?"

"And unattached."

I made a mental note to remind the admiral that loose lips sink ships.

"So am I," she said brightly.

I said something polite and hit the road. Didn't really want any more coffee, after all.

"Do you have any grandkids?" Sal Molina asked Jake Grafton. They were in the basement of Molina's Bethesda home. Molina was sitting on the floor putting a tricycle together. Parts were strewn around, and he had the directions within easy reach. Grafton found a clean spot on the sofa and sat down.

"Not yet," Grafton said. "Amy is still looking for Mr. Right."

"That damn guy is hard to find," Sal admitted. With his glasses in place, he glanced at the directions, then selected a washer and cotter pin from a small pile and began installing a rear wheel. "Talk to me," he said. "Alexander Surkov."

"Surkov was Oleg Tchernychenko's chief lieutenant, and presumably Tchernychenko told him about the data-mining op we put in Tchernychenko's company. Tchernychenko trusted him, and we needed a bag man, a man to carry money, around Europe and the Middle East to our soldiers. So through Tchernychenko, we used Surkov. I thought he would be better than an American at delivering the money."

"But you didn't trust him?"

"He was in a position to betray my people."

"What do you think? Did he sell us out?"

Grafton took his time with that question. "Surkov was living very well in the U.K., even for an expatriate with serious connections, making serious money. It's possible he was selling information to anyone with cash to buy."

"To al-Qaeda? Abu Qasim?"

"Perhaps. Or he may have sold information about Tchernychenko's business to one of his boss' competitors. Or to the Russian government. In any event, he deposited a hundred and fifty thousand pounds in his London bank three weeks ago, a check drawn on the account of a shell corporation based in the Seychelles. The check was good."

"How likely is it that the Russians poisoned him?"

"The two men who ate dinner with him are the most probable villains, but one wonders if the orders really came from Moscow." Grafton told Molina about his meeting with Janos Ilin as Sal finished with one of the tricycle's rear wheels and began on the second one.

"The amazing thing," Grafton concluded, "is that I had a man watching Surkov when he was poisoned. That is, assuming the British police's theory that he was poisoned at the restaurant holds up."

"You had a tail on Surkov?"

"We couldn't watch him around the clock — we don't have the resources — so we were doing the best we could with what we had. We monitored his landline and cell phone. Tommy Carmellini bugged his apartment and his car. Tommy was also keeping a discreet eye on who he met."

"Why?"

"We lost two men last month. One of them and his girlfriend were tortured, then murdered. They took down Abdul-Zahra Mohammed, who had been running a money-laundering operation through a Russian company Tchernychenko has a finger in. The al-Qaeda guys aren't stupid. Sooner or later they are going to investigate that connection, and Surkov, the greedy hustler, would be a logical place to start."

Sal Molina shook his head and tossed the pliers into the toolbox. "Jake, this takes the cake. If Ilin learns that one of your men saw Surkov get it, he's going to smell a dead rat and get curious."

Grafton was undaunted. "Oh, I suspect he already knows."

"Did he mention it?"

"Oh, no. Yet look at it — Surkov is murdered in London and isn't even in the ground before we have a senior Russian intelligence officer looking up a senior American intelligence officer to pass on a back-channel message. 'We didn't do it,' they say." Grafton threw up a hand. "There are U.S. ambassadors all over the globe, the Russians could have made a beeline for the State Department, the Kremlin could have called our president on the hotline. Why me?"

"I'm with you," Molina muttered.

"Ilin must know that a man who normally works for Jake Grafton was present when Surkov went down. He then assumed that the CIA is or was interested in Surkov. So I took Tommy Carmellini, the op who was watching Surkov the night he was poisoned, to meet Ilin, who looked him over and told him he had heard his name. That convinced me I was right. Guys that senior normally ignore the grunts."

"If the Russians didn't kill him, who did?"

"That's the problem — it could have been anyone. One of his dinner companions, someone in the kitchen or serving, Marisa Petrou — who may be Qasim's daughter and was right there eating dinner — or anyone else in the restaurant. Carmellini was there observing, but he didn't make a note every time someone passed that table. For heaven's sake, they sat there on and off for almost three hours."

Sal Molina finished the tricycle and levered himself off the floor. He sat down in a chair facing Grafton.

"Do I understand this correctly? You think it's possible that Surkov sold out the Winchester group for money and someone killed him?"

"Yes."

"One of the group, or the person he sold them to?"

Grafton shrugged.

"Proof?"

"I'm not in the proof business," Grafton said testily.

"What does Winchester say about all this?"

"I'll find out tomorrow. I'm seeing him then."

"He may be having some serious second thoughts," Sal Molina mused.

"Too late for that," Grafton snapped. "I tried to tell him, and you, that once he was in, he was in until the crack of doom. As they say in Vegas, he and his friends are all in, with everything piled in the middle of the table."

Molina rubbed his forehead. "Everything else going okay?"

"Jerry Hay Smith, the Mouth That Roared, is writing a book about the conspiracy."

Molina closed his eyes for a moment. When he opened them, he eyed Grafton. "Is it any good?"

"Fair. Not much dialogue and it's short on action, but it has its moments."

"Is the president in it?"

"Only by inference. Winchester has kept his mouth shut, which is a minor miracle."

"I'm not going to ask how you got hold of it."

"That's good. You should take care of your blood pressure."

"You in it?"

"Yep. I can't decide if he thinks I'm the hero or the villain. Could go either way, I suppose."

"He know you're CIA?"

"Yes. I had to tell them."

"Terrific."

"I thought so, too."

"Sheikh Mahmoud al-Taji, the London cleric — what do you know about him?"

"He's a terrorist," Jake Grafton said curtly.

"Are you sure?"

"As sure as you can be about these things. We have two informants in the mosque, and they tell us al-Taji is not only preaching, he is recruiting terrorists, using donations to help fund weapons acquisition and training, and meeting with various like-minded souls to discuss possible terror targets in Britain. Our spies don't know what targets they've picked or how close they are to doing something. They're not yet in the inner circle."

"The British know this?"

"We've shared everything with them. The crown is prosecuting him because he's a

140

public nuisance and questions were asked in Parliament, but MI-5 isn't sharing intelligence with the prosecutors. They couldn't use any of it at his trial, of course, without betraying our people inside the mosque. They'd be dead within an hour."

"Why not pull these people out first, then put the sheikh away in a drafty old English prison?"

"I've talked to the head of clandestine ops about that, and he's talked to Bill Wilkins. Ethnic Middle Easterners who speak the language, have the guts and smarts to go undercover and are loyal Americans to the core are hard to find. We hoped these guys would help us catch bigger fish. If we pull them out and then help convict the sheikh, they're finished as undercover men. Even worse, it will be literally impossible to ever get another man into a London mosque."

"Okay. What does your friend in London say about the Brits' dilemma?"

"He says the government doesn't want any more London subway attacks or anything along those lines. They want the sheikh out of the country or silenced."

"Silenced how?"

"Not murdered. That would inflame British Muslims. My British friend is sort of hoping, off the record, of course, that the sheikh will have a fatal accident or die a natural death."

"A natural death would be best," Sal Molina said, nodding.

Jake Grafton shrugged.

"Can we help with that?"

"Perhaps."

Hunt Winchester and Simon Cairnes had lunch with Jake Grafton in the dining room of Winchester's yacht club in Newport in front of a big picture window. Through the window the diners could see the bay and whitecaps marching in rows under puffy clouds. On the dock below the window, flags snapped in a nice chill breeze. The bay was empty of boats.

When Grafton suggested that they meet in a place where no one knew Winchester, the industrialist made a rude noise. "The yacht club," he said. "I'll get us a private room. And Simon wants to talk to you." The room contained twenty tables, but Grafton, Winchester and Cairnes were the only diners today.

"I feel like a fool sneaking around some dump bar or coffee shop, hoping no one will recognize me," Winchester told Jake now after he took an experimental sip of white wine. "As if I were a criminal." After a moment's thought he added, quite un- necessarily, "I don't like that feeling."

Simon Cairnes shook the admiral's hand, then seated himself.

Grafton also sipped wine. It was dry and cold. He glanced at the label on the bottle. French wine, of course. He carefully placed the glass on the table and watched the shadow and weak sunlight play upon the waters of the bay. In the yacht basin below the clubhouse — an old mansion with creaky wooden floors — the piers were empty. Off to the left, boats hauled out for the winter sat on blocks.

"There won't be any other customers," Winchester told them. "I reserved the whole restaurant."

"Umm," Jake Grafton said.

"So tell us, are you getting any useful information from our records?"

"Some," Grafton said, nodding. "All we get are leads, which must be investigated. Right now we have about seventy-five people devoted to that effort. Our allies also have significant resources checking out the leads we have passed them. Every now and then we learn something we didn't know."

"That's the way life is," Cairnes muttered.

Winchester wanted more. "Have you or have you not found any of those bastards?"

"We have."

Hunt Winchester smiled wanly and settled back in his chair. He removed an envelope from the inside pocket of his sports coat and placed it in front of the admiral. "There's a hundred thousand in there. For services rendered to date. I know you work for the government and don't want money, but we want you to have it."

Grafton picked up the envelope, took the cash out and divided it into two stacks. He put a stack in each of his side pockets. He found a pen in a shirt pocket and wrote on the envelope, *Received $100,000 for consulting services.* He signed it and put the date under his name, then passed it across to Winchester.

"A signed receipt?"

"You can tear it up if you wish."

Winchester folded, then pocketed the envelope.

A waiter brought menus. The admiral didn't pick his up. He sipped wine, idly watched Winchester and Cairnes examine the menu and looked out the window.

When Winchester lowered the menu, he said, "I assume you want to talk about Surkov."

Grafton nodded.

"I've been watching the news," Winchester

continued. "Hell of a note! Tchernychenko knew the guy, trusted him." Winchester shook his head. "And for the life of me, I can't figure out why anyone would use a radioactive isotope to murder someone."

"A bullet would have been just as fatal," Grafton mused. "Arsenic just as deadly. They chose polonium to send a message, Mr. Winchester."

"To whom?"

"To you, of course. To you and Tchernychenko and Mr. Cairnes and your other friends."

Winchester's eyes widened. He searched Grafton's face. "You're serious, aren't you?"

"Last month two of our men were killed. I told you about them. Ricky Stroud was killed shortly after assassinating Abdul-Zahra Mohammed in North Africa. Nate Allen was tortured and murdered in Rome, shortly after he returned from North Africa. His girlfriend was also tortured and murdered."

Winchester nodded. Cairnes didn't turn a hair. He was watching Grafton with narrowed eyes.

"Nate may have talked." Grafton took a deep breath. "Probably did. Probably told them everything he knew so they would stop torturing his girl and end it sooner. If I had been Nate, I would have talked."

The admiral finished his wine and poured another glass from the bottle. "Al-Qaeda must know those men were working for me. They'll be looking for a leak. And if they think of Tchernychenko's company, they'll come looking there."

The waiter entered the room and walked over to the table by the window for their order. Winchester picked up the menu again and stared at it. Cairnes ordered by saying, "My usual."

"A chicken salad sandwich on wheat toast for me," Jake Grafton said. "Put some mustard on it."

"Yes, sir." The clouds were momentarily gone, and outside the sun drenched everything with a cold, clear light, making the colors extraordinarily vivid.

Winchester finally ordered a salad. "And a double bourbon on the rocks."

When they were again alone, Winchester asked, "Did Surkov betray us?"

Grafton told him about the check from the Seychelles corporation.

"You've got your fingers in a lot of pies, don't you?" Simon Cairnes said, eyeing the admiral askance.

"So if Surkov betrayed us to al-Qaeda, why did they kill him?" Winchester asked.

"To send you a message. Have you received it?"

When Winchester didn't reply, Jake turned his gaze to Simon Cairnes. "How about you, Mr. Cairnes?"

"I got the message from those Islamic Nazis years ago," Cairnes said, his face coming alive. "They want everyone on earth who doesn't worship God as they do dead and in hell. They're perfectly willing to do the killing. When the slaughter is over, they intend to rule the dungheap. Now *that's* the message, by God. The question is, When are the damn fools in Washington going to get it?"

"When the American people get it, and not before," Grafton replied. "That's the way things work in a democracy."

"You're probably right," Cairnes said softly, "but still . . ." He paused to gather his thoughts. "When I was a boy, a teenager, I lied my way into the United States Army. Completed training and wound up in a replacement pool in France in January 1945. That spring I was seventeen years of age, just a pimple-faced kid, when I walked into the concentration camp at Dachau. Saw the people starved, saw the ovens, saw the ashes, tried to get food and water down people and had them die in my arms. Our

147

captain had us round up the local German civilians and march them through the camp, made the bastards look.

"Now the Arabs say the Holocaust didn't happen. The reason they say that is because they're fascists, Islamic Nazis, and like the German Nazis, they plan on killing everyone on earth who doesn't agree with their religious dictates. Do you hear me? They plan on murder on a scale Hitler couldn't even conceive of."

"Is that why you agreed to be a member of this group?" Grafton asked as he examined the moisture on the side of his wineglass.

"I'm an old man, Grafton. Lived a long time and seen a lot of things. There's not much the government or the courts or anybody else can do to me now that is going to cause me much grief. Lawyers can keep me out of jail — I can hire an army of them. I've made a huge shit-pot full of money, more money than I ever dreamed of, because I read the newspapers and talked to people and I could see how the future was going to go. I invested in the trends that I saw. I've been terrifically right a lot more times than I've been wrong, and I've made more money than a hundred men could spend in their lifetimes. For the last ten years I've been chairman of a bank — but you know all that.

"Now let me predict the future. The civilized world is headed for a major war with fundamental Islam. Our enemies think America and its European allies are weak, ineffectual, no match for committed holy warriors ready to fight God's battles and die doing it. So they are going to push and murder and chip away at the West until the only thing it can do is fight or die. And it will fight — you and I know that, even if the fundamentalists don't. We'll fight and we'll win, of course, yet a great many people will die. Organized religion as we know it will be one of the casualties, which will be a tragedy. A great many enormous crimes have been committed in the name of God, yet in the main, through the centuries religion has been a civilizing influence, a force for good in countless lives."

Cairnes tapped his glass on the table. "If we can prevent that war from happening, Mr. Grafton, we can save this world that you and I have lived our lives in. We can save Christianity and Buddhism and Hinduism and Islam and all the rest. We can save this civilization based on religious principles. That, I think, is a goal worthy of all that we are, all that we have, all that we can do during our lifetimes."

"And you, Mr. Winchester?" Grafton said. "I know about your son. Is revenge the goad that drives you?"

Winchester looked belligerent. "I want some of it, yes. But I agree with Simon — these bastards have got to be fought, and the longer we wait to fight, the worse it is going to be. Everything we do —"

Cairnes butted right in. "Hunt is a fallen-away Catholic. He doesn't give a damn about religion. They can put all the Bibles and hymnals and theology books in one big pile and burn them for all he cares."

"You know that isn't true, Simon," Winchester protested heatedly. "Just because I don't go to church anymore doesn't mean that I am ready to dump on anyone else's religious beliefs."

The waiter entered the room with the lunches on a tray. After they all were served and the waiter had left, Cairnes looked at Grafton and rumbled, "Maybe you'd better tell us the real reason that you're in this."

"In my spare time I work for the government, as you know. That is a job I also know how to do."

"Your bosses, they know about us?" Cairnes gestured vaguely at Winchester and himself.

"That's really none of your business."

"Maybe you're with the CIA and maybe you're not."

"Think what you like."

Cairnes stared at him from under shaggy brows. "I think you tell a lot of lies."

"If I ever tell a lie, Mr. Cairnes, you'll never catch me at it," Grafton shot back.

"He came highly recommended," Winchester said. "That's good enough for me."

"I'll find out," Cairnes vowed. "Before I'm through I'll know more about you than your mother did."

Jake Grafton got busy on his sandwich. When he finished, he told them he needed some money transferred and the names of two more data-miners he wanted them to hire.

That evening, when he got home to his flat in Rosslyn, Jake Grafton gave the cash he had received from Huntington Winchester to his wife. "Tomorrow," he said, "I want you to go to Navy Relief and give them this money as a donation. Every dollar. Get a signed receipt and don't lose it."

Callie Grafton looked at the stacks of bills, which were held together with rubber bands. "Selling drugs these days, are you?"

"It's worse than that," he said heavily.

"This is the worse mess I've ever been in."

"I doubt that."

Jake Grafton made a noise, then started to say something. He changed his mind, went to the window and looked out. The lights of Washington were beginning to come on. Finally he wandered off toward the den.

"Jack Yocke returned your call," she said loudly. "He's in his office this evening."

Callie began counting the hundred-dollar bills on the kitchen table. She had married her husband after the Vietnam War, when he was a Navy lieutenant flying A-6 Intruders. Since then she had watched him shoulder increasing responsibilities, and she had occasionally been a part of them. She trusted his judgment implicitly, and yet . . . all this money? What was he into this time? She was curious, but she would never ask. Jake would tell her what he could, when he could. Through the years she had learned to live with that. People come as packages, and she was wise enough to know that in Jake Grafton she had gotten a good, solid man.

In a few minutes her husband was back. She was still counting.

He watched for a moment. "The man who gave me that," he said, "thinks money makes the world go around."

"You didn't have to take it," she replied without looking up.

"Yes, I did. He did what he thought was right. Sometimes you have to let people do that."

Ten minutes later Grafton called Jack Yocke, who was a columnist with the *Washington Post.* Jake had known him for years. At the start of their acquaintance, Yocke thought he was going to get information from Grafton, but finally gave up on that idea. These days the information only went one way — from him to Grafton.

After they had said their hellos, Grafton got around to the reason he called. "What do you know about Jerry Hay Smith?"

"He's not with the *Post.*"

"Umm."

"Won a Pulitzer fifteen years ago."

"Sixteen," Grafton said.

"I stand corrected. His column used to be syndicated in eighty-nine newspapers, if my memory serves me correctly. Only fifty-some carry him now."

"Fifty-two."

"What don't you know that you want to know?" Yocke said sharply.

"What do you think of his ethics?"

"Well, he has some, I suppose. A few,

anyway, that he keeps in a closet somewhere and dusts off occasionally."

"Has he ever gotten in trouble over stories?"

"Depends on what you mean by trouble. He tries desperately to get stories that other people don't have — that's one way you can get ahead in this business. Incidentally, that's what I try to do. I don't read his column on a regular basis, so I don't know what pies he has his fingers in, but yes, he's had a reputation for years of crossing the line to get a scoop. A couple of times he's been accused of playing fast and loose with the truth."

"He had any big stories lately?"

"Not that I can recall. Why do you ask?"

"Just curious. Thanks for your help."

"By the way, what are you doing for amusement these days?"

"This and that. Why don't you come over for dinner some evening?"

"Okay."

"Callie will call you when the schedule fits."

"I'll bring a date."

"Thanks, Jack."

London was enjoying a wet, cold, miserable winter. The English find this sort of thing invigorating, or pretend to, anyway. I reminded myself that the concept of central heating came late to this little isle.

After a flight across the pond, which took all night and left me bleary-eyed and feeling hungover, I went directly to the CIA's office in Kensington. There I met the two guys Grafton wanted me to work with, Speedo Harris, an MI-6 op, and Nguyen Diem, an FBI special agent.

Harris was clean-cut, modestly athletic and meticulously groomed. He looked like Central Casting's version of a metrosexual. "Speedo?" I asked.

"School name, you know. It seems to have stuck. Bathing suit incident, of course."

"I see." I turned to Diem, who was a darn big Vietnamese, almost my size. Goes to show what a high-protein diet will do. As we shook he said, "The Great Carmellini. I've heard about you."

I found myself liking the guy. "Lots of wonderful things, I'll bet."

"Actually, no."

"You got a cute nickname, too?"

"Per."

"I would have never guessed."

"Why'd they send you over here for this?" Diem asked.

"I'm tech support. Bugs and such."

"The Company doesn't put tech-support guys on ops."

"Normally, no, but the boss, Admiral Grafton, knows me. I keep his BlackBerry humming."

"And his cigarettes lit."

I could see that Diem and I were going to be best buds. "Just keep your mouth shut and do as you're told. Got it?"

"Yeah."

"And you?" I asked Harris. "Ops with the Yanks?"

"Short straw."

"Did you bring the file on the Petrou family château?"

"As you requested," Harris replied. Grafton told me to start with Marisa, and since Marisa hung out a lot at the château — and since I didn't have any better ideas — I figured that was the place.

One of the places the news of Alexander Surkov's spectacular murder came ashore was the Petrou château outside of Paris. Isolde Petrou read about the latest developments in *Le Monde* as she ate her breakfast at her desk in her bedroom after working out in her private gymnasium. Breakfast was unsweetened tea, dry wheat toast and yogurt.

When she was dressed and ready for the office, she found her daughter-in-law, Marisa, reading the newspaper at the desk in her bedroom. She had come in, apparently, while Isolde was in the bathroom.

"The police have found radioactivity in various places from Moscow to London," Isolde Petrou said. "Do you still think the Russians are innocent?"

"There is no such thing as an innocent Russian," Marisa shot back, "but the Russians didn't kill Surkov. You know it and I know it."

Isolde stood before the mirror as she donned her earrings. "He must have known everything — the names of the seven, the amounts we are contributing, the source of our intelligence, who Grafton's soldiers are — everything. He knew even more than you know."

Marisa folded the paper and placed it squarely on the desk. She looked at her mother-in-law's image in the mirror and said, "You are in danger of your life. You all are. If *he* got to Surkov, *he* knows, and if *he* knows, you and your friends are in mortal danger."

"How did he find out?"

Marisa drew a deep breath. "I will not insult your intelligence. You are in an illegal, criminal conspiracy to make war on al-Qaeda. Your own government would prosecute you if they knew. While the conspiracy may be small, the number of people necessary to carry your war to the enemy grows with every passing day. But I'm telling you nothing new — you know all this."

Isolde Petrou turned to face her daughter-in-law. "So who betrayed us?"

"We'll probably never know."

Isolde seated herself beside Marisa and searched her face. Marisa met her gaze. From this distance she could see the hairline scars under Marisa's makeup that the plastic surgeon had been unable to eradicate.

"Why did you marry Jean?"

Marisa grimaced. "He was the only man who asked."

"You could have done much better."

Marisa said nothing to that. After all, Jean was Isolde's son. He was what he was and words wouldn't change it.

"What should we do?"

"You and the other six? Or you and me?"

"All of us."

"Kill him before he kills you."

When Isolde left the room, Marisa sat thinking about the dinner at which Surkov was poisoned. It was Jean who suggested they go to dinner that evening at that restaurant in Mayfair. When she saw Surkov, whom she wasn't supposed to know, she started to walk right by his table. It was Jean who recognized him, who stopped and chatted briefly with the three men as she stood there smiling and nodding, trying to pretend they all were strangers.

What was on that table? She racked her brain, trying to remember. She had stood there looking at the faces and . . . Had the drinks been served? Certainly there were glasses of water in front of everyone. An appetizer?

Could Jean have dusted polonium on Surkov's water glass or cocktail?

If he did, why would he do it?

Even as she asked herself the question, she realized that she knew the answer. What if her husband, Jean, not Surkov, betrayed the members of the Winchester conspiracy to Abu Qasim? He knew his mother was involved. Qasim knew about Jean, of course. Perhaps they had a way of contacting each other.

She and Jean both knew Surkov, had met him before on one or two occasions. Was it she or Jean who said, "Oh, there's Surkov"? Perhaps she had. She tried to remember exactly what was said when they paused at

Surkov's table to chat. Had the two men made eye contact, or did they avoid it?

If Jean did it, where did he get the polonium?

From Abu Qasim, of course!

If he did it, which seemed unlikely. Yet even if he didn't poison Surkov's water, why did he suggest that particular restaurant for dinner?

The whole thing had Abu Qasim's fingerprints all over it.

Very neat, you must admit.

She hadn't an iota of proof. Yet.

Her husband was in Paris this morning at the ministry, so she went to his bedroom. The maids were finished. She locked the door and began searching.

CHAPTER SIX

After we got to France, my colleagues and I set up surveillance of the Petrou château and quickly learned the routine.

The château sat on about eight fenced acres of rolling countryside, twenty-two miles from the Louvre, and had at least twenty-eight rooms, not counting the dungeon, or basement, as the case might have been.

In residence were old Madame Petrou, the banking executive, young M. Petrou, the statesman, and young Madame Petrou, the lovely, loyal Marisa.

Twelve people worked there more or less full-time — *twelve,* in this day and age! — so the place was never empty. There were maids, a cook, a gardener, two security guys who carried guns, two chauffeurs and at least two people that we couldn't classify. One of them might have been a personal secretary, who handled bills and telephone calls and such, and the other might have been the wine cellar guy. We couldn't decide. From time to time tradesmen came in vans and cars. One of them, we concluded, was a hard-body female personal trainer who routinely wore skin-tight spandex. To summarize, there were people in the main house day and night, every day, and someone was always awake.

There were kennels for the dogs, a stable for a couple of riding horses, a garage for the cars, quarters above the garage for one of the chauffeurs and a couple of outbuildings for general storage.

There was even an old cemetery on the grounds, where presumably family members who didn't want to lie with the common herd in a public burying ground could spend eternity among kin. Or maybe they buried the help there when they keeled over on the job. One or the other.

"It's like a private hotel," Per Diem remarked on our third day of observation from the top floor of a nearby country inn. We had large binoculars mounted on tripods that we used to look at the main gate and at the château, which was about a half mile away. In the summer this view would be obscured by leaves, but this being winter, we could see fairly well. We also took walks along the perimeter fence, rode along it at odd times in a couple of cars we were using, and studied satellite and aerial photography, which the CIA office in London had provided.

The real key, however, to keeping track of the goings-on at the château was a radio-controlled drone that a team of U.S. Air Force recon specialists kept airborne over the grounds during daylight hours. It flew at about one thousand feet above the grounds, was essentially silent and broadcast a continuous video feed, which we monitored in the comfort of our digs at the inn. When the winter winds were steady off the Atlantic, the drone flew into the breeze and seemed to hover over the estate. We could even switch back and forth between ambient-light video and an infrared presentation.

Each morning Madame Petrou, the old madame, left in a chauffeured limo, off to the banks to lash the executives and make more money. About the same time son Jean left in a little gray two-seat Mercedes, a much newer version than the one I drove back in the USA. Around eleven or so, Marisa departed in a cream-colored sedan of some type, Italian, I think. Marisa returned first, the old madame came rolling in about three, the hard-bodied trainer showed around four and left at five thirty, and Jean came home about six. They held to that schedule for the first three days, anyway.

"Knowing how the upper crust lives is broadening," Speedo observed. "I can feel my horizons expanding."

"Comes the revolution," I told them, "I'm going to get me a place like that. Maybe even that one."

We amused ourselves by trying to estimate what Isolde paid every month to keep the place afloat. If Marie Antoinette only knew!

I was going to have to go in there and bug the joint, so I was trying to figure out how to minimize the risk of being caught and get the bugs into locations where we might actually hear something useful. We didn't have a blueprint of the interior, with the bedrooms and offices — if there were offices — marked, so I was going to have to sniff around some when I got in, which meant I needed some time in the place.

A call from Jake Grafton set the date. "The Petrou family bank is hosting a dinner this coming Thursday for the officers of all the Petrou banking enterprises." He told me the name of the hotel where the dinner would be held. "There will be a cocktail party prior to that," Grafton said. "According to our sources, all three of the Petrous will be there."

"Someone's been pumping the secretaries."

"I think so."

"How come I don't get jobs like that?"

"I'm getting some pressure on this, so we need to make something happen."

I wasn't sure exactly what he meant by that, but I had a fair idea. "Okay," I said slowly.

"You got the hardware you need?"

"Yes, sir. We helped ourselves from the attic in Kensington."

"Keep me advised, Tommy," Jake Grafton said.

"Yes, sir."

There I was, yessiring Grafton like I was a boot seaman. There is something about the guy that causes that reaction in me. I fight it, but every now and then I can't help myself.

After I hung up I spent a tough five minutes sharpening a wit, then issued orders to my two troops. They were unhappy, of course, but it has been my experience that my many bosses don't lose sleep worrying about the state of my morale, so I didn't worry about theirs. If they got too blue, they could write a letter home to Mom.

Marisa Petrou was across the street from the ministry when her husband, Jean, came out of the building a little after twelve with several colleagues, on their way to lunch. On Monday and Tuesday he had lunched with colleagues at a nearby café, which was apparently their usual haunt. To prevent him from recognizing her in the event he should glance her way, she was wearing a wig, a scarf, dark glasses and a long coat she had purchased Monday morning.

Wednesday, however, he came out alone and turned right on the sidewalk instead of left, toward the café. She followed along at a discreet distance, just keeping him in sight.

Her searches of his bedroom and office at the château had turned up nothing suspicious. Not that she really expected to find anything, but one never knew. Jean was not organized. When he met people, he habitually wrote their telephone numbers on matchbooks, which he snagged whenever he saw one because he couldn't remember to carry his lighter. She had seen him do it often. Yet she found no matchbooks at the château with telephone numbers. His computer was benign. She had checked the

166

numbers on his cell phone while he was in the shower; she knew most of them. She had called the others on a pay telephone and had recognized none of the voices.

Still, the worm of suspicion was gnawing mercilessly at her, so she was following him.

Marrying Jean had been a huge mistake. She had known it within weeks after the ceremony, a civil one, naturally. The best part of the marriage was Isolde, who had accepted her daughter-in-law as if she were her natural child. For a woman who had never known a mother, it was a wonderful experience. They talked and talked about every subject under the sun.

Why Isolde had the misfortune to have an ineffectual son like Jean was one of life's mysteries.

Jean stood at the curb, obviously looking for a taxi. Marisa felt a moment of panic. She turned and had the good luck to get the first empty one that passed. She had the driver wait while she fiddled with her purse. When a cab stopped for Jean, she pointed at it. "Follow that taxi, please." She handed the driver a twenty-euro note. He shrugged and put his car in motion.

Relieved, she settled back in the seat.

Jean's taxi crossed the Seine and entered the Left Bank area. Marisa's driver almost missed the light, but he managed to keep the other car in sight. When Jean's taxi stopped in front of a café, she ordered her driver to pull over and handed him another twenty-euro note, then bailed out.

Jean looked up and down the sidewalk, saw Marisa and apparently didn't recognize her, glanced at his watch, then entered the café. Marisa lit a cigarette and began window-shopping.

Seven minutes later she saw a reflection of a figure she recognized in the window of the shop she was facing. He was wearing an expensive homburg and a fine wool coat. His tie and white shirt were just visible under his chin. He walked quickly.

Her back was to him. He walked purposefully, a man with a destination and an appointment, and turned into the café that Jean had entered.

Abu Qasim!

On Thursday morning I managed to be riding by the gate when the guard opened the door of the guard shack and headed for the personnel door in the fence. Speedo was watching the drone video and helped me with the timing. When the guard disappeared up the path, I hopped out of the car with my backpack and went over to the

168

guard shack. Yep, the door was locked.

If the routine held, I had about ten minutes before the day guard arrived. I wanted to be inside the grounds by then.

The four Dobermans on the grounds of the Petrou château dictated the time of my entry. The security types took care of the dogs, which spent the night outside roaming the grounds doing doggie things and looking for something to kill. Every morning the security man going off duty would rattle the dog dishes and the Dobermans would come at a dead run. He put them in a dog run, fed and watered them and left them there. With the dogs put away, the main gate could be opened and closed when people wanted to come and go. The residents of the château, the hired help and the various tradesmen could walk to their vehicles or stroll the grounds without risking a dog attack.

When the Dobermans weren't on duty, security cameras were used to guard against intruders. Day and night, the guards spent their time, when they weren't taking care of the dogs or making rounds, in a small building that was actually outside the main gate. That was, I suspected, the location of the video monitors. The guards gained entry to the grounds via a personnel door in the fence so they wouldn't have to open and close the main gate, thereby risking letting a dog loose upon the countryside.

I had studied the photos I had made of the lock on the personnel gate, clicking them off with a telephoto lens as we cruised by in a car. It was a simple keyed lock. Diem went into Paris and visited a couple of stores that carried that brand. He bought one, and I worked on it with the picks back at the inn while Speedo and Diem did the watching. The lock on the security shack was pretty run-of-the-mill. I didn't know what kinds of locks were on the doors of the château, or on the interior doors, in the event I found one locked, but I had my usual assortment of picks and files.

Now, as I stood in front of the door on the guard shack, the chips were down. I managed to pick it and get inside within a minute, which was better than I expected. There were three monitors mounted so the guy at the desk could watch them. I traced the coaxial cables back to a computer, which routed the various feeds to the monitors, probably on a program that the guard could select at the keyboard on his desk. The feeds were also recorded digitally on some kind of continuous loop arrangement.

I found the power wire to the computer

and unplugged it from a backup battery that supplied power when the grid shut down, plugged it into a box that I had brought and taped the box under the table the computer rested on. The power wire from the box I ran to the battery and plugged in.

"It's hooked up," I said into my headset. "The computer is booting up again."

"Okay." Per Diem's voice.

A couple of cars went by on the street.

I glanced outside at every car. If the day guard arrived while I was in the shack, I was going to have to go through him to get out, and if that happened, we could kiss the day's program good-bye. And, of course, my next entry attempt here would be exponentially more difficult.

When the computer had managed to reboot itself and the video was again on the monitors, I said into my headset, "Kill it."

Diem did so with a radio transmission that the box picked up. The monitors went dark.

"It worked," I said as I strode out of the shack and headed the five steps toward the personnel gate. "I'll call you when I get inside."

"There's a car coming. The day guard, I think. You have about half a minute."

I'm the second-best lock picker alive, but I wasn't good enough to go through the gate lock and be out of sight inside the grounds within half a minute.

I bounded toward the gate and leaped. Got my hands on the top, which was about nine feet high, and scrambled up. One leg over, then the other. Nine feet is a long way to the ground. Praying I wouldn't break an ankle, I jumped. Hit and rolled. Got up and zipped behind some evergreens that helped screen the buildings from the road. I paused there to inventory parts.

Sure enough, I was barely out of sight when the day man's car rolled to a stop beside the night man's Fiat. He got out, stretched, reached back in the car for a bag that undoubtedly held his lunch, then strolled over to the shack and unlocked the door.

When he was inside, I boogied for the main house, making sure that I kept the pines and spruces between me and the guard shack. Anyone looking out a window in the big house could have seen me sprinting across the lawn, but I was betting that anyone up and about in the half hour after dawn had other things on his or her mind. Like the bathroom, or coffee, or cooking breakfast for the lady who paid the bills.

I wanted inside that house, and quickly. The guard in the shack was probably diddling with the computer, trying to figure out what was wrong with it. I didn't want him finding my radio-controlled control box and figuring out that someone had sabotaged the thing. Nor did I want to meet the night man on his walk from the dog pen to the gate.

I was approaching the front door of the château, under the overhang where the limos discharged their passengers and the doorman greeted them. Going through the front door would be nice, but not just now. I wanted something on the second story, a window perhaps.

Sure enough, on the west side of the building was a second-story balcony. I climbed a vine, got a handhold and swung myself up. One of the windows was open a crack.

I had a set of night vision/infrared goggles in my backpack, so I pulled them out and put them over my head. These things would allow me to see heat sources inside the room, things like people or lapdogs or even cats. I toggled the switch to turn them on — and got nothing. Took them off and examined them. The earpiece was cracked. That roll after I dropped off the personnel gate — I probably broke these things then.

I stuffed them back in the pack, listened

at the window that was open an inch, then used my fingers to open it wider. There was a set of drapes. I eased them aside and looked. Someone was still asleep on the bed. Taking no chances on talking, I clicked my mike twice for Diem.

"Got it," he said. He would turn the computer in the guard shack back on and stop that worthy's search. We hoped.

The light in the bedroom was dim. A little light leaked through the gap in the drapes, and there was a five-watt glowworm in the bath. That was it.

I dug into my backpack, selected a bug and pinned it to the drape as high as I could reach. Then I oozed across the room to the door to the hallway. It was unlocked. I twisted the knob as carefully as humanly possible, all the while looking at the sleeping figure in the bed. She turned over.

It was Marisa!

Still asleep.

I opened the door enough to examine the hallway — empty — slipped through and closed the door behind me by carefully twisting the knob, pulling the door shut, then slowly releasing the knob.

Out here I could hear noises. Someone was awake.

"They're opening the main gate," Diem

said in my ear.

I would have liked to bug every room in that mansion, but there was no way. Without night vision goggles, I was letting it all hang out. Someone could open a door or come around a corner at any moment and find me. Whoever it was would know that I wasn't supposed to be there.

I went to the top of the staircase and listened intently. Fortunately my ears are as good as my eyes. I started down the stairs, keeping to the side so a step wouldn't creak.

I found the library easily enough, so I bugged it. Likewise the dining room.

Neither room felt as if the folks who lived there spent much time in it. I needed to find the rooms where they lived.

After a glance into the larger rooms on the main floor, I went back up the stairs. Moved swiftly along the hallway, listening at each door. Found one standing open. It was an office. I went in.

There was an attached bedroom, and it was big. This, I guessed, was the master suite. Or where the young Petrou male slept alone. I bugged the office, then moved into the dark bedroom.

There was someone in there asleep, all right. I could hear the heavy breathing.

The sleeper was not Jean, but Isolde Petrou, and she had black blinders on her eyes to shut out the daylight oozing around the drapes. I put bugs on the drapes and one on the head of the bed.

"Two cars going through the gate," Diem said in my ear, loud enough to wake the saints asleep under the Vatican. "Maids, I think."

My heart kicked into a gallop. Madame Petrou didn't stir.

The other Petrou was the one I wanted, the son. I sallied forth to find him.

I did. He was awake and in the bathroom making noises. Moving as quickly as I dared, I planted three bugs in the bedroom and two in the adjoining office. I was ready to step into the hallway when I heard someone coming.

I got behind the open closet door. There was a knock on the bedroom door; then it opened and the butler came in with a tray that held a thermal carafe. I saw him through the crack between the door and the jamb. There was someone right behind him, though, someone I had seen from a distance often enough to know him, the night security guard. He was wearing his pistol. Uh-oh.

Young Petrou stepped from the bathroom — he was wearing a robe — and the three of them began babbling in French. I knew enough of the language to get the drift; there was an intruder on the grounds, maybe. The night man saw a man's footprint in a damp area without grass as he walked back across the grounds after feeding the dogs. It looked as if the man might have been running toward the château.

"A footprint?" Petrou was incredulous.

"A man's footprint," the guard said meekly.

I couldn't believe my bad luck! Who would have thought that the security guards were Apache trackers? Next he was going to tell the master of the house my height and weight.

"When was it made?" Petrou demanded.

"It wasn't there yesterday."

"You're sure?"

"I didn't see it yesterday, monsieur," the guard said, a servant to the boss. He wasn't going to insist on anything and risk getting fired. He was merely doing his duty. All this was in the few words he spoke.

"This morning you noticed it?"

"Yes, monsieur."

"Have *you* seen anyone?" Petrou asked peremptorily. Presumably to the butler, who answered with a negative.

Petrou sighed. Then he took a noisy sip of

something, perhaps coffee or hot chocolate. "Search the house and grounds," he said without enthusiasm.

The guard left in a hurry, passing me behind the door. The butler wasn't far behind. He began going into rooms along the hallway. Of course, he had already been in this one, so he wasn't going to search it again.

I stood there trying to evaluate the situation as Petrou took his cup and returned to his toilet in the bathroom. Presumably the guards were going to search the grounds and outbuildings. I wondered if they were going to close the main gate and turn the dogs loose. By God, I hoped not.

I looked at the soles of my shoes. Tiny crumbs of dirt remained on them. Wonderful, wonderful. Presumably more crumbs were scattered everywhere I'd been in the house. I wondered if the staff were sharp enough to notice and, if they did notice, competent enough to mention it to the imperious monsieur.

I slipped out from behind the door, opened the bedroom door and got into the hallway. With the door shut behind me, I trotted down the hallway as quickly as I could without making any noise. I heard the butler thrashing about in one of the rooms. He was going to awaken the house-hold, if anyone was still asleep. This hallway and the downstairs were going to fill up fast.

I heard someone climbing the main stair, so I ducked into the first room I could reach. It was a bedroom. Empty. I went to the window and looked out.

"Per, kill the computer," I whispered into my headset.

"Done," he said.

I opened the window and leaned out. The night man was at least a hundred feet away looking in a gazebo partially surrounded by evergreens. I didn't see any dogs.

Now he was getting a cell phone call. It was so quiet out there in the country I could actually hear it ring. He answered it, mut-tered something and walked quickly away in the direction of the main gate.

When he disappeared around the corner, I dug from my backpack the controller/repeater we used to turn the bugs on and off and to boost their transmissions so that they could be received at a distance of several miles. I turned it on, then tucked it into the ivy vines as far as I could reach to my left. It appeared to be out of sight.

That done, I went out the window onto the sill. I managed to get the window closed behind me, then slowly put my weight on the ivy vines that had been using the wall for a trellis since Napoleon was in diapers.

If you've ever tried to pull ivy off a wall, you know how firmly it is attached. On the other hand, if you've ever tried to climb a wall covered with it, you know how loosely it is holding on. I got maybe three feet down when I felt the ivy starting to rip loose. I turned, pushed off and dropped the twelve feet or so to the flower bed. The dirt was soft, which was fortunate, yet there was a trimmed rose bush strategically placed that had carnal knowledge of me. Moments like that separate us real men from the wannabes. Blinking back tears, I inspected the tracks I had made in the soft, black, manicured earth, tracks Inspector Clouseau could have found.

There was a fallen limb lying nearby that the gardener hadn't cleaned up, so I used it as a bunker rake. Did the best I could with it, tossed it aside and took off for the back fence, trying to stay behind evergreens as much as possible.

It wasn't until I was over the fence that I keyed the mike and told Per Diem to turn on the guards' computer again.

After I got cleaned up, Band-Aided and presentable, Speedo drove me off to the

Paris World Hotel, where the Petrou function was to be held that evening, for my first day on my new job as a waiter.

Getting hired on the banquet service staff had taken some serious finagling, which meant that I had paid the head dog a large bribe. The unemployment rate in France is about 20 percent for young men my age, so I had to give him a really good reason to bypass all the people on the waiting list and hire me immediately even though I didn't have a French work permit. I even agreed to provide my own uniform, which meant that a London tailor had to be flown to Paris and work all night. When I spend U.S. taxpayers' hard-earned dollars, I go all out.

Of course, when I got to the hotel, the maître d', Henri Stehle, was nervous. I was worried that if I dropped any more cash on him he was going to smell a serious rat, so I told him that I desperately needed to make it in Paris to prove to my parents that I wasn't the playboy they thought I was. "I've had experience in good restaurants" — what kind of experience I didn't say — "and I can do the job. Just watch me. In a week you'll think I'm the best employee you have."

He wasn't sure. He was a man of medium height, in his middle forties I would guess, who was trim without looking like a gym rat. "That work permit —" he began.

"I'll have one by next week. I've already talked to the authorities."

Mollified, he had me work with the people setting up for the banquet. It looked as if there were going to be about a hundred people at this feed; Madame Petrou, the banker, was picking up the whole tab. I figured it might be tax-deductible for her, so I wasn't overwhelmed with envy.

The afternoon passed quickly. I learned how to keep the towel over my left arm, practiced serving the way the other waiters did and managed to fit right in. This wasn't as easy as it sounded, because most of the staff were older than I and had worked at this hotel for years. In short, they were true professionals. They were also a decent lot and helped me with little tips. It was obvious to them that I was a neophyte, but I was hoping that only the pros would notice. I saw Henri checking me out a time or two, and he seemed less anxious than he was when I arrived earlier. He really didn't have anything to worry about — any waiter could spill a bowl of soup in someone's lap, and if it happened, he could soothe ruffled aristocrat feathers and fire the guilty worker swine. He knew that and so did I. Life would go on.

Henri had me carrying a tray of champagne flutes, full, when the first guests began dribbling into the room where the cocktail party was being held. A string ensemble was playing chamber music in one corner. I offered champagne to everyone; some folks took a glass, some didn't. I worked the crowd, listening to the French, English and German flowing back and forth over the classical music, and tried to actually understand some of it. That effort, I found, interfered with my champagne duties, so I gave it up and concentrated on not spilling my tray, offering a drink to newcomers, and ensuring drinkers didn't hold empty glasses very long.

I was hard at it when the Petrous came in. They had already shed their coats at the check rack outside, so I went over and offered champagne. I was hoping Marisa would make eye contact, but it didn't happen. She was upper crust straight through to the backbone, a blueblood who ignored the help. She took a glass off the tray and never even glanced at my face. She smiled at someone she knew and held out a hand.

I offered Jean a snort of the bubbly, and he took a glass. His mother ignored me completely. I moved along. They wouldn't have noticed me if I had had two noses.

My plan was quite simple: I wanted Marisa to notice me at some point in the evening, to actually see my face and recognize it as the mug of Tommy Carmellini, CIA officer. Then, when she got home, I was sorta hoping she would talk with her husband and mother-in-law about the fact that the CIA had someone at the party, in a place, of course, that our new microphones could pick up the conversation.

Once they all knew the CIA was interested in them, I thought things might happen. For one thing, Marisa might report that fact to Abu Qasim. Grafton was tired of waiting for something to happen — he expected me to force the issue.

Only Marisa didn't cooperate. I would have bet my pension that she didn't notice my face during the cocktail party.

When Henri announced dinner, the entire hundred must have been there. The buzz of loud conversation drowned out the chamber music. As the guests filed in to dinner, I ditched my tray and headed for the kitchen to help serve the first course, which was fish. Five or six of the guys were joking near the serving table in French, talking about the banker who had brought his wife and his mistress. I asked what he looked like, and he was described to me.

Then we were on. Out of the kitchen we marched, one behind the other, with three dishes on our left arms and two on our right.

I concentrated on serving, on doing the job I was supposedly hired to do. Every now and then I sneaked a glance at Marisa at the head table; she was never looking my way.

If she didn't spot me, I was going to have to think up something that ensured she did. Not that I wanted to do that — I was hoping she wouldn't think I knew that she had seen me.

When we were on the main course, which was beef, I realized that she might indeed have seen and not recognized me. The thought was a shock to my healthy male ego, yet I had to admit, it made sense. We've all run into someone from our past so unexpectedly that the face doesn't register, right?

On the other hand, we did go to bed together once, and she certainly recognized me when she saw me in Paris for the G-8 conference; she was getting out of a limo and I was the last man alive she expected to see, yet she placed me immediately. Perhaps she had seen and recognized me tonight and didn't want to let on, so was now studiously ignoring me.

I was cogitating on this when I almost put a carafe of water in a graying matron's lap.

No doubt I was overthinking this. Truthfully, this whole gig was a half-baked idea. Grafton would have laughed if I had told him what I planned. The fact that Speedo Harris and Per Diem thought this plan was lousy was the real reason I insisted upon it.

After we waiters had served the main course and were again charging the wineglasses, I worked my way toward the main table, which was round, with eight people seated at it. Marisa was listening to some crusty old gentleman on her left regale her with stories he thought were funny. She was smiling when he roared with laughter. I wondered how much champagne he had had. He was sure slurping down the wine.

Beside her Jean Petrou was working on his grub and looking sour. To Jean's right, Isolde Petrou was engaged in conversation with a lady of the same age, one draped in pearls.

I poured some wine for the woman across the table, then glanced at Marisa. Her face wore a look of shock, even horror! She wasn't looking at me, though. She was looking past me, toward the door to the kitchen. I glanced back . . . and saw Henri Stehle standing there, looking this way.

When I turned around, Marisa's face was back to normal. Then, amazingly, Jean Petrou seemed to pale. If I hadn't been looking right at him, I wouldn't have seen it. He turned pale, his eyes unfocused, laid down his fork, seemed to take a deep, deep breath . . .

"Waiter, I'd like some more wine, please," the man nearest me said.

I was frozen, unable to answer.

Jean Petrou grabbed at his throat, as if he were having trouble breathing. Marisa stared at him —

I set the wine bottle down and rushed around the table. I got to Marisa first, grabbed her wrist. She looked me straight in the eyes. Her face was a study in confusion.

"Don't eat another bite," I said. "He may have been poisoned."

Now she recognized me. I saw it in her eyes. Beside her, her husband was getting into the dry heaves.

"Make an announcement," I ordered. "No one here should eat another morsel. Stand up and say it."

I released her wrist and bent down to check on her husband. He was pasty. I grabbed his wrist; his heart was going a million miles an hour. I jerked his hands from his throat, then rammed two fingers into his mouth as deep as they would go. He vomited on the table. Then I lifted him from the chair and laid him out on the floor as Marisa stood and made a loud, clear statement about possible poison in the food. Pandemonium broke loose. If Jean Petrou just had severe indigestion, I was going to be in big trouble.

A man rushed over, pushing me aside. "I'm a doctor," he said in French.

I stood and looked toward the kitchen door. Henri Stehle was still standing there, looking our way. He made eye contact with me, then turned and disappeared into the kitchen.

The diners were all talking at once, jumping up, trying to leave. The whole crowd had panicked.

I heard the doctor say, almost to himself, "He's been poisoned, all right." Then I was gone, elbowing and shoving and pushing my way toward the kitchen.

Chapter Seven

I charged through the crowd to the door of the kitchen and slammed it open, knocking three people out of the way. There was a crowd there, one that had heard the hubbub from the dining room and had come to the window in the kitchen door to see what was going on.

I scanned the faces. "Where's Henri?" I roared in English, then had to do it again in French.

Two of them pointed toward the door to the stairway that led down to the employees' dressing room and entrance to the hotel. World Hotels Inc. didn't want the help mingling with the paying guests.

Down the stairs I went as fast as I could go. I certainly didn't know if it was Henri Stehle that Marisa looked at with loathing, but if he didn't know her from Eve, he wouldn't have rabbited for the underbrush when we locked eyes.

He wasn't in the male employees' dressing room. There was a man there dressing for the desk, so I asked, "Henri?"

He shook his head no.

I slammed into the women's. Two startled females. One sucked in a chestful of air and screamed. It was a nice effort, a real ear-splitter. I asked the other, "Henri?"

She shook her head, so I split. There were two offices on the hallway. I tried the door of the first, which was the employment office. Locked. I made a fist and punched out the glass, then opened the door and looked around the space. No people.

The second office, payroll, I think, was also locked. If Henri wasn't in there, he was quickly getting away. I ran down the hallway and out the door to the street.

He was running, maybe a hundred feet away, really booking it. Obviously he hadn't planned on a fast getaway.

I sprinted after him.

Now, I wasn't stupid enough to think, just because Abu Qasim's natural daughter made a face at this guy, that he had poisoned her husband. Oh, no! For all I knew, this guy was a Mossad agent, and the daughter of the worst al-Qaeda scumbag west of Baghdad recognized his nasty, infidel face.

There were a few people on the street,

light traffic, and the people turned to stare at Stehle, then me, pounding along.

Honestly, when I saw ol' Jean Petrou going down, I thought that his lovely wife had probably poisoned him. After all, she was going to be a seriously rich widow if they buried Jean in a few days, and they were recently separated because they didn't like living together. She might be able to work up a tear for Jean's funeral; then again, maybe not.

These thoughts went through my empty head as I thundered down the street after the fleeing Henri Stehle. No doubt he was cussing me as an ungrateful wretch — and he'd be right.

I was gaining on him. I'm no sprinter, but I have long legs and I work out, and I was closing on the guy.

Behind me I heard the shrill tweet of a police whistle. Stehle didn't stop, so I didn't.

I wondered if he was armed. I wasn't, and I'm not bulletproof.

I had closed the distance to maybe twenty-five feet when he went around a corner. I took it wide, just in case he wanted to stop and take a wild punch as I came pounding along.

He didn't swing. He was jumping in the back seat of a sedan. He didn't have the door closed, but the car was already in motion. I leaped, caught at the door to prevent it from closing.

He looked at me, kicked at my hand, and the car accelerated away as somebody in another vehicle slammed on his brakes. Stehle's driver had almost caused a collision.

I vaulted over the stopped car's hood, grabbed the driver's door and jerked it open. A woman driver, buckled in. "Police," I roared.

I reached across, popped the buckle and pulled her out. The car began to roll. I confess, I wasn't gentle. I dropped her and jumped behind the wheel and slammed the door shut. The sedan with Stehle in it was a half block ahead, accelerating quickly. I floored the gas pedal.

Stehle's car — a Peugeot, it looked like — took the next left. Of course the light was changing, and I had to slow, but there was just enough room so I poured the coal on and away we went, him still a half block ahead. I had the pedal to the metal, but the three squirrels under the hood could give me no more.

Three more turns and we were accelerating down the boulevard in front of the hotel. The clown ahead went screaming by the two police cars with flashing blue lights parked near the entrance and an ambulance easing up with flashing lights and siren moaning. As I roared by I got a glimpse of a nice little crowd gathered on the sidewalk.

Henri Stehle was in no mood for quiet conversation — that was obvious. The guy driving the Peugeot wasn't, either.

Soon we were out on the boulevard by the Seine, weaving through traffic and blowing through stoplights. Pedestrians were dodging and jumping every which way. I used my horn freely, but still . . . We were going to kill someone if this kept on.

I got a glimpse of his license plate — I was that close. An *A* and an *F.* Couldn't get the numbers.

I could hear a police siren, one of those French whee-hoo, whee-ooh jobs. Glanced in the rearview mirror and, you guessed it, he was behind me.

The Peugeot ran a red light and managed to miss a truck pulling out from the left. I wasn't so lucky. It was the truck fender or the pedestrians streaming across the street on my right. I took the fender. Whump!

I wasn't buckled in and nearly went through the windshield. My ride turned 180 degrees and slid to a tire-squalling halt. Gray smoke was wafting up around the crumpled hood.

Somehow I managed to get the ignition off. I seemed to be all in one piece, although I had taken a lick on the forehead and something wet was oozing into my left eye. I wiped at it. Red shit. Fuckin' A, man!

The driver's door didn't want to open. It was jammed. I was kicking at it when two cops grabbed hold, and with our combined efforts it swung free. The fuzz leaned in, placed rough hands on me and dragged me out onto the street.

Before I could explain my status as a civil servant of their old ally on the other side of the gray Atlantic, they had cuffs on me and jerked me to my feet, then slammed me against my wrecked ride. One of them helped himself to my wallet while the other felt me all over for a weapon. As if I could have hidden a pistol in that tight, tailored waiter's outfit.

I looked up the street. The Peugeot had stopped and was sitting up there with the brake lights on. Even as I looked, the right rear door opened and Henri Stehle got out. He had something in his hand. When he began walking back this way, he held it down beside his leg.

Uh-oh.

I may not be the brightest bulb in the box,

yet I am not the dimmest. I instantly arrived at the conclusion that ol' Henri figured I had almost gotten him caught and he'd decided to ensure it didn't happen again.

And here I was all handcuffed, without even a slingshot to even the odds.

I kneed the officer in front of me and, as he doubled up, put my knee into his face. He went down. The other one I backhanded — not too hard because I was wearing cuffs and couldn't really get the leverage to whack him good. He staggered. I popped him on the chin, then bent down and pulled his pistol, a nice little automatic, from his holster. There was a lanyard on it. That broke when I gave it a hell of a jerk.

People were shouting and fleeing, giving us some room.

I took two steps to give myself a clear shot at Henri, thumbed off the safety and tried to calm down enough to get a good sight picture. He wasn't waiting. He opened fire. Two pops, then he turned and ran back toward the Peugeot.

I don't believe in fair play, giving a sucker an even break — none of that crap. I'd rather shoot someone in the back than the front, because he won't be shooting at me while I do it. Besides, Henri had already had two free ones. I started whanging away with the cop's little popper — bang, bang, bang — as Henri scrambled into the back seat of the Peugeot. Once again, the door was still open when the car accelerated away.

I said a couple of nasty Anglo-Saxon words I happen to know and tossed the cop's shooter at him. Good thing. The other cop had his pistol out and was bent down a little working on the safety. He couldn't see too well because of his broken nose.

I held up my hands, still cuffed, so he wouldn't drill me when he got it all together. It took him about fifteen seconds to figure out I was just standing there, not trying to get away or murder anyone. When he did, he whacked me on the side of the face with his pistol.

None of us were having a good night.

"Your husband died on the way to the hospital, Madame Petrou." The French detective spoke with all the sincerity of a funeral director, Marisa thought. He was a senior detective, very senior, an officer named Marcel Gaillard. He was so senior that he had two young detectives with him, one of whom took notes in shorthand. The other . . . well, he seemed to be there in case the great man needed a glass of water, or tea, or a more comfortable chair.

"The doctors are very sure he was poisoned, but they won't know what kind, of course, until . . ." Gaillard sighed delicately.

"Until the autopsy is completed."

"Yes. You understand, under the circumstances, we —"

She nodded and took a deep breath. "A glass of water, please."

The junior member of the trio trotted right off. On the other side of the room, two gray-headed men were questioning Isolde Petrou. Marisa thought she recognized one of them from the newspapers, a cabinet minister.

"Now, unfortunately," said Gaillard, "it is my duty to ask you some very personal questions. I do not mean to offend you, but these are questions the examining magistrate will insist that I ask."

"I have told you everything I know, everything that happened, from the moment we entered the hotel until I sat down with you. Your man here has written down every word. I can't imagine that there is anything more to discuss."

"Unfortunately there is. Permit me, please. How would you describe your relationship with your husband?"

"We were separated, then we decided to

live together as husband and wife once again. My affection for Jean was — I had affection for him." Marisa paused, then added, "I know of nothing to add to that statement."

"And his relationship with his mother?"

"Ask her."

"We shall, we shall, madame, but I ask you now for your impressions."

"They had a great affection for each other and a mutual respect."

Marcel Gaillard nodded. "A few more questions, then we will stop. Your late husband's will will soon be a matter of public record. Perhaps you can tell me how much — in very general terms — you expect to inherit from him."

"I have no expectations. I will await the reading of the document."

"I see."

"I mean no disrespect, monsieur, but there are family trusts that Jean's father set up. I have no knowledge of these matters. I received a generous allowance."

"And I ask you again, do you know anyone who, for any reason, might have wished that your husband were dead?"

"No."

"Very well, madame. Thank you for your patience. I express my condolences."

"Am I a suspect?" Marisa asked.

"I am but a policeman, madame. I merely gather evidence for the magistrate, who will undoubtedly have information from many sources to weigh. I bid you good day. You may go."

Marisa stood. She walked over to where her mother-in-law sat. Isolde saw her coming, yet sat listening to the two men before her.

They fell silent as Marisa approached. She was in time to hear her mother-in-law say, "I will instruct the staffs of the various banks to cooperate fully. Harass them and our customers all you wish. Now, if you gentlemen will excuse me, I have had quite enough for one old woman. I need rest."

The two women were escorted from the hotel. When they were in the limo for the ride to the château, Isolde said, "Who was that at the door to the kitchen?"

"I thought I recognized him, but perhaps not."

"Did you tell them that?"

"No."

Isolde drew a deep breath and exhaled audibly. "Jean was a good son. He did his best. He was not a brilliant man, nor did he have the head for business his father had, but he tried. God knows he tried."

Marisa didn't reply.

"Who was that waiter that made Jean vomit? The detectives questioned me again and again about him. Was I supposed to know him?"

"I recognized him," Marisa said softly. "He is a CIA officer. His specialty is planting listening devices."

"The château, you think?"

"Possibly. And this car."

Isolde Petrou turned her face to the window. She had nothing more to say.

Marisa looked at her hands. Flexed them.

She thought about Jean, but they were just thoughts. She didn't love him, never had, which had made marriage difficult, to say the least. Oh, he was nice enough, but only that. A nice man. She had married him because . . . well, because he was a nice man, and at that time in her life, that was what she thought she needed. She had been so lonely . . .

Growing up as the pretend daughter of Georges and Grisella Lamoureux had been horrific at times. When she was little she didn't understand why she couldn't live with her real father, who came to see her occasionally, once a year or so. She had asked him that question, repeatedly, and he had said that it was best that she stayed where she was. Of course, where she was was at a Swiss boarding school. On vacations she visited the Lamoureuxs in France, or wherever Monsieur Lamoureux's diplomatic career had taken him.

Once, when she was seven or eight, her real father remarked in the way of explanation that his business was dangerous. "That is why you must tell no one, hint to no one, not even your very best friend, that you are not the daughter of the Lamoureuxs. I am just your uncle, come to visit."

The name he was using then was Alain Thenault. He wore impeccable suits and was always perfectly barbered and smelled of a subtle, no doubt expensive, scent, the kind that was popular among wealthy French businessmen just then. At his request, she called him uncle, in case someone might overhear.

"But what of Mama?" she asked on one visit. She could still remember the moment and the place, spring, in the school's garden, on a little bench seat as the sun and breeze caressed the early flowers. "Why can't I live with her?"

"It is not possible," he said curtly. "Let us not speak of her again."

So she wondered, on those lonely nights when the lights were out and everyone else at the school was sound asleep, Why could she and her father not speak of Mama? Was she dead? *Who was she?*

In her imagination she could see her mother, a beautiful woman, French, of course, with a wonderful smile and a gentle touch. Someday she would meet her — she knew it and wanted it to be so — and they would have so much to talk about, and she would love her mother and her mother would love her. On those endless nights long ago that had been her favorite fantasy.

Of course it never happened.

And never would. She knew that now. She didn't know who her mother was and never would know.

Her mother was probably dead. In fact, one suspected she killed herself when she realized what a monster she had married.

Remembering those days when she was a child, thinking these thoughts, Marisa rode silently through the streets and suburbs of Paris with Isolde Petrou, who was also lost in her own thoughts.

Henri Stehle lived in a walk-up flat in Montmartre. It was four in the morning when he rounded the corner and stood looking at the door to his building. There were no policemen in sight.

Dare he risk it? His clothes and money were in his apartment.

That fool American waiter! Chasing him. Of course he would tell the police that Stehle ran, and the police would want to know why.

Running was so stupid. He had panicked.

Fortunately he had seen his friend Alain sitting there at the curb in his car, waiting for him.

They had had such a good thing going, selling cocaine to rich tourists.

Standing in the dark doorway, Stehle tried to light a cigarette as he thought about the police and the money. He had drunk half a bottle of wine in the past hour, yet still his hands shook. He had to light three matches before he got his cigarette burning satisfactorily.

He wanted the money in the apartment. It was his! He had earned every sou. But what if the police came while he was upstairs? He waited . . . watching and smoking — and shivering. He had left his coat at the hotel. What a fool he was!

Henri Stehle went over the events of the evening one more time, running through every scene in his mind's eye. That crazy American!

Mon Dieu, who would have thought something like *that* might happen? It had been so unexpected, he had reacted without thinking.

Shooting at the American had been foolish. Silencing him was futile — he really knew nothing — but the crazy American had chased him, ruining everything. It was so frustrating!

Even now, the thought of that athletic man behind him, running to catch him, elevated Stehle's heart rate. He looked up and down the street again.

Think about the money! Forget the American and the police and all of that. Think about the money and the future and all the photographs you are going to take.

He puffed nervously on his cigarette. Well, the truth was that every minute he waited made it more likely the police would catch him upstairs. The sooner the better.

He screwed up his courage, tossed away his weed and walked to the entrance of the building, trying to walk normally. Through the door, up the stairs.

In front of his door he paused. Listened. Not a sound from within.

He used his key and pushed the door open. Closed it behind him. As he reached for the light he saw the man sitting in the chair. Startled, he stood motionless. In the weak light coming through the window from the streetlights he couldn't see the man's face.

"Who — ?"

His words stopped coming when he saw the pistol. Saw the silencer. In the intermittent light from the streetlights and store signs, he saw the deadly little hole in the snout of the silencer.

He stared, frozen, as the man extended the pistol, pointed it right at him, then, mercifully, everything went black.

CHAPTER EIGHT

I was uncomfortably ensconced in a jail cell at the Préfecture de police when the door to the cell block opened and George Goldberg, the CIA station chief for Paris, came in. He was a big guy, rumpled and overweight, a former All-American tackle who was three times brighter than the average football player. He wasn't smiling.

"When they said they had Carmellini, I didn't believe it. But here you are."

Obviously, we had met before. Like last year, when al-Qaeda tried to assassinate the heads of government of the G-8 nations at Versailles.

"You look a little worse for wear," he said as he examined the bleeding goose egg on my forehead and the welt across my cheekbone. It was also cut a little. I figured the front sight of the officer's automatic did the damage.

"It isn't the years, it's the mileage," I muttered.

Goldberg spoke to the uniformed policeman with him, and the cop unlocked my cell door. He took off my cuffs as Goldberg plodded away. I followed George out of the lockup.

The cop went off somewhere, and George led me to a desk, where I had to sign some forms for two glowering cops. I didn't read the forms, merely signed everything they pushed at me. They gave me back my belt, bow tie, shoelaces and the contents of my pockets. I counted the money in my wallet.

"Get out of here," one of them growled in French, nodding to his left, toward the door that led to the street.

Dawn was breaking on a miserable winter day when we came out of the prefecture's courtyard. Goldberg had a car and driver waiting. He had some stroke with someone.

When we were in the back of the car and it was rolling, he said, "Jean Petrou died in the ambulance on the way to the hospital. They couldn't revive him. And Henri Stehle, the head of food service at the hotel, can't be found."

"I sorta had that impression. The police learned everything I knew in fifteen minutes, then we spent three hours going over

207

it again and again. I refused to tell them why I was working in the hotel, and that seemed to irritate them."

"They're very unhappy with you."

"Anyone else take a fast hike?"

"Three of the staff seem to be missing. No one is sure just when they left. The police were hoping you would confess to the murder. They know that you were Johnny-on-the-spot when he had his first attack."

I shrugged.

"You want some food?"

"Yeah. And a bath and a plane ticket home."

"Admiral Grafton will be here this afternoon. All I can do is grub and a bath."

I was bathed and shaved, had had a nap and was accoutered in trousers, a white shirt, a tie and a sports coat when I was admitted that afternoon to the secure spaces in the basement of the U.S. embassy in Paris.

The place looked like an old-fashioned bank vault but was called a "skiff" — a Sensitive Compartmented Information Facility, or SCIF. Elaborate physical and electronic safeguards had been installed to prevent electronic eavesdropping. The air was conditioned, of course, and bore the unmistakable faint aroma of light machine oil. The windowless cubicles lit 24/7 with fluorescent lights overhead, the odor and the constant low-grade whir of fans moving air made the SCIF feel like a world within a world, a place detached from the places where normal people live. In short, the dump looked and felt like a prison. And believe me, if the people outside ever locked the door, we weren't leaving until the resurrection of the dead.

Grafton was tucked into a little office in the SCIF about the size of a bedroom closet. He had a desk, the chair he sat in and two more little folding chairs. The furniture almost filled the space.

"I hear you had a long evening," he said as he inspected my welts and bruises.

I dropped my fanny into the folding chair on the left and sighed. "You want to hear it again?" I knew he would have been briefed, probably by George Goldberg. Two newspapers lay on his desk. Marisa was on the front of one and Isolde the other. I tilted my head so I got a better look. Isolde looked distraught, haggard, and Marisa looked overwhelmed. Lovely. Vulnerable. How did she manage that, anyway?

"All of it," Grafton said, nodding.

When you report to Jake Grafton, it's like

talking to a voice recorder. He merely sat and listened, didn't ask any questions while I spoke, nor did he do facial expressions or gestures to keep me talking. He listened. Listened so well that I always got the impression he could repeat everything I said pretty much word for word.

When I ran dry he scratched his nose a few times and sat digesting it all. At last he said, "This Henri Stehle . . . he worked for the Paris World Hotel for about a month. The police say his references and his address are fake. The prior employers he gave as references never heard of him, and he doesn't live at the apartment house he said he did. The concierge doesn't recognize the photo the hotel took for his building pass."

"Guess World Hotels Inc. really checked him out."

"The police inspector told me Stehle was the right age, had good references and knew how to cook French cuisine. The hotel manager let it go at that. Stehle didn't handle money. He did an excellent job until last night."

"So he poisoned Jean Petrou?"

"No proof of that. You didn't serve the head table, did you?"

"No."

"Turns out Jean and his mother both

ordered vegetarian plates. Isolde has been a vegetarian since her university days, and Jean has had some kind of stomach trouble the last few months. The food that remained on Jean's plate contained a powerful heart medication, digitalis; the other didn't."

"The plates were identical?"

"Apparently. The waiter was told in the kitchen who they were for. He served Isolde first, and she got the plate in his right hand because he's right-handed. The plate in his left hand he put in front of Jean."

I wasn't liking what I was hearing. "If the people in the kitchen didn't know which person the plates were going in front of, they couldn't have poisoned them. Have I got that right?"

"That's a working theory, anyway."

"So the implication is that either the waiter, Isolde or Marisa poisoned him. The waiter could have poisoned the food as he brought it to the table —"

"Difficult but not impossible," Grafton said.

"— Or more likely, Isolde or Marisa put something in his grub when his head was turned."

"Oh, I didn't tell you. The police have heard that Isolde was a heart patient several years ago. They are checking with her physicians to see what medication she was on then and is on now."

"I don't think Marisa did it."

Grafton chuckled. He had a dry chuckle, sort of like a rooster might make when looking at his favorite chicken. "Umm," he said.

"Why would his mother want to pop him off?"

"Darned if I know," the admiral muttered. "The French police are investigating. A very wealthy family, large stock positions in banks in four countries, board positions, family trusts — one suspects that with Jean's death large sums of money will change hands."

"So what are the women saying at the château?"

"Nothing at all. They got home, packed their bags and left in the limo for an unknown destination. Right now they are somewhere in Germany."

I said a nasty word. I was thinking of all the effort I put into bugging the joint. Okay, okay, the job took less than an hour, but I had to set it up and think about it for a week. *That* was the time and effort that was wasted.

If Grafton had any sympathy for me, he didn't let it show. He appeared to be thinking about something else.

There was a photo on Grafton's desk of Henri Stehle. This was the photo the Paris World had taken for his employee pass. I picked it up and scrutinized it carefully. Stehle didn't look much like the old man I had seen here in Paris last fall. Yet the more I stared, the more doubts I had. Perhaps he and the old man were indeed one and the same.

"Abu Qasim?" I asked Grafton, waggling the photo.

Grafton shrugged. "Possibly," he muttered.

"Come with me," he said. He picked up a file from his desk and led me to a conference room, where the real work is done in a SCIF. Speedo Harris and Nguyen Diem were there going over police reports and slurping coffee. Unfortunately the American embassy was the only place in France that served American-style coffee. British though he might be, Harris was swilling his like a Yank. He and Diem inspected my war wounds and made appropriate comments.

Admiral Grafton summarized my adventures of the previous evening. "Gentlemen," he continued, "we have a hell of a mess on our hands. The Russian government says it had nothing to do with the murder of Alexander Surkov, a murder that is being inves-

tigated by the British police and Interpol —
and the nuclear angle is being investigated
by half the police forces in Europe. Last
night's murder of Jean Petrou is being
investigated by the Paris police. The only
link between them is the presence at both
poisonings of Marisa Petrou, who is possibly the daughter of the most wanted terrorist in America and Europe, Abu Qasim."

He paused, and Speedo Harris asked, "*Is*
she his daughter?"

"Maybe, maybe not."

"That comment could be made about
bloody near every young woman on earth,"
Harris observed trenchantly. The Brits were
like that, trenchant, yet I don't think Harris
had a very high regard for the admiral.

Grafton wasn't normally one to take much
crap from subordinates, but he didn't
bother to squash Speedo this time. "Very
perceptive," he said agreeably.

"So what is your theory?"

"I want to know if there is a link between
these killings. What, if anything, did Alexander Surkov and Jean Petrou have in common?"

"Marisa Petrou killed them both," Speedo
suggested.

"Or Abu Qasim," Per Diem mused.

From a pocket Grafton produced a photo

and handed it to Diem. I recognized the face from the newspapers — Alexander Surkov. He also produced envelopes, one of which he handed to each man. "You both are now liaison officers officially attached to the U.S. State Department, which means you work for me. Those letters will get you cooperation almost anyplace if you say please and thank you. Visit the various agencies investigating these killings. I want to know what they know. Got it?"

Each opened his envelope. Diem was the first to whistle. "Is this really the FBI director's signature? On a letter with my name on it, even."

"Your career is blooming like a rose."

"My letter is signed by the head of New Scotland Yard," Speedo Harris said solemnly, staring at the paper. Then he looked at Grafton with new respect. "You have some pull somewhere."

"Somewhere. Now hit the bricks. You have my telephone numbers."

I thought Speedo was going to salute, but he didn't. As he and Diem exited, George Goldberg came in. He handed Grafton another copy of the Stehle photo. "Twenty-three percent," Goldberg said. He nodded at me and left.

Grafton tapped the photo on his fingernail, then handed it to me. "Better hang on to that. You may need to wave it around somewhere."

"Okay."

"The folks at Fort Meade" — that would be the National Security Agency — "say that this photo and the one you took last year of the old man in Paris are of the same person, to a twenty-three percent certainty."

I took a good look at the Stehle photo. His face had actually been too close to the camera when it was snapped, and so the lens distorted the image slightly. Was that the reason the probability was only 23 percent, or . . . "He looked old last year," I remarked.

"He can make himself look any way he chooses, but he can't change the dimensions of his skull, and those are the dimensions the computer measures."

"Twenty-three percent. Even Vegas gives better odds than that." I put the photo in a breast pocket of my sports coat. "I don't think Marisa poisoned anyone," I added.

"Why?"

I hunted through the attic for a reason I could articulate, and couldn't find one. None of it made much sense. Why in the world would Qasim want Isolde Petrou dead? Or playboy son Jean? On the other hand, I could think of a dozen reasons why Marisa might feel relieved that Jean was on his way to another place. I bulled ahead anyway. "Instinct, I suppose. She's not the poison type."

"Thank you, Dr. Freud," Grafton said dryly. "She and her mother-in-law are on their way to Germany. Get a car, pack your toothbrush and hit the road. Check in with the duty officer this evening — she'll tell you where those women have come to rest. I want you to get as close to Marisa as humanly possible and stay there."

"You think Abu Qasim might try to kill her?"

He frowned. "I don't know what their relationship is." He rapped on the table several times with a knuckle; then his features softened and he looked me right in the eyes. "I want Qasim dead or alive, and I don't give a damn which it is. Marisa is your bait goat. Take a pistol with you."

"Okay." I stood to go.

"If I were you," Grafton added casually, "I'd watch what I ate around those women."

George Goldberg had four pistols in the safe behind his desk. I looked over his selection and took a new Springfield Armory EMP 1911 automatic with a three-inch barrel, in

9 mm. I've have trouble hitting anything at a distance, but within twenty-five feet, the bad guys had better watch out. The one I took had a clip welded on the left side of the frame so that a right-handed guy could stick it down between his trousers and shirttail in the small of his back and hook the clip over his trousers, anchoring the gun in place. George gave me an extra magazine with hollow-point shells already in it, and I put it in my trouser pocket. I worked the slide a few times, tried the safety and trigger, then loaded the thing, left it cocked and locked, and put it where it was supposed to go.

"How do I look?" I asked George.

"That sports coat doesn't really go with those trousers."

"The next time I go shopping, I'll take you along."

One of the embassy staff took me to the airport to rent a car. Since Uncle Sugar was paying the tab and I have a certain image to maintain, I rented a Porsche 911. As I drove it back to Paris to pack and check out of the hotel, I decided that I would buy one of these if my old Benz ever went lame and I had to shoot it.

I was late getting out of Paris and got caught in rush hour. It was dark and raining by the time I had cleared the last of the suburbs. The pistol in the small of my back felt like a rock, so I put it in the pocket of my sports coat.

I called the duty officer in the embassy, as per Grafton's instructions, and was told the women had gone to a castle on the Rhine River.

"A castle?"

"Yep. It's owned by Wolfgang Zetsche, who is the chairman of the largest shipping firm in Europe." She named it. "He retired as CEO last year." She gave me directions to get there.

"Better get me a room in a hotel or inn nearby for tonight."

"Already did." She gave me the name of the place and more directions.

As I drove toward Nancy and the northeast corner of France, I thought about what I should do. I almost called Jake Grafton to get his opinion, then decided not to. If he had had instructions he would have given them to me before I left the embassy. I was on my own. Or semi on my own, anyway; he was as close as my cell phone.

Jake Grafton spent most of the evening in the SCIF on his telephones. He had three on his desk — two encrypted landlines and an encrypted satellite phone. He had received telephone calls from Per Diem and Speedo Harris, giving him the latest info on both the British and French investigations of the two poisonings. He also had a computer on his desk, which he used to send encrypted emails. He was pounding keys this evening, talking via the Internet to Sal Molina, who was at his desk in the White House.

If Alexander Surkov sold the identity of the Knights Winchester to al-Qaeda, which then poisoned him, the radioactive trail is a ruse designed to frame people with a known grudge against him. On the other hand, if the Russians really did it, it follows that the Knights have nothing to fear. If that is the case, who murdered Jean Petrou? Was it really an attempt to kill Isolde, Huntington Winchester's best friend, or did Isolde and/or Marisa decide they had finally had enough of dear old Jean?

Wolfgang Zetsche is at his country home on the Rhine, and Isolde seems to be on her way to join him. Where is Oleg Tchernychenko? I am informed the Swiss banker is in Zurich at his bank. And where are the three Americans? I suggest you get the FBI to keep tabs on them. If al-Qaeda is really after these people, we need to get them to a place where we can guard them, and catch anyone who tries to assassinate them.

Grafton sent the message. Five minutes later he had a reply.

The Knights Winchester? Who thought that up? Tchernychenko is fishing in Scotland, and the three Americans are in the States, although scattered. I asked the FBI to locate them yesterday. If Surkov did indeed sell out the six Knights, he also betrayed your teams. And you.
  Keep me advised.

It was midnight on a dark, rainy night when I reached Strasbourg and crossed the Rhine into Germany. As I drove up to the border crossing, the gates were wide open and the man under the awning was just waving traffic through.

The Rhine River is the border between France and Germany from Basel, Switzerland, downriver to about Karlsruhe. Wolfgang Zetsche's castle wasn't really on the Rhine; it was about two miles up a tributary on the German side of the stream near the town of Rastatt. The hotel the folks in Paris had booked me into was in Rastatt, but I wanted to see the castle. I drove through town and took the river road toward the Rhine, trying to see through the night rain and mist. Visibility was terrible, and if it had been any worse, I would have missed Zetsche's country retreat. It was a castle, all right, built on a rocky outcrop that forced the small river into a horseshoe bend to get around. From outside the gate, I got the impression of sheer walls of stone, a flat roof, all set amid huge trees behind stone walls that were at least fifteen feet high in the lowest place, higher elsewhere.

I turned around in front of the closed gate and headed back to Rastatt. The distance was only about a third of a mile.

Zetsche had obviously done well in the shipping business. Make that very well. So how did he know Isolde and Marisa? Why would they come here, of all places, immediately after the death of the good son?

Rastatt looked centuries old, with three- and four-story medieval buildings along a twisty, narrow street paralleling the river. The lights from the windows and poles reflected off the wet pavement. Not a single pedestrian this time of night. All the good burghers were home in bed.

The hotel wasn't old — it was a modern brick structure of five or so stories that sat right on the street. An alley led to a parking garage behind it. I parked the Porsche on the second deck, rescued my junk from the trunk, locked up the car and went inside to see if the computer recognized my credit card.

It did. After I had dumped my stuff in my room, I went to find some dinner. Back in my room I had a nice hot shower and scrubbed my teeth. I was exhausted. In less time than it takes to tell, I was in bed with the light off. Then my cell phone rang.

"Yeah."

"Hey, Tommy." It was Jake Grafton.

"Yes, sir."

"The police found Henri Stehle this evening. He was floating facedown in the Seine about ten miles downriver from the center of town."

"So he's not the guy we talked about." That would be Abu Qasim, of course, but I wasn't going to say it over the air.

"Our luck doesn't run that way. Or mine doesn't, anyway."

"Oh, man! She was looking right at him, I thought. You should have seen the look on her face — recognition, horror, loathing, it was all there."

"She might have been looking at Stehle, who might have reminded her of someone. Or she might have been looking at someone else, one of the waiters, perhaps, or one of the guests."

"Or the real Henri Stehle wasn't there."

"They're checking on that. In the meantime, Wolfgang Zetsche's hovel by the river — you know where it is?"

"Drove by a little while ago."

"Better get over there and spend the night. I want him to be alive in the morning."

I must have been tired, because the only thing I could think of to say was, "You want me inside or out?"

"Inside, of course. As close to Zetsche as you can get."

"Of course."

"Try to keep Marisa alive, too."

"Maybe you'd better send the Marines."

"You're it, Tommy."

Oh, man! The news just kept getting worser and worser.

" 'Bye," he said and hung up.

I turned the light on and rolled out. Back when I was a callow youth, if I had known how miserable the hours would be while working for the CIA, I would have just told that recruiter to send me to prison instead.

How does that old song go? "If I'd shot him when I met him, I'd be out of prison now."

CHAPTER NINE

I left my car in the garage and walked to the castle. I was dressed in black trousers, a black pullover shirt, dark sneakers and a black sweater, and carried my gear in a navy blue knapsack slung over one shoulder. My hand-cannon was tucked in the small of my back and my cell phone was in my pocket, set to vibrate if anyone called. That "anyone" would, of course, only be Jake Grafton or a duty officer in London or Paris. Swine that I am, I hadn't even given my mother this number.

As I saw it, my job was relatively straight-forward. The admiral said he wanted Wolfgang Zetsche and Marisa Petrou alive in the morning. I had to get into the house and find those two people, then ensure no one with mayhem on his mind got to them during the hours of the night. On the other hand, if they had already ingested poison, there wasn't much I could do about it except get them to a hospital quickly after they got sick but before they died. I decided I would worry about poison if and when.

It wasn't dark and stormy, but it was dark and gloomy and dripping that winter's night. I was the only person on the street, which was probably a good thing — people have a nasty habit of calling the police when they see a man dressed all in black sneaking around outside in the middle of the night. Presumably Johnny Cash didn't sneak.

My entrance to the castle had to be over the wall that separated the grounds from the road. The river was on the other three sides, and I wasn't about to swim it.

At fifteen feet tall, it was a heck of a wall, constructed of fieldstone and, fortunately, not smooth. I scanned the trees and top of the wall as I walked along on the other side of the road. I didn't see any security cameras. Which didn't mean there weren't any — only that I didn't see them. Anyone with a lick of sense who planned to burgle the place would case the joint during the daytime; working for Jake Grafton, I didn't have that luxury.

Two cars went by. I ducked out of view behind a tree one time, and into the entrance to a stairs that led to a house on a hill the other time. I walked the entire length of the wall, looking it over as carefully as I could.

I stood across the road in the entrance to another set of stairs that led up behind me and listened for traffic and voices. Nothing.

With the knapsack firmly in place on my shoulders, I took a deep breath, trotted across the pavement and free-climbed the wall. I learned this skill in high school when two friends and I took up rock climbing, kept it up through college and still liked to take climbing vacations whenever life allowed.

I crouched on top near a large tree limb that barely cleared the wall. Opened my backpack, got the infrared goggles on and scanned the grounds. Nothing in infrared, so I switched to ambient light. There were two cars parked in front of the place and another in front of a garage beside the house. Lots of large trees, a few shrubs and two flower beds. The windows of the building — from this angle it didn't look as formidable as I first thought — were blank, with only one light showing in one window on the third floor. There were dormers on what appeared to be the fourth floor. Each corner of the building had a round, silo-like structure festooned with windows; presumably these round rooms were bedrooms. No crenelles or merlons. After I had examined the ground and house as well as I could from this angle, I switched to the trees. Security cameras and motion detectors would probably be mounted high. I didn't see any.

I slithered down the limb until it reached the trunk of the tree, then dropped about two feet to the ground.

Knelt and looked some more. Listened. I could smell smoke. Someone had a fire going.

A vehicle — it sounded like a car — stopped on the other side of the wall and sat there with its engine running for about a minute, then drove on.

A sprint took me to a bush under one of those round turrets that decorated the corner of the building. I got busy with the goggles on the infrared setting, scanning the grounds, then the house. The nifty thing about the goggles was that they could detect heat sources through windows or normally insulated wooden walls. Unfortunately Herr Zetsche's country home was constructed of stone, and a lot of it. The heat sources were too well masked for the goggles to find. Couldn't even find the hot water tank or the fire in the fireplace. I did see a plume of heat emanating from one chimney.

I went around behind the building, trying to stay in the deep shadows under and behind the shrubbery. As I made this trip, rain began to fall. Not a night mist, but rain. The walls above me were wet and getting wetter. I had made it up the rough boundary wall, but free-climbing this cut limestone in the rain was a bit more than I thought I could handle. No sense in finding out how deep a crater I would make in Germany if I fell two or three stories.

The servant's entrance was down five stairs and had a small projecting roof over it. I went to work with the picks I kept in a small folding wallet on my left hip. The door had two locks. After checking the door for alarms and not finding any, I opened the top lock first, then went to work on the bottom one.

The continuous gentle patter of raindrops on the little roof above my head was broken only by the faint, distant moan of a train whistle. Once, twice, three times it called, then fell silent. I fervently wished I were on it.

The telephone rang in Jake Grafton's Paris apartment. Not the encrypted portable satellite telephone he carried with him everywhere, but the regular unsecure land-line.

"Hello."

"Admiral Grafton? How are you this evening?"

"I don't know who you are. In five seconds I'm hanging up." Grafton began counting silently.

At three, the man said, "Jerry Hay Smith."

"How'd you get this telephone number, Mr. Smith?"

"If you'd been in the newspaper business as long as I have, Admiral, you'd have some sources, too. I called to find out what you know about Alexander Surkov and polonium 210. Not for publication, of course, but because I think I am entitled to know."

"Buy a newspaper."

"Admiral, I have read the wire service reports and everything the newspapers have chosen to publish." Smith was confident, smooth, a man who just knew that everyone on the planet was dying to talk to him. "I'm also calling about another murder that hasn't yet made the press here in the States, a Frenchman named Jean Petrou. His mother is a personal friend."

"This is a ridiculous conversation," Grafton said, tossing off the words. The thought that Jerry Hay Smith was probably recording said conversation crossed his mind. "Why would you think I know anything that isn't in the press?"

"Because you're a CIA officer. And because you are . . . consulting, shall we say, with Mr. Winchester. Who murdered Jean Petrou?"

"You are misinformed, Mr. Smith. I know nothing about your matter." Grafton put the telephone back onto its cradle.

Apparently Smith was working on his memoirs or his book. Or a column for tomorrow's paper.

Grafton made a mental note: Jerry Hay Smith was going to be a problem.

Wolfgang Zetsche was in his late fifties, a brilliant, vigorous athletic man about five and a half feet tall, one with little patience for what he viewed as the lesser lights of the species. He listened to Marisa now with thinly disguised impatience, almost as if he were ready to interrupt to complete her sentences.

The room they were in was huge, a drawing room full of stuffed furniture and exhibits of artifacts and curiosities Zetsche had gathered on his many expeditions to far corners of the globe. He was currently between wives. The future Frau Zetsche number four sat in a chair near Isolde, her eyes fixed on Wolfgang.

Near the group was a television upon which the four of them had been watching the late evening news. Several minutes had been devoted to the murder of Jean Petrou, and several more to recent revelations in the still unsolved murder of Alexander Surkov. Now the audio was muted, although images of talking heads and policemen shimmered across the screen.

"Ha," Zetsche said when Marisa paused for air, "you think an assassin could reach me here, in my own house?" He strode to a nearby desk and jerked open the right-hand drawer. From it he removed a pistol, a wicked black automatic. He pulled back the slide until he saw brass, then let it go home with a metallic thunk. He held it up where Marisa could clearly see it. "If those Islamic zealots want to come, let them come!"

He jammed the pistol into his pocket, then looked at Isolde, sitting in a nearby chair. "I am sorry for my manner, which is insensitive. I know you have come far in your hour of grief to warn me, but I need no warning. You have met the assistant butler and my personal chauffeur — they are trained bodyguards, expert in armed and unarmed combat. I will speak to them. The four of us are safer in this house with them than we would be alone in a bank vault. Trust me — it is true."

Marisa glanced at the future frau to see how she was taking all this. Apparently she knew all about her fiancé's involvement in a conspiracy to rid the world of Islamic Nazis. The wonder was that Wolfgang Zetsche hadn't been interviewed about it for a major newsmagazine.

It took me maybe three minutes to open both of the locks, three minutes listening to the wind in the treetops and water gurgling down an old downspout just a foot away from this entrance . . . and glancing around occasionally to ensure I was still alone.

I pulled the door open and had started to step inside when I saw something moving out of the corner of my eye. I was wearing the night vision goggles set on ambient light, so I turned my head and looked. The ambient light presentation is green, for technical reasons that are a bit beyond me, so I saw green trees and green rocks amid a green world. Nothing was moving now.

A flip of the switch and the goggles reset themselves to display infrared images. Not a single image of a warm-blooded creature did I see.

Well, something had moved and caught my eye.

Or perhaps it was my imagination, the way I was turning my head. The field of view in the goggles is limited, and usually the clarity of the images is some degree of fuzzy, so sometimes an overactive imagination can lead you to think you see things that aren't really there.

I stepped through the door and closed it behind me. Turned both bolt handles to ensure it was again locked, then adjusted the goggles on my head and took a look around.

I was in a hallway with stone walls, part of the basement, and a wooden ceiling. I looked up . . . no people visible. I felt something under my feet — a mat. For wiping shoes. I put it to its designed use.

Moving forward, slowly and silently, I searched the basement. It seemed deserted. Quickly found the hot water tanks — there were three — and the hot water pipes leading away to faucets all over the building.

As soon as I was sure I was alone in the basement and had a general idea of where the doors were, I crept up the stairs. At the top of the stairs I had a good view through the walls, which were apparently made of some kind of thin, painted particleboard. I saw dim, ghostly figures moving some distance away, through several interior walls, it seemed. I also found the fire, which was in a room where there appeared to be four people — three sitting, one standing. Two more people were in what I thought might be the kitchen area — I could see a heat source that might be a coffeepot or teakettle — and one or two people were upstairs; no, make that three.

The nearby hallways being empty, I opened the door as quietly as I could and sneaked through. There were lights in the hallway, dim night-lights mounted halfway up the walls. I raised the goggles to my forehead. The ceiling was at least twelve feet above the floor, and dark chandeliers dangled every few yards.

I opened the door to the room adjacent to the room with the fireplace. As I walked in, the light coming through the doorway revealed a giant bear standing on his hind legs, every tooth bared, about to rip my head off with his paws.

I recoiled, then realized the bear was stuffed. A leopard gathered to leap stood on a table in one corner; deer, elk, caribou and antelope heads shared the walls with shelves full of books. There were four stuffed easy chairs, a bar and a table for playing cards. A gun cabinet filled with hunting rifles and shotguns stood between the two exterior windows.

I pulled the door closed and checked in infrared in all directions to ensure no one was marching for this room. Then I hunkered down beside a bookcase and put a stethoscope microphone against the door that separated the two rooms. Fortunately the four people on the other side of the door were making no move to come this way: With only the one wall and some books between us, I could see their figures fairly well.

The earpiece had about ten feet of cord. I unwound it and slipped the earpiece into my right ear. I heard voices from the next room.

". . . the person who betrayed us. Obviously someone did. We must find that someone." A man's voice speaking accented English, the lingua franca of our age.

"It might have been Surkov," a woman said tentatively. That accent sounded French. Was that Marisa?

"If he had been the one," the man said positively, "they wouldn't have murdered him. Why kill your source of secret information? Oh, no! I think the traitor is one of us. Or perhaps Grafton."

Grafton? *Jake Grafton?* I thought that Grafton betraying the group, or any of them, was about as likely as me winning the Irish Sweepstakes, considering the fact that I had never bought a ticket.

I stood there amid the stuffed beasts in the Dead Zoo frozen into immobility, wondering what in the world these people were going to say next.

"This undertaking was always hazardous." That was an older woman speaking, a French accent. I thought perhaps Isolde Petrou. "There are occasionally moments in history when a handful of determined people can make a difference. I do not know if this is one of those times, but I feel it is our moral duty to fight this great evil that is attacking the people of the earth. If they win, civilization will collapse and we will enter a new dark age. If we win, the adherents of Islam will eventually learn, as have the believers of all other faiths, how to live in a secular world, at peace with those who believe differently. The politicians wish to bury their heads in the sand, as usual. They will do nothing until the entire house is on fire. Huntington Winchester was absolutely right — it is the moral duty of those with the courage and means to grapple with this great evil."

"I had thought," the man said softly, so softly that I had to strain to hear, "that with the death of National Socialism in Germany, fascism was once and for all defeated. It wasn't. The Islamic strain is even more virulent than the Italian and German varieties. My parents — you knew them, didn't you, Madame Petrou?"

"I did."

"They were Nazis in the thirties, rejoiced when Hitler took over, hated the Jews. Oh, yes, they admitted it later, when I was a boy. They were just children in the thirties, innocent, foolish and proud as all children are, but when they saw the devastation of Germany, when they realized that Hitler had murdered millions of people in concentration camps, then . . . they lived with the guilt of their earlier approval all their lives. I saw that guilt. It haunted them. This stain was on Germany, on Germans, this foul, evil, bloody stain . . ."

He paused and, listening but not seeing, I thought maybe he was trying to regain his composure. "We are all committed," the man said forcefully. "We are all convinced we are doing the right thing. But there is a traitor among us and we must ferret him out."

"Or her." That was a female voice I didn't

recognize. Perhaps the future ex–Mrs. Zetsche.

"I am ready for bed." Marisa.

"Of course," the man said. "My body-guards will be in the hallway all night." So the man was Zetsche. He apparently rang a bell. In less than a minute I heard and saw someone enter the room. "Werner will escort you to your rooms. We will discuss this matter tomorrow at breakfast. *Gute Nacht*."

They rose from their chairs in the living room and made their way toward the hall-way as I wrapped up my cord and stowed the stethoscope mike.

I was walking around that trophy room in high dudgeon, tired, wishing I could spend twelve hours in bed, silently cussing and revisiting my decision to stay married to the green paycheck, when I got a glimpse through one of the windows of a man walking across the lawn. Just a dark figure, strid-ing purposely.

Now what?

I thought about calling Grafton and giv-ing him a piece of my mind, then decided against it. I checked the pistol in my waist-band.

I'd feel a lot better about all of this if I got busy and shot somebody.

CHAPTER TEN

As I climbed the stairs behind the four people from the living room, staying so far behind them I was out of sight, I was adjusting the gain and contrast knobs on the goggles. I was smack up against the limitations of the technology: I could see the four people in front of me, and I could count two more images of what should be people, faint images, merely blobs of color. In infrared, the lights in the hallways looked like stars.

When the four people in front of me went into bedrooms — at least they looked like bedrooms, with hot water radiators for heat and attached bathrooms with hot water pipes — I looked for an empty bedroom beside them to hole up in. The building reminded me of an old hotel that had been renovated. How this architectural monstrosity survived World War II was a mystery. Maybe it was damaged and restored. I found an empty bedroom and went in.

With the door closed, I tried to find the other people who were in the house. Located three, this time. I was still diddling with the knobs when the goggles died. One second they worked, then the various heat sources faded away to nothing. Didn't take me long to figure out that the battery was as dead as Adolf Hitler.

I sat there in the darkness cursing my luck. That didn't do a lot of good, so I installed three stethoscope microphones so I could at least listen to the goings-on in the rooms around me and in the hallway. What I heard was two women in the bathroom.

Zetsche and his girlfriend were in the bedroom beyond the Petrous. All I could hear was murmurs, which might have been conversation or something else, such as television audio. Difficult to say. Of course, even if I did hear them, they would probably be talking in German, which wasn't one of my languages.

I used the facilities myself, then settled down on a chair with the earphones in my ears. Without the goggles, this was the best I could do.

Before long the Petrou women fell silent. Conversation continued, still inaudible, for about an hour from the room beyond that; then it, too, faded away, leaving the big house in silence.

The night crawled along. Occasionally I heard measured footsteps — one of the bodyguards, I concluded, walking the hallways. Between footsteps there was no sound except the gentle patter of raindrops on the windowpanes. Amazing that the microphones picked that up so well.

One o'clock came and went. I tried to keep my eyes open by debating the issues. Was Marisa an assassin, was this really the line of work for me, and should I punch Jake Grafton in the nose the next chance I got? Unfortunately there were no clear answers; my eyelids got heavier and heavier and I slept.

For Marisa, nights were the worst. When the house was dark and silent her memories came flooding back, and her fears and anxieties and private hurts.

"Why won't you tell me about my mother?" she demanded of her father during a rare visit. She had been a teenager then, thirteen or fourteen, sure that she knew the difference between right and wrong, sure of her ability to heal a broken world.

"There is nothing you need to know," he said, in that condescending, self-righteous manner that she had grown to despise.

"I am not a child," she retorted hotly. "Tell me the truth and I will live with it, as you do."

"I am your father and you are still a child, a young woman. You must learn to trust my wisdom. I have made the right choice."

"You ask for trust and yet you have none. Where is the justice and wisdom in that?" She had been tart in those days, argumentative. Her teachers even wrote notes to her putative parents, Georges and Grisella.

"I am a man and you are a woman. And I am your father."

"What you are is a misogynist." If he expected her to surrender, he didn't know his daughter.

"What I am is a Muslim," he retorted firmly. "I believe in Allah. I believe that the Prophet set forth the relationship between men and women in the holy Koran, and the relationship between father and daughter. I demand your respect and obedience to my will."

"You may demand it, but you would be wiser to earn it."

That was the first time she had seen him angry, out of control. "*You* would be wise to hold your tongue, child," he said firmly.

For the first time in her life, she was frightened of him. The beast within had been revealed. He was like a prophet from the Old Testament, a visionary who saw only good and evil, and if you were not among the good, the obedient, then you were evil. It was in his eyes.

She saw it and remained silent.

She had seen the inner man. At that moment she knew the truth, knew him for the righteous, bigoted fanatic that he was.

Oh, her poor mother! To marry such a man! To sleep with him and have his child! And to gradually learn the truth, as she must have. It was like a nightmare from Shakespeare.

Tonight, in Wolfgang Zetsche's house, she thought of those moments, relived them as she had many times in the years since.

"You are my daughter and will obey me," he had said with cold steel in his voice. Yet it had been his eyes that held her mesmerized. Eyes are wonderous things: Most people use them to look out at the world, yet the eyes of her father allowed the world to look at the man within. At least, they did on those rare moments when he lost control and his face no longer obeyed his will. Then one could see the raging passions and illogical fanaticism on full display.

It had been a sobering moment for her, a glimpse of the truth at the core of her life. She didn't know anything of her mother, except that she must have been a woman, and her father was insane. She felt as if she were an alien who had just landed on planet Earth and upon meeting the natives asked aloud, Who *are* these creatures?

It wasn't long after that, Marisa reflected tonight, when her father began to discuss Islam, the holy Koran, Allah and the infidels and Paradise and all of that. Her first reaction was amazement. That a man she had known all her life and seen as a pillar of the community should believe this garbage, as he obviously did, was nothing short of astounding. It was as if her roommate had announced she believed the Grimm fairy tales were all true, every word.

Tonight as she stood at the window looking out into a black, wet universe, Marisa wondered yet again, for the ten thousandth time, about her mother. What had her mother thought when her father first told her of Islam and the jihad against the infidels?

Indeed, what *had* she thought?

Perhaps he killed her, Marisa mused, and not for the first time. Perhaps Mama said something, something that revealed that she didn't share any of his beliefs or any of his passions. Perhaps the rage was more than he could handle.

I awoke with a start. The house was deathly quiet. Even the rain had stopped. I glanced at my watch, which had hands that glowed in the dark. A few minutes after three in the morning.

What had awakened me?

I listened on each earpiece — there were three.

All silent.

I removed the penlight from my pocket, made sure it was on red light, then clicked it on and shined it around the room.

I came out of the chair slowly and carefully, trying to make no noise. Went to the bathroom, eased the door closed and flipped the light switch on. The room stayed dark. No power.

Back to the door to the room. I eased the lock to the open position and opened the door as slowly and quietly as I could. The hallway was dark as a pharaoh's tomb and just as quiet.

Standing there, listening, I let the darkness and silence creep over me as I tried to make sense of it.

The power should be on. There should be night-lights. And guards. Those two studly hunks with guns — where were they?

I stepped into the hallway and eased the door closed behind me. Pulled it until the latch began to engage, but didn't let it click home. Taking my time, staying to the side of the hallway, I worked my way to the Petrous' door and pressed my ear against it. Someone in there was snoring gently.

On to the next door, Zetsche's. Couldn't hear a thing.

Where were the guards?

I went to the head of the stairs and looked downward. It was like looking into the eternal pit. Not even a candle glowed in that vast darkness.

I went down the stairs as slowly and smoothly as I could, alert and listening and looking. And nervous. Something was really wrong . . . and it gave me goose bumps.

Maybe I have an overactive imagination. I can't sit through a horror movie because it scares me too much. I'm easily overstimulated, as one former girlfriend acidly pointed out.

If the circuit breakers had popped, the emergency generator should have kicked in. If Wolfgang owned one. I was betting he did and it was in the basement. Fortunately I knew how to get there since I had come in that way. I didn't dare show a light. If the guards were prowling around and saw a light, they might get twitchy and start shooting once they concluded that I wasn't their employer or one of his guests. At the very least they would try to subdue me one way or another and call the local police.

Working strictly by dead reckoning and feel, I found the door to the stairway to the basement where I'd entered . . . and it was open.

I certainly didn't leave it that way.

Perhaps one of the guards . . .

I stood there with my eyes closed, every other sense alert. A minute passed, then another.

Reached for the railing and started down.

Right then I would have given a month's pay to have the agency-issue night vision goggles working properly and riding on my pointy little head. The problem with technology is that when you need it most, it fails you. There must be a deep philosophical lesson lurking in that truth, but I wasn't smart enough to figure it out just then.

At the foot of the stairs I paused again to listen and feel the darkness. I had a decision to make. Unless I used the penlight, I was going to have to find the power box by feel, which might take all night and would certainly be noisy as I careened around like the proverbial bull in the china shop. It really was no decision at all — I had to use the penlight. Just in case, I pulled the little 9 mm from my waistband and checked that the safety was on. Yep. Cocked and locked.

I scanned the light quickly around the room, which I had seen on my entrance, then scanned every inch of the walls. No box. There were doorways, however, yawning blackly because the doors that would have closed them were blocked open.

Before I went exploring, I looked at the outside door that I had come through. The locks were open. I pulled the door open and saw pry marks on the jamb. The jimmy was lying right there, a tool about eight inches long with a flat end.

Whoever did this was no artist. Now I realized why the house was so quiet: The rain had turned to snow — a skiff lay on the lawn. Snowflakes sifted down even as I scanned the penlight around . . . and saw no footprints. My spine turned to ice; perhaps the person who jimmied the door was still inside.

After pushing the door shut, I crossed the entryway and shined the little light into the first room, trying to shield my body behind the doorjamb as I did so. Washing machines and dryers . . . tables for folding sheets and towels and whatnot.

The second door led to a room full of shelves bearing what appeared to be bulk food supplies, bags of flour, boxes of cans . . . and another door yawned in the far wall.

I moved that way, holding the flashlight away from my body, just in case someone was in there with a gun and he — or she — got twitchy. I looked into the room and saw the body.

A man . . . on his stomach. He was lying completely relaxed. The walls were lined with stacks of cardboard boxes; his body lay against the left stack.

The far wall had no door, merely an opening. I walked forward, the pistol in my fist leveled in front of me, my heart thudding like a trip-hammer. A glance at the body was enough. I rolled him over. He had been shot in the forehead.

I paused at the edge of the opening, my body as plastered against the wall as possible, and swept the little pool of light from the penlight around. No living persons were there, but there was a body lying under the gray power box mounted on the wall. This man looked dead, too. These men were, I assumed, the guards.

I didn't enter the room, merely ensured it was empty of living people, then turned and retraced my steps back through the basement.

I didn't dawdle, nor did I hurry. The two people Grafton sent me here to keep alive, Marisa Petrou and Wolfgang Zetsche, were upstairs and, presumably, so was the killer.

Back up the stairs I went, adrenaline pumping, my heart pounding.

Nothing in the lower hallway, but I could not afford the time to search every room. There was a small stand in the hallway. I grabbed the glass vase on it and placed it on the second stair going down into the basement. Then I headed for the stairs that led to the second floor and went up two at a time, the penlight slashing the darkness.

Outside the door to Zetsche's bedroom, I paused. Listened at the door. Put my ear against it. Nothing. Not even a snore. Oh, man.

As silently as I could, I applied pressure to the doorknob. It rotated in my hand.

I dropped to the floor, then pushed the door open.

Something screamed and rushed me, smacked into me and ran down the hall. I almost lost it right there. In the glow of the penlight I caught a glimpse of a yellow tail disappearing down the stairs. A cat!

Looked into the room. Saw the bed, the covers, mounds in the middle. Shined the light around to see if there were any other humans there. Dressers and chairs and drapes on the windows.

There was a door standing open. Bathroom.

I looked at the covers. One person was face up . . . the wide, open eyes of Wolfgang Zetsche stared at me. The knife was jammed dead center in his chest. His mouth was open. His eyes weren't tracking the light. Dead.

Beside him in the bed the woman lay facedown.

Blood everywhere. She hadn't died instantly.

I stepped toward the bathroom, illuminating the interior with the light.

Standing there wide-eyed, white as a ghost, was Marisa Petrou. She had a gun in her hand, and it was pointing at me.

Blinded by my flashlight, she demanded harshly, "Who are you?"

"Tommy Carmellini."

She wrapped both arms around her chest,

the pistol apparently forgotten. The gun looked like a little Walther, not a cannon but deadly enough to do the job at close range. I grabbed it from her unresisting hand and tossed it into the bedroom.

I ran the penlight over her hands and arms, trying to see if she had blood on them, then inspected her robe, a white cotton thing that went from her neck to her ankles. I jerked her arms down and pulled the front of the robe open. She started to resist and stopped. I saw no blood, which only meant that she had no big stains. If she knifed those folks, there might be tiny droplets that a lab could find.

I turned away and went back to the bed. Touched the blood. Fresh as a flower. Still oozing around the knife.

"They're dead," she said without inflection. If there were ever a superfluous comment, that was it.

I grabbed a corner of the sheet and used it to keep my fingers from touching the handle. Pulled at the knife. It was really jammed in there, and apparently stuck. I headed for the hallway. Whoever had jimmied that door was probably still in the building, and I was in the mood to do some shooting.

"Wait," she called. "Don't leave me here."

I ignored her. Checked the hallway, then stepped out into it and went directly to the door of the room Marisa was sharing with Isolde.

I tried the knob. Locked. Spun around and found she had followed me. Barefooted, she was quieter than the damned cat.

"Unlock it, quickly now," I demanded. I grabbed her arm and pulled her up in front of the door.

She had the key in her pocket. She put it in the lock. I shoved her aside and opened the door.

Isolde Petrou was very much alive and sitting up in bed. "Marisa?" she asked.

I backed out. Paused to think.

If the knifeman was still in the house, he was probably downstairs. I walked along the hallway to the head of the grand staircase. Stood there in the darkness listening and looking. Couldn't see anything . . . or hear anything.

I'm not sure how long I stood there, trying to become one with the night and the old building . . . trying to feel the presence of other human beings.

Finally I could stand inactivity no longer. I began easing my way down the staircase, one slow step at a time, pausing after every step to look and listen.

Four bodies — and Marisa standing near two of them holding a pistol. I thought it unlikely she scared off a killer with that popper she had in her hand. Did she lead the killer to Zetsche, or was she holding Zetsche at gunpoint until the killer arrived with his sticker? Or was she trying to find the knifeman to shoot at him?

I heard the cat running along the hallway below me. Then silence again.

Something scared it.

It sounded as if the cat came from behind the staircase, from the kitchen and dining room area. The Dead Zoo and parlor were in the other direction.

I gained the lower floor and stayed low, hunkered down, looking and listening. Unfortunately all the outside windows were in rooms one entered from this interior hallway, which was as black as Hitler's heart.

Time was passing, and if the killer was out of the house and making a getaway, my sneaking around inside hunting him was going to prove unproductive, to say the least. On the other hand, acting as if he were gone when he wasn't seemed like an excellent way to become victim number five.

I decided to give him a few more minutes. Time was riding him the hardest. For all he knew, Marisa or I had called the cops. I wondered if she had.

Something was out there in that hallway. I could feel it.

Something that moved, then stopped for a while, then moved again. Something that was as alert as I was. I could feel him . . .

The sound of glass breaking shattered the silence. The vase! Then another sound, a tumbling. A heavy weight, thump thump thump.

I sprinted for the door to the basement staircase. Got there with my penlight just in time to see a formless shape moving at the bottom of the stairs. The bastard had tripped over the vase and tumbled all the way to the bottom.

I rushed the first shot. The little pistol kicked viciously. The muzzle flash blinded me and the report nearly blew my eardrums out. Unable to see a damn thing, I pulled the trigger three more times as the small automatic tried to tear itself from my hand. Blind and deaf, I stopped shooting and used the light again, trying to see if there was anything still down there at the bottom of the stairs to shoot at.

I was peering into the darkness, the gunpowder smell heavy in my nostrils, when I heard a noise behind me. Started to turn, and something slammed into my head.

■ ■ ■ ■

Stunned, I went to the floor. Dropped the penlight. In the glare I could see a white shape above me, drawing something back to whack me again. I kicked. Got her in the knee. She fell heavily. It was Marisa.

I rose, retrieved the penlight and staggered down the stairs. Glass crunched under my feet. A splash of blood in the entryway.

The door was standing open. Lying ten feet out into the snow was a man. I walked out, held the pistol ready to drill the bastard again and turned him over with my foot.

He had been hit twice. Once in the back and once in the arm. Scanned the light around . . . and saw a set of tracks leading away from the house. A man's tracks, it looked like, running. So this clown I shot was number two.

I killed the light and moved to one side. Squatted, trying to make myself a small, invisible target. Nothing seemed to be moving. I looked, letting my eyes adjust, as I held the pistol in both hands, ready to shoot.

The only sound was my breathing.

Whoever he was, he was over the wall and gone, or he was out there behind a tree, waiting for a fool — me, for instance — to come looking for him. Then he would drill the searcher and leave at his convenience.

Like most folks, I have done my share of foolish things and will probably do some more dumb stuff in the future. Not this night, though. I didn't like the odds.

I slipped over to the man lying on the white, wet ground, bent down, put the pistol against his ear and felt for a pulse in his neck. There wasn't one.

I shined the penlight full in his face. His mouth was half open. Lifeless eyes stared into infinity.

He might be an Arab, I thought, and young. Not over twenty-five, I would say. I took another quick look, trying to decide. Ethnic identifications are not my thing, and after all, this guy was dead. *Perhaps* he was an Arab. Or perhaps not.

I went back inside, leaving the door open, and mounted the stairs. Marisa was standing in the hallway. If she still had a gun, it was in her pocket. I hit her with the back of my hand and she slammed into the wall. Didn't go down.

"You're in this to your eyes, you fucking bitch."

"You don't know anything," she hissed, then turned and ran.

I was standing there with my cell phone

in my hand, holding the penlight in one hand and trying to focus on the little keypad, trying to get my breathing under control, when a man came running down the hallway. I put the light on his face.

The butler, I thought.

"What —" he began, but I cut him off.

"Herr Zetsche and his girlfriend are dead. Murdered in their bed. One of the killers is lying in the snow. Call the police."

His mouth made a big O. I gave him a little shove in the chest. "Go, find a phone and call the police. Now!"

He went.

Jake Grafton answered on the third ring. I gave it to him as quickly and succinctly as I could.

He took a second or two to process it — no more.

"Come back to London," he said. "Get out of Germany as quickly as you can."

"I've left fingerprints all over. The local fuzz will alert every cop and county mountie between here and California."

"I'll call them. Leave before they arrive." Then he hung up.

I stood there with the dead phone pressed against my ear, trying to think. He didn't give a good goddamn if the assassin came back after Marisa. He must know she did it, or was in on it.

Well, I had a few minutes. One or two, anyway.

I put the phone in my pocket and went storming back upstairs. The door to the Petrous' bedroom was closed and locked. After I retrieved my gear from the bedroom next door, I used my foot on Marisa's chamber. Two kicks and the doorjamb shattered. The door flew open.

Marisa had lit a candle. The old woman was sitting in a chair, wearing a robe. Marisa was on the bed.

"Why'd you do it?" I demanded.

"I thought you were shooting at one of the guards."

"You lying bitch! Why'd you open the basement door to let the knifemen in?"

She stared at me. "You don't know that."

"I make my living opening locked doors. That door was opened from the inside. The jimmy marks were made so it would look like the door was forced. It wasn't."

She lowered her head and remained silent.

I grabbed a handful of hair and lifted her head so I could see directly into her face and she could see into mine.

"Four people murdered, and *you* helped kill them. One woman and three men. Let me tell you how it is. If another person dies with you in attendance, I'm coming after you. There isn't a hole on this planet you can hide in. And when I find you, I'll kill you sure as God made little green apples. And you can tell that to your pop."

Then I left. There was nothing else I could do.

CHAPTER ELEVEN

When Khadr dropped over the wall and lit like a cat on the sidewalk, Abu Qasim put the car in motion. He stopped by Khadr, who climbed into the passenger seat.

"I heard shots," Qasim said.

Khadr took a deep breath and exhaled slowly as he collected his thoughts. Khadr was not his real name, of course. In fact, Abu Qasim didn't know his real name. He was a professional killer from somewhere in the Middle East, spoke five languages fluently, had some education and was an excellent actor, with the ability to fit into almost any crowd. If he had any religious convictions, Qasim didn't know about them. Khadr killed for money. For the right price, he would kill anyone. Qasim paid his fees because Khadr was good, very good. Holy warriors on jihad would do their best, but when Qasim wanted it done right the first time with no screw-ups, he hired a professional like Khadr.

"I was jimmying the door when I heard someone turn the lock. Obviously I was making some noise, and apparently the man heard it. There were two locks. I stood back, and when he opened the door and was silhouetted by the light behind him, I shot him. I stepped inside, and the other guard was coming down the stairs. I shot him, too.

"I dragged the corpses into a basement storeroom and found the electrical distribution box, turned off the power, waited for my eyes to adjust, then went upstairs.

"Zetsche and his woman were asleep. I killed them with a knife. On the way out someone began following me. We played cat and mouse for a while, then I slipped down the stairs to the basement. Someone had apparently put a vase on the stair. I saw it, but the man behind me didn't. Then someone started shooting — killed the man chasing me, I think."

As they drove, Abu Qasim thought about his next move. Finally he said, "There is a man in Zurich, a banker named Rolf Gnadinger . . ."

The snow was sticking on the grass, but the wall to the Zetsche estate was merely wet and slick. I fell onto the sidewalk, a drop of about five feet, and twisted my ankle a little bit. Cussing under my breath, I limped off toward town. The road was also wet — the flakes were melting as fast as they hit.

Up in the parking garage, I threw my bag into the front trunk of the Porsche and lit her off. If the law found me before I got out of Germany, I was going to spend a few miserable days as a guest of the German republic. My clothes and razor and tooth-brush were in the hotel — I certainly didn't want to waste time retrieving them. I'd just replace that stuff somewhere and put the bill on my expense account. Screw the taxpayers — that's my motto.

On the way out of town I passed an ambulance running lights and sirens going the other way. They need not have hurried; none of the people at the Zetsche estate needed a fast ride to a hospital.

I didn't relax until I crossed the Rhine River bridge into France. That's when the reaction to too much adrenaline and a fumbled assignment hit me hard. At one point I had to pull over and rest my head on the steering wheel as the windshield wipers slapped and squeaked and a rain-snow mixture pattered gently on the roof of my ride. My face throbbed where that cop slugged me, and I was exhausted.

A dead battery in the night vision goggles and my inability to stay awake had cost four people their lives. Oh, I know, I didn't kill them — the assassin who did had already gone on to his reward, whatever it might be. Still, the story should have had a different ending. Those people should still be alive.

Marisa Petrou! She had to be the one who opened the door for the assassin. Even if she wasn't, she sandbagged me, trying to help him escape. That gorgeous bitch was in this mess right up to her plastic surgery scars.

I should have slapped her harder. Should have knocked her damned head off.

Grafton knew she was involved in the Surkov killing, and I'd bet ten dollars against a doughnut that she poisoned her husband. Tens of thousands of women have murdered their husbands since people stopped living in caves — maybe millions. It's the ones who don't kill their man that we should wonder about. Naturally, I made a fool of myself by defending her to Grafton. "She isn't the type." Ha!

A sleety dawn was threatening to smear itself all over France when I realized that I couldn't go any farther. The next pull-off was a truck rest stop. There was even a Mc-

Donald's. I found a spot under a tree — behind a semi where the car couldn't be seen from the highway — killed the engine, locked the doors and went to sleep.

The workday was well under way in London when Jake Grafton called Sal Molina on the encrypted telephone — getting him at home and waking him up — and gave him the news: Wolfgang Zetsche was dead, as were his girlfriend and two employees. The killer had been shot dead by Tommy Carmellini. Before he could tell it all, Molina began asking questions.

"Abu Qasim?"

"I haven't had a chance to do a debrief yet. Tommy's driving back to London. He said the man he killed was young, maybe twenty-five."

"German police?"

"I've talked to the German intelligence chief. Given him all I can."

"Do any of the police or intel agencies know of the link between Surkov, Petrou and Zetsche?"

"The police know Marisa Petrou was present at all three killings, and Isolde at two. Tongues are starting to wag. To the best of my knowledge, they don't know what the link is, but they are looking."

"Did one of those women kill those people? Or any of them?"

"I don't know."

"Lot of damned help you are."

"My job is delivering bad news."

"You're really good at it. Call me when you get some more." The connection went dead.

Jake Grafton called Speedo Harris and Per Diem into his office. "Let's hear it," he said. Unlike the president's aide, he listened to everything the British and FBI officers had to say before he asked questions. The murder of Alexander Surkov with polonium was still getting the bulk of the various police agencies' investigative assets — for political reasons, if nothing else — and the revelations were aired on television and radio as fast as the agencies dribbled them out. Politicians postured and wrung their hands.

"The agencies are trying to find out everything they can about Marisa Petrou," Per Diem said. "She was at the scene of three murders in what — twelve days? That's bound to attract some notice. They are also interested in Tommy Carmellini. The Brits know he is a CIA officer, and they are asking questions. I suspect our good friend Harris may have put them on Carmellini's trail."

Speedo didn't turn a hair. "I was asked about Carmellini and answered truthfully," he told Jake Grafton, who nodded his approval. "Carmellini's popularity with the French authorities is on the wane, however. The French officer I spoke to made some regrettable comments. Positively nasty, I dare say."

"Tommy rubs them the wrong way," Diem added, quite unnecessarily.

"The officer I spoke to at New Scotland Yard was less than complimentary about you, Admiral," Harris continued. "He snarled something about you playing your cards very close to your vest. 'All take and no give,' he remarked."

Grafton nodded. "Oleg Tchernychenko," he said, changing the subject abruptly.

It was midafternoon when I rolled into old London town. I was so tired my eyes watered. I parked in front of the office and went inside to see the boss.

"Where have you been?" Jake Grafton barked.

"Fleeing the scene of a crime."

I must have looked so bad that he took pity on me. His frown disappeared and he said, "Get a bath and change clothes. You and I are flying to Scotland this evening."

"It's January in Scotland," I pointed out. "Have you any idea what the weather is up there?"

"Invigorating. Go! Hurry. There's a plane waiting."

By golly, there was, too. It was past teatime and the sun was long gone when we climbed aboard, but in minutes we were droning through the clag over England. Grafton sat beside me so we could talk, but I didn't even try. I put my head back and went promptly to sleep.

When he woke me up — by shaking me — we were on the ground and taxiing.

Speedo Harris was behind the wheel of the car that was waiting for us. He muttered something pleasant to me, but I didn't quite catch it and wasn't in the mood to ask him to repeat it. I grunted and sat there watching as we rolled out of the suburbs and off into the wild Scottish night. The wind blew fiercely and the rain fell sideways, drumming on the car's sheet metal. Every now and then the car shook from the impact of a gust of wind. I pulled my miserably thin coat tighter and wondered what this trip was all about.

"You got our man cornered in a hole up

here?" I asked Grafton.

"Tell me about last night. Everything you can remember."

I flicked my eyes over to Speedo, who could be relied upon to repeat every word to his MI-6 bosses. Grafton nodded, almost imperceptibly. So he was sharing. Make that: He was sharing what *I* knew.

So I went through it, minute by minute. I had enough wit left to omit any mention of threatening Marisa. If she got shot, stabbed or poisoned, I didn't want Jake Grafton and MI-6 and every spook agency in the free world suspecting me. Who knows? I might even decide to shoot, stab or poison her myself before I got a whole lot older. A man has to keep his options open.

When I finished my narration, he asked, "Did she kill Zetsche?"

"I dunno. I've run through it a hundred times today, trying to decide. I don't even know if she opened the servant's door. Anyone in the house could have opened it. Anyone could have killed the juice. All I know for a fact that I could swear to is that she was standing in Zetsche's bathroom with a gun in her hand — with him in bed with a knife in him, dead as old dog food — and she sandbagged me downstairs a few minutes later, when I was about ready to drill the villains. Villains plural."

"Tommy," Grafton said gently, "I hate to have to tell you this, but the man you shot was Isolde's chauffeur."

"Aaw . . ."

"He must have been following the assassin, chasing him, when you opened fire. It was a tragic, regrettable accident."

I didn't know what to say. Even if I had known, I doubt if I could have got it out. That moment had to be the lowest point in my life.

"Of course," Grafton continued after a few moments, "he might have been the one who admitted the assassin to the house. He might have been in that stairwell to lock the door after he left when you opened fire."

I stared at him. Finally I found my tongue. "Why in the world would he lock the door behind the killer? With four dead bodies cluttering up the place? They jimmied the jamb to make it look like a break-in; they even left the pry bar lying there so the police would be sure to find it. Locking the door behind the guy would show the world that there were two people involved."

"I don't know, Tommy. Maybe the chauffeur was playing solitaire in the dark and heard the killer leaving and chased him. Maybe he went downstairs to check on the power and the killer rushed by him."

Maybe, perhaps, could be —

Infuriated, I spluttered, "What's the answer? *What* is going on?"

"Damn if I know," he said and shrugged.

Jake Grafton, spymaster. Yeah, dude, he's got it all figured out. Right.

As I sat there contemplating strangling *him,* my eyes settled on the back of Speedo Harris' perfectly barbered head. The thought occurred to me that Jake Grafton probably knew a lot more than he wanted MI-6 to know.

Yeah. That was it. He was mushrooming everyone, including me, keeping us in the dark and feeding us shit.

I scowled at him and he pretended not to notice. The jerk!

Did you ever meet someone with an ir-repressible, volcanic personality that stunned you and left you gasping? I've met a few — Jake Grafton's understated person-ality is like that on those rare occasions when he lets the tiger come out to play — but none measured up to Oleg Tcherny-chenko, whose inner fire overwhelmed and dazzled everyone within range.

We were in an old mansion on the wind-swept moors. It was as big as a medium-sized Holiday Inn but much better decorated. More comfortable, too. The big room that the guy at the door brought us to had a roaring fire going in a huge, blackened fireplace, but since Tchernychenko was holding forth in front of the fireplace, keeping us frozen with his eyes and voice and facial expressions, I didn't get a chance to look around much until later. Whoever owned the joint — I doubted if this Russian did — was very much into World War I. Helmets and bayonets and uniforms were mounted high on the walls, along with other memorabilia from that period, such as silver cigarette cases engraved with the autographs of German aerial aces, old newspaper front pages, photos of the princes and belles of the age and the like. Everywhere there were books, hundreds of them, thousands.

As I said, though, for the first five minutes I didn't see any of it. I was staring at Tchernychenko and his mane of graying hair. It seemed as if he were about to whip out a white baton and conduct the orchestra, but no. He did his conducting with voice and eyes and facial expressions and presence.

"Grafton!" the Russian boomed. "When I heard that name I told them to let you in — there couldn't be two Jake Graftons sneaking about, now could there? Of course, the hour is late, but we arrive when we arrive, eh?"

I rolled my eyes at the boss, who didn't even look my way. Fortunately Speedo was in the kitchen with the help, so tomorrow the boys and girls at MI-6 weren't going to be puzzling over Tchernychenko's remarks. At least I hoped Speedo was there. Then I wondered if Jake Grafton cared.

"Ah, yes, Grafton." Tchernychenko didn't have much of an accent — if anything, he sounded to me as if he were British, or had wasted much of his life hanging around them.

"MacGregor!" he roared. "MacGregor! Come take some orders and bring these gentlemen a drink."

Since we were in Scotland, we drank the local stuff — neat, of course. Even adding water would have been sacrilege.

Grafton had trouble getting a word in edgewise, so he let Tchernychenko run on. He was ranting about the Islamic fundamentalists, "Islamofascists," he called them.

"Amazing as it sounds to a logical mind, many British leftists are very sympathetic to the fascists, even though they are xenophobic, misogynic, homophobic, antidemocratic religious fanatics who are willing to murder anyone who doesn't believe as they do. Add the British instinct to root for the underdog to a generous dose of anti-Semitism and it's positively breathtaking what they can explain away. British intellectuals have a lot to answer for, including their fascination with Communism in the twentieth century. They are going to again cover themselves with glory, I fear."

He paused a moment for air, then said, "They need another Churchill and they haven't one."

Grafton moved right in. "We came tonight to discuss the Surkov murder with you."

"Alexander Ivanovich . . . a tragic figure." Tchernychenko shook his leonine head. "Polonium, so he would suffer. A lesson to every Russian."

"He accused the Russian government of poisoning him," Grafton murmured.

"They did it, of course."

"Not some terrorists, perhaps?"

"Oh, no. Putin and that crowd are trying to make the expatriates come to heel. A few spectacular poisonings will bring them around, he thinks. One of these days he'll snap his fingers and they'll obey like trained dogs."

"And you — how do you stand with the Russian government?"

"They will not shed tears at my funeral," Tchernychenko said curtly and took a mighty slug of Scotch.

"If the real enemy is terrorists and they get you, you'll be just as dead," Grafton pointed out calmly. He had a way of saying things that would freeze your blood if a normal person said them, yet from him the remark seemed candid but harmless. That was an illusion; nothing about Jake Grafton was benign.

"No one unknown to me can get onto the grounds. I have four men on duty every hour of every day."

"Russians?"

"No. British. There isn't a Russian alive who can be trusted to disobey Putin . . . me included." He chuckled, as if that comment were funny. "I know these men and pay them well. They are loyal and extremely competent. They know the stakes, and they know that in the long run Putin and the terrorists will lose. Tyranny and fanaticism burn with a white-hot flame for a short time, then they always sputter out. No one trembles today when one mentions Hitler or Joseph Stalin — no one. Would you like more Scotch?"

For the first time, Grafton glanced at me. "Tommy, would you please check on

Speedo? See that he gets a drink and is properly entertained."

I rose and went off to find the British op. When I glanced back as I went through the door, Grafton and Tchernychenko had their heads together.

I will tell you frankly, I didn't believe the Russians iced Surkov, or Jean Petrou, or Wolfgang Zetsche. I had a name and wasn't letting go: Abu Qasim.

Or, maybe, Marisa Petrou. For husband Jean, at least. A little of Mom's heart medication in hubby's vino and voilà! Life is looking up.

After visiting the kitchen and ensuring Speedo was being properly attended to, I wandered through the house, looking at the stuff from World War I. The downstairs held four large rooms with twelve-foot ceilings, each with a massive fireplace. Little rooms were arranged down the west side of the building: kitchen, pantry, a few bathrooms and a couple of small sitting rooms that now contained televisions. I inspected the entire ground floor and the outside doors and staff door and the view from the windows. Just plain old Scottish night was visible out each window, black and windy and wet. The portraits on the wall and the black windows stared at me as I walked along, looking at this and examining that. The floorboards creaked and groaned with every step.

The sound of the wind whispered through that Scottish mansion. Every few moments I paused, closed my eyes and listened to the song of the wind and the rattling windows. Drafty old place. Cold, too. Fifty-five degrees would be my guess, almost cold enough to hang meat. I was fast losing any secret desire I might have had way back when to live in a castle or McMansion. My warm, cozy little apartment was going to look sooo good.

After I had checked out the downstairs, I went upstairs and sniffed around. The rooms were smaller, still chilly and drafty, stuffed with loaded bookcases, and the only bath was at the end of the hallway. Eight bedrooms, three sitting rooms and one bathroom. My mom wouldn't have liked it.

I wondered about Isolde's chauffeur. Was he a good guy who tried to capture a villain, or was he one of "them," a holy warrior trying to earn glory in the next world by committing mayhem and murder in this one?

That Marisa . . .

Maybe I shot the wrong man in that castle near the Rhine. If I was supposed to get a guilt trip over that possibility, it wasn't working. I didn't feel anything, not guilt, angst, remorse . . . not even relief. Okay, okay, I'm lying again. The truth was I felt guilty and in over my depth. Yet when I ran through the events of that evening in my mind, I couldn't see what I could have done differently.

I was getting more than a little peeved at Marisa. She knew the answers — all the answers — and she wasn't talking.

The 1911 Springfield felt good in my pocket, a nice, solid, deadly lump. I got it out and exchanged the half-empty magazine in the grip of the thing for a full one. Checked that the hammer was back and the safety was on, then wedged it back under my belt.

"Wolfgang dead," Tchernychenko muttered. "Murdered."

"With a knife, apparently," Jake Grafton said smoothly, "and you may be next."

The Russian made an unpleasant noise with his lips and teeth. "I'm safe as it is possible to get here in this house." He waved his hand dismissively. "Some Arab knife artist or mad bomber isn't going to dash across these highlands in the dead of winter and through four armed men. On the other hand, if Putin wants me dead, there isn't much you or I or anyone on earth can do about it. There isn't anyplace on this planet one can hide from *him.* The polonium — it was a warning. So we would know and fear him."

"Perhaps," Grafton said slowly, "you are misreading this situation. I have been told by a man I respect that the Russian government had nothing to do with Surkov's death."

"The Russian government? Those mice that serve at Putin's pleasure? Perhaps they didn't. But Putin — I have incurred <u>his</u> wrath before. He is consolidating his power in Russia. He wants to become a czar, to rule Russia." Oleg Tchernychenko waggled a finger at Grafton. "I think he will do it. Yes, sir. I think he will do it. Beholden to no one, with a mandate he wrote himself, he will rule as Stalin did, as Lenin did, as Czar Nicholas and Catherine the Great did.

"You people of the West, of these little green islands and the lands across the Atlantic, you don't understand. You have your elections and make polite noises and debate endlessly and vote. Let me tell you, sir, they don't do that in Russia. Never have and probably never will; certainly not in our lifetimes. And, Admiral, they don't do that democracy twaddle in the Middle East. God speaks to the imams and they tell the faithful and the faithful charge off to die gloriously as soldiers of God — and kill a few infidels, if at all possible. Those simple fools have never asked why God needs their help, nor will it ever occur to them to ask.

"On the other hand, Putin doesn't need God's help. He can build his empire with his own two hands. He can poison Alexander Surkov in Mayfair and all the power and might of Great Britain can't save his life. We Russians, we understand the basic laws of political physics."

Jake Grafton said nothing. He sipped at the last of his Scotch.

Tchernychenko wasn't finished, however. "There is a man, Sheikh Mahmoud al-Taji, who runs a mosque in London. The British court released him today — it was on the telly this evening. He will not be jailed or deported."

"I heard about that."

"He's a terrorist."

"Do you know that for a fact?"

"I have my sources. Rumor has it he is trying to buy weapons and explosives from Russia. I have friends — I hear these things. Why would they say them if it were not true? And why the British government didn't accuse him of that I can't imagine. So now he is free to stand in his mosque and preach his poison. 'To die in the name of Allah should be the goal of every believer.' That is his mantra. The court didn't convict him because he didn't say 'to kill and die in the name of Allah.' The judge is a fool."

Grafton didn't reply.

"What are you going to do about him?" Tchernychenko demanded.

"What should I do?" Grafton asked softly.

"Have him killed. Send your soldiers after him."

"He is a religious leader. As far as I know, he hasn't raised money for terrorism, hasn't plotted terror strikes, hasn't enlisted soldiers in the war of terror. I, too, have heard rumors, but they are only that, rumors. All he has done that the British could prove is rant in a mosque."

"He is inflaming the rabble. Surely you can see that?"

Jake Grafton rubbed the stubble on his chin. It had been a long time since he shaved this morning. "We've assassinated five men. All five were actively engaged in terrorism. True, they preached in mosques and argued politics, too, but first and foremost, they were directly responsible for murder of the innocent."

"You can't draw that line and defend it," Tchernychenko roared. "Your Abraham Lincoln noted that there was no difference between the wily agitator who induced a soldier to desert, and the soldier who did indeed desert."

"No, sir," Grafton said forcefully. "Lincoln did not say that there was no difference. He asked if he had to leave the hair on the head of the agitator untouched. He did not answer the question, he merely asked it. Now I tell you, if we try to kill everyone who disagrees with us politically or on religious grounds, we are going on a fool's errand. We'll be up to our armpits in blood, to no avail."

"Maybe that is where we should be," Tchernychenko said heavily. "The time has come when we must take sides and choose a course."

"We cannot murder everyone who disagrees with us," Jake Grafton said curtly.

"I wished the Islamic fascists believed that," Tchernychenko shot back, undaunted. "On the other hand, Putin understands he cannot kill everyone, but he can kill the people who irritate him the most. Corpses make wonderful examples."

I was sitting in a stuffed chair in the big

room across from the main entrance, well back from the light, dozing, when I sensed that someone had entered the room. I tightened my grip on the Springfield as I pried my eyelids open. It was Jake Grafton. Tchernychenko was behind him.

"Hey, Tommy, time to go."

I came erect and pocketed the pistol. We collected our driver, said our good-byes and stepped out into the windy night. The temp had dropped some while we were there.

As we rode away in the car with Speedo behind the wheel, driving on the wrong side of the road, Grafton said, "Did you get the bugs in place?"

"Every room in the joint," I muttered, "including the one you spent the evening in. Best job I've done in years."

"And the retransmitter?"

"Stuck it on the side of the house. Leaned out a second-floor window. No way to hide it, of course."

Grafton didn't say anything. Each bug would transmit a tiny signal to the retransmitter, which could boost the signal and broadcast that signal and up to thirty-one others at once, to the satellite. The satellite could send the collected signals to Langley or Fort Meade, whichever seemed to have less work, or both. There the signals would be monitored and recorded for study by computers and humans at a later date.

I sat looking out the window into the black Scottish night. Blacker than the doorway to hell. Blacker than the Devil's heart. Black and formless. Black, black, black.

CHAPTER TWELVE

After the plane landed at a London airport and the engines were secured, Grafton motioned me to remain in my seat. He went forward, said something to the pilot, then came back and sat down across the aisle from me as Speedo and the crew filed off the plane. The lights and air-conditioning, powered by an auxiliary power unit in the tail of the plane, stayed on.

When we were alone in the airplane, he said, "The key is Marisa Petrou. She knows this bastard better than anyone else alive, and I've got a hunch she knows what he's planning."

"What is that?" I asked, to prompt him.

"Oh, he wants to kill Winchester and the others, me, you . . . and the president. He wants to assassinate the president."

I gaped.

"Qasim wanted to kill him last year in Paris," Grafton explained, "and I doubt

287

if he's given up on that dream. Qasim believes that decapitating the head villain, the Devil incarnate to their way of thinking, would shake Western civilization, maybe crack the foundations, as the assassination of Archduke Ferdinand did in 1914. Baldly, Qasim wants to trigger a world war. He thinks Islam will rule triumphantly when it's all over, in a century or two. Death to all the infidels. The victory will be Allah's."

His eyes swiveled to me again. "We're going to kill him first," he said, not so much to me as to himself. He was taking a vow. Then he repeated it, and I could feel the cold steel in his voice: *"We're going to kill him first."*

The moment passed. Staring off into space, he took a deep breath, exhaled slowly, then looked at me again.

"Tomorrow morning I have a job for you. Then, tomorrow afternoon I want you to go back to France, find Marisa and stick to her like glue."

This was the second time he had given me this order. Of course, he was the one who told me to get out of Germany. "She won't like it," I pointed out.

"Figure something out."

"Okay," I said, as if hanging out with

unwilling females were one of my many skills.

"This time, if you must shoot someone, bring the women with you."

"What about that Russian back there?"

"It's impossible. He refuses to use good sense. He commutes back and forth to London, thinks three or four bodyguards will keep him safe."

"It would take fifty men to properly guard him."

"I have precisely two. I have them watching the estate, looking for anyone sneaking in. That's the best I can do."

"Who are they?"

"You don't know them."

"I know most of the people in the Company's Europe operations," I said brightly.

"You don't know them," Grafton repeated.

"There's still a whole hell of a lot I don't know," I said reasonably, trying to be a good soldier. Or sailor. That was the only way anyone on this earth was ever going to get anything out of him.

"What else do you want to know?"

"Maybe you ought to tell me if Isolde's chauffeur was a bad guy or an innocent bystander whom I just happened to murder."

He smiled a little bit and said softly, "That

I don't know, Tommy. You did the best you could. We'll all have to live with it that way."

I felt like a fool and must have reddened. My face seemed hot. "Sorry," I said.

"Keep swinging at the strikes," he muttered.

He got out of his seat and led the way up the aisle toward the door.

It was a gray, rainy dawn — the English are good at these and do them often — when I rolled out the next morning. My roommate, the up-and-coming GM junior executive, was still in his room, presumably asleep. I made coffee and stood at my window looking at the world, which from this perspective consisted of four brick buildings identical to the one I was in.

I decided they should find the architect responsible for this masonry crime and cut off parts. Still, the neighborhood was nicer than most of Manhattan, the areas that people live in, and the streets had less garbage piled up. Cities, I decided, were an acquired taste.

I was trying to keep my mind off terrorists and murders and Jake Grafton. Even so . . . A glance at my watch got me going.

A half hour later I hailed a taxi on the main street a block from my building. The hackie spoke English, the taxi was clean, and he knew how to get to the address I gave him.

If prostitution is the oldest profession, then espionage is the second oldest. Man's desire to know other folks' secrets is certainly as old as the desire for sex. And every spy needs a handler, so he — or she — came along at the same time as the spy.

The case officer, or handler, is the spy's contact with his world — the world he grew up in or the world he chooses to serve, for whatever reason — when he is in enemy country. In addition to putting the spy in place, supplying him with the tools of the trade and telling him what information to get, the case officer must be the spy's emotional support, his anchor, his source of strength and resolve. Some spies need more moral and emotional support than others, but all of them need some of it. Providing it is the case officer's most important function; without that support, the spy won't be very effective or stay in place very long.

As Eide Masmoudi's and Radwan Ali's case officer, Jake Grafton met with both men periodically, as seldom as he could, yet as often as he thought they needed him, and whenever either of them asked for a meet. Communications went through the courier,

Kerry Pocock, who was a regular visitor to Harrod's gourmet food department.

One might think in this day and age cell phones would be the communication method of choice, but they weren't. People would see the agent talking on the cell phone, which recorded every number called or received. Sooner or later a suspicious person could examine the phone. However, both men did have cell phones, and both had memorized emergency numbers to call, just in case. But once they called one of those numbers, they had to dispose of that phone immediately.

Spy-handler meets were dangerous. London, and all other European capitals, were buzzing with Muslims, most of whom were not religious extremists or terrorists in any sense of the word. Yet since the villains looked like everyone else, one had to make sure the meet was as private as possible. In addition, it had to fit into the spy's day and lifestyle in a way that wouldn't arouse suspicion.

Jake Grafton and Eide Masmoudi were meeting today in one of the men's rooms at Harrod's. MI-5 supplied a van and tradesman's coveralls, which I donned. I parked the van in the back of Harrod's at the loading dock, off-loaded my service cart with mops and pails and signs, and went inside.

I started in the men's rooms on the first floor and worked my way up in the building, keeping an eye on the time.

I was in a third floor men's scrubbing out a toilet when Jake Grafton came in. I went out into the hallway, made sure my OUT OF SERVICE signs were prominently placed and got busy scrubbing the door. Two minutes later Eide came down the hallway. He was a little guy, maybe 130 pounds, with dark skin and big eyes and black hair. Although he was wearing trousers and you couldn't see them, I knew he had a set of really big balls. Our eyes met, I nodded once, and he went into the men's room.

As the minutes passed, I worked on that door, then began mopping the hallway. Spilled some water to give me something to work on.

People came to the end of the hallway and looked at me and the OUT OF SERVICE signs and went away. I usually glanced at them, then pretended to pay no attention. The customers were wearing coats, usually, and Harrod's employees were not.

I got the floor clean and stopped to inspect it. By golly, here was a career possibility for me if the spook business ever went south.

Then I dumped more water on the floor and set about mopping it again.

Jake Grafton listened to everything Eide had to say before he produced a computer-generated picture of what Abu Qasim might look like. "This man — have you seen him?"

Eide took his time studying the picture, a three-by-five on photo paper. "Perhaps," he said. "A man in the mosque, last week. Then again . . ."

Grafton pocketed the photo and produced a small bottle with a screw cap. It held about an ounce of liquid. He held it so Eide could see it. "Some evening, when the sheikh is dining in the mosque, I want you to pour this in whatever he is drinking."

"He drinks only water and tea."

"Whatever."

"What is it?"

Jake Grafton took a moment before he answered. "It's a chemical that will combine with another chemical that is already in his body and cause his heart to stop. The two chemicals combine into what the chemists call a binary poison."

Eide was dubious. He didn't reach for the bottle. "Is this stuff poisonous?"

"Not unless you have that other chemical in your system, and you do not. Nor does anyone else who could be reasonably expected to eat at the mosque. Al-Taji does. The chemical in this bottle will kill him."

"Where did he get the first chemical?"

"During his trial he drank water, along with the other people at the defense table. The first half of the binary cocktail was in the water and was absorbed into the fat cells in his body. It is still there, and will be for some weeks before it becomes inert or is flushed from his system."

"And this second chemical will combine with the first?"

"Yes. By itself, it's harmless. Also tasteless. You could drink all of it and it wouldn't harm you. This amount is enough to treat about ten gallons of liquid. It will only prove fatal to someone who has that first chemical in his body. Together they are a binary poison."

"If an autopsy is performed, will this poison be found?"

"Very doubtful. Conceivably it could be, but only if the toxicologist knew precisely what he was looking for."

"You are asking me to kill Sheikh al-Taji." That wasn't a question but a statement.

"Yes."

Eide Masmoudi searched Jake Grafton's face. He knew al-Taji was a terrorist, a killer who plotted murder of the innocent — he had been writing the reports for Grafton. Masmoudi believed men like the sheikh perverted Islam, insulting the Prophet and everyone who believed. Even worse, they betrayed Allah.

"To pervert the holiest of holies is a great crime," he whispered. Still he did not reach for the bottle. He stood there staring at it.

"If you use this," Jake Grafton said, "you and Radwan will have to leave the mosque."

"That wasn't the original plan."

"No, it wasn't," Jake admitted, "but I'm the case officer, and I can change the plan. I'm changing it. These people are beyond paranoid — they're criminal psychopaths. They'd kill a dozen innocent people hoping that one of them is guilty. Hell, they'd kill a hundred, just for the publicity. I don't want you and Radwan to take a risk like that. If you agree to use the poison, you two are out of there. As fast as your feet can take you."

Eide Masmoudi was a very brave man. He took his time framing his next question. "If this poison, this binary chemical, works as you say it will, al-Taji will merely have a fatal heart attack. Is that correct?"

Grafton replied, "The doctors tell me his heart will probably stop while he is asleep."

"He isn't the only villain in that mosque. The place is full of throat-slitters and holy murderers. They pervert Islam. They make it into something evil, a crime against man and Allah." He searched for more words, then said, "They'd kill the queen of England if they had half a chance. Anybody. They'd murder anybody who'd get them in the newspapers."

Jake Grafton nodded. "And they'll kill you if you give the slightest hint — the tiniest hint — that you are scared or worried or have something to hide. They'll kill you believing that if you're innocent you'll wind up in Paradise, so your murder really isn't a sin. Isn't that right?"

Eide acknowledged that Jake Grafton had stated the case correctly.

"So if you take the bottle," the admiral continued, "you and Radwan are leaving."

Eide eyed the admiral. "You're the case officer. *I* take the risks."

"Don't fuck with me, kid. I make the rules and give the orders. You'll bleed same as everybody. We'll use you later on something else. We're not retiring you — you'll get your chance to make a difference. There're thousands of these sons of bitches out there running around loose, and we need all the help we can get. Now tell me, yes or no?"

Eide took his time. Finally he took the bottle from Grafton's hand and pocketed it. "For my mother," he said.

Jake Grafton nodded.

Eide Masmoudi walked out of the men's room.

For his mother, Jake thought, who was murdered in the World Trade Center on September 11, 2001, by suicidal fanatics. A man couldn't have a better reason to fight.

Rolf Gnadinger was still at his office at the bank in Zurich when he received a telephone call from Oleg Tchernychenko. Gnadinger had financed numerous oil field deals for Tchernychenko and Huntington Winchester in the last ten years. They were willing to pay top rates — and did — in return for loans granted with a telephone call and closed within hours. Speed was the name of their game, and Gnadinger had made millions for the bank because he was willing to play. He was willing because he trusted both men, who were solid as rocks.

After the telephone encrypters were turned on and had timed in, Oleg said, "I had a visit yesterday from Jake Grafton. He told me this Abu Qasim villain is real and evil as a heart attack. He believes Qasim killed Alexander Surkov and Wolfgang

Zetsche and may have murdered Isolde Petrou's son, Jean."

"Have you talked to Hunt?" Rolf asked.

"Yes. He is plainly worried, but put a good face on it. These deaths are evidence, he said, that our war against the terrorists is hurting them. 'Money well spent,' was his phrase."

"I have taken precautions," Rolf assured Oleg. That was a lie, one that came readily to his lips. He was being more watchful than he used to be, but that was the extent of it. The truth was that he didn't want to think of someone hunting him. To kill him. He refused to even look at that vision from the ancient, primeval past. *After all,* he told himself, *I am just another face in the crowd.*

"So have I," Tchernychenko responded. "I'm too good a client for you to lose. And truth be told, I don't want to go to the trouble of breaking in another banker."

They said their good-byes and hung up. Gnadinger spent a sober moment staring at the telephone. Then his gaze wandered to the portraits on the wall. The chief operating officer of the bank rated a big corner office, with lots of wall space, which he had filled with portraits of his predecessors.

He studied them, one by one. He had joined the bank in the mid-1960s, about the time the furor over the money the Holocaust Jews deposited in Swiss banks began to bubble. His predecessors had been officers and employees of this bank, or other Swiss banks, when those deposits came in during the late 1930s and early 1940s. They met the German Jews, shook their hands, accepted their money. Then the Nazis murdered them. The banks kept the money.

That is, they kept the money until the survivors and relatives of the Jews got organized and raised a huge stink. Even then, the banks held on to the bulk of the funds by demanding records that the officers knew didn't exist.

The portraits were of the men who refused to return the money. Gnadinger glanced at every face. When he was young, Gnadinger wondered what those men thought about themselves in the wee hours of the night when they were alone with their consciences . . . and with God, if indeed He had survived the Holocaust. Gnadinger had watched for decades as they wrestled with their consciences, or refused to do so, assuring any who asked that they were absolutely certain they were doing the right thing, the right thing for their banks, the right thing for Switzerland. They were right, *right, right!* Except for the stinky little fact that they weren't.

Hitler murdered the Jews, seven million of them, whole families, whole clans, and the Swiss banks profited from that stupendous crime.

The Islamic terrorists were out to do it again, those new Nazis, who prayed to Mecca five times a day and murdered infidels when they weren't on their knees with their foreheads on the carpet.

Rolf Gnadinger had no intention of winding up like one of those men in the portraits.

He finished the paperwork on his desk, arranged it neatly in piles and in-baskets and files just so, the way the secretaries knew he would arrange it. He had climbed the banking ladder by being logical and detail-oriented, and he was now. Even his anxiety couldn't force him from the habits of a lifetime. He finished his workday around six thirty in the evening by signing some late-afternoon correspondence, then capped the pen, put it in its place in his drawer, locked the drawers of his desk and rose from his chair.

It had snowed early this morning, but this afternoon had been unseasonably warm, with sunshine and slush in the streets and melting icicles. He stood at the window for a moment looking at nature's handiwork, which hadn't intruded into the quiet offices and corridors of the executive suite.

He donned his coat and arranged his hat just so, then opened the door and left his office. He nodded at his secretary as he glanced at his watch. He was leaving right on the dot, at his usual departure time, not a minute too early nor a minute too late. Timing is everything in life, a wise man once said.

Gnadinger rode the elevator down from the executive suite to the main floor of the bank, where he found the tellers finishing their accounting and filling out their day sheets. The guard at the door touched his cap as Gnadinger approached, then turned to unlock the door.

Well, Oleg was right: He needed a bodyguard. Tomorrow he would call the security service that had the bank contract and ask for a man with a gun. If the man was competent, no one would realize he was an armed bodyguard. The banker reminded himself to demand a man who looked and dressed as if he belonged in Gnadinger's social circle. No tattooed or pierced persons, please.

The uniformed guard opened the door for Rolf; he stepped outside into the evening gloom. The temperature was still well above freezing. The sidewalks were shoveled, the icicles on the building were dripping copiously, and slush filled the gutters.

He looked around nervously. Away from the safety of the office, outside in raw nature, with water and wind and slush and people moving randomly, Oleg's warning about assassins seemed more real, more possible. He set off along the sidewalk toward the parking garage that held his car as he glanced warily at pedestrians and passing cars.

Really, in the twenty-first century, in safe, civilized Switzerland, in this ancient old city by the lake, the nightmare of killers and murderers and religious fanatics seemed like something from one of those trailers for a horror movie that he would never watch. A lot of people did watch the horror films, of course, to be titillated, because even they could not accept at a gut level the fact that the evil depicted on the screen might be a part of the world in which they lived.

The banker paused at the door to the garage. Took a deep breath and opened it. The stairwell was empty, the overhead light burning brightly. He climbed the stairs, his leather shoes making grinding noises with every step, noises that reverberated inside that concrete stairwell.

His car was on the third level, right where he always parked. In fact, the parking place had a number and was reserved for him: The bank rented it by the year.

No one was in sight amid the cars when he came out of the stairwell. About half the spaces were empty. He forced himself to walk calmly toward his car. He already had the keys in his hand, his thumb on the button of the fob that would open the locks.

His eyes moved restlessly, looking for a lurking figure, anything out of the ordinary. Of course he saw nothing.

Fear is a corrosive emotion, and Gnadinger knew that. In time he would become more and more jumpy, more and more nervous, as the acid of fear worked on his nerves. He knew that, too.

Approaching the car Gnadinger pushed the button on the fob. He heard the click, audible and distinctive in that concrete mausoleum, as the door locks released.

Then he realized that someone might have put a bomb in his car. He stopped, stood frozen, waiting, wondering what he should do. He realized that he was holding his breath, waiting for the bomb to explode.

It didn't, of course. He stood there in that ill-lit, dingy garage until he felt foolish; then he opened the door to the car, the interior lights illuminated just as they should, and he climbed in. Closed the doors and locked them and put on his seat belt. Inserted the key into the ignition.

The bomb might be wired to explode when he turned the ignition!

Several seconds passed before a wave of disgust washed over him and he turned the key. The engine caught immediately and the vehicle's headlights came on automatically. So did the CD player, from which emanated the lively tones of classic jazz, which he had listened to on the way to work this morning.

As he put the transmission into drive and inched out of his space, Rolf Gnadinger chastised himself for being a fool. Oleg had spooked him, and his imagination had done the rest.

Yet the killer or killers might come one of these days. Someone had murdered Tchernychenko's aide, and Wolfgang Zetsche, and Isolde Petrou's son. Someone from the Kremlin? Perhaps the Kremlin had ordered Surkov's murder — he had immediately assumed that when he first heard the news, but why would the Kremlin want Zetsche dead? Or young Petrou, a French diplomat?

Terrorists, he thought. Yes, indeed. Fanatics. Throat-slitters. Suicidal bombers and mass murderers.

He needed a professional bodyguard, he told himself again. Someone trained to be watchful for all these threats. The bodyguard could worry about all this stuff and Gnadinger wouldn't have to.

The traffic was moderate at this hour and threw up sheets of spray that the wipers had difficulty with. Gnadinger kept busy punching the windshield wash system every few moments.

His neighborhood of renovated older homes was also quiet. Only a few cars passing on the streets, no pedestrians. His house was empty tonight. His wife was in Rome on a shopping expedition with their daughter, who was grown with children of her own. They had planned this trip for months.

And today was the maid's day off. The maid was from somewhere in North Africa — he didn't know where; the employment agency had sent her, and his wife had dealt with them. What the maid did on her day off, where she went or whom she talked to, he had no idea.

He pushed the button to raise the door on the two car-garage, the new one that he had had built after he and his wife bought the house ten years ago. The old one was a ramshackle wooden affair, ready to fall down, and he had gotten tired of looking at it. The new one had the same facade and design as the old house, so it looked as if it had been there forever.

Much better, he thought as he walked out of the garage and lowered the door with another button on his key fob.

Fifteen paces took him to his front door. As he walked he eyed the icicles hanging dangerously from the eaves. He needed to have the maintenance people remove those tomorrow.

As he looked for the door key on his ring, he heard a noise behind him, very slight. Startled, he turned immediately.

A man coming at him, with something in his hand! Before Gnadinger could react, he jabbed the thing downward into Rolf Gnadinger's chest.

Stunned and amazed, Gnadinger glanced down and saw the butt end of an icicle protruding from his chest. He grasped it, tugged futilely . . . and looked into the face of the man who had stabbed him. The man smiled.

Rolf Gnadinger could no longer stand. He felt himself sinking toward the ground, too weak to remain upright. His vision became a tunnel. Through that long, long tunnel he saw the man walking away. Then the tunnel closed completely and the darkness became total.

CHAPTER THIRTEEN

Harry Longworth and Gat Brown were dirty, cold and bored. They had been sleeping in a hole, eating MREs and pooping in another hole for ten days now, and they were thoroughly sick of it. The cold, the wind that never stopped and the blowing dust didn't help.

"One more day of this," Harry Longworth said. "Then tomorrow we call for an extraction and hike to the pickup point."

"I've got a better idea," Brown retorted. "Let's call this morning and start hiking tonight. Get picked up tomorrow afternoon and by tomorrow night we'll be in a bath, eating real food and drinking real beer. A tub full of hot water, real soap, aaah."

"Pussy."

"If I had some I wouldn't know what to do with it."

"If nothing happens by this time tomorrow, we call then."

The men were hidden on the side of a canyon that wound its way into the mountains. The crest of a rocky ridge was a thousand feet behind them. To their left the Hindu Kush rose in peaks covered with snow.

They listened to the weather on their shortwave radio every day. If snow was forecast, they would have to leave. They had had a window of dry air, though, cold as the devil, with not a cloud in the sky or a flake of snow. They huddled in their hole, watching, shivering, enduring, cursing, telling each other the same old lies.

Below them, against the far wall of the canyon, sat a cluster of six houses and barns, ramshackle affairs made of stones and wood and cinder block. Smoke rose from several chimneys. When the wind was just right, they could smell the smoke and the aroma of cooking meat. Of course, they couldn't risk a fire. Although it was wide, the canyon wasn't particularly deep. On its floor were flats with grass for goats and small gardens.

They were there to watch that village complex. So far, for ten days, nothing of interest had happened.

Beside them on a bipod was the .50-caliber sniper rifle, complete with scope.

The darn thing weighed thirty-one pounds and shot 1.71 ounce slugs a half inch in diameter and two and a half inches long.

Brown lay on his back as Longworth kept watch. Occasionally Longworth glanced through a spotting scope at the village, but mostly he just watched. They were hidden in an acre of leafless brush, and the view outward was restricted. Ten days ago they had ensured they had a good viewing hole through some judicious pruning of branches. Not much, just enough.

They had counted four men in the village and given each a nickname. There was also one woman and two children. The man they wanted wasn't there.

"I don't think the bastard will ever come," Brown said. "More bum information, and we do the big camp-out. I don't care what anyone says, at least we can out-camp these bastards."

"Right."

"I don't know how these people stand living in this wasteland. No wonder they're hot to die and get to Paradise."

"Next life's gotta be better than this one."

"You Jesus freaks keep saying that, and without a shred of evidence," Gat Brown said, delighted that Longworth had given him this opening. To keep from dying of boredom, they had been debating religion for days. Longworth was a born-again Christian, and Brown was an atheist, or so he said. He wasn't really, but he wanted to keep the conversation alive, and one way was to never agree with Longworth.

There was a man on the ridge behind them. He had climbed up there at dawn and was hiking along the ridge, looking. He had a rifle of some kind. With his back to the village, Brown tracked his progress with binoculars. "They're expecting something to happen," he muttered.

"What?" muttered Longworth.

"Why don't you admit it?" Brown asked, his eyes glued to the binoculars. "All religion is bunk, theirs and yours and everyone else's. The whole religious house of cards is built on the premise that man is a special animal, and he isn't. We're cousins of the monkey, and he doesn't fret about getting to heaven or worry about going to hell."

"You're an idiot," Harry Longworth said mildly and closed his eyes, pretending to sleep.

An hour later Longworth said, "Well, look at this. Truck coming."

Gat Brown checked the sentry on the side of the ridge one more time, got him located on the skyline, then crawled to his hole in the brush for a look. He swung up his binoculars. The vehicle was coming up the canyon, trailing a plume of dust. An old flatbed truck of some kind.

"This might be it," Harry said.

"That guy up behind us. When we shoot, think you can take him? He's about three hundred yards away."

Longworth crawled to a place where he could see the ridgeline. He located the sentry. "Okay," he said, and checked his M40A3 bolt-action rifle in 7.62mm NATO, which was lying on a blanket. Then he returned to the spotting scope.

Brown settled himself behind the big Fifty and ensured the safety was on. He swung the scope crosshairs onto the huts, checked that both legs of the bipod were level and the horizontal line in the scope was also level. Beside him was the case that held the .50-caliber Browning machine-gun cartridges. He opened it, pulled four more cartridges out so they lay loose upon the padding.

After a little fidgeting, he settled down to watch the scene through the scope, which had a twenty-six-power magnification.

The range to the huts was 1,639 yards. They had used a laser range finder to establish that, and had lased every path and promontory below them, just in case the people in the huts discovered them and decided to come up here for a look-see. This would be a long shot, but Gat Brown had made shots at this distance before. His longest was almost 1,700 yards.

Shots at these ranges, even with the big Fifty, were difficult. The scope had to have a lot of magnification so that he could actually see what he was aiming at, yet the high magnification made it difficult — actually almost impossible — to hold the crosshairs steady. His breathing, the beating of his heart, the uneven heating of the air — everything made those crosshairs dance nervously even though the thirty-one-pound rifle was on a bipod. Hitting a man-sized target at that range was a job for an expert, which Gat Brown was.

"Wind from your left, maybe eight knots," Longworth said. He had the binoculars on the truck again. "Three guys in the cab, I think. Hard to say."

Brown adjusted the rifle to account for the estimated wind. He liked to hold a centered crosshair on his target, but at this distance, there were no guarantees. The wind was just an estimate, and it wouldn't be uniform over the 4,900 feet the bullet had to travel. He had adjusted the horizontal crosshairs for the trajectory days ago.

"Guy with binoculars beside Hut Two," Brown murmured. "He's glassing this slope."

The village men glassed the slopes every day, and twice in the last ten days they had hiked along the valley floor and ridges with dogs, just looking. Brown and Longworth were well hidden, and the dogs hadn't gotten a sniff.

"This may be it," Harry said again, trying to keep the tension out of his voice.

Brown instinctively pulled the rifle tighter into his shoulder, settled himself, forced himself to breathe easily and regularly. He was steady as a rock when the truck rolled to a stop near the huts.

Two men who had been inside came out to greet the new arrivals. Longworth examined each of them carefully through the spotting scope, which had a thirty-six-power magnification. He didn't touch the scope, which sat on a tripod — merely held his eye as close as possible and looked.

The driver of the truck . . . his back was to them, and he walked around the front of the truck, disappearing from view. The man getting out on the passenger side . . . Brown got a profile. The other man, who had been riding in the middle of the bench seat, also got out and for a moment stood behind the other passenger. Then he stepped away and Brown got his best look at the first man to exit.

"It's him," he said softly and flicked off the safety. "The guy in the brown coat."

"That's our man," Longworth agreed, his eyes glued to the spotting scope. "Any time you're ready."

Brown took a deep breath, exhaled, steadied the rifle on that brown coat. The bearded man wearing it was talking to a man from the hut. This would be a quartering shot into his left rear side.

With the reticle in the scope twitchy, yet more or less centered on the target as steady as a trained rifleman could hold it, Brown began squeezing the trigger, which was adjusted for an eighteen-ounce pull. So gently and steadily did he caress it that the shock of the report and recoil took him by surprise. Automatically he worked the bolt, ejecting the empty cartridge as the deep, booming echo of the report rolled back and forth across the valley.

"You got him," Longworth said, his voice taut. He abandoned the spotting scope and swiftly crawled to his bolt-action. He looked for the sentry on the ridge.

The man wasn't there.

Terrific!

Gat Brown shoved a fresh round into the chamber and closed the bolt, then settled back into shooting position and again looked through his rifle scope. Two men were kneeling by the man who was down. He steadied the crosshairs on the nearest man and squeezed the trigger again. In front of him the brush quivered from the muzzle blast.

At the second report the ridge sentry's head popped out from behind a boulder. He looked around, still uncertain of the sniper's location. Longworth got his rifle on him, settled into a braced position on one knee and brought the crosshairs to rest. Then he squeezed one off. The sentry went down.

"A hit," he told himself. He didn't see the bullet strike, but the shot felt good. A good shooter has an instinct about these things. He crawled back to the spotting scope.

When Brown again looked through the scope, he saw two men sprawled beside the flatbed.

"Put a couple in that truck — see if you can disable it — and let's saddle up," Harry Longworth said.

The truck was a much easier target than a man. Where do you suppose the designers put the gas tank?

Brown steadied the big Fifty, held the crosshair where he thought the tank should be, and squeezed the trigger ever so gently.

The rifle spoke again, the brush shook, and again the booming echo rolled around the valley.

"You hit it," Longworth said tightly. "One more."

Brown fired again, trying to angle a bullet through the truck to hit the engine block.

"That's shooting!" Longworth exulted. "Now let's get outta here while we still can."

"Amen to that," said Gat Brown. They taped a delayed-fuse bomb containing a half pound of plastique to the rifle. Then they tossed the spotting scope and ammo beside it, triggered the chemical fuse, grabbed their personal weapons and the rucksacks containing the radios and water and boogied. They left the uneaten MREs and the sleeping bags for the holy warriors.

On their way across the ridge they passed the dead sentry. He had taken a bullet in the left chest.

Two hours of running and trotting later, they were on the other side of the ridge and into the valley. Another hour of hard trotting took them to the mouth of a small canyon they had passed through on their way to the village. They went up the canyon almost a mile, then separated, one man taking one side of the defile, one the other. They came back down the canyon to a place about five hundred yards or so from the entrance, a place where the canyon widened out and there was little cover. The likelihood of an ambush was much greater at the mouth of the canyon; when it didn't happen there, the pursuers would be less wary when they reached this spot, which at first glance didn't seem to offer much in the way of cover. There wasn't — for them.

Harry Longworth fired up the satellite telephone and called for the extraction. He used code words. When he got an acknowledgment he turned the telephone off again to save the battery and stowed it in his backpack.

He arranged his M40A3 and ammo so they were handy. In his backpack were two grenades; he placed them beside the ammo. Making himself comfortable, he removed an energy bar from a jacket pocket, tore off the wrapper and munched on it between swigs of water as he scanned the rocks and ridges and stunted vegetation huddled down for the winter.

The village men would probably be along after a while, following the dogs. If they came, when they came, Harry Longworth and Gat Brown would kill them. The dogs, too.

Per Diem was driving, and I was in the right seat. We were following Marisa Petrou's limo. Actually the car belonged to Isolde. Apparently she had found a new wheelman after I accidentally on purpose terminated the last one. Shit happens, I'm here to tell ya.

Paris is not an easy town to follow a car in because there is too much traffic and too many traffic lights. If you stay back, inevitably someone gets in front of you and you miss a light and the car you are following disappears in the sea of traffic ahead. So we weren't trying to finesse Marissa's chauffeur — we were right on his tail. He didn't seem to notice. Drove the boulevards without a care in the world.

I wondered where Marisa was going. If she was going to meet Abu Qasim . . . well, I should be so lucky. Jake Grafton had given me orders: "If you see him, shoot him. I don't care where it happens or what else is going down. Shoot him dead. Use the whole magazine if you have time."

That order certainly seemed clear enough. Of course, my chances of bumping into Abu

Qasim were about a zillion to one: I had a better chance of winning a Powerball lottery. Even if I did see him, odds are I wouldn't recognize him. I certainly didn't want to pop any bankers or boyfriends or members of the bar, even if they were French. I had made up my mind — no more accidental homicides.

I almost left the gun in my hotel room, then thought better of that impulse. Strangulations are brutal and messy. Bullets would be better.

Diem was a good driver. He seemed aware of all that was happening around him and checked the rearview mirror regularly. I glanced back from time to time, too. When people are too easy to follow, a suspicious fellow might wonder if there is a reason, such as someone trailing you. Not this time.

We drove into the heart of the city, crossed the bridge and pulled up in front of police headquarters. The limo stopped, and Marisa got out. There was a photographer on the sidewalk, and he snapped her picture. She didn't look at him, just walked past pretending she didn't see him and went inside.

"Wanta go in and see who she's talking to?" Diem said.

"Ha, ha, ha." I opened the door. "Follow the limo. I'll call you on your cell if she grabs a cab."

I got out and headed for a vantage point across the street, where I could keep an eye on the front door of the prefecture. Knowing Marisa, I didn't think there was a chance on earth she would use a side or back door. Found an empty bench in front of Notre Dame, inspected it for pigeon doo and parked my fanny.

Gusty wind, temp in the fifties, gray clouds scudding overhead . . . fortunately I was dressed for the weather. I turned my coat collar up and pulled my hat down tight. Tried to keep the eyes moving and the brain in neutral, which was difficult.

I could see about a thousand possible permutations on how this thing would play out, one of which was that we actually managed to kill Abu Qasim and get him stuffed for display in the CIA museum. One out of a thousand. About six hundred of the possibilities had Grafton winding up in a federal prison. Of course, if that happened, I was probably going to get tossed in an adjacent cell, because I knew all about this vast criminal conspiracy lodged in the rotten heart of the American government and didn't blow the whistle.

The photographer on the sidewalk across the street made call after call on his cell phone. Before long another photographer arrived. A half hour later a television crew, complete with supporting truck, arrived. After they were set up, the reporter — a woman — talked into a camera for a while, then they waited. Ten minutes later another guy showed up carrying two camera bags, one on each shoulder. They formed a gauntlet that everyone leaving the building had to pass through. Several people did, and the media let them pass unmolested.

Marisa was in there for an hour and a half. The limo appeared at the curb, and the driver got out. Diem in our rental was a hundred feet behind. I walked over and climbed in just as Marisa came out the door and the photographers sprang into action. Inquiring minds want to know. One would think she specialized in hot love scenes for the cinema. She marched determinedly through the crowd, didn't say boo to the lady with the microphone — which she stuck in Marisa's face — and climbed aboard the limo. Away we crept, off through traffic, back to the château Petrou out in the country.

"What was that all about?" Diem wanted to know. "Why the star treatment?"

"We'll buy a paper this evening."

When we did, we discovered that Marisa

was the prime suspect in her husband's murder. Of course, the police didn't state in so many words that she was *it,* but she was answering questions before the examining magistrate. Again. She had access to the poison that did him in, opportunity and lots of motive. The dirty laundry of Jean and Marisa's marriage was smeared all over the paper for the world to read. And she was young, beautiful, rich and slightly exotic. If she managed to beat the rap, she could probably get a movie contract.

I studied the photo in the paper, which was a full-face close-up. I saw a lovely woman with her emotions under tight control. I looked for a hint of guilt or innocence, and didn't see a trace of either one.

The holy warriors came in late afternoon, when the canyon was deep in shadow. The temperature had dropped to about twenty degrees, and the breeze was off the Hindu Kush. One man was on the point. He stayed on their trail, such as it was — a few scuff marks, here and there a partial footprint — wary as a nervous deer. He passed completely in front of Longworth and disappeared to the left, up-canyon.

He and Brown waited. Longworth's watch seemed to stop. He breathed shallowly so his breath vapor would dissipate without rising as a cloud.

When they came there were four of them and two dogs on leashes. They walked well spread out. Harry Longworth studied them through binoculars. They were carrying AK-47s.

He ran the binoculars over the far ridge, looking for any sign of movement. Seeing none, he laid down the glasses and picked up the sniper rifle.

The line of searchers passed directly in front of him, the nearest man about eighty yards away, and continued on up the canyon. Fifty yards farther on they began crossing a flat place almost devoid of rocks.

That's when he shot the man on the left. He heard the high-pitched crack of Gat Brown's M-16, again and again.

All four men and the two dogs were down when Harry Longworth saw a flash of movement on the far side of the canyon and heard a burst of three shots.

The point man! He had doubled back.

The wind blew and the evening got darker in the canyon.

Finally, when Longworth was convinced the point man wouldn't move, he did. Harry's bullet caught him and he slid down a steep, naked slope and came to rest against a small stone.

It was full dark and bitterly cold, with the wind working up to a gale, when Harry Longworth found Gat Brown. He piled some stones on him as he said a little prayer. Brown always pretended to be an atheist — and perhaps he was — but now, Harry Longworth thought, he was with Jesus. Maybe.

The problem with religion is that you don't really *know.*

Longworth took Gat's weapon and rucksack and left him there in that rocky canyon in the foothills of the Hindu Kush.

The next day Marisa didn't come out. I wondered if our bugs were working. The CIA had someone at Ft. Meade listening to the household drivel on a real-time basis. Grafton had insisted upon it. I called Grafton's assistant, Robin Cloyd, the lady of the jeans and sweatshirts and big hair, on an encrypted satellite phone.

"Hey. This is Tommy."

"Well, hello there, world traveler. Where are you today?"

"France. What are the spooks hearing from the Petrou château?"

"Oh, lots and lots of stuff. Should I send you a summary on your BlackBerry?"

"Yeah." We spies were really into twenty-first-century gadgets. "But let's cut to the chase. Is there anything there that I should know about?"

"Well . . . I am scrolling through this stuff . . . The agency uses a program that reduces speech to text, so we get it untouched by human hands." She hummed a little bit, then said, "It all looks very benign. When are you coming home?"

"My birthday. For sure." I was lying, of course; I had no idea where I would be tomorrow. "Let me know when Marisa sounds as if she might go out."

"Of course."

"Great."

"Thanks for calling, Tommy."

Robin Cloyd was a strange woman. As I repacked the satellite phone in its little case, I wondered about her.

The third day of our vigil, Marisa set forth again in the limo. We were forewarned by a call from Robin, and were waiting in our rental when the limo appeared. I checked with the binoculars. She seemed to be alone.

"How do you stand all this excitement?" Diem asked as we rolled along.

"Too lazy to work and too stupid to steal. You know that old song."

"Yeah," he admitted.

I kept waiting for Diem's personality to grow on me, but so far it hadn't germinated.

It was raining that day in Paris, a steady rain from a dreary sky, matching my mood. Marisa's chauffeur didn't try to lose us, which was good, because he would have succeeded. He dropped Marisa at one of the big department stores on the right bank of the Seine. She was just disappearing through the doors of the retailing temple when I bailed out of the rental and charged off after her. I was hoping she was here to meet someone, and I figured Jake Grafton might like to know who it was. For that matter, so would I.

It was warmer and drier inside, with women huddled over the scent and makeup counters and talking in low tones. Marisa was waiting on the elevator, facing the door.

I waited until the door opened and she entered, then jumped on the escalator.

She went up to the eighth floor and into the restaurant. I found a vantage point outside that allowed me to see her through the plate glass windows. She took a seat at a small table in the corner, all alone, studied the menu and ordered when the waitress came around. If she was supposed to meet someone, she wasn't waiting. Hmmm.

There were three other couples dining there and several single ladies. Two ladies went in and were seated while I dawdled. Half the tables were empty.

I waited ten minutes, just in case, then went inside. The maître d' smiled at me, and I pointed at Marisa in the corner.

I walked over and joined her.

"I thought you'd never get here," she said and gave me a hint of a smile.

"You were waiting for me?"

"I was unsure of the best way to get in touch with you. While I was sitting in the bath, I wondered, should I just name a place and time and ask you to meet me? Or should I go somewhere and wait until you arrived? Which would you prefer in the future?"

"I called the newspapers before I came in. The photographers are gathering outside."

The waitress brought her a bottle of white wine from the Rhone valley, and an extra glass for me. The waitress poured. The wine was dry and delicious.

"So," Marisa said when the waitress trotted off, "are we going to sit here telling each other lies, or will you give me the real reason that you are following me?"

"The real reason. Honest injun, cross my heart and hope to die. My boss told me to."

"Aah," she said, as if that explained everything.

The waitress brought a menu for me, but I refused it. "Whatever she's having," I said, nodding at Marisa. "Bring me the same."

The waitress smiled, sure she was in the presence of true love, and went away happy.

"If you don't mind," I said, "when the lunch comes we'll trade dishes, just in case."

She was sipping wine as if she had waited all week for this taste, yet she kept her eyes on me. Now I saw what I hadn't seen in the photos — she looked stressed.

"Of course, if you brought your polonium with you, you can just sprinkle it all over my grub before I taste it. I've heard it gives you a thrill that Mexican hot sauce never will."

She put her wineglass on the table, and I reached for her hands. Held them both — they were cold — then released one. Sure enough, she had a slight tremor. She withdrew the unattached appendage, but she held on with the other. Her hand felt solid, sensual. For a prime suspect, she felt mighty good.

"Or you can haul out your Walther and start blasting," I said. "I'm sure everyone will understand. You do have a good lawyer, don't you?"

She didn't say a word. Didn't turn a hair. I didn't know if she ever played poker, but I wouldn't bet ten cents with her holding cards.

"Did you poison your husband, was it your mother-in-law, or was it that swine Abu Qasim?"

Now she withdrew her hand and gave me a wan smile. "Mr. Carmellini. Tommy. I know you mean well, that you are a soldier for good and righteousness and those other American things." With her French accent, the words really sounded cool. Corny, but cool. "I wish for you to deliver a message to Admiral Grafton."

I sipped wine as I thought about things. "Okay," I said. "Shoot."

"He knows all the names, including yours, and he plans to kill all of you."

"My name?"

"Those are my words for Admiral Grafton."

By "him" I figured she could only mean Abu Qasim. A cold chill slid down my spine. Four days ago Jake Grafton had predicted murder as Abu Qasim's goal, and had named the targets.

After a moment's thought, I asked the obvious question. "How did he learn the names?"

"My husband told him."

"I'll give Grafton the message," I said.

She appeared sincere, the mask gone.

Or she was one hell of an actress.

I wondered which was the case.

"Thanks for the wine." I rose, nodded at the startled waitress and walked out.

If you thought I was going to have a relaxing lunch with the prime suspect in a husband poisoning, and perhaps another, you're nuts. I wouldn't have even touched the wine if I had seen her hand near the bottle. Marisa could pay the lunch tab. I figured she could afford it.

Sheikh Mahmoud al-Taji met his visitor in a safe room in the basement of the mosque. His visitor had entered the mosque in full robe and headpiece, so no one had gotten a good look at his face. Even if they had, he was heavily made up, wearing a full beard.

This basement room was the safest place for private conversations. The room was completely suspended upon shock absorbers in the middle of a larger room and surrounded with insulation. Installed on the floors and walls of the basement were amplifiers that broadcast the sounds from within the mosque above.

"It is good to see you again, Abu Qasim."

"I need to pray. Will you pray with me?"

The two knelt on the rugs and prayed to Allah, the all-merciful. When they had finished, they sat upon the rugs and conferred in low tones.

"It was as you said it would be," al-Taji said. "The English courts did not convict me. Truly, we can use these people's laws against them. They are tied up in their own contradictions."

Al-Taji thought that the English were stupid, with their insistence on the rule of law. He took a moment now to expand upon that theme. It was Allah who ruled, and his words given through the Prophet were supreme. The English had lost their god somewhere along the way, and were the worse for it.

Abu Qasim knew Western society was more complex, but he didn't choose to discuss it with the sheikh. They had more important things to occupy them.

"The Americans killed Rameid," Qasim said, "in his refuge at the base of the mountains. Killed him two days ago with a long-range rifle."

Al-Taji was taken aback. "May he rest in peace," he muttered.

"I, too, am a hunted man, as you know. One suspects that you also are a target."

"But the English did not convict me!"

"They did not convict Rameid, either," Abu Qasim pointed out, "or Abdul-Zahra Mohammed or the others. They use the law when it suits them and the bullet or the knife when that suits them. Underestimating the infidels is a grave mistake. They are in league with the Devil, as you know."

"I have given my soul to jihad," al-Taji said forcefully, "and Paradise awaits. I am at peace. *Inshallah.*"

They sat there the rest of the afternoon discussing the secret army that hunted them, and its leader, Jake Grafton. Discussed and planned and plotted revenge, which, as every man of the desert knew to the depths of his soul, is life's sweetest experience.

As he contemplated the prospect, Sheikh Mahmoud al-Taji smiled.

CHAPTER FOURTEEN

"She says he knows all the names, including yours, and he plans to kill all of you."

I was talking on the encrypted satellite phone to Jake Grafton, who was somewhere in America, I thought; he flitted around like a moth on crack. He was silent after I gave him Marisa's message. He was silent so long that I thought maybe we had lost the connection. "You still there?" I asked.

"Yeah. Gimme a moment to think."

More silence.

Finally I said, "Looks like your crystal ball is giving you good dope."

"I have to see some people here. I'll call you tomorrow about noon your time. Okay?"

"Sure."

I was staying in a cheap hotel on the Left Bank — the bedroom was so small that I had to crawl over the bed to get to the bathroom — and eating in cheap restaurants. The steady decline of the dollar hadn't been reflected in the per diem rates. If it got much worse, I was going to be living under an overpass and pushing my stuff around in a stolen shopping cart.

Since Per and another guy from the embassy had the night watch on the Petrou château if Marisa decided to sally forth — or if someone tried to get in to do the Petrou women — that evening I played tourist, strolling the sidewalks along the Seine and wishing the season were summer. It wasn't. Still, Paris was full of lovers, bundled up and strolling arm in arm, looking at the lights.

I like Paris. You can have Chicago if you wish; Paris is my kind of town.

An hour before dawn Oleg Tchernychenko awoke and looked out the window into the Scottish night. The wind was rattling the pane, and raindrops were spattering themselves against the window. He dressed quickly and went downstairs to brew a pot of tea.

As the kettle warmed, he wandered through the old house looking at his books. He had thousands, which filled shelves in various rooms from the floor to the ceiling. Books. They were the great discovery when he left Russia fifteen years ago. Books. The Communists didn't like books, except politically correct tomes by Russian authors, which weren't, to Tchernychenko's mind, real books at all. He made this momentous discovery in Great Britain, in the bookshops and libraries that dotted the streets and neighborhoods.

He had been lucky. One of the first books he found was Winston Churchill's *History of the English-Speaking Peoples,* in four volumes. Inside he found civilization. Churchill told of conquests and kings, religious passions and wars and the differing visions that led the world forward, in fits and starts. Churchill's six volumes on the Second World War were a revelation; one almost wondered if that were the same war the Communists had talked about all those years.

He read Charles Darwin, William Shakespeare, the Brownings, and Alfred Lord Tennyson. And everything else he could get his hands on, from Robert Louis Stevenson, H. G. Wells, H. Rider Haggard and J. R. R. Tolkien to Tom Clancy, Dan Brown and J. K. Rowling.

Tchernychenko walked along, fingering the books on his shelves. He smiled when he reached the little paperback mysteries by

Agatha Christie. He had them all — every one.

When the tea was ready, he poured himself a cup and stood at the kitchen door watching the dawn. The sky began to gray. As the light improved he could see the clouds scudding swiftly over the grass-covered hills, churning endlessly, driven by the wild wind.

He glanced at his watch. On Saturday the limo was coming from London to pick him up, him and his two bodyguards, who were still upstairs in bed. He certainly didn't need to be in London to work. Still, he had a few hours before he needed to start making telephone calls and taking care of business.

He had leased this house in the Highlands because he loved Scotland — loved the hills and waving grass and rocks and sky, loved the weather in all four seasons. Five miles west was the coast, steep, rocky cliffs hammered since time began by the restless sea, with sheep making a precarious living on the headlands. Here and there were little cottages, hunkered down, a part of the earth. Scotland was wild, visual and sensual; when he was in London or Europe and thought of it, he always smiled, as one does thinking of an old lover fondly remembered.

When he finished his tea, Oleg Tchernychenko donned his rain gear and Wellingtons and prepared for a hike. He paused at the door. Putin was sending fatal messages to people who displeased him — Tchernychenko had few friends in high places in Moscow — and Abu Qasim and his fanatics wanted him dead. When he heard Jake Grafton's message, he had known the admiral spoke the truth.

He looked again at the cold rain and December wind, blowing in off the Atlantic. It was a bad day for assassins, who were probably home in bed. On the other hand . . . He went back to his den and found the double rifle a Scottish neighbor had once used on an expedition to Africa. The rifle was a tangible reminder that in a free society a man could get a wild hair and journey to far corners of the earth to stalk the great beasts, for no reason other than he wanted to go. There was something magical about that — almost mystical. That a man could envision a life different than what he led, and go forth to seek it; say what you will, that is *freedom.*

He loaded the rifle — with big, heavy yellow cartridges topped with big, heavy lead slugs — made sure the safety was on and set out with it under his arm. His destination was the low ridge to the north of his house. Last year on its rocky crest he had found a rusted sword. From that vantage point a man could see for miles, if the visibility was good enough. Perhaps in olden days a soldier had waited there, on watch — and perhaps had died there. Personal tragedies are quickly submerged in the river of time, and are irretrievably lost.

As he walked with the rain stinging his cheeks and the rifle heavy under his arm, Oleg Tchernychenko scanned possible hiding places and thought about life and death.

Alexander Surkov, his aide, was dead of polonium poisoning. Grafton thought Surkov had sold out Tchernychenko and Winchester and the others to Abu Qasim. If Surkov did that, he knew he was signing their death warrants. Tchernychenko didn't believe that Surkov was capable of such an evil.

Thinking about it as he walked along, Tchernychenko was sure he was right. Surkov would never do a thing like that. The Seychelles check . . . aah, that was a different matter. Alexander Surkov was perfectly capable of working both sides of the road to Moscow if there was money in it for him, and probably he had.

If he did, he had probably crossed Putin or one of his friends, which was a dangerous thing to do.

Oleg Tchernychenko had also crossed Putin, in fact, many times . . . and Abu Qasim. Putin was inevitable, a thing that was going to happen. Qasim — well, that was a conflict he had sought. He had known Huntington Winchester for years, at least ten. They had done business and developed a mutual respect. He and Winchester had spent long evenings together, several of them here in Scotland. They had become fast friends, and their conversations had covered the gamut of the human experience.

So when Winchester lost his son and asked for help against the religious fanatics, Tchernychenko had readily agreed. It was time to fight those tyrants, too.

Of course, they could strike back. He had always known that.

He was in no hurry to die. Since leaving Russia, Tchernychenko had discovered that life is sweet. He had come to see the grand sweep of life, the human struggle, the changing earth down through the ages. Come to see it and become part of it.

He had had a good life. No thanks to the Communists, the tyrants or the religious fanatics, all of whom sought to impose their vision of life on everyone else.

Oleg Tchernychenko paused, turned his face to the wind and closed his eyes and let the rain pound his face.

Well, damn them all.

Sure enough, the next day at noon, Jake Grafton called me. "Go see her again this afternoon," he said, "and get some more. Then call me. Make her sell you."

"Why don't I —"

"Please, Tommy. Just follow orders."

"It's really great being on your team, by the way, being one of the guys in the huddle. But if you expect me to catch a ball, you're going to have to tell me what the play is."

"Indeed."

That was Jake Grafton, Mr. Consensus.

I called Robin Cloyd at Langley to find out what was going on just then at the Petrou château. She was supposed to be reading — or at least scanning — the printouts sent over to Grafton's office by the CIA of the conversations picked up by the bugs I had planted last week. It seemed a lifetime ago.

"So what's happening today in Marisa's life?" I asked.

"Let me get my notes," she said. "How's the weather there?"

"Clear and chilly."

"Oh, I wish I were there," she said warmly. "France sounds so romantic."

"I'm sure."

"I'm hoping, on my next vacation —"

"This call is costing the taxpayers serious money," I pointed out. I was quickly learning that it was necessary to keep her focused.

"Ah, here are my notes. Marisa and Madame Petrou had lunch together a few minutes ago. This morning — morning in France — they visited madame's attorneys. They were talking about attending a concert tonight."

"Thanks." I broke the connection. Speedo Harris was there with me at our vantage point in the inn, so I decided to take him along. He could watch the joint from in front of it.

Twenty minutes later I presented myself at the security shack in front of the main gate and presented my card. I had several in my wallet to choose from, so I selected one that said TERRY G. SHANNON, WORLD TRAVEL CORP. My cell phone number was printed on it. The guard, a portly fellow well past middle age, wearing a holstered pistol, went back inside to call the main house.

A while back I thought about having a card made up, TOMMY CARMELLINI,

SPIES AND LIES, for occasions such as this, but knew my many superiors at the agency would frown when they learned of it, as would happen eventually. People pass cards around or discard them in the oddest places.

In about two minutes the guard moved to the door as the gate opened and waved us on. He kept my card, probably as a souvenir.

Speedo parked the rental car in front of the house and remained behind the wheel as I got out. He picked up a novel and settled in. I glanced back at him as I stood at the door. He was yawning and listlessly turned pages. Being chauffeured around was a new experience for me. I wasn't sure that I liked it.

Abu Qasim watched Tommy Carmellini through binoculars from his vantage point on the second floor of the château across the road from the Petrou mansion. It was fortuitously empty; the owners were spending the winter at their condo in Martinique, as they did every year.

"He's here," he said to the man sitting on the couch across the room. That man, who went by the name of Khadr, removed an automatic pistol from his right-hand coat pocket and a silencer from his left. He pushed the silencer onto the barrel and twisted it ninety degrees, locking it in place. He pulled back the slide, checking for the gleam of brass, and ensured the safety was on. Then he stood and reached for his long coat, which lay on a nearby chair.

Qasim also reached for his coat. He already had his gloves on — he had never taken them off — so there were no fingerprints to worry about.

"Let's go," he said.

Khadr followed him from the room.

The butler opened the door at my knock and ushered me in. We crossed the giant foyer and tackled the stairs. Marisa was seated at a small round table in a dayroom on the second floor, reading a newspaper and sipping something hot. A television provided background noise, which would make it more difficult for the NSA wizards to wring conversation from the bugs, but not impossible. The old madame wasn't in sight.

Marisa didn't get up. She gestured toward a chair across from her. "Is this seating okay?" she asked innocently. "Or should we sit somewhere else for better reception?"

I dropped into the indicated chair. "I relayed your message to Jake Grafton, and he sent me back for more. Do you want to confess to me or wait to tell him in person?"

Before she could answer, the maid came in. She was actually wearing a French maid's uniform — I kid you not — and carrying a jug of something hot on a tray.

"Chocolat, monsieur?" she asked as she refilled Marisa's cup. I shook my head. I wouldn't have swallowed anything in that house for all the money in Switzerland.

When the maid was out of the room, Marisa said, "You and I need to stop needling each other — that is the word for it, isn't it? Needling?"

"That word fits," I admitted.

"We need to sign a peace treaty."

"Smoke the pipe and bury the hatchet, eh?"

"Smoke . . . ?"

I waved it away and looked her over as I tried to spin the brain up to speed. She had wide cheekbones, deep brown eyes set wide apart and a magnificent mane of dark brown hair brushed over to her left side, exposing her right ear, upon which a small diamond earring could be seen. She wasn't wearing any rings on her hands. I didn't know the protocol for widows, but I didn't recall ever seeing her with rings. She had long, slender fingers and perfectly manicured nails, of course. Whatever Marisa's problems were, they didn't include nail-biting.

So what were her problems? Presumably she had inherited enough money to live on. If she didn't get prosecuted for killing ol' Jean, life should be looking up. And I seriously doubted that a murder prosecution was in her future, not unless the French fuzz had a digitalis bottle with her fingerprints on it.

I sat there musing about her problems and enjoying the view — she was a beautiful woman — while she sipped chocolate.

Abu Qasim drove down the driveway to the road. A small truck was coming, so he waited until it had passed and the road was empty before he turned north and drove the twenty-five yards to the Petrous' guard shack. As the car rolled, Khadr removed a ski mask from a coat pocket and pulled it on. It was knitted wool and covered his face, leaving only small openings for his eyes, mouth and nose. Khadr got out of the car as the guard settled his cap upon his head and made ready to leave the warmth of the little building.

As the guard walked out the door he saw Khadr, and began fumbling for the pistol that was in the holster on his belt. Khadr shot him with his silenced pistol. The man's hat flew off and he collapsed in the doorway.

The assassin pocketed the pistol and dragged the guard's body back inside the shack. He pushed the button to open the gate and closed the door behind him.

After a glance at Qasim, Khadr walked up the driveway toward the Petrou château. Qasim sat in the car, watching. He saw that Khadr was holding the pistol with its long silencer down beside his right leg.

"Why don't you level with me," I said to Marisa, "and tell me what's on your mind?" Of course she wouldn't tell me the truth, but I was curious about what the story would be. Grafton obviously was, too, and he was even more of a cynic than I was. Maybe because he was older. Wiser. Meaner. More twisted.

"Who plans to kill whom?" I prompted.

She scrutinized my dishonest phiz, undoubtedly trying to figure out what I knew. The answer, of course, was very little, but I didn't want her to know that.

"From your lips to Grafton's ears, through me," I said and tried to look trustworthy.

"Admiral Grafton understands the message," she said finally.

I raised my hands and shoulders, then

lowered them. "He sent me with instructions to get the complete story from you. He doesn't tell me what he knows and doesn't know. I simply do as I'm told."

"I see."

"Then we're getting somewhere. Who is the killer?"

"Abu Qasim."

"Your father?"

She said nothing. Merely stared at me. Okay.

"So who is Abu going to kill?"

"Jake Grafton and the others."

"More progress. Who are the others?"

"You don't know or you are trying to find out if I know."

"Read it any way you like. Gimme names."

"My mother-in-law, Oleg Tchernychenko, Jerry Hay Smith, Huntington Winchester, Rolf Gnadinger, and Simon Cairnes."

"Why these people?"

"They are funding Grafton's war on al-Qaeda." I took a deep breath and exhaled. So she knew all about the intrepid little band of heroes who were financing a private war on terror. Even worse, according to her, Abu Qasim knew.

"Wolfgang Zetsche?"

"So you aren't as ignorant as you wish me to think. Qasim had him killed."

"And Alexander Surkov?"

"The Russians, I imagine."

"But you don't know?"

"No."

"Your husband?"

"Qasim."

"How do you know?"

"He might have poisoned Jean by mistake, while he was trying to poison Isolde, or intentionally because he was afraid we would learn that Jean betrayed Isolde and the others to Qasim and demand that Jean tell the authorities. I just don't know."

"But you didn't see Qasim poison the food?"

"No."

"I have a suggestion. Why don't you just tell me what Abu Qasim told you and the part you are supposed to play in his drama?"

She sprang from the chair and reached for her purse. I was ready to break her neck if she pulled out that Walther, but she extracted a pack of cigarettes and a pack of matches. Her hands shook as she tried to get a cigarette lit. It took two matches to get the thing ignited. Being a gentleman and all, perhaps I should have lit it for her, but I merely sat and watched.

Was she selling out her father?

Or was she doing precisely what Abu

Qasim had told her to do, which was tell this tale to Grafton, via Carmellini?

I had been hanging around Grafton too long — I was even beginning to think like him.

If she was merely obeying orders, what did Qasim expect Grafton to do with the information? What was it Qasim wanted Grafton to do?

The problem, I decided, was that I didn't know which side Marisa was really on.

Of course, maybe she didn't know, either.

Khadr walked up behind the car sitting outside the Petrou mansion and raised the pistol as he came alongside. The window was up. He fired through it, hitting the driver in the head. The driver slumped forward onto the steering wheel.

Khadr walked on, up the walk, up the steps, across the stoop, and rang the door-bell. He waited.

If Marisa was acting, I thought she should have been on Broadway. She sat on the edge of her chair, her feet under her, and sucked on her weed. Inhaled deeply and blew smoke all over. She repeatedly pushed her bangs back out of her face, over and over, unconsciously.

351

"Will he try to kill Isolde?" I asked gently.

"I don't know."

"You?"

She eyed me. "I don't know." She looked down and sucked some more on her cigarette. After a moment she said, "If they knew I was talking to you and Grafton, they would."

"They?"

"You don't think he's working alone, do you?"

"I guess not."

When the door opened, Khadr shot the butler once, right in the face. He stepped into the foyer.

The maid was there, carrying a tray with a silver pot. She started to scream. Khadr shot her, too. The first bullet hit her in the body and she fell, dropping the tray. Dark liquid splattered all over the floor.

Khadr walked into the room and shot the maid in the head as she lay on the floor. Then he turned and walked out of the château.

Down the steps, past the car with the dead driver, and down the winding driveway to where Abu Qasim was waiting.

Marisa finished her cigarette in silence,

stubbed it out and took a deep breath. She looked calmer, more herself.

I rose from my chair. "I'll go call Grafton, see what he says."

"*Au revoir,*" she said automatically.

"I'll be right back."

She looked up at me, pinned me with those dark brown eyes and said, "Every time I see you it's as if I'm seeing a ghost. They want to kill you so badly . . . you're a dead man walking, Tommy Carmellini. So *au revoir,* in case we never meet again."

I walked the hallways to the main staircase and started down. About halfway down I saw the butler, who was sprawled near the front door. The door was wide open.

I stopped — frozen — looking and listening. The Springfield seemed to find my hand automatically. I looked down and left . . . and saw the maid, lying on the floor with her legs akimbo. Spilled chocolate all over the floor, a lake of it. The platter had broken. Why hadn't I heard it break?

I guess my brain locked up about then. In my mind's eye I could see Speedo behind the wheel of our rental car, parked outside. Speedo Harris, MI-6. Good God!

My legs carried me the rest of the way down the staircase, across the foyer and out the door without any thought on my part. The rental car was parked out there on the brick pavement. I could see Speedo's head slumped over the wheel.

No one else in sight. No cars, no people, no dogs, no airplanes going over, only a deathly silence.

I walked around the front of the sedan to the driver's door. The window was up . . . and had a hole in it. The steering wheel was holding Speedo up. His eyes were open, staring at nothing.

Amazing the things you think about at a moment like that. I stared at Speedo's head and saw the entry hole for the bullet that killed him. Just a little spot of red, right above his left ear. His paperback novel was on his lap.

Well, at least Marisa didn't kill him; she had been with me ever since the butler showed me to the upstairs sitting room.

But somebody shot him, sure as hell. Hanging around with Carmellini was the equivalent of a death sentence. Jake Grafton oughta be locked up for sending me to guard anyone.

I felt a yell coming on. If the shooter was upstairs doing Isolde and Marisa . . .

I charged for the porch, took the steps three at a time. I was yelling then — I couldn't help myself. Howling. I jerked the damn door open and ran inside, ready to shoot the first person I saw.

I saw no one alive. The butler and maid were lying just as I had first seen them.

I charged for the stairs and went up three at a time, still yelling. Raced along the hallway and jerked open the sitting room door. There sat Marisa, staring at me as if I had lost my mind. Maybe I had.

"Where's Isolde?" I roared. I was waving the pistol around, looking to make sure she was the only one in the room.

She didn't come fast enough to suit me. I grabbed her arm and threw her toward the door.

"Quick, goddamnit!" I was trying to speak normally, but it wasn't working. The words came out as a shout. "Someone shot the guy I came with and the butler and maid. He may be in the house. *Where is she?*"

Marisa gathered herself and ran. I followed, two doors down, through a hallway that led to a corner room suite. The old woman was sitting there at her desk working on something.

I looked around the room, in the bath, in the closet. God, I was so ready to shoot somebody. I don't recall ever being so frustrated or keyed up.

"Get your passports and your purses and any medication you have to have. Quickly, now. We're leaving."

"Where — ?" Marisa asked.

"London. A safe house. That's the only place I know that killers can't get to you."

Marisa said something in French to the old lady, and by gum, she jumped up and ran into the bathroom. In thirty seconds she had her purse and her passport from the desk and was ready to go. I wondered if her late husband knew what a jewel she was.

It took about the same amount of time to collect Marisa's stuff, and then I was leading them down the stairs.

When we saw the butler and maid sprawled out, Isolde stopped dead. She began spewing French at Marisa. She bent down, gently touched the butler's white hair.

I thought this wasn't the time and place for long good-byes, and reached for her. Marisa put a hand on my arm.

Isolde Petrou got down on her knees beside the butler and seized his hand. Tears were running down her cheeks and she was biting her lip. "No, no, no," she muttered. After a moment she hoisted herself up and went over to the maid, who was lying on her back with her eyes open, staring at infinity. Isolde got down on her knees again, closed her eyes, touched her cheek, said her name, said good-bye.

Marisa reached for the older woman's arm, helped her to her feet, nodded at me. Together, they followed me.

We went out through the kitchen toward the garage, taking our time, looking for anyone at all. Didn't see hide nor hair of the cook or gardener or wine cellar dude. I wondered if they were all asleep . . . with bullets in their heads. No time to look — they were alive and well or they weren't. I was going to keep these two women alive or die trying.

I put Marisa in the front seat of the Mercedes limo and Madame Petrou in back, then hunted through the chauffeur's quarters over the garage for the keys. It was like an anxiety dream. Lurking around somewhere, maybe, was an assassin, and I couldn't find the damned keys. I kept expecting to wake up any second in a cold sweat.

Just when I was ready to admit defeat, I found the keys hanging on a nail at the head of the stairs. Don't know how I missed them coming in.

I shot down the stairs, punched the garage door opener and stood to one side, watching, as it rose at its usual pace. It made a noise going up. Needed oil.

No one in sight. I dove into the car, backed out smartly and got going down the drive. The gate was open. I slowed and looked into the guard shack.

I intended to drive on by, then thought better of it. Slammed on the brakes, jammed the transmission into park and turned it off. Took the keys with me, just in case. I didn't trust Marisa far enough to throw her. The last thing I wanted to see was her and Isolde disappearing down the road while I stood there surrounded by corpses, looking stupid.

One glance into the guard shack was enough. The day man was facedown on the floor.

I got back into the car, jammed the keys into the ignition and lit that thing up. As we roared away, I got out my cell phone and pushed the 1 button. In about a minute I had Robin Cloyd. "Tell Grafton that some-one killed Speedo — a bullet in the brain — and at least three of the Petrou household staff. I have both the Petrou women in their limo, and we're heading to London."

"I have been listening to the audio from the bugs."

"Call the police. Maybe they'll get lucky."

"I've already talked to the admiral."

"Where is he, anyway?"

"Here." That would be Washington.

"Put him on."

"He'll call you in a few minutes."

The connection went dead.

Marisa was watching the road and checking the rearview mirror on her side of the car. She had her purse in her lap, and the top was open. I grabbed it and glanced inside. Sure enough, she had that Walther in there. I took it out and put it in my pocket, then dropped the purse in her lap.

"I didn't kill anyone," she said.

"Maybe not in the last fifteen minutes, I'll grant you that. And I certainly don't want you shooting me."

"I am not going to shoot you, Tommy."

I adjusted the rearview mirror in the middle of the windshield to keep an eye on madame in the back. Maybe she poisoned her son and maybe she didn't. She was biting her lip, looking out the windows . . . Once, when I glanced in the mirror, I caught her wiping her eyes.

"Honestly, I'll feel better having the gun in my pocket," I told Marisa.

"If you don't slow down, we're going to be killed in a car wreck."

Those big Mercedes Benzes sure can roll. I let off on the gas and took a deep breath and tried to get my thoughts in order.

Poor Speedo. He was a dweeb, but still . . . to die like that.

I wondered if he even saw it coming.

Jake Grafton took the call from Robin Cloyd at Sal Molina's desk in his tiny White House office. On the other side of the desk was CIA director William S. Wilkins, and he was in a sour mood. He knew far more than he had before about Huntington Winchester and his friends, and the president's aide's personal direction of this operation.

As the admiral listened to Cloyd's summary of events at the Petrou château on the other side of the Atlantic, Wilkins snarled, "You're a fool, Molina. I don't give a pinch of rat shit what commitment the president made to Huntington Winchester. Involving the agency in a hare-brained scheme like this — one that is bound to blow up in your faces — strikes me as a classic case of rotten judgment."

Molina looked unperturbed. "In the president's judgment — and mine — the possible rewards justified the risks. Yes, the risks are substantial, but we are going to have to take risks if we expect to have any chance at getting the terrorist masterminds."

William Wilkins shook his bald head. "I'm not a fool and I'm not an optimist. I have spent thirty years assessing risks in covert operations, and believe me, this one meets none of the criteria for approval."

He was wasting air, and he knew it. During the last twenty years the agency had lost the trust of many of the politicians in Washington. It had missed the impending collapse of Communism in the late eighties and early nineties, assured the establishment that Saddam Hussein had weapons of mass destruction and been overly optimistic about the prospects for some kind of political settlement between the three major groups in Iraq after Saddam was removed, to name only three of its blown calls.

The agency's record of penetrating terrorist organizations and combating them effectively was even worse. This was the unspoken fact that hung in the air now, although neither Wilkins nor Molina was willing to voice it, and was undoubtedly one of the factors in the president's decision to provide support to Winchester's quixotic quest. Knowing the political forces at work merely deepened Wilkins' gloom. Amateurs mucking about, getting killed or scared and squealing to the press, weren't going to get it done. Other than filling some coffins with their own corpses, their main accomplishment would be triggering another congressional investigation, destroying the president politically and throwing even more mud on the agency.

As he sat watching Grafton on the phone, avoiding Molina's calm scrutiny, William Wilkins contemplated retirement. The hell of it was, it was *his* agency, and, by God, *his* country, too.

"I'll call him in a few minutes," Grafton said and hung up the telephone. He glanced from face to face, then told them of the events in the château and of Carmellini's departure with both women.

"What is your recommendation?" Molina asked calmly. The man would wear that expression when they lashed him to a post in front of a firing squad, William Wilkins thought savagely, and wished *that* day would really come.

Grafton deferred to his superior. Wilkins was having none of it. He held out his hand to Grafton and opened it. "The floor is yours," he said through clenched teeth.

"I think we need to inform the French government of what just transpired," Jake Grafton said, "and get those two women out of the country. My recommendation would be to bring them to the States, collect the other members of Winchester's group and put them in a location where we can trap whoever will come after them."

"How do you know anyone will come after them?"

"Marisa Petrou told Carmellini that Abu Qasim plans to kill them all." Grafton didn't mention that Marisa had said that he, the admiral, was also on Qasim's list.

"He's doing a fine job, so far," Wilkins said acidly.

"Not a safe house?" Molina asked.

"We want Qasim to find them. I was thinking the Winchester estate, in Connecticut. We'll use some security, not too much. Qasim must see this as an opportunity, not a trap."

"Has the thought occurred to you, Grafton," Wilkins said, "that you may be doing precisely what Qasim wants you to do?"

"Yes, sir. I think it very probable that he wants us to gather all these people in one place so he can kill them in a spectacular manner."

That comment caused Sal Molina to lose control of his face for a moment. He found himself staring at Jake Grafton.

"And you're going to do it?" Wilkins growled.

"To kill a tiger, you need a goat."

"What if this Marisa Petrou is a double agent?"

"If she tells Qasim where she is, that might be a plus," Grafton said.

"The eternal optimist," Wilkins said acidly. Sarcasm was a poor weapon, he knew, but he couldn't help himself.

"Did she or did she not kill her husband?" Molina asked.

"She might have."

"She might have killed Zetsche, or helped."

Grafton nodded in acknowledgment.

"She might be an assassin," Sal Molina said, eyeing Grafton carefully.

The admiral nodded again.

"So how are you going to keep Winchester and his pals alive if she is? All she has to do is poison the soup."

"Carmellini and I will be inside with them. We'll keep an eye on her."

William Wilkins snorted.

"Your comments, Mr. Director," Sal Molina said politely.

"I wish you people hadn't told me about this," the CIA director said. "I would rather have just read about it some morning in the *Washington Post* as I drank my coffee. I would have had my heart attack there on the spot and quietly died."

Then he rose from his chair and walked out of the room.

■ ■ ■ ■

The silence that followed was broken when Jake Grafton said, "He's right, you know."

"I do know," Sal Molina said forcefully. His icy composure cracked again; his face fell, and he reached up and rubbed his forehead. "If this blows up, as William so eloquently predicted, I'll resign and take full responsibility."

"I just want to do my time in a country-club prison," Jake Grafton said with feeling, "with the stock fraud artists, Ponzi schemers and inside traders. Those drug dudes are bad company, so I'm told."

"What about Tchernychenko?"

"He refused to take serious precautions. He has two competent bodyguards, he said, and he promised to call Gnadinger, pass on a warning."

Molina said a cuss word.

"We'd better get cracking," Grafton said, "before Abu Qasim kills them all."

CHAPTER FIFTEEN

I received a series of calls on my cell phone from Jake Grafton as I drove past Paris and headed for the ferry to England. We were a few miles northwest of Paris when Grafton informed me that the U.S. ambassador to France, the French intelligence service — the DGSE — and the French police had been told about the murders that morning at the Petrou château. The police demanded that Marisa and Isolde Petrou return to the château. With Grafton's concurrence, I kept driving northwest. I started watching for police cars — and saw them everywhere. They took no notice of us . . . yet.

Nor did anyone seem to be following us. I spent so much time looking in the mirrors I almost crashed twice.

Twenty minutes later Grafton called again. The French police, he said, were now only demanding that the Mesdames Petrou not leave the country. The police had found four bodies and six people alive, huddled in the basement, where they had fled after a masked gunman had killed the butler and one of the maids. He also told me the Swiss banker, Rolf Gnadinger, had been found dead the day before yesterday on the stoop of his house. Stabbed to death with an icicle, apparently. The Swiss police were investigating.

When Grafton hung up, I informed the women. "You'll need a new butler, maid and day security man," I said. "Bet you have a hard time finding new people."

Marisa didn't say a word, which didn't improve my mood. The problem here, I decided, was that Jake Grafton had given me only background without telling me who was really doing what to whom. These women probably knew enough to write a book. The old woman hadn't said ten words to me, and Marisa only went in for cryptic comments to be passed on to Grafton. I felt completely out of the loop. The darkness was stygian.

A black Porsche got behind us and settled in. I changed lanes, and he did, too. Not that I could see the driver, because the windshield was slanted too much and the sky reflecting on it made it opaque.

I sped up. He stayed right with me.

Fearing the worst, I slowed down. A minute later the Porsche passed me — the driver, a woman, was using me to clear the road of police looking for speeders. I had been doing ten over.

"And Rolf Gnadinger is dead. Murdered. On his porch, apparently."

"Rolf?" That was Isolde.

"Yes, ma'am."

Isolde Petrou had been hit hard today, and she winced as she took this body blow. Marisa turned and looked at her. They stared at each other for a long moment before Marisa turned around.

In the next call Grafton said the coast was clear; I could take the ladies to England. "Roger that." I flipped the phone shut.

"You're off the hook," I informed Marisa in a nasty tone of voice. "You won't have to spend tonight in jail."

She turned her head and gave me The Look. She had, of course, heard my side of the calls, which mainly consisted of a series of grunts and yessirs. In keeping with my role as loyal, obedient slave, I hadn't asked any questions.

After checking again for tails, I glanced at Marisa. She was examining her hands. Probably looked the same as they had this morning, I suspected. Her face looked thinner, though, and drawn. The second time I looked, I could see some of the hairline scars, little white lines, that the plastic surgeon had apparently been unable to eradicate from her adventure in Paris last year.

"So," I said conversationally, "is Abu Qasim your father?"

"He says he is."

"Well, he oughta know. He was there at the conception or he wasn't."

Silence followed that flip remark. Okay, okay, that was ill-advised.

"Do you believe him?" I asked, glancing her way again.

She took a moment to reply. "I used to. It doesn't matter now."

"There's such a thing as DNA testing, you know."

Those brown eyes swiveled my way. I met them and then put my attention back on the road, where it belonged. Every so often I glanced her way, trying to decide if she was part Arab. She was a lovely woman, perhaps a shade darker than your average French chickadee, but so were a lot of women. Dark brown hair, almost black, those big brown eyes, perfect lips. No hook nose — nothing like that. Just a nose. Actually, a nice nose.

"It'd be nice to know," I said after a while.

"No," she said softly. "It would not."

Isolde Petrou leaned forward and put a hand on her shoulder.

Eide Masmoudi didn't tell his fellow spy, Rahwan Ali, about the bottle of binary poison in his pocket. In his life as a spy he had learned that a secret is a secret only as long as no one knows it. The fact that Jake Grafton knew about the poison didn't count — he had supplied the stuff. Anyway, Eide thought he knew Jake Grafton, and the admiral would never tell a soul. Rahwan wouldn't, either, for the simple reason that his life was also on the line. Still, if he didn't know, he didn't have to carry the secret around. The other thing Eide had learned was that secrets had mass and radiated energy. The more powerful a secret, the more it radiated, like a glowing pile of plutonium, and when a secret reached critical mass, the possessor had to tell *somebody.*

Eide was surrounded by young men, Muslims from the mosque, who couldn't keep secrets. They lived in rented flats, as many as could be packed into a small apartment. The mosque was the center of their lives, where they worshipped, where they hung out, where their friends were. They told everything they knew to their comrades, every hint they picked up, everything they heard, everything anyone said. After all, they were involved in a great quest, were planning glorious deeds that would earn them entrance into Paradise. So of course they talked to each other, incessantly. The mullah, al-Taji, and his lieutenants, knowing this, told them as little about the planning of the glorious deeds as possible. Still, the young men got hints, and they speculated. These speculations and hints were the raw intelligence Eide and Rahwan passed to Jake Grafton, and he forwarded them on to his opposite number in MI-5.

Eide's secret was giving off light and heat in his pocket — he thought everyone could see it. Could see the bulge in his trousers, could feel the heat, could see his guilt. Could see in his face that he was a traitor to jihad, their holy war against the infidels.

Not that he believed in jihad, because he didn't. His mother's death — murder — had convinced him. Jihad was an evil, a betrayal of Allah.

Still, the sooner he got rid of this bottle, the better. And the sooner he got out of this mosque, this gathering of the Devil's disciples, the better.

He thought about getting out a lot now.

Going back to America, back to Brooklyn. Back to the friends he had known all his life, the mosque where he had grown up, the cleric there who had been his friend and mentor ever since his father died in a construction accident, eight years ago. A year after his father's death, his mother was murdered.

He had watched the television in horror as the World Trade Center towers collapsed. He knew she was in there, on the fifty-second floor. That was where she worked.

He remembered that day as the most horrible of his life. He had stayed glued to the television . . . and his mother never came home.

They never even found her body.

Later, in the days that followed, when the police would let spectators pass, he had gone to Ground Zero and stood looking. That was the horror the jihadists wanted, that they planned and plotted and schemed for as they dreamed of murder and Paradise, with houris who would give them sexual pleasure beyond their wildest fantasies. Because they murdered infidels — and fellow Muslims if they happened to get in the way.

Shit happens, the people in Brooklyn said.

Yeah, Eide Masmoudi reflected. Indeed it

does. And simpleminded fools who have no idea of the harm they are causing make it happen.

Still, the bottle was hot in his pocket. He was going to kill a man with it.

That was no small matter.

Nor was the fate awaiting him if the holy warriors who followed al-Taji found out — or even suspected — he had been the agent of the great man's death. In their anger they would torture and murder him as fiendishly as they could. They were like children, or savages, assuming that torture and murder of their enemies would solve the problems they saw in their world. When you hate enough, they thought, you can change the world. Hate was their motivation and their salvation. Hate enough and Paradise awaits.

Allah would watch over him, Eide thought. His life would go as Allah wished. God is great. *Allah akbar.* Put your trust in Allah and go forward. At least the holy warriors had that right; in fact, that was the only thing they had right.

All he needed was an opportunity. So far it hadn't come.

Let it come soon, he prayed.

Jake Grafton had two men shadowing Huntington Winchester, so it was a simple matter to call them and find out where he was. New York City, they said, in an office building on Madison Avenue, across the street from Madison Square.

The helicopter that had brought him from Washington deposited him at the West 30th Street Heliport. He went to the street and hailed a taxi.

So that was how he came to be sitting in Madison Square when Huntington Winchester and two people, a man and a woman, came out of the building across the street and paused to shake hands. There was a limo waiting for Winchester, but before he could get into it, one of Jake's men spoke to him and nodded at Grafton, sitting on a bench across the street. After speaking to the limo driver, Winchester jaywalked and joined the admiral on his bench. The two attorneys, if that was what they were, managed to flag down a taxi and climb in.

"Lawyers?" Jake asked, nodding toward the departing taxi.

"I'm putting a couple of their kids through Harvard," Winchester said. "Divorces are the cost of socially sanctioned sex. Hell, everyone I know is divorced, getting divorced or wishes they were divorced."

Jake Grafton, who had been happily married for many years, didn't bother to comment.

"That man over there who spoke to me and pointed you out — he works for you, doesn't he?"

"For a few days. I needed to keep tabs on you, and the folks at the FBI were kind enough to help."

"He's an FBI agent?" Winchester was incredulous.

"He's still standing over there. Go ask to see his credentials."

Winchester waited for a break in traffic and jaywalked again. The FBI man glanced at Grafton, who nodded, then produced his credentials for Winchester's inspection.

When Winchester returned to the bench, he dropped beside Grafton and said, "Why didn't you just call me?"

"We'll get to that," Grafton replied. He stood and glanced behind him to see who might be listening. That glance was not lost on Winchester. "Let's take a walk," the admiral said.

They walked through the park, and there was another limo waiting on Fifth Avenue. The driver held the door open for Grafton and Winchester as they approached.

"My wheels," Grafton said, and motioned for Winchester to get in first. When they were rolling south down the avenue, Grafton said, "We can talk here."

"So this isn't some kind of giant scam," Winchester said glumly.

"Jerry Hay Smith said it was?"

"Yes."

"I'd take anything he says or writes with a grain of salt, if I were you."

Winchester rubbed his eyes with his fists. Finally he took them down and took a deep breath. "I've been a fool," he said savagely.

"We both have," Grafton said. "I should never have agreed to this charade." He smacked his thigh with his fist. "Well, I did and you're in it now, right up to the roots of your hair."

Hunt Winchester stared at the admiral. "*What* am I in?"

"We're trying to find a terrorist," Grafton said softly, "named Abu Qasim. And now he's trying to find you."

Winchester couldn't believe his ears. "Me? Find *me?*"

Grafton nodded.

"Why?"

"He wants to kill you," Jake Grafton said, smiling to take the sting out of his words.

Grafton brought him up to date on events in Europe. When he fell silent, a badly shaken Winchester said, "I need to think.

How about taking me back to my hotel?"

"Sorry. I have a suite reserved for you in a different hotel, under another name, and two FBI agents are waiting there. They'll be just outside the door all night."

Huntington Winchester tried to say thank you, but it wouldn't come out. He nodded instead.

Oleg Tchernychenko and his two bodyguards rode in the back of the limo. The bodyguards rode on the jump seats facing aft, and Tchernychenko rode facing forward. As usual, he used his limo time to read contracts and proposals and memos from his small staff.

The limo driver, who had been with Tchernychenko for two years now, was a retired policeman. He drove too fast and, when he got stopped for speeding, never got a ticket.

The driver had brought the limo to Scotland from London to pick up Tchernychenko, who refused to fly unless there was no other way to get to where he had to go. As they rode the motorway south, the driver and bodyguards kept a wary eye on traffic.

They were well aware of the fact that criminals and terrorists had a variety of ways to stop a limo and kidnap or murder the occupants. A handful of determined men would be very difficult to thwart, especially since this vehicle was not hardened, wore no armor or bulletproof glass. The bodyguards had automatic weapons — old Sten guns, for which they had permits — on the floor at their feet. In holsters under their arms they wore pistols. The driver was also armed. They were competent, alert, fit and ready.

They had been in the car a little over an hour and were rolling along at about seventy miles per hour when the bomb under the floorboards exploded. It contained almost five pounds of plastique and sprayed glass and auto parts in every direction. The main frame of the car and the engine and what was left of the passenger compartment skidded along the road, smoking. The two rear wheels were blown completely off the vehicle. As the wreckage decelerated amid a shower of sparks and smoke, it caught fire.

Cars and trucks on the motorway swerved desperately. One large truck went into a guardrail and overturned. Another car smashed into it.

The burning wreckage of the limo came at last to rest on the edge of the pavement. There were no survivors.

Jake Grafton heard about the limo bombing

an hour and a half later. "A bomb in his car," the London station man said. "Probably set off by radio, perhaps a cell phone. They won't know for sure for days."

"You're sure it's Tchernychenko?"

"It was his car, and they've found a wallet they think is his. The bodies are in badly burned bits and pieces. Not much left for the coroner."

"I see."

"I'm sorry, Admiral."

"Damn it all to hell, so am I."

The safe house that the agency's London office wanted the Petrou women in was actually a guest cottage on an estate in Kent. I don't know who owned or lived in the big house, but they avoided the cottage and anyone who stayed there.

It was dark when we arrived. The key was in the usual hiding place, so I didn't have to pick the lock or do the Santa thing down the chimney. I aired out the place a bit and looked through the cupboards. Essentially bare, although there were containers of salt, pepper and baking soda. I left the women there and went looking for grub in a nearby village. Bought bread, milk, wine and cheese, cold cuts, some stuff in cans and tea — all the essentials.

When I got back to the cottage, the women were making beds and sweeping up. It was gratifying to see two aristocrats hard at the household chores. Maybe there is hope for mankind, after all.

I made a sandwich of meat and cheese and poured myself a glass of wine before either of the women had a shot at the groceries.

As I sipped vino, I reported to Grafton via cell phone. "Stay there tonight, Tommy," he said. "Leave your telephone on. Call the office and let them know where to find you."

"Got something going down?" I asked. "Something besides assassins with their hair on fire hunting Isolde and Marisa?"

"If the duty officer calls, someone will need you badly."

"Yes, sir."

I thought I knew who that someone might be. Grafton could have told me, of course, but he didn't, which was par for this course. No need to burden ol' Tommy with excess information.

I rendered a snappy salute as I put the phone in my pocket. When the wine was gone I went back into the kitchen, where Marisa was cutting cheese. I would have liked another glass of wine but didn't want to open another bottle.

Just to be on the safe side, I went outside

for a stroll around the house. The night was overcast, with a gentle cold breeze. Every now and then a spatter of rain dampened things down. I pulled my coat collar tight and shivered. Little squares of light shone from the cottage windows, dimly illuminating the yard. There was also a small light by the front door, one apparently activated by a light sensor. I tried to memorize where the bushes and trees and decorator rocks were, just in case.

The possibility that someone followed us from the Petrou château, or picked us up when we exited the ferry, worried me. I hadn't seen anyone behind us for the last two miles, but that didn't mean we weren't followed. It meant I didn't see anyone. These guys were killing people; certainly they were capable of setting up a rolling surveillance with three or four or five cars. With two-way radios and cell phones, anticipating my destination, the chore would not have been difficult. Even now they could be out there in the darkness, planning an assault.

How much paranoia can one man stand?

I wondered if I should stay inside or outside tonight. If I could sit against the house, under a bush, out of this wind . . . Then I yawned, which decided the issue. I was whipped. If an assassin showed up, he was going to have to wake me if he wanted a fight.

A button on the limo's key fob locked the vehicle's doors. I tried them just to be sure.

When I got back inside, I made sure the outside doors were locked and tried all the windows. They were locked, too. I made a pit stop, then flaked out on the couch and used my coat for a blanket. I could hear the murmur of women's voices in the bedroom — there was only one — but I couldn't make out the words. Nor was I curious. I must have lain there on the couch tossing and turning for a whole minute before I drifted off.

Eide Masmoudi was in the kitchen, fixing dinner, when the opportunity came. Suddenly he was alone. The water pitcher was on the counter beside him, full. He didn't wait, didn't hesitate. He pulled the bottle Grafton had given him from his trouser pocket, poured the clear liquid into the water pitcher, and put bottle and cap back in his pocket. Twenty seconds, max.

He was taking the lamb from the oven when he heard the door open and someone came in. He didn't turn around.

The person paused. "Looks good," he

said. Eide turned. It was Sheikh al-Taji. He leaned toward the platter, took a deep breath and said again, "Good." He actually smiled. He seemed to be in an excellent mood.

Then he was gone.

Eide got back to the task at hand. Radwan came in to help carry the food to the table in the dining room. The men filled their plates, then sat cross-legged on the floor to eat, as if they were in a tent somewhere in the great wastes of the desert.

Radwan served the water, then got a plate and joined them. Sheikh al-Taji was in a fine mood. He held forth on this and that, discussed obscure points of the Koran, mentioned the glories of jihad, shook his head over the tribulations of the believers in Iraq and Afghanistan. It wasn't a conversation, it was a monologue.

Eide filled his glass and forced himself to drink the water. He watched in fascination as the sheikh sipped at his, and wondered how much he had to ingest to get a fatal dose. Well, he told himself, he would soon find out.

The dinner went well. The senior lieutenants remained behind with the sheikh as Radwan and Eide and several other young men carried the dishes and pans to the kitchen and began washing everything.

All the while Eide wondered if he and Radwan should leave.

Radwan knew nothing of the poison. Only he, Eide, knew.

Still, one second's loss of control of his face, one second's hesitation in answering a question . . . and Grafton had said that everyone would be under suspicion. Everyone.

He and Radwan were both spies, with huge secrets to hide. Could they do it?

That was the nub of it. All through training, all through the early days of this assignment, Eide had wondered. Could he do it? Radwan had once admitted that he also had secret doubts. A man would not be human if he didn't.

Marisa lay in bed beside her sleeping mother-in-law staring into the darkness. She had often lain awake in the night as a little girl at the boarding school, looking at the darkness and wondering about her mother. And how she came to be the "daughter" of Georges and Grisella Lamoureux.

Grisella was a woman with a cold, brittle personality, a person who took every pothole in the road as a personal affront. A forgetful maid, a sloppy waiter, all the usual jolts and abrasions of life she regarded as personal insults; consequently she was never happy. Her face habitually wore a frown. Needless to say, she was never pleased with her "daughter," Marisa, who was incapable of being the model of childhood perfection that Grisella envisioned; indeed, that she demanded.

Consequently Marisa often thought of her real mother when the other children were fast asleep, saw her in the glow of her imagination. Her real mother was a beautiful, kind, understanding, gentle woman who laughed a lot and loved her little Marisa. Although in fact Marisa had no memory of ever seeing her mother, over time she convinced herself that this woman she saw in her dream was indeed Mama.

Being a child, she finally told the dorm lady all about Mama, about how she looked, how she wore her hair, her smile and laugh and touch. The dorm lady told the headmistress, who mentioned it to Uncle when he came.

She remembered Abu Qasim staring down at her as the headmistress talked, the look in his eyes.

Years later she wondered about the hold Qasim had on Georges and Grisella, the hold that would make them pretend to be parents of someone else's daughter. Was it money? Grisella certainly liked her jewelry and fashionable dresses . . . and after all, in the diplomatic service Georges undoubtedly had to keep up appearances.

Or was it something else, a dark secret, blackmail?

When she was a teenager Marisa loathed Grisella and favored the blackmail theory. The woman was capable of anything, she believed. Grisella had probably murdered someone, a deranged lover, perhaps — any lover of hers would have to be deranged — and somehow Abu Qasim had learned about it. Qasim . . . yes, with his air of knowing all, back then she thought him capable of blackmail. Years later she found that he was capable of the most heinous crimes imaginable. Blackmail would have been a misdemeanor for him.

Had Qasim murdered her mother?

Tonight, in the cottage in Kent, Marisa Petrou lay in the darkness turning that possibility over and over in her mind, as she had done for thousands of nights, ever since she was a child.

It was almost midnight when Eide Masmoudi and Radwan Ali met on the sidewalk outside the mosque. There was a trash can

on the street corner, full but not overflow-
ing, and as he went by he stuffed the tightly
capped bottle in there. Just having it on his
person was a huge risk — he had carried
the damn thing far enough.

They crossed the street and were walking
down the sidewalk when Radwan glanced
over his shoulder. "What did you put in the
trash?" he asked.

Eide looked back. Someone was reaching
into the can, pulling out trash. He didn't
recognize the figure under the streetlight.
"Who is that?"

"Looks like Omar to me, that suck-up
from Libya, the one who's always spying on
everyone. He must have seen you put something in there."

Eide jerked at Radwan's arm and kept
walking. "I put a bottle in there," he said.
"Jake Grafton gave me a small bottle with a
chemical of some kind to pour in the drinking water. It will kill the sheikh, stop his
heart. Maybe tonight."

Radwan stared into Eide's face.

"It'll look like a heart attack," Eide said.

Radwan stood paralyzed, trying to process
it. Eide grabbed his arm and forced him to
keep walking. "Grafton wants us out of
here. Now."

"Oh, man . . ."

"I'm going to call Grafton and set up a meet. He'll send us back to the States."

"All my stuff is in our flat," Radwan protested. "My money, everything. I gotta go by the flat and get my stuff."

"Let me call Grafton first." Eide removed his cell phone from his pocket and punched in a number he had memorized. They continued along the sidewalk.

As Eide waited for the phone to send the call through, Radwan said, "Man, if the sheikh croaks and we rabbit, the holy warriors are going to smell a rat. They're going to be really pissed. I mean, like, *really* pissed."

Eide snapped the telephone shut. "So what do you want to do?"

"Man, if that asshole just drops dead of a heart attack and we sit there with our mouths shut, looking innocent and heartbroken, who's to know?"

"Grafton said the risk was too great."

"He doesn't think we have the balls for this."

"I don't know that I do," Eide said as he forced himself to put one foot in front of the other. He had his cell phone in his left hand, his right in his pocket, and was staring at the sidewalk.

"Well, by God, I do," Radwan Ali declared. "These jihad fools are pissing on believers everywhere. They're pissing on the Prophet. They're pissing on *Allah!*"

"It's that kind of world."

"Allah will help us. He'll give us strength. The truth is we are on *His* side. Do you believe or don't you?"

I came awake when I heard someone moving in the room. My pistol was a lump in my pants pocket, and Marisa's Walther was in my coat. I lay frozen, listening. The glow from the light outside on the stoop gave the room a smidgen of illumination.

"Are you awake?" Marisa's voice.

"Yeah," I said. I moved then. I reached into my pocket and got the pistol in my hand. Slid it out. Since I had my overcoat over me she couldn't see what I was doing.

I found her with my eyes. She was wearing some kind of robe and was barefooted. Since she hadn't had a chance to pack when we left the château — yesterday? — presumably she found the robe in a closet. She held the robe shut with her arms, which were wrapped around her chest.

Marisa sat down in the stuffed chair across from me, so I relaxed a little. If she intended to stick a knife in me, she was going to have to come flying out of that chair to do it. She used a hand to brush hair back out of her face.

"I want to talk to Jake Grafton," she said.

"Umm." I checked the luminous hands of my watch. About 2:30 a.m. here, 9:30 p.m. last night on the East Coast. "What about?"

"Abu Qasim."

"One of his favorite subjects," I admitted. What the heck. Grafton rarely said anything interesting, and Marisa might. After all, Grafton told me to pump her. I got my cell phone out, flipped it open and pushed the button. Grafton's cell number came up. I pushed the green button and listened to the rings. He got it on the fourth one.

"Yes, Tommy."

"Marisa wants to talk to you."

"Everything okay?"

"Quiet as a grave."

"Okay, put her on."

I threw the coat back and stood, reached, handed the phone to Marisa. Her eyes swept over the pistol I had in my right hand and fastened on the cell phone. She grasped the thing in both hands and said, "Hello."

I went to the window by the front door and looked out. At least the limo was still there.

When I turned around Marisa was walking toward the kitchen, whispering into the telephone. I got a few words, but only a few.

I debated following her — after all, she was using my phone — but didn't. I dropped into the chair she had vacated, put the pistol back in my pocket and yawned. Her voice was merely a low murmur.

Ten minutes passed, then fifteen. I was starting to nod off sitting up when Marisa came back and handed me my phone.

"Thank you," she said.

When she turned away I caught the glistening of tears on her cheeks. I reached out, grabbed her, pulled her gently onto my lap. She didn't resist. I wrapped my arms around her and she laid her head on my shoulder.

After a while I realized she was asleep.

CHAPTER SIXTEEN

It was the pounding on the apartment door that awoke Eide Masmoudi. He slept beside Radwan Ali on a foldout couch, while the other two men who shared the apartment shared the only bed in the only bedroom.

Ali was also instantly awake. It was only a few minutes after five in the morning . . . still dark outside.

As the pounding sounded through the apartment, Ali leaped from the bed and stepped around the kitchen counter. Masmoudi put on his trousers and shirt, then unlocked the door.

Three men from the mosque burst into the room. One of them was Omar from Libya. When Eide saw him, he knew he and Radwan were in big, big trouble.

The other two, Osama and Fawaz, were older men, trusted confidants of Sheikh al-Taji.

Before anyone could say a word, the

bedroom door opened and Eide's room-mates appeared wearing trousers and T-shirts. In the kitchen area, Radwan was pulling on his trousers and shirt.

"Sheikh al-Taji is dead," Osama roared, his eyes on Eide.

"How . . . ?" asked one of the men from the bedroom.

"Poisoned," Fawaz thundered.

"Poisoned?"

"He died in his sleep. Omar saw this man" — Fawaz's arm shot out, his finger rigid, inches from Eide's face — "throw away a bottle when he left the mosque. He fixed dinner. Hours later the sheikh died in bed."

"What bottle?" Radwan asked.

Omar pulled it from his pocket and displayed it.

"That had eyewash in it," Radwan said disgustedly. "I saw him use it."

"Eyewash?"

"Medicine for the eyes," Radwan said. He lifted his chin and made a pouring motion with his hands.

"It has no label," Osama objected. The doubt was beginning to creep into his voice.

Eide shrugged. "It came off."

"I say the bottle held poison," Omar roared, loud enough to wake the sleepers on the floors above and below.

Eide held out his hand, took the bottle. He unscrewed the cap, sniffed the bottle, then licked the top. Ran his tongue around it. Then he tossed it at Omar. "And if I don't die, then what?"

"But the bottle is empty," Omar shouted. His eyes shot an appeal for help to Osama and Fawaz.

"How do you know the sheikh was poisoned?" one of Eide's roommates asked.

"He was a healthy man. Healthy men don't die in their sleep."

"Sometimes they do," Radwan said conversationally.

"Wash for the eyes . . ." Osama scrutinized Eide's face, then Radwan's. "The sheikh is dead. He may have been murdered. If he was . . ." He faced the roommates. "No one leaves this room. We'll be back."

With that Osama pushed his way toward the door. Fawaz followed. Omar was last, still holding the bottle. He didn't look at Eide or Radwan.

When the door closed, Eide looked around at the other three. "He was a great man, and the infidels feared him. Rightly so. They are right to be suspicious."

"It is the will of Allah," one of the roommates said, then headed for the bathroom.

In five minutes everyone was back in bed.

That was when Radwan whispered, "If they go to a pharmacy and look at eyewash bottles, they will see none like that one."

Eide looked at Radwan and Radwan looked at Eide.

"There are no pharmacies open at this hour."

"The one on Regency Street might be."

"Wait," Eide whispered.

He let fifteen minutes pass, fifteen slow, agonizing minutes, then they got slowly out of bed, as soundlessly as they could, and put their clothes back on again. Radwan went to the kitchen and took two paring knives from the drawer while Eide looked out the window at the fog that muzzled the streetlights and filled the space between the buildings. One knife Radwan handed to Eide, who put it in his coat pocket. They found their wallets, their cell phones. Carrying their shoes, they tiptoed toward the door, opened it as quietly as possible and went through, then pulled it shut.

They paused on the stairs and put on their shoes, then continued down the three stories to the street.

When they exited the building, they almost knocked Omar down. He was leaning on the stoop railing.

The collision was unexpected, but Omar's

reaction told both men precisely where they stood. Omar had been left to watch them. "Traitors," he hissed and grabbed for Radwan.

Radwan slashed at Omar's throat with his knife; blood gushed forth. Omar sank to the bricks of the stoop, holding his throat. He fumbled for his cell phone. Eide had already started to run, but he whirled and came back, grabbed the cell phone from Omar and kicked him in the face. Then he and Radwan ran into the fog.

After they had covered several blocks, they slowed to a walk and Eide used his cell phone to call Jake Grafton. While he was on the phone, out of the corner of his eye he saw movement. Fawaz and Osama came walking out of the fog toward them down a side street.

Oh, bad break!

Eide and Radwan sprinted for their lives.

The cell phone vibrating in my pocket woke me. I had been sleeping in the chair. Marisa was asleep on the couch, where I had placed her sometime during the night. I had covered her with my coat.

"Tommy," Jake Grafton said when I answered, "Tom and Jerry need your help." Since this was an unsecure line, Grafton was using code names. Tom was Eide Masmoudi and Jerry was Radwan Ali.

As he talked, I went to the window and looked out. The stoop light was glowing into thick fog. I looked at my watch; dawn was still an hour or so away.

After he hung up, I went over to the couch. Marisa's eyes were open and she was looking at me. I bent down and whispered, so we wouldn't wake Isolde in the bedroom.

"I have to go out. Going to take the limo and leave you two here. Don't make any telephone calls, don't go out, don't answer the door. I'll be back in a few hours, I hope."

She nodded.

I put on my coat and covered her with hers. Her eyes stayed on me.

Her little Walther was a lump in the left pocket of my coat. I took it out, checked the safety and handed it to her. "Just in case," I said.

She put the pistol in the pocket of her coat, then pulled the coat up around her chin. Those big brown eyes stared at me.

"He will try to kill you," she whispered. "Or he will send a professional killer named Khadr. He has used him before. Khadr was probably the one who killed the people yesterday at our château, I think."

I bent over and kissed her on the lips, then

left. Made sure the door latched behind me.

If she poisons me one of these days, I am going to regret that kiss right up until the lights go out. Still, it tasted mighty good.

The holy warriors were right behind Eide and Radwan. They couldn't see them, but they could hear their running feet whenever they paused for a few seconds, and they could hear them shouting at each other, checking alleys and side streets.

Radwan was breathing hard — and running slower. Eide's years of recreational jogging had left him in much better shape.

"I can't go much farther," Radwan huffed at one point.

"Run or die," Eide shot back.

They kept running.

The issue was decided at a major street. They darted across . . . and a speeding car loomed out of the fog. The driver slammed on his brakes and lay on his horn. Eide managed to avoid it, but the fender smacked Radwan's left leg a horrible thump and spun him to the pavement. As the car screeched to a halt, Eide checked his friend, grabbed his arm, tried to pull him up.

Radwan moaned.

Now Eide saw. His left leg was broken. The thigh bone was snapped and the leg bent at a horrible angle.

"You can't carry me," Radwan said between clenched teeth. "Allah is with me. Save yourself."

Eide grabbed Radwan and pulled him toward the car. Radwan wrapped his arms around Eide's arm and pulled himself upright by sheer strength of will. Eide reached for the passenger door handle, which was locked, immobile.

"Hospital! Open the door," he thundered at the driver, who was staring at him with a gaping mouth. He must have seemed a terrible apparition, a brown man sweating profusely, every muscle in his face and neck taut, trying to get into the car.

The driver floored the accelerator. Radwan lost his grip on Eide and fell to the street with a groan as the car roared away into the fog.

"Leave me," Radwan implored. "Save yourself."

Eide looked around desperately. He heard the running feet again. There was just no way. "We'll meet again in Paradise," he said.

"Go." Radwan pushed at him.

Eide turned and ran.

Outside the cottage I paused by the car to listen and look. The air was chilly, at least twenty degrees colder than it had been yesterday evening when we arrived, so the fog was almost a solid. Dark, of course, in that hour before first light, and quiet. Every now and then I caught the distant low rumble of a jet running high, but nothing else.

I tried to remember what day this was, and decided it was Sunday.

The only light in that dark soup was the little glow of the light above the front door.

Was there anyone out here in this stuff?

I closed my eyes and concentrated on what I could hear.

Nothing.

I opened the car door and got in, started the engine and fed gas.

Sunday morning, and the roads were nearly empty, which was fortunate, since I drove way too fast for the conditions. I parked at a subway station on the outskirts of London and took the next train in. I kept looking at my watch. Six thirty a.m. in St. James' Park, the third bench in from the southwest corner, Grafton had said.

Should I be precisely on time, or early? I thought early, if I could make it, and as I trotted toward the entrance to the park, I thought I would get there with maybe ten minutes to spare.

■ ■ ■ ■

Eide Masmoudi found the bench in St. James' Park that he had told Grafton about and stood in the fog trying to catch his breath. He checked his watch. A few more minutes. The big American would be on time — of that Eide was sure. Tommy Carmellini. Eide had seen him on several occasions but had never spoken to him. Jake Grafton trusted him, and that was enough.

He threw himself on the bench and stared about him into the fog. After a few seconds he found that he couldn't sit.

He stood, shifted from one leg to another, walked around a little, listened and peered into the opaque gloom that swirled about him. He held his cell phone in his hands, just in case.

The sheikh was dead, he told himself. That was something positive. The sheikh and the others were so happy last night. They killed somebody . . . with a car bomb, probably. Like children, they were delighted by explosions, which fascinated them: The split second of extreme violence appealed to their imaginations and their souls. He didn't get much of what they said, just a few whispers, then they would laugh.

He didn't know who they killed. Not that it mattered to them. They killed *someone,* some infidel, and they really didn't care who. Just murdering someone made them feel good, empowered, important. They were like dogs, pissing on the pillars of a great civilization that they neither understood nor felt a part of.

He thought about Radwan. If only the driver hadn't panicked!

Inshallah. It would be as Allah willed it.

Eide took a deep breath and exhaled. He forced himself to think about his mother. She was in Paradise with her husband, that he knew, and he silently thanked Allah for that.

He heard someone coming.

By some quirk he could hear soft footsteps approaching. On the sidewalk . . . from the direction of the corner gate. Grafton's man would come from there, probably.

He turned to face that way. A figure solidified out of the fog, a man wearing a business suit. Out for a stroll this morning, carrying an umbrella in his left hand, wearing a soft hat . . .

"Good morning," he said in perfect English as he walked the last few feet toward Eide, who was still standing in front of the bench.

"Hello," Eide said, visibly relaxing.

Now the man's right hand swept up. He had a pistol in it. Eide saw the pistol with its fat silencer too late to react.

Eide forced his eyes from the black hole in the front of the silencer to the man's face, which was partially hidden under the hat brim. It was a hard face, he could see that.

The man was going to kill him — he knew it and accepted it.

"I would pray," he said.

"If you wish."

He looked about, wondering in which direction Mecca lay. It didn't matter, he realized. He went to his knees, bent his head to the sidewalk and began to pray.

The bullet caught him in the back of the head. His body toppled. The man took a step closer and shot him again in the head. Then he picked up the spent brass cartridges and pocketed them.

Another man loomed out of the fog, but he approached the bench from behind. He, too, had a pistol in his hand.

"Quickly," the first man said. "Sit him on the bench and give me his cell phone."

They pocketed their guns and lifted Eide onto the bench. With the cell phones in hand, the first man led the second into the fog behind the bench. He stopped and checked the telephone numbers Masmoudi had called last.

"He called Jake Grafton," Abu Qasim said. "So someone will be coming to meet him here, and soon."

"Should we kill him, too?" Khadr asked.

Abu Qasim pocketed the telephone as he considered. "No, I think not. I want you to stay here. Move forward just enough so that you can see the bench and anyone who arrives, and if he examines the body of the traitor, shoot him. Make sure you get at least one bullet in him. Then flee."

"He will probably be armed," Khadr pointed out. In his entire career he had never been in a gunfight, and Tommy Carmellini was the only man who ever managed to fire a shot at him. He did not relish the prospect of giving Carmellini another chance.

"Perhaps," Qasim acknowledged.

Khadr said no more. Had anyone but Abu Qasim told him to do this, he would have refused.

With his umbrella firmly in hand, Abu Qasim walked away into the fog.

The morning looked like wet concrete when I came out of the subway station, although the sky was trying to get lighter in the east.

The fog swirled like smoke when disturbed. Not many people out and about yet — not any sane ones, anyhow. The moisture felt cold against my cheeks and forehead, almost like a wet cloth. Damp and cold and clammy.

I felt my phone vibrating.

"Yeah," I said when I got the button punched and the thing against my ear.

"They aren't answering their cell phones," Grafton said. "They may have turned them off so they won't attract attention."

"That's one possibility," I agreed as I strode through the wrought-iron gate that marked this entrance to the park.

"Be careful, Tommy," he said, and the line went dead.

I put the phone back in my shirt pocket and put my right hand into my coat pocket, where I had the Springfield stowed. It felt solid, reassuring, as I walked along in that dark gray, wet, gauzy world.

I found the first bench beside the sidewalk easily enough. Eide and Radwan were supposed to be on the third one. Needless to say, I didn't know how far that was from where I stood. Ten yards, fifty, a hundred?

I stood by the bench, near a light pole, listening to the silence. There was a background of muffled traffic noises, the occasional rumble of a subway train that went under the street I had just left . . . and . . . a plane, somewhere high and far away.

Now I heard steps. A man. Hard leather heels, walking purposefully, striding along the sidewalk.

Even as I turned in his direction he appeared out of the gloom, a man in an overcoat wearing a soft brimmed hat and carrying an umbrella. He nodded at me and strode on. I listened to his steps fading.

I walked the way he had come, looking for the second bench. It was perhaps twenty yards past the first one. I got my first glimpse of the darker shape of it from about fifteen feet away. The light on the pole above it was lit, illuminating the fog for a few feet around.

Never in my life had I seen fog that thick. It seemed to be getting thicker as the dawn progressed, if that was possible.

I walked on.

Barking. Actually it was yapping, just ahead. A little dog, yapping at something. And a woman's voice, scolding the dog.

Now I saw them, coming toward me. She was tugging the dog along on its leash. It didn't want to come. It was looking behind her, still yapping, worried about something. "Now, Winston," she said.

She saw me and flashed a grin.

I gave the dog room. Getting dog-bit sets a bad precedent for the week.

The third bench began to take shape as I approached. A man was sitting on it.

Two more steps and I could see him fairly well. His head was down, with his chin on his chest. He was totally relaxed, as if he were asleep.

Another step closer. It was Eide Masmoudi. He didn't stir as I approached.

"Hey," I said.

He didn't move.

I froze. Ran my eyes around. Listened.

So where was Radwan?

Another two steps . . . I could see Eide better. His eyes were open.

I stepped off the pavement, walked up behind him. That's when I saw the two red spots behind Eide's right ear, about two inches apart. Two small-caliber bullets in the brain.

Tom — Eide Masmoudi — was extremely dead.

As I stood there trying to process what I was seeing, I felt a cool breeze on my cheek. The wind was picking up. There was more light — the sun was above the horizon and illuminating this mess.

Eide hadn't been shot sitting here. Someone had arranged his body on this bench. That struck me as unusual. Most killers, I thought, did their thing and got the hell out of Dodge.

This killer had lingered. He had taken the time to arrange the body so at first glance Eide appeared to be sleeping. Why?

The cool wind on my cheek was clearing the fog. Visibility was rapidly improving. I could see trees, stark black things without leaves, and rocks . . . bushes, and the second bench. Empty.

The killer didn't want anyone calling the bobbies immediately because he was still here! That realization hit me like a hammer, and I ducked down behind the bench.

As I did so I heard a pffft of something passing by my head. I knew what that was, by God — a subsonic bullet.

I jerked the pistol from my pocket and ran toward two big rocks that I could see twenty feet behind the bench. Dove through the air and landed behind them as something spanged the rock and went zinging away.

I tried to glue myself to the back of the biggest boulder.

So the killer was still here and he wanted big dumb me. Lovely. Just fucking lovely!

I had no idea where he was. I found out real quick, though. The next shot came from ahead of me — I saw the muzzle flash, just a small wink — and the bullet hit me in the left shoulder. A stab of pain went through me.

I crawled around the rock as fast as I could go. At least two more shots whacked into the rock, maybe three, before I managed to get the stone between me and the shooter.

I worked my left arm and hand. Nothing broken, but my shirt was getting cold and wet from blood and the wound stung like hell.

I figured he was using a small-caliber auto pistol with a big silencer, the same weapon he had used on Eide. Without sights, the weapon would be impossible to shoot accurately at any distance. He had managed to do a number on me with it, though.

I still had my Springfield in my right hand, and it had sights. And a three-inch barrel. Perfect for shooting someone ten feet away, but not quite what the doctor ordered for a Sunday morning shoot-out in the park.

At least I knew where he was. Or where he fired from. No doubt he was moving.

I got my feet under me and went running out to my right, away from the rock toward a set of trees that would allow me to work back to his shooting position.

I felt something tug at my coat as I ran.

Got a glimpse of him just before I got to the trees, so I snapped off an unaimed shot just to keep him honest — and to alert any police who might be strolling through the park on Sunday morning.

The fog was lifting, but there was still some, so the report didn't sound all that loud. Sort of a loud pop.

I didn't stop behind the trees, but tried to keep them between him and me as I closed on him.

I had the pistol in both hands now, and I wanted to shoot. Caught a flash of him running the other way — he wasn't waiting for the cops — so I cut loose. Fired three times.

After the last shot I didn't see him, so I ran in that direction. If he was lying on the ground waiting, he was going to get a free shot at me, but unless he drilled me between the eyes, I was going to kill him with this 9 mm.

He wasn't on the ground as I came thundering up. I looked all over, the pistol ready in my hands as if I were Jack Bauer, but he had disappeared. Made a tactical retreat, I suspected, running like a rabbit. But which way?

Not a soul did I see, any way I looked. What I saw was short dead grass and naked black trees and stick bushes and some rocks and paved paths — sidewalks — in every direction. Here and there a bench for better days. The sun was a faint ball in a skuzzy gray sky, hanging in the trees. Visibility up to maybe a half mile, a chill wind taking the sweat right off my brow . . . and my shoulder hurt like hell. I guess I relaxed a little.

So the punch in the chest when the bullet hit almost took me off my feet.

There was a ditch maybe seventy or eighty feet ahead, and the shooter was in it. I got a glimpse of a head sticking up, and maybe a smidgen of the pistol. Then another round sailed by my cheek and I realized that I was going to have to find cover or die.

Scared the hell outta that guy, so I did.

I ran toward the nearest tree and got behind it. Damn thing was pretty skinny, but it seemed to cover the essentials.

A bullet had thumped me in the chest, so I wondered how badly I was hit. I reached inside my coat, found the sore place . . . and my cell phone. I pulled it from my shirt pocket. It was ruined. A bullet had smacked it and was stuck in the thing, with just the base sticking out. Looked like maybe .22 caliber. I dropped the phone back in my pocket. Checked the sore place with my fingers, didn't feel blood.

I ooched one eye around the tree and looked for my would-be killer. Didn't see him. I scanned the grass where the ditch should be. He had gone in one direction or the other, but I didn't know which.

He was certainly a ballsy bastard — I'll give him that. He was whanging away with a silenced .22, trying to wound me just enough that he could safely approach and deliver the *coup de grâce,* as he did to Eide Masmoudi.

I wondered if the guy was Abu Qasim. Or that killer Marisa had warned me about, Khadr.

So what did he expect me to do? Stay hidden and call the police? I would if I had a phone; he didn't know he put it out of action, though.

I didn't figure he would stay around long. I looked right and left, waited for him to come out of the ditch or creek, whatever it was.

Just when I was ready to give up and charge his last position, I saw a dark shape run up the bank to my left, maybe a hundred yards away, onto a paved sidewalk. He galloped off into the trees.

I was tempted to go after him but didn't.

All he had to do was duck behind a tree and wait for me to get within range.

I put my pistol in my pocket and headed back for the bench where Eide had started his eternal sleep. My shoulder hurt with every step, and my chest ached.

When I got there a female police officer was checking the corpse, ensuring he was dead. The radio in her hand was squawking continuously, a stream of unintelligible noise. An older man with a big dog straining on a leash was watching her.

When the bobby glanced at me I said, "The guy who did it to this guy is gone. How about calling an ambulance for me?"

"What's wrong with you?" she said sharply, frowning at my criminal mug.

"He got one in me. It's bleeding and hurts like hell. And have your dispatcher call MI-5."

The dog barked at me. Barked and snarled and barked some more. Lunged forward on his leash.

The cop was on her radio, so I asked the guy who was holding the hound back, "Did you see anything?"

"I arrived just a moment ago. Out for a stroll to exercise old Jack."

"Then get the fuck outta here," I said nastily.

A wounded look crossed his face, but he left, dragging the dog.

CHAPTER SEVENTEEN

When his cell phone vibrated, Jake Grafton removed it from his pocket and looked at the number. The call was from the agency office in London. He was sitting in the library of Huntington Winchester's house in Connecticut. Winchester was there, as were Simon Cairnes and John Hay Smith. They watched him punch the button and say, "Yes."

"Boss, Carmellini. They got Tom. He was dead when I got to the meet — two bullets in the brain. Have no idea where Jerry is. And the shooter got one into me. He also killed my cell phone. I've been to the hospital for a Band-Aid and am back here at the office."

"How bad are you hurt?"

"Silenced twenty-two bullet. Went into my left shoulder a couple of inches. Missed my tiny little heart by a mile. They dug it out. I'll be okay. Doc told me to take some aspirin and call him tomorrow."

"Go get Marisa and Isolde and bring them to the States. Have the people there make travel arrangements. Catch the first possible flight."

"Okay."

"Keep me advised."

"Yeah."

"I'm sorry, Tommy."

"Hated to see him like that. I never even spoke to him, but he seemed like a hell of a guy."

"He was."

"I threw a few slugs at the shooter, on the off-chance. I don't think any of them connected."

"Get some more bullets."

"Yes, sir," Carmellini said, and the connection broke.

Jake Grafton put the telephone back in his pocket and looked at the three men seated in the chairs around him. He tried to smile; it came out a grimace.

"So," he said. "Where were we?"

" 'Get some more bullets.' Want to tell us what that was all about?" Jerry Hay Smith asked. He wore what was left of his hair in a Trump combover.

"One of my men shot at a man and missed," Jake Grafton said. "He'll get another chance."

Simon Cairnes and Jerry Hay Smith stirred uneasily. They had been summoned last night to come to Winchester's house immediately. It was now — Grafton glanced at his watch — ten after five in the morning.

"I agreed to contribute money to help Winchester," Cairnes said, "and I've done that. I've given Hunt every penny he asked for, almost a million dollars total. I'd like to know where the money has gone and what you've managed to accomplish."

"My men — your employees — have assassinated six prominent terrorists."

"That's just a number. Gimme some names."

Jake Grafton recited them.

"What I want to know — what we all want to know — is this: Is Islamic terrorism less of a threat today than it was three months ago? Have we made any difference at all?"

"That," Grafton acknowledged, "is precisely the right question. And the answer is unknowable."

Simon Cairnes stirred uneasily. His gaze swept around to Winchester and Smith. "You two want to say anything?"

Smith piped up. "Last night you called and invited — no, demanded! — that I come immediately to Winchester's house. So here I am. Tell me whatever it is you think could not wait for business hours."

"Do you have a cassette recorder in your pocket?" Grafton asked pleasantly. "Or are you using a cell phone with an open line?"

"I don't have to answer that," Jerry Hay Smith said, with a bit of belligerence creeping into his voice.

"You do if you ever expect to have that recording admitted as evidence in a court of law. Now I'm asking you again, are you making a record of this conversation?"

Smith glowered. "Yes," he muttered.

"What court do you think we're likely to wind up in?"

"I think someone might sue me for libel, and I want a recording to protect myself."

"What do you think of that, Mr. Cairnes? Are you aware that Mr. Smith is writing a book about you, Mr. Winchester, and the other people in this venture? He's up to sixty-seven thousand words, by the way."

Simon Cairnes' face was a mask of cold fury as he stared at Jerry Hay Smith, who was staring at Grafton. "How did you learn that number?" the journalist demanded of the admiral through clenched teeth.

Before Grafton had time to answer, Huntington Winchester roared, "For Christ's sake, Jerry," and leaped from his chair. He squared himself in front of Smith with his fists clenched. "Writing a book wasn't even mentioned when you told me you wanted to help rid the world of these Islamic fascists. You've put ten thousand dollars into this venture, and Cairnes and I and the others have contributed almost four million. So what is this? A shakedown? Blackmail? Either we buy your goddamn screed for a price you set or you'll publish and ruin us — is that your game?"

"Hunt," Smith said, trying to keep his voice under control, "I'm a journalist. That's what I do. I made you no promises about keeping your venture, or my participation in it, a secret. When this has played out I'll decide —"

He got no further because Hunt Winchester reached down with both hands, jerked him erect, then planted a straight right on his chin. Smith missed the chair and sprawled on the floor, half stunned.

"By God, that felt good!" Winchester exclaimed.

He reached for Smith again as Cairnes said, "Hit the bastard one for me."

"Gentlemen, gentlemen," Grafton said. He clapped his hands once. Winchester froze with Smith half off the floor.

"You can beat the crap out of Mr. Smith any old time," Grafton continued, "but right now why don't you gentlemen sit here like reasonable adults and listen to what I have to say?"

Winchester dropped Smith back onto the floor and began feeling his pockets. Smith tried to push him away, and Winchester slapped him. He felt some more, then reached into a jacket pocket and pulled out a small digital recorder. He walked away from Smith, looking it over, then tossed it into the flames in the fireplace.

"I'll sue you for assault, Winchester. These men are witnesses."

"Didn't see a goddamn thing," Cairnes rumbled.

Smith climbed back into his chair while Winchester stood in front of the fire staring at him.

When Smith was safely back in his chair, he wiped his face on his sleeve, felt his jaw, then said to the admiral, "I want to know who the hell you really are."

"The name is Jake Grafton."

"Who the fuck do you really work for, Mr. Grafton?"

"I told you when we first met, Mr. Smith: the Central Intelligence Agency. I might point out that I am a covert employee. As you probably know, revealing that fact to anyone not authorized to know it is a federal felony, punishable by imprisonment."

"Got that, Smith?" Cairnes snarled at the journalist, who was still probing the tender place on his jaw.

"I got it."

"Publish and be damned, you little bastard," Cairnes roared. He grabbed his cane like a baseball bat. "I won't pay you a fucking nickel. And I hope the feds send your sorry, traitorous ass to prison. *Judas!* Betraying your friends for money —"

"Gentlemen, gentlemen," Grafton murmured. "You're in this lifeboat together. Save the recriminations for the ten-year reunion. Right now you have a more pressing problem."

"Oh?" That was Cairnes.

"The name of your problem is Abu Qasim, a smart, wily, vicious man who specializes in murder and mayhem in the name of Allah. He has killed, or ordered killed, Alexander Surkov, Wolfgang Zetsche, Rolf Gnadinger and Oleg Tchernychenko."

Their faces fell. "Oleg?" Winchester gasped.

"Murdered with a car bomb yesterday in England."

"Isolde Petrou?"

"She's still alive and under armed guard."

Jerry Hay Smith mopped his face with a handkerchief. When he had composed himself, he said, as if they had been discussing pop music in Mombasa, "What has Oleg's murder got to do with us?"

Grafton's face wore a savage look when he said, "Qasim intends to kill you, too, Mr. Smith. And Winchester and Cairnes. So far, his batting average is a thousand. I called you here to see if we could find a way to keep you three out of Qasim's reach — and alive — for a few more days."

They were interrupted by a knock on the door. Winchester opened it, admitting the cook and the butler carrying trays. They served coffee and an egg soufflé, then left.

As the four men ate, Hunt Winchester said to Grafton, "I notice that Jean Petrou wasn't on your list."

"The list is not complete," Grafton said softly, thinking of Eide and Radwan. "I doubt if we'll ever learn all the names of Qasim's victims."

"What I want to know," Jerry Hay Smith tossed in, "is how a request Huntington Winchester made to his friend the president got him — and us — up to our eyeballs in the middle of a fucked-up CIA operation. And how we wound up funding the goddamn thing."

Grafton took another forkful of soufflé and swallowed it before he said, "You're just lucky, I guess."

"Tell us about Abu Qasim," Cairnes urged. "Everything you know."

It was early afternoon when I arrived back at the safe house. My shoulder was throbbing, and I was in a black, foul mood. I had my hand on my pistol, which was in my right-hand coat pocket, when I got out of the car. Fortunately the morning fog had dissipated, the air had warmed nicely, and I could see that there were no armed men lurking behind the nearby shrubbery.

I knocked on the door. Seconds later Kerry Pocock opened it. She had her hand down beside her leg. I glanced down and saw she was holding a large, wicked-looking automatic.

"Hello, Tommy. Do come in."

I did so, and she shut the door and threw the bolt.

Marisa and Isolde were dressed and sitting in chairs. Everything they owned was in their purses.

Marisa's brown eyes swept over my messy coat, then went to my face. The coat had some blood on it — mine, unfortunately —

and a few seriously dirty spots.

"What happened to you, Mr. Carmellini?" Isolde asked. She leaned forward, looking at me intently.

"I met a man in a park," I said evasively. I was unwilling to say more. They could see that, I guess, and left it there.

"They're ready to go," Kerry said in her take-charge way. She should have been a grade-school teacher instead of wasting her talents in MI-5. "They were hoping you might detour for a small shopping expedition on the way to the airport."

I glanced at my watch. We had five hours until the plane was due to leave. "Why don't you come with us and bring your shooter? You can escort the ladies to your favorite shops while I wait outside. I don't want either of them going to any shop they've ever visited before."

"When I am in London, I *always* shop at Harrington and Jones," Isolde Petrou announced. "We'll go there."

Pocock looked at me for a decision. Getting the senior Petrou to do what I wanted her to do was going to be a challenge, but I didn't think this was the time and place to draw a line in the dirt. With women, one has to carefully pick his battles. I tried to smile gracefully and nodded my okay.

"Perfect," said the indomitable Pocock to the mesdames. "Ladies, let us depart."

Later that morning Jake Grafton answered the door to the Winchester estate. He recognized the men on the stoop: Harry Longworth, Ramon Martinez, Will Tschudi, and Nick Metaxas. They were Americans, except for Metaxas, who was a British adventurer. All four were lean men with short haircuts and heavily tanned skins. Longworth was in his early forties, the other three in their thirties.

"Come in, gentlemen."

When they were inside with the door closed, Grafton shook each of their hands. He held on to Longworth's as he said, "Sorry about Gat, Harry. We're going to miss him."

Harry Longworth just nodded. He looked glum, but there wasn't anything more to say.

Grafton led the four into the study, just off the main room, and sat them down. "I think it possible that Abu Qasim or people working for him may try to kill the people in this house. It could happen any time — today or two weeks from now. I want to trap and kill them."

He went on, briefing them thoroughly and

telling them what he wanted. It took half an hour. When he finished, he said, "Any questions?"

Harry Longworth shook his head from side to side.

Whenever he received an assignment, Ramon Martinez tried to come up with a point the briefer missed. This morning he couldn't think of a thing.

"You've covered it, sir," Will Tschudi said. Metaxas nodded.

"You've got my cell number. Talk to me. I don't want any surprises, none at all."

He meant that he didn't want them to surprise him. They seemed to understand perfectly.

"Let me introduce you to the principals."

He led them into the main room. Sitting around the fireplace in the library area were Winchester, Cairnes and Smith. "Gentlemen, these are the men who are going to keep you alive."

He pronounced everyone's name as the four former soldiers got a good look at the three men seated in the chairs. Facing those three, he said, "If you see these men, ignore them. Do not speak to them or acknowledge their presence in any way. Do you understand?"

"Who are these guys, Grafton?" Jerry Hay

Smith said belligerently.

"They are shooters, Mr. Smith. Snake-eaters, snipers, commandos, clandestine soldiers, whatever you want to call them. They've been working for you."

"I feel like a worm on a hook," Smith complained.

"That's an excellent analogy," Grafton muttered. He nodded to the former soldiers, and they filed out of the room.

"I assume they have some weapons," Cairnes said.

"That's a safe assumption," Grafton said, glancing at his watch. He addressed Winchester. "I have to go to Washington for a few days. I'm leaving you in good hands. You managed to talk to all of your domestic staff?"

"Yes."

"My people will be here this afternoon to replace them. Mr. Longworth will admit them. If you have any questions, Winchester, call me."

"I want to know how long this state of affairs — we three as prisoners — is going to go on," Winchester said in a no-nonsense tone. "This is a ridiculous situation, the three of us huddling here like fugitives in the United States of America, guarded by gunmen while foreign assassins are stalking us to commit murder."

"If they are," Smith said sourly. He was a sour man.

Grafton's gaze went from face to face. "I'm asking you to cooperate with us for a few days. If you're tired of living and want to take your chances, go home. I'll send flowers to your funeral."

That seemed to stifle them. For a moment, anyway. Grafton shook his head and walked out of the room.

"We are prisoners," Smith said to his companions.

"Now you know how the president feels," Cairnes shot back.

"Grafton talks to you like you're a boot recruit," Smith said to Winchester, who got out of his chair and went to the window, where he stood looking out. Smith continued, "Personally I find it galling to take orders from some civil servant weenie without the backbone or wit to make it in the real world."

"He should have scribbled himself rich and famous, like you did, eh?"

"Don't patronize me, little man," Smith roared at Winchester's back. "I won't take crap from you just because you know how to run a few fucking factories."

"Oh, shut up, Jerry," Simon Cairnes said

disgustedly.

Winchester ignored them both and headed for his private office.

We wound up in first-class seats on our trip westward across the Atlantic. The Company put us in business class, but Isolde threw a ladylike duck fit when she heard that, so I upgraded us, using my credit card. If the Company bean-counters took offense when I turned in my expense account, I decided, I'd send a bill to Isolde. She would probably frame it and hang it on a wall.

I had an aisle seat with Marisa on my left and Isolde in a window seat on the other side of the plane. On the aisle beside Isolde, and across from me, was a college-age youngster who was fashionably disheveled, with tattered jeans, an earring and sproutings of facial hair and pimples. I decided he was harmless and ignored him. He must have decided I, too, was harmless, and old as dirt, so he ignored me — donned his iPod earphones and tuned out.

I felt sort of naked sitting there unarmed beside two women with targets on their backs. I had given Marisa's Walther and my Springfield to Mrs. Pocock to hold until I returned to the sceptered isle, someday. A pistol in your pocket won't make you bulletproof, but in our uncertain age it can be a comfort, a metal pacifier, if you will, or a crucifix for the ungodly.

My shoulder was aching, so I rubbed the bandage and helped myself to another two Tylenol, which I swallowed without water. Marisa watched without comment.

We had been airborne about an hour and were flying above a cloud deck when she said, barely loud enough to hear, "What happened this morning?"

So I told her, whispering. I saw the kid across the aisle glance my way. He couldn't hear a word with those earphones on, but must have assumed Marisa and I were lovers.

When I finished a recitation of events, she had no comment. I had a few, but I didn't voice them. Really, someone who supposedly knew what he was doing whanging away with a silenced .22-caliber pistol at that range? I hadn't seen him carrying a rifle, and the police search didn't turn up one. So it had indeed been a pistol, a weapon designed for point-blank murder.

He was lucky he hit me. Well, hit me twice.

I wondered why he shot me in the first place. He didn't have a chance in a hundred of killing me.

He certainly didn't panic. That was out. A

diversion? From what?

I decided that a diversion was the likeliest possibility. The man who had killed Eide Masmoudi might have been leaving in another direction.

So I had botched that assignment, too. I seemed to be having a long dry spell at the plate.

"You're lucky you aren't dead," I muttered to Marisa.

"Sometimes I wonder," she responded.

"Who are you, really?"

"Just a woman. That's all I know about myself. I am a person with an unknown past and an unknown future."

"That pretty much describes most of us," I observed.

After she picked at the complimentary meal and drank a glass of champagne, Marisa settled back with a pillow under her head and went to sleep. The flight attendant saw her and brought a blanket, which I arranged over her.

Isolde sat staring out her window at endless clouds and sky. After a while she removed several reports of some kind from her large purse and immersed herself in them. Once in a while she made a note in a margin. She must have grabbed those when we skedaddled from the château.

She was a tough old bird. Still, son Jean, friends Zetsche, Tchernychenko and Gnadinger dead, with the fearless, feckless Tommy Carmellini standing guard . . . Standing up for your principles was turning out to be damned expensive. I wondered if she thought signing on with Huntington Winchester was worth the cost.

I read the newspaper I had bought in the airport, then leafed through the in-flight magazine, which was full of info on cool vacation places I'll never have the time and money to visit. Nothing in there on the sewers of Cairo, where I'd spent some time this past summer. After a while my eyelids got heavy. I reclined the seat and drifted off.

"Two more dead?"

"Yes. Oleg Tchernychenko and his two bodyguards were killed when his limo blew up on a motorway. Rolf Gnadinger was stabbed with an icicle, apparently. The maid found him dead on the front stoop of his house outside Zurich."

"Jesus Christ," said Sal Molina, shaking his head sadly. He took a moment to gather his thoughts. They were sitting in his cubbyhole office at the White House. "Any more news?"

Grafton told him about Sheikh al-Taji,

Eide Masmoudi and Radwan Ali. "The British police found Ali an hour or so ago. He and his two roommates had been tortured to death. Their landlord found them in their London flat. Blood everywhere."

"Al-Taji's death was in the morning briefing. What will the autopsy show?"

"That he died of heart failure. These things happen."

"Why did they murder the roommates?"

"Guilt by association, I guess," Jake Grafton said forlornly. "Needless to say, the Islamic militants are claiming that the sheikh was assassinated by agents of the CIA."

"You've fucked this up, Jake."

"That's an accurate description, I suppose."

Molina picked up a pen and bounced it off the desk. "Guess we had better go see the man."

"Before we do, let me see the president's schedule for the next several weeks."

Molina dug the document out of a locked drawer, then sat silently while Jake perused it. When Jake handed it back, he said, "I don't like what you're thinking."

"Let's go see him."

Molina put the schedule away, then led the way to the Oval Office. Two senators were with the president, so they had to wait.

Ten minutes later the senators left and, after murmuring something to the receptionist, who would hold the calls and keep any scheduled visitors waiting until they came out, Molina led Grafton in. The private secretary was there, and Molina waved him out. He closed the door behind him.

Both men took seats on chairs facing the president, who was seated at his desk. The president listened in silence as Jake summarized events in Europe and the U.K. over the last several days. He didn't interrupt or comment, merely listened. He was used to listening to bad news, Jake thought, and no wonder — he heard a lot of it.

When Jake finished speaking, the president sat in silence digesting it. "So where do we go from here?" he asked.

"I'll resign, if you like," Grafton said. "Wilkins wants me out, and you've got to admit, he's got good reasons."

The president waved that away. "I don't remember you promising results. As I recall, you told Sal you thought it was worth the risks to get a shot at Abu Qasim. Still feel that way?"

Grafton searched the president's face, then Molina's. His gaze returned to the president. "Qasim wants a big strike. He *needs* a big strike. He wanted your head

434

last fall in Paris, and I think he still does. If he can also get Winchester and his pals, fine. But they are small fish and you're the whale."

"I've been called a lot of things, but never that," the president said with a grimace.

"What is Qasim going to do next?" Molina asked.

"That's just it — we don't know," Grafton explained. "So far he has been looking for an opening, going after Winchester's pals one by one as the opportunity presented itself. He isn't doing it to intimidate or terrorize us; he's doing it to keep his organization intact and his holy warriors motivated by showing them that he — and they — can successfully fight back. And that is precisely the reason Winchester and the others wanted in — to prove that *they* could fight back. Every group of people since the dawn of time has looked for ways to successfully resist their enemies. That motivation is what makes us human."

"Which gets us where?"

"Abu Qasim will take any opening that presents an opportunity to hurt us at minimum risk to himself. Our challenge is to trap him."

"Are we talking one terrorist or two? Or ten or twenty?" the president asked with a frown. "How many?"

"I don't know. But believe me, one good one is more of a threat than a hundred mediocre ones."

Molina and the president had run out of questions.

Grafton continued, addressing the president: "On Thursday of next week you are scheduled to appear at a political fundraiser in New York. It's probably been announced and been in the newspapers and on the Internet for weeks."

The president nodded.

"You're going to China this weekend for three days. That was probably also publicized."

This time Molina nodded.

"The rest of your schedule for the next two weeks looks benign. No public events, just the usual preparation for the next session of Congress, budget talks and so forth. I think it's possible that Abu Qasim may make a try during your New York visit. I'd like to help him out, with your permission, by including Winchester, Smith, Cairnes and Isolde Petrou as invited guests at the fund-raiser. The press secretary can put their names on the list and give it to the press. I suggest that Sal call Winchester and extend invitations."

"I thought no one knew what Qasim looks like."

"No one but his daughter, Marisa. Carmellini is sitting on her. She'll be at the fund-raiser with Tommy and me."

The president rubbed his chin. "Qasim was in Europe, you think?"

"Probably still is. He'll be coming this way — you can bet the ranch on that."

"Any chance Homeland Security or the FBI can pick up his trail?"

Grafton shrugged. "I've talked to the secretary of Homeland and the FBI director. I have another meeting with Homeland and my boss, Wilkins, scheduled for tomorrow. We can only hope."

It went without saying that the Secret Service would pull out all the stops searching the hotel where the fund-raiser would be held. They would even use radar to look at the structure of the building.

"Are you going to be able to keep Winchester alive until then?"

"I'll try."

The president looked at Molina. "Sal?"

Molina shrugged. "This mess will probably go nuclear before then. If the press gets wind of this . . ." His voice trailed off as he scratched his forehead. He looked at Grafton. "Got any other ideas?"

"No."

"Darn." Molina said it softly, almost inaudibly.

The president came to life, sat up straight. "Do you trust Marisa Petrou?" he demanded of Jake.

"Within reason, I suppose. I'd give her a quarter for a parking meter."

"You're lying," Molina said acidly. "You wouldn't trust her with a wooden nickel."

Jake Grafton didn't respond.

The president smiled grimly. "Admiral, remind me to never, ever play poker with you. You're going for the whole pot with nary a pair. You don't even have an ace. You've got nothing but a lousy black queen."

Grafton nodded.

"I can't wait until the wolves in Congress get their fangs in this," the president said. "It's going to be one hell of a circus." He shooed them both out.

CHAPTER EIGHTEEN

I awoke on the descent into Dulles. The sky was dark, full of clouds. Soon the glow of Washington's lights lit the clouds from underneath; then, as we continued to descend, the sea of lights became visible from horizon to horizon. Marisa woke up and busied herself getting put together while I got glimpses out the window.

As the wheels squeaked on the runway, the flight attendant, a woman, came on the PA: "Let me be the first to welcome you to the United States." As a cheer erupted from the tourist section, Marisa smiled at me.

A man from the Company met us when we came out of customs/immigration and drove us straight to Jake Grafton's condo in Rosslyn. While Isolde and Marisa were nibbling snacks in the kitchen with Callie Grafton, the admiral motioned me into his den. He sat and listened while I went through everything that had happened, in minute detail, since we had last seen each other.

When I finished my litany of stupidity and death, he didn't say anything, so I added, "I'm sorry, Admiral."

"You don't owe anyone an apology, Tommy. Not me, the dead people or the gods. You did the best you could. That's all any of us can do."

"Well, we have them here in the States now. With all those gun-toters at Langley to help us, a mouse couldn't get through to them."

He took a deep breath and his eyebrows rose, then fell. "Unfortunately I can't get all those gun-toters. I can't get any of them. Wilkins and his deputies nixed that. They have zero confidence in me, and they say that if indeed we do have a squad of dedicated terrorists heading this way, the Company needs all its security personnel in place and on the job to prevent a terrorist event at Langley. Hard to argue with that."

I was incredulous. "Can't you get anybody?"

"I brought back some of the guys that have been hunting in the Middle East, the ones I could pull out without blowing their covers. The FBI has loaned me a couple of people, and I have you. If you can get your pal Willie Varner to help, we can add one more to the list. That's about the crop."

I felt nauseous. "Why don't you get Sal Molina to tell Wilkins to cooperate or ship out?"

"If I did that, I'd be finished in the Company. It was Wilkins' call and he made it. Period."

"So we salute and soldier on."

"Something like that."

I lost it then.

Grafton waited until I ran down, then said, "The women are sleeping in the guest bedroom tonight. You're on the couch. Tomorrow morning, go see Willie."

He opened a drawer and took out a pistol, a 1911 Colt automatic in .45 ACP, which he passed across the desk. I popped the magazine out, then pulled back the slide and checked for brass. It was loaded, all right. I snapped the magazine back in and looked it over.

"It was my father's," the admiral said. "He carried it during World War II. I want it back."

"He ever have to shoot anybody with it?" I asked as I tucked it into my belt.

"He once told me he did, then refused to answer questions about it."

"Marisa said Qasim wants you dead, too."

"By God, I hope so," Grafton said fiercely.

"I hope he attends to it personally instead of sending his mechanic's assistant, Khadr."

"He might also decide that Callie will do in a pinch. Or your daughter, Amy."

Jake Grafton nodded once. His lips were compressed into a straight, thin line. "I've been thinking about that, too," he murmured. "Come on, let's do the tour."

He led me into the hall and told me about his neighbors' condos. There were actually four on each floor. The usual elevator shaft had two elevators, and beside it a stairwell. Anyone could get into the stairwell on any floor, but only the lobby and basement doors could be opened from the inside without an access code, the admiral told me. We were on the eighth floor. First we climbed the stairs to the top floor — actually the fourteenth floor, although it was marked 'ROOF' — Grafton keyed his secret code into the keypad that unlocked the door, and we stepped out onto the roof.

The surrounding buildings were a couple of stories lower, so this one stuck up out of the skyline a little. The flat roof was surrounded by a chest-high rail. About half the area was covered by a wooden deck that stood up maybe six inches above the asphalt goo that made the roof waterproof. Vents and pipes stuck up everywhere, a metal forest. Three barbecue grills were chained to pipes so they wouldn't blow away. Someone had put a few flowerpots up here, and now, in the dead of winter, the plant carcasses they contained looked forlorn. It didn't take us long to see all there was to see.

We clumped down a flight, then rode the elevator to the lobby level, where we went out the main entrance. The lobby door was locked. People could key in their access code to unlock it or could buzz someone in the building; the front door could be unlocked from any condo. Once in the lobby, one could enter the stairwell or summon an elevator.

"The Homeowners Association has talked for years about putting a keypad system in the elevators, but they haven't gotten around to it," Grafton said. "The elevators will take you to any floor."

A security camera looked at the lobby, which contained a listing of the building's tenants and a bank of mailboxes, nothing else.

We went outside and walked down the alley to the back of the building, which faced east, as did Grafton's condo high above. On the back of the building at ground level, the basement level, was a loading dock, which allowed furniture to be moved into the basement and elevators via a sliding overhead metal door, now padlocked shut. Beside the big door was a personnel door with the lock in the doorknob. I examined it. It was a run-of-the-mill commercial lock, easy to pick or, if you lacked the talent for that, to break with a pipe wrench on the knob.

The building on the north side butted right up to this one, so to complete our circumnavigation we had to go around both buildings.

When we were back at the front entrance to Grafton's tower, the admiral asked, "What do you think?"

"Without a squad of armed people on duty around the clock, it's indefensible," I replied. "They can post a sniper to shoot into your place, break into an adjoining condo and plant a bomb, bomb your front door and come in shooting, or just burn the damn building down with you and all your neighbors in it. If they don't want to bother with bombs or fire, they can stay outside and gun you and yours on the street when you come out."

"That about covers it, I guess," the admiral said thoughtfully.

"If I were you, I'd get the authorities to evacuate everybody until we get Qasim. Tell people there's a sewer leak or rabid rats or infected cockroaches. Whatever."

"That won't work," Grafton said. "We can't evacuate America until we win the war on terror."

I knew he'd say that. "Your best bet is to post some guys outside to spot them coming in."

"That's my assessment, too. Would you go to see Willie in the morning?"

"Okay."

Stretched out on Grafton's couch with a pillow and blanket, I couldn't sleep. Between the nap I had on the plane, the time zone changes, and a mild case of constipation from all that sitting, there was no way the sandman was going to find me. I lay there tossing for a while, then sat up in the darkness for a while, then went to the window and looked out. Amazingly, snow was falling. Wasn't sticking, just falling. If this kept up, they would cancel the government tomorrow.

I was standing there in my underwear when Marisa came padding out wrapped in an old robe she had borrowed from Mrs. Grafton.

"Can't sleep, either?" I asked.

"No."

She stood beside me for a few minutes

watching the snow fall into the lights. "When I was a girl I loved to watch snow come down," she said. "I seem to have gotten out of the habit."

"Was that in Switzerland?"

"Yes. I spent my childhood at a boarding school. They must have taken me there when I was still in diapers. Adults came and visited me occasionally, and took me out for dinner and movies, but I lived there, in that little world, behind walls."

"Did Abu Qasim ever visit?" I asked.

"Oh, yes."

"Tell me about him."

She remained silent for so long I thought I had crossed an invisible line; then she began to speak. Slowly at first, then faster and with more assurance. She literally began with the first visit of Qasim that she could remember and went through it almost hour by hour. Then the next, and the next, and so on. She remembered his every word, every gesture, every grimace, where they went, what they did, where they sat, what they ate — all of it. Two hours later she finally ran down. I gave her a drink from a bottle in Grafton's kitchen cupboard and sent her off to bed.

The snow had turned to rain, and the wind had kicked up.

446

One thing's for sure, Tommy, I told myself. *She really hates that son of a bitch.*

After breakfast, I borrowed Grafton's car and went off to visit my business associate, Willie Varner, who was better known in some quarters as Willie the Wire. You met him earlier on one of his bad days, at our lock shop. We're partners, although my name is on the shop lease and the contractor's and fidelity bonds since Willie is a convicted felon.

He greeted me like a long-lost brother. "Where the hell you been?"

"Europe."

"That's a big place."

"France, England and a little slice of Germany called Rastatt."

"Sounds bad. That a city or jail or what?"

"Town."

"Well, you got back to civilization just in time. We got a contract to install the locks and burglar and fire alarms in a whole subdivision they're buildin' over in Virginia — three hundred town houses, somethin' called Sherwood Forest Hills, although it's in an old cow pasture, flatter'n Florida, and there ain't a tree in sight."

Willie rubbed his hands together. "Big money in contractin', boy, and we're gonna

447

get a chunk. Can't believe this fell in our lap, but fall it did. Got Scout and Earlene signed up to help do the work. With you helpin', it'll go a little faster." I knew Scout and Earlene, a couple who did some electrical contracting in the city. Earlene was a former WNBA player, and Scout had done a stretch in the pen.

"When we're done," Willie added, "I'm goin' to Vegas for a week or two."

Willie had been up the river a couple of times for burglary. After he got out the second time, we opened this lock shop. He was a wizard with a hairpin, a natural talent, who could open about any lock around. Me, I used picks, and since I didn't have natural talent, made up for it with old-fashioned grit and persistence.

"Man, we'll have to find someone to do it for us," I said, using the imperial "we." After all, I owned half the business. "I need you on a little job I'm working across town."

He couldn't believe it. He told me how much we stood to earn doing the subdivision. "Tommy, this is major money, a real score. *Honest money,* too! We only got this job because the original sub got busted for drugs and, on top of that, the damn fool had a pistol in his pocket. He's sittin' in jail. Needless to say, his contractor's bond went up in smoke. We got called at the last minute. I demanded twice what the man offered, and he was over a barrel and said yes. Maybe I oughta feel a little ashamed at takin' advantage, but I don't. His fuckin' problem! Big opportunity for us. We get that stuff in right and workin', make these dudes happy, and we got a shot at biddin' major subdivisions all over. Jesus, Tommy, they're buildin' out the whole northern half of Virginia, houses sproutin' outta those old farms like toadstools after a rain."

I waited until he ran down. "Let Scout and Earlene do the work. We have a contractor's bond and they don't. They'll make some serious money and we'll pocket some and get the call on the next subdivision."

Willie sat down on a stool and eyed me suspiciously while I fired up a table saw and began making wedges out of a two-by-four. "You still workin' for that sailor, Grafton?"

"Yeah. I'm sitting on his family for a week or so. It's possible some bad dudes want them dead."

"Man, you went to the hospital twice for that man. How much of his shit you gonna shovel?"

"It's three times, and the answer is, It's Uncle Sam we're working for, not Jake Grafton."

"Yeah. Right! Next thing you'll be tellin' me that it's raghead suiciders who want to do them."

I couldn't help it. My face must have been a study.

Willie took one look at my puss and groaned. "Oh, Jesus, Tommy, tell me it isn't true!"

It was true, though, so I twisted his arm and he cussed me out and argued. "I been to the hospital twice myself on your adventures, Tommy. Don't want to go again. I'm too damn old, man."

"There's no risk involved. I just need your eyes and street smarts."

"No guns. I don't do guns or knives. Tried that last year and it didn't work. Denzel Washington I ain't."

I appealed to his patriotism and greed. We were on the side of the angels. He would make money on the subdivision contract and he would collect some government money, too. Finally greed won out and he agreed to help. "Only to keep Mrs. Grafton alive, you understand." We called Scout and Earlene and made a deal. Willie said he would be ready to go to work tomorrow.

"Let's go see him now," I said. I flipped off the saw, brushed the sawdust off my clothes and put my wedges in a paper bag. There was a nice hammer lying there, so I added it to the bag.

"Busy now." He waved at all the projects on the bench.

"Now," I insisted. "Get your coat."

He was subdued and well behaved by the time we rode the elevator up to Grafton's condo. In the elevator he spotted the bulge under my coat. "You packin'?"

"Yeah."

"Oh, man, no guns you said. Push the down button, you lyin' sack of . . ."

I didn't, of course. The admiral was glad to see us. He took us into the study and closed the door. When we were seated, he asked Willie, "Did Tommy tell you why we need you?"

Willie gave me an evil look. "Just gave me some shit about an easy job, no guns or knives, no violence of any kind. I knew he was lyin', of course. He ain't told the truth for one whole day in his whole miserable life. He's the only man I know who tells more lies than I do."

"I'm taking our houseguests to Connecticut," Grafton said, ignoring Willie's bullshit, as I habitually did. With Willie, it becomes second nature. "But Callie, my daughter, Amy, and Tommy will be here alone. It's possible that someone may try to kill Callie or Amy. If the hitter is a professional, he's probably going to case the place, try to establish who is here, figure out the women's routine, all of that, before he decides how to make the hit. I need someone in the street to find and identify the watcher. You, I hope, will be my someone. The job will last about a week — no more. If and when you spot a watcher, you'll call Tommy on his cell phone. He'll take over from there."

"Man, they'll probably just burn the whole place down with everyone in it. You oughta get your wife outta here."

"Callie, Amy and Tommy will be here," Grafton said in a tone that ended the discussion.

"Just watch and call Tommy?" Willie said, eyeing Grafton.

"That's it," Grafton reiterated. "I'll get you a lapel mike and earphone. He'll hear everything you say. You'll also need some props, some reason to hang out on the street. You need to be out there wandering around, watching but not appearing to be watching."

Willie nodded. "I can do that."

"What props do you need?"

"Just a brown bag and a bottle. Watched

winos all my life. I can do that for a few days."

"You're on the payroll. Contract wages. Stop by in the morning and I'll give you the radio."

"I need some old clothes. Go to the Salvation Army this afternoon and get myself an outfit."

"You need to be out there pretty much around the clock."

"Gonna be tough money," Willie said. "Tough money, this time of year, sleepin' on the street."

"Just don't drink too much of that poison," I warned.

"Sort of a government-paid toot," Willie said philosophically. "Might be a nice little vacation, after all."

After he met Callie and shook her hand, and she thanked him for agreeing to help, he left to make his arrangements. Grafton went over to Langley for a few hours, and I did some general hanging out in his den.

He was leaving in the morning for Winchester's estate in Connecticut, and taking Isolde and Marisa with him. Callie and Amy and I were staying here, with Willie watching on the street. Although that sounded like a half-baked, desperate plan to me, I couldn't come up with a better one.

The problem was that Qasim and his helper — make that helpers, because I had no idea how many he had or could recruit here in the good ol' U.S. of A. — could attack in dozens of different ways. Qasim and company certainly weren't stuck on a particular MO. Already they had used poison — chemical and nuclear — bullets, a knife, an icicle and a car bomb. About the only methods they hadn't used were fire and a nuclear explosion, and I suspected that with Qasim's help they could arrange those things if they put their heads to it. Which was, of course, precisely why Jake Grafton, Sal Molina and the president wanted Abu Qasim dead and in hell.

Hell, I had to agree, would certainly be the place for him.

Marisa agreed, too. That conversation in the wee hours last night had been a revelation for me. She hated the bastard. Had he been just a figure from her childhood, she might have gotten over it in the hustle and bustle of life, but he came back . . . and she obeyed his orders in a terrorist attempt on the G-8 leaders. So now she hated him. And feared him.

Or so she said. Of course, he also sliced up her face.

I got up from Grafton's little leather couch and examined the titles on his bookshelf and fingered his mementos while I went over that conversation again, trying to decide if Marisa had told the truth. The possibility that she was a world-class actress couldn't be eliminated or excluded. Traitors have marched through the human drama since the dawn of time lying to everyone around them while they were committing treason. Such people are the lifeblood of intelligence agencies, including mine, and our most precious assets.

Isolde came in about that time. We chit-chatted for a bit about America and her previous visits, then I asked her point-blank: "Does Marisa really hate Abu Qasim, or is she lying?"

The Frenchwoman looked me squarely in the eyes as she said, "Never have I seen someone hate another so much. It is a poison, and if she doesn't somehow neutralize it, it will destroy her."

She thought about that for a moment, then added, "I, too, have hated, but not like that. Not with the entire total of my being, not to the absolute depth and length and breadth of my soul." She got up from her chair, looked around the room once more, then said, "Hatred has mutilated and twisted Abu Qasim. I don't want Marisa to end up as he is, disfigured, foul, obsessed to the brink of insanity, *evil!* That would be a horrible fate."

"Good to see you again, Admiral," Robin Cloyd said when Jake Grafton walked into the foyer of his Langley office and the security door closed behind him.

"Good morning," he said and walked on through to his private office. His desk was orderly, with the items demanding his attention carefully arranged in a pile. The urgent stuff that needed his immediate attention was on top, and the routine stuff on the bottom. Cloyd did the arranging, and her judgment was impeccable.

She also had his telephone call slips in a pile. Right on top was one from the director of MI-5. Jake sat down and dialed the number on the encrypted telephone that was on his desk. Three minutes later the British officer was on the line.

After a few social pleasantries, the director said, "Little development I thought you should know about. We got into Alexander Surkov's security box at his bank. Found a wad of currency and four passports for four different people. None of them had Surkov's photo on them. Two were American, one British and one from the Ukraine."

"Real passports?"

"Our boffins think not. They look good, very good, good enough to fool any immigration officer who has only a minute or so to look at them, but our experts think they might be products of the SVR." The *Sluzhba Vneshnei Razvedski,* Russian foreign intelligence, was Janos Ilin's outfit.

"You don't say," Grafton murmured.

"No way to know for certain," the British officer continued, "but one suspects Mr. Surkov had a lucrative little sideline supplying documents to unfortunates who found themselves inconveniently without."

"He knew people in Russia," Jake said thoughtfully. "That was what he had to sell."

"The names on the passports don't seem to be in our database, so we're seeing what we can do with the photographs and addresses. In the meantime, we're keeping this discovery under our hats. It won't be released to the press or shared with law enforcement."

Grafton thanked him and said good-bye.

Robin stuck her head in. "It's almost time for your appointment, Admiral."

Grafton glanced at his watch, then headed for the door. "See you in a bit," he said.

The room beside director William Wilkins'

office was a multimedia theater cleverly disguised to look like a conference room. When buttons were pushed, walls retracted and displays popped up, rather like the cockpit of the starship *Enterprise.* Today the gadgets were hidden.

Grafton made small talk with the head of the Secret Service, Abe Goldman, while they waited for Wilkins and the secretary of the Department of Homeland Security, who were in Wilkins' office behind closed doors. An aide stuck his head in, saw that Grafton and Goldman were there and disappeared, presumably to relay the news to Wilkins, who came in a few minutes later with the secretary in tow. Grafton and Goldman popped to their feet.

"Stay seated, gentlemen." Wilkins had no regular chair, but parked his bottom wherever the mood struck him, a habit that led to small side bets among the department heads who regularly attended meetings here. Today he took a seat directly across the table from Grafton. The secretary, who was Goldman's boss, seated himself with an empty chair between him and Wilkins. In the bureaucratic shuffle that followed 9/11, the Secret Service had been removed from the Treasury Department and put in the new Department of Homeland Security.

"So, Jake, tell us this fairy tale you sold the president," Wilkins began.

Grafton stated that he believed Abu Qasim was going to attempt to assassinate the president, and gave his reasons, including the history of his attempts to bring Qasim to bay. He discussed the murders of Zetsche, Tchernychenko and Gnadinger, and devoted several minutes to discussing the break-in and murders at the Petrou château in France.

Wilkins let him talk without interruption.

When Jake finished, the secretary spoke right up. He was a veteran of the Washington bureaucratic maze and was fairly good at reading between the lines. "There's a whole lot here you haven't told us."

"He can't and won't reveal ongoing covert operations," Wilkins said heavily.

"But what's the logical thread between these murders and an assassination attempt?"

"Abu Qasim tried it last year, and he may try again."

"That's a logical fallacy. Does the president know more than you're telling us?"

"Yes."

"So you're selling us another pig in a poke," the secretary grumped to Wilkins, who didn't smile. "Another fucking hunch."

After the moment of silence that followed that remark, Grafton continued, "I had a telephone conversation this morning with the head of MI-5. He says Alexander Surkov, the Russian émigré assassinated with polonium in London, had four passports in his safe deposit box at his bank that may have been made in Russia. The working assumption in London is that he was a dealer in fake paper, which he got from a contact in the SVR."

"And that tidbit leads us where?" the secretary said heavily.

"Tchernychenko, Surkov's boss, was killed by a car bomb Saturday. Perhaps by Islamic extremists. Perhaps at the urging of Abu Qasim, who may have been a Surkov client."

"This is a house of cards," Goldman observed. "Surkov's murder could have been ordered in Moscow, and so could Tchernychenko's. I've heard about Janos Ilin's little disclaimer and request to Grafton, and it was a farce. All you people are doing is reading tea leaves."

"You want sworn testimony, go to the federal courthouse," Wilkins shot back. "This is a spy agency. This is about as good as it gets, guys."

Goldman took a deep breath, then exhaled. "Okay," he said heavily. He turned to Grafton. "When and where, do you guesstimate?"

Jake told him. Twenty minutes later the secretary and Goldman departed, leaving Wilkins and Grafton alone in the conference room.

"How confident are you that it will go down the way you told those two?" Wilkins asked the admiral.

"This isn't just my guess as to his intentions. Marisa Petrou also thinks this is the scenario." He paused, then decided that the time had arrived to show all the cards to his boss. "I think she might have killed her husband, who was probably selling information to Qasim. I think she has made some kind of deal with Abu Qasim to keep him from killing her mother-in-law, Isolde. He may have told her to tell me this tale, but I doubt it. I think she is telling the truth *as she believes it to be* about his intentions. The bottom line is that she wants Abu Qasim dead. So do we."

"Is she or is she not his daughter?"

"I don't know, and I don't believe she does. Sometimes she thinks she is, sometimes she is sure she isn't."

Wilkins rubbed his forehead with his fingertips as he digested that remark.

"You know," he said conversationally, "I've been in this business for twenty-five years. Without a doubt, this is the goddamnest tangle I've ever seen, and I've seen them all."

"Yes, sir."

"And letting the president get these *amateurs* involved . . . Damn that Molina, with his fingers in every pie!"

Wilkins took a deep breath, exhaled slowly, then said, "Tell you what — if Homeland doesn't snag our buddy Abu in the interim, or if he doesn't make his try on the president next Thursday night as you have so persuasively predicted, I want your resignation on my desk on Friday morning."

"Yes, sir."

Grafton's condo was on the eighth floor of his building, and it occupied the entire eastern end of the floor. Looking out the living room window, I could see over the buildings on the east side. See the roofs and the apartments they contained. Could see the spire of the Washington Monument in the distance, a white phallic symbol poking up above the trees.

The main bedroom where the Graftons slept was on the northeast corner. Marisa was asleep in the adjacent guest room when I tiptoed in. Looking out the window, I could see more of the same. I drew the curtains and tiptoed out.

When I wandered into the kitchen, Callie was there with Isolde, gabbling in French. I knew that Callie, a language professor at Georgetown University, loved opportunities to gas with native speakers of one of her languages. She and Isolde, a smart, dynamic, experienced executive with a wealth of life experience almost as broad as Callie's, would soon be fast friends, I suspected.

Each of them was working on a glass of white wine. Callie offered me a glass, but I refused. A door off the kitchen led to a tiny balcony which jutted out from the building on the east side. The kitchen windows on the south side of the room faced apartments in the buildings across the way, each with its private balcony and its windows.

This condo was a sniper's wet dream. I lowered the blinds and drew the curtains.

"Surely they won't be here so soon, Tommy," Mrs. Grafton said.

I didn't think so, either, but I said, "Can't be too careful."

She and Isolde went back to their cookbook, which was open on the butcher-block island in the middle of the room, and switched to English, in deference to my presence. Apparently dinner was going to be a production.

I watched them until Callie looked my way again. "Hanging out here with Abu Qasim on the loose is going to be very dangerous," I said.

She smiled tightly. "I know."

"And lately I haven't been doing very well at the bodyguard gig. Actually, I've been doing terribly."

"Isolde and Marisa are still alive," Callie pointed out.

"They're alive because Abu Qasim didn't want to kill them. Then. If and when he gets around to it, they're going to have a serious problem. As you and I do."

"Marisa told me that he'll probably send a colleague named Khadr," Callie said. She got busy removing food from the refrigerator.

Isolde was standing beside the cookbook watching us and listening. Now she said, "She thought Khadr was the gunman who attacked my château."

Here it was again: Ol' Marisa knew a lot, to hear her tell it, and one suspected she knew a lot more that she wasn't telling. That sure put a damper on the conversation.

I watched the two of them dice vegetables

and cut up a chicken for a casserole.

"I'll say it one more time," I said to Callie. "I think you should go with your husband to Connecticut, or at least slip off to visit friends in the wilds of California or wherever."

"I know you and Willie will do your best."

"My best hasn't been very good. That's what I'm trying to tell you. Besides, even if I were Superman, I'm only one guy. Who knows how many of them will come after us? Hasn't it occurred to you that they want me, too? Kill me, then the coast is clear to wax you, and every other person in this building. Every move I make leaves other options open for them. Surely you can see that."

"Amy will be joining us for dinner," Callie said, glancing at me, "and she'll be staying with us for the next week or so. Jake thought that wise."

End of conversation.

So Grafton was betting the farm on Willie and me. I silently cursed him for a damn fool, then went back to the den and sacked out on the couch for a nap. It took a while, but I finally drifted off. Got to dreaming about killers setting off bombs against the door and rushing into the room with guns blazing. Started thrashing. Woke up suddenly covered with sweat.

In addition to Amy Carol Grafton, there were two other guests for dinner, a journalist named Jack Yocke and a lady friend he brought along. I had read Yocke's stuff for years in the *Post* and recognized the name. He was a tall, gangly guy, articulate and full of opinions. Apparently Grafton and Yocke had known each other for years. When Grafton introduced us, he pronounced Yocke's name as Yock-key: I had seen it in print a hundred times but never heard it pronounced before.

"We talked about having dinner together, what? Three months ago?"

"Four, I think," Grafton said apologetically. "Hard to fit you in between golf and bowling."

"You retired guys," Yocke said wryly, glancing at me. I could see that he knew Grafton was about as retired as I was.

"After the murder of Jean Petrou," Yocke said as he scrutinized Grafton's face, "I am amazed that the French authorities allowed them to leave the country."

Grafton shrugged.

"I suppose you don't want their presence in the States to make the papers?"

"Publish if you wish, but don't use my

name. And don't question them."

At the dinner table Yocke entertained us with unprintable inside dope on the goings-on among the politicos around town. I pretended I cared.

Yocke's girlfriend or significant other, as the case might have been, seemed nice enough. Her name was Anna-Lynn Something — I didn't pay much attention to her last name. If she had any idea of the tensions swirling around the table, she ignored them. She seemed happy and laughed with Callie and Amy and told political jokes.

Marisa and Isolde were more subdued, yet they held up their end of the conversation. Me? I didn't have much to say. I was a bit overwhelmed at the guard-duty assignment and pretty steamed at Grafton.

At one point I asked him, "Do you own this place or rent it?"

"We own it," he said.

So anyone with a computer and access to the Internet could get his address from the public records. Terrific!

Marisa, who was seated on my left, put her hand atop mine for a moment and smiled at me.

Amy Carol was a schoolteacher, fourth grade this year, in her late twenties. She was dating a stockbroker who lived and worked in Baltimore. The Graftons, I gathered, had high hopes that this guy was The One. Callie asked Amy about her beau and subtly pumped her for information, which Amy supplied in little dribs and drabs, just enough to be polite. Parents!

After dinner, while we were lingering over the dessert Anna-Lynn had brought and some coffee, Grafton asked Yocke if he could have a word with him in the den. They left for a tête-à-tête.

Marisa smiled at me again, and I smiled right back. What the hey, a guy can only die once. The coffee was excellent — life was beginning to look a little better.

In the den with the door closed, Jake Grafton said, "I have a story for you."

"Oh, happy day!" Jack Yocke shot back. He found a chair and dropped into it.

"But there are ground rules," Grafton continued smoothly. "You have to agree to all of them or I won't give you the story."

Jack Yocke stared at the admiral across the desk. "There's a quote about a gift horse that comes to mind."

"Here are the rules. First, you can't print the story unless and until I give you the green light. Second, you can't quote me. Third, you have to write and print the story as I give it to you — no changing or editing or speculating."

"Uh-huh. How much of the story will be true?"

A smile crossed Grafton's face. "Some of it, anyway."

"I've heard, simply a rumor, you understand, that you work for the CIA in a covert capacity."

The smile stayed on Grafton's face. His gray eyes, Yocke noted, weren't smiling.

"I'll look like a fool," Yocke continued, "if the real story comes out and it looks as if I've been had."

"Your story will be the real story," Grafton replied. "No one will call you a liar."

"Can I quote you as an unidentified source?"

"You can attribute the story to unidentified sources. Plural. No quotes."

"Are there real people named in your story?"

"Yes."

"May I interview them?"

"Only after you print the story I give you. They'll substantiate every word of the printed story."

"Well," said Yocke, after thinking it over, "I can agree to this: I'll listen to your tale, making no commitment to publish. I will

469

talk this matter over with my editor. If and when you tell me I can publish, the editor and I will decide then if we'll run it."

"Subject to the other provisos?"

"Yes."

"Don't tell him my name."

"I won't."

"I can live with that."

Jack Yocke took a notebook from an inside jacket pocket and placed it on the desk in front of him. He removed a cheap ballpoint from a shirt pocket, clicked it, checked that the point was out, then looked at the admiral, who began to talk.

When Grafton finished twenty minutes later, Yocke went over the names again to ensure he had them spelled correctly. He asked questions to clarify a few points, then reluctantly closed the book.

"So your houseguests are involved?"

"Yes."

"May I question them now?"

"No. We went over that."

Yocke stowed his book and pen and leaned back in his chair. He rocked it back on its two rear legs and sighed. "This story is nothing but speculative fiction. By your own admission, the climax is uncertain and may never happen."

"Ah, but if it does . . ."

"What if it doesn't?"

"Then this conversation never took place. You tear up your notes and we get on with life."

Jack Yocke pursed his lips as he digested that remark. "You know, I've been a reporter in this town for eighteen years, come March. I've been lied to a million times, tooled around, stonewalled, cursed, cajoled, flattered, threatened, insulted, demeaned, beaten up and made a fool of. At least a dozen people have tried to bribe me. I've even had a gun waved in my face. But, I must admit, *this* takes the cake. This is a first."

"Your memoirs are going to be a great read."

"Got anything else to add to your tale?"

"No."

"Let's rejoin the party. I could do with a cup of coffee."

CHAPTER NINETEEN

Abu Qasim flew into New York's JFK Airport just like the tens of thousands of passengers who arrive from all over the world every day.

If the FBI were waiting, he told himself, they would be in the terminal as he exited the jetway. They weren't. He walked along as if he were being watched, because he might have been. He tried to show ordinary curiosity, not too much, not too little. After all, this was supposed to be his first visit to the country.

Qasim queued in an immigration line and casually glanced around, just to see if anyone was paying any attention to him. No one made eye contact with him. The clerk at the desk ahead ignored him.

All around were Americans returning from abroad, some with children, and people from every corner of the earth. Behind him some English visitors were plotting a shopping strike on Manhattan.

When his turn came, the clerk glanced at his immigration form — he was here on business, he said — and ran the passport he had purchased from Surkov through the scanner. The clerk, a woman, unwrapped a stick of gum and popped it in her mouth as she waited for the computer to decide if he was on a wanted list. Or if his passport was a fake.

Abu Qasim kept breathing regularly, trying to look bored. Then she stamped the passport and handed it back. "Have a nice visit," she said perfunctorily and motioned to the next person in line.

His luggage was on the carousel. He retrieved it and joined the customs line. He had nothing to declare, he told the agent when he passed him the form. The agent pawed lightly through his stuff, then closed the top of the suitcase and scribbled something on the form. Abu Qasim was waved on.

On the other hand, he reflected, perhaps the FBI was trying a finesse. Perhaps he would be followed until he revealed members of his network, then arrested.

Perhaps.

He went outside and got in the line waiting for a taxi. Night had already arrived, and the temperature was in the low forties with a breeze. A light rain was falling. Traffic at the airport was unbelievably bad.

So many cars . . . so many infidels, white, black, brown and yellow, the women brazen and wearing suggestive clothes, talking loudly. He had been to New York many times before, but each visit was a shock to his nervous system. One woman jostled him and said, "Sorry, honey."

Abu Qasim rode into Manhattan with a driver from Pakistan who ignored him. This was fine with Abu Qasim, who had no desire to reveal his knowledge of languages. This man might be in the pay of the FBI.

He gave the man a three-dollar tip when they arrived at Pennsylvania Station. Not too much, not too little, so the man would have difficulty remembering him if someone asked about him a few days from now.

At Pennsylvania Station Qasim bought a twenty-dollar subway pass at a machine, then went through the turnstile carrying his bag. He rode the subway north into the Bronx, got off and went into an alley.

When he came out, he was no longer wearing his suit and tie but was in jeans, a short coat and a cheap baseball cap with no logo. He left the suitcase in the Dumpster behind which he had changed. Someone would grab it, he hoped, and soon. If the authorities had placed a beacon in the bag, they could chase it wherever.

He reboarded the subway and rode it under the streets of Manhattan, Queens and Brooklyn until almost eleven that night. At one point he exited the station, then walked to the next station, where he got on another train that took him back into the heart of the city.

When he was absolutely satisfied that no one was following him, Qasim got off the subway in Brooklyn and walked a half mile through the rain to a row house. He checked the number, knocked on the door and was admitted. When the door closed behind him, the man there embraced him.

"Ah, you arrive! Allah be praised. Did anyone follow you?"

This question annoyed Qasim. Of course no one followed or he wouldn't be here, but he kept his good humor and answered politely.

"You must be hungry," his host said. "Let us pray, then eat."

The host went by the name of Salah al-Irani in the movement; this was, of course, not his real name. During dinner they were joined by four young men from the host's mosque, and the host, an Iranian, entertained them all with his taxi-driving adventures. He had been in the United States for four years and had saved enough money to have his son join him. Allah be praised.

Proud that his house should be graced by such an important man as Abu Qasim, al-Irani talked loudly about the importance of Arab nationalism, which had been impeded, he said, by Western influence. Jihad was the weapon whereby foreign influences would be defeated — and Israel destroyed — and a great Arab nation created, an Islamic nation, of course. After delivering himself of several impassioned statements in this regard, he then took pains to impress upon his guest the extent of his temporal prosperity, which derived from his vast competence at driving a taxi in this rich nation, the United States.

If Abu Qasim thought the conflict between his statements ironic, he gave no sign. He well knew that many Arabs thought agreement on lofty principals was real progress. And, after all, in this world a man must eat.

When dinner was over, the four young men from the mosque left after voicing their fealty to jihad, leaving al-Irani alone with Qasim.

"I have heard of the deaths of Abdul-Zarah Mohammed and the others."

"Sheikh al-Taji in London. They killed him, too."

"Inshallah."

"No doubt, but the enemies of Allah are many and strong. I have come to seek vengeance against our enemies, who are here, in America."

"What can we do to help?" Salah al-Irani asked softly.

After breakfast at Grafton's condo, Jake motioned to Marisa, who followed him into the den. He closed the door and motioned to a seat.

He dragged a chair around to face her. "It's time," he said, "to level with me."

Marisa's expression didn't change. "I have told you the truth."

"What did Abu Qasim tell you to do?"

"He has told me nothing."

"He made you a promise," Grafton said, looking straight into her eyes.

She didn't reply.

"Do you really think he'll keep it?"

"I don't know what you are talking about."

"If you don't tell me the truth — and all of it — you are actually helping him. Do you understand that?"

"I have told you all I know." She met his gaze levelly.

"I hope so. If people die because you didn't, you are the one who has to live with it."

When she didn't respond, he rose from the chair and went to the door. He held it open.

After Marisa walked out, he brought in Isolde Petrou.

"Madame, the time has come for you to tell me all you know . . . or suspect."

"*Mon amiral,* you flatter me."

"Oh, no. Marisa has talked to you. I think she knows more than she has told me."

Madame Petrou sighed. "Marisa is a woman with deep wounds, as you know. I think she has told you more than she has told me. But whatever the case might be, I believe she has told you all she knows. Or all she wishes to admit she knows, even to herself."

After Grafton had thought about that one, he said, "I would like for you and Marisa to accompany me to Winchester's house in Connecticut. We'll leave in an hour or so and stay there until Abu Qasim is caught or dead."

The French lady cocked her head slightly to one side, as if sizing him up for the first time. "You have not impressed me with your competence, Admiral."

"If you have any suggestions, please make them."

"This Carmellini — he is obviously in love with Marisa, and —"

"I doubt that," Grafton said, interrupting.

"I know about these things, Admiral. I have eyes and I am French. He is not warrior enough."

"And Qasim? Do you know him? Ever met him? Seen him?"

"I only know what Marisa has told me, as you do. And I have seen his victims. He is vicious, ruthless, and enjoys what he does."

Grafton watched her facial expressions as she spoke.

"I think you are very clever, Admiral. Carmellini is brave and bold and tough, but not clever."

Jake Grafton just nodded.

"Qasim is full of hate," Isolde said. "You aren't."

Jake Grafton had had enough. As he rose from his chair he said, "I'm getting there."

Willie Varner showed up about nine that morning. I couldn't believe it when I opened the door — he looked as if he'd been sleeping in alleys for about ten years. He even smelled. "Oh, Lord," I said.

"Paid a guy twenty bucks for these," Willie told me. "He thought I was crazy."

"I think so, too."

I took him to the den so Grafton could admire his transformation. After he oohed and aahed, the admiral gave Willie a little radio. The mike went on his clothes — I had to get close to pin it on — and the earpiece went in his left ear. There were no wires. The electronics that made this thing work were in a little box that went in one of Willie's pockets.

We both talked on the radios a bit, just testing them; then Grafton gave Willie some spare batteries, which he pocketed, shook his hand, and said, "Good luck — and thanks."

Willie nodded and left. I locked the door behind him and went back to the den. Grafton had two pump shotguns lying on the couch, so I took one and loaded it with five shells containing No. 4 buckshot while he loaded the other.

"I'm counting on you," he said.

"Bet they don't even come," I replied brightly.

He just glanced at me, then went off to see his wife. I sat down in one of the chairs with a shotgun on my lap.

Crazy. He was nuts and his wife was

nuts and so was I. All three of us crazy as bedbugs.

After Grafton and the women left for Connecticut, I sat at the kitchen table with Callie pretending to look at the morning paper. Mostly it was SOS, the Same Old Stuff. Jack Yocke's column was about the upcoming fund-raiser next week at the Walden Hotel in New York. His column was about politics, which I scanned without much interest. Politics is like weather — everyone talks about it, but no one can do anything about it.

I remembered the Walden Hotel, which was an old place, renovated a few years ago, with a great corner bar, a body exchange for the hip and trendy, and windows, where you could get a libation and watch pedestrians stroll the avenue if there were no thirsty young things in sight. Apparently the hotel had a big ballroom, which I had never been in.

Callie went off to her bedroom to do some reading, and I wandered the living room and den, bored silly. Maybe I should resign from the Company, get on with my life. I was making big plans about what I'd do if I quit or got fired when the doorbell rang.

With my pistol in hand, I looked through

the security hole. Robin Cloyd. Just who we needed!

I put the shooter away and opened the door. "Good morning," she chirped, then marched right in, frizzy hair and all.

When I had the door bolted again, I turned around. "What do you want?" I asked without curiosity.

"The admiral sent me over to help you."

My expression must have showed how unlikely I thought it was that she could be of any help whatsoever, so she kicked me in the balls.

That doubled me over. She kicked me again in the side, a pretty healthy lick, and I toppled onto the floor. Being a lean, mean, fighting machine, I had the good sense to stay there. Of course, I was down to about 10 percent effectiveness just then.

"Where'd you learn to do that?" I managed between gasps.

"I was an unarmed combat instructor in the Marines," Cloyd said airily, "back in my wilder days."

"Glad I didn't know you then."

She pulled a pistol from her purse, just so I could see it. "And I know how to use this."

Callie had bolted from the bedroom to see what the rumpus was about, and now she and Robin helped me into a chair. Then

Callie led Robin by the arm off to the kitchen to get a cup of coffee. "Jake said you were coming by. I'm so glad to see you."

I waited about five minutes until the pain had eased to a dull throb before I headed for the bathroom to check for bruises. Man, was I sore!

Damn these women, anyway.

The mood was gloomy at the Winchester estate when Jake Grafton and the Petrou women arrived in midafternoon, even though the gauzy winter sun was brightly illuminating the room through the big picture windows. All the men were into the sauce, Grafton noted, which apparently had a good deal to do with it. Winchester said a perfunctory hello to the women, nodded at Grafton and poured himself another drink.

Winchester's collie was lying on an empty chair when Grafton and the Petrou ladies came in. She leaped off the chair and came over with tail wagging to make friends. Jerry Hay Smith snarled at Grafton and ignored the women. Simon Cairnes just glowered at everyone from the sofa in front of the big television — he had CNBC on — and puffed on his cigar, almost as if he were daring someone to object to his smoking in the house.

Carrying a suitcase in each hand, Grafton led the women upstairs to locate a bedroom.

When he came back down, Winchester cornered him. "I want to know what the hell is going on."

"Don't we all?" Grafton tossed back.

"Seriously, what's the damn government doing to catch those terrorist assholes? That sunuvabitch Qasim?"

"We're working on it."

"I'll just bet."

"Even while you sleep."

"You'll still be working on it even when we're dead," Smith called from behind the bar. He was apparently mixing martinis.

"We're trapped like rats on a sinking ship," Cairnes said nastily. "The only bright spot is a well-stocked bar. When we get it drunk up, I'd just as soon go to prison — the company will be better."

Grafton scrutinized each face. "Tell you what. If you three don't behave yourself and act civil to the ladies, I'm going to pour all that liquor and wine down the sink."

Cairnes pulled a revolver from his pocket and waved it around a little. "Just try it, sailor-boy." He replaced the revolver in his pocket and turned his attention back to his brandy snifter.

"How do we know," Smith called as he

added olives to a glass, "that one of those Petrou women won't poison us, like they did Jean Petrou?"

"And to think they volunteered to do the cooking," Jake said grimly. He headed for Winchester's private office to call Callie and the folks at Langley.

Khadr arrived that evening at JFK on a flight from Paris. Qasim was waiting outside the terminal when he wandered out pulling his suitcase. Qasim almost didn't spot him amid the throng of people queuing up for taxis and piling into waiting cars and limos. When he did, Khadr was looking around exactly like a tourist on his first visit to America, which this was. That might be a problem, Qasim thought.

Eventually Khadr joined the taxi line. Qasim didn't see anyone paying the least attention to him.

Finally Khadr's turn came and he climbed into a taxi, which went trundling off into the night and was soon lost amid a sea of taillights.

Qasim went back into the parking garage and rode the elevator to the fourth deck, where his borrowed car was parked. He was waiting outside Grand Central Station when Khadr came out of the south entrance precisely at 9:00 p.m. He pulled up and got out to open the trunk. Khadr put his suitcase in and climbed into the passenger seat, and away they rolled.

"Any problems?" Qasim asked.

"I hate air travel," Khadr said.

"Welcome to the United States."

"That is what the pilot or flight attendant said when we landed." Khadr flashed a mirthless grin. "That passport worked like a charm. They didn't even search my suitcase."

"Perhaps because they already searched it in Paris before you boarded the airplane."

"Perhaps," Khadr acknowledged.

"You saw the other suitcase in the trunk. We'll stop at a filling station when we get to Brooklyn. Put your clothes in it and leave yours in the men's room."

Khadr nodded his understanding.

Jake Grafton went outside after dark to check on his troops. He found Harry Longworth beside the barn sitting in a foxhole with a rifle wearing a nightscope cradled on his lap. Only the top of his head was aboveground. On the edge of the hole lay a handheld night vision device. He was wearing gloves, camouflage pants, coat and hat, and lined rubber boots. A slender boom mike ran from an ear to the vicinity of his mouth.

Grafton squatted beside the hole. "Comfortable?"

"Oh, you bet. Thirty or forty degrees warmer here than the Hindu Kush. This is like a vacation."

"I hope so. So tell me where your people are."

"Two sleeping. Nick and I are on watch. All four of us are on in the two hours after dawn and after dark. That's about the best we can do."

"You got food and water and all that?"

"Bottled water and MREs, sir. Poop in a hole. We can't risk a run to town or over to the main house."

"Isn't there a kitchen in that chauffeur's apartment over the garage?"

"Maybe. We don't want to be seen going in or out. Even at night."

"This should be my last time coming out."

"Okay."

"Those big windows in the other side of the house — someone with a rifle or grenade launcher could have a field day."

"Nick's over there in a hole in a big thicket, and we have some remote, wireless infrared sensors in the trees." He showed Grafton the vibrator in his pocket that would be activated by the sensors. "Last night some neighborhood dogs set it off twice. They run through here occasionally when the guy up the road lets them out for their evening constitutional. Watch where you walk on the grass. There are also a couple of cats in the barn, and they prowl at night, too, although they haven't yet set off a sensor."

"How about people moving around?"

"The guy who takes care of the horses comes every morning and works in the barn and corrals and piddles with the nags until he gets tired of it and goes home. Yesterday he was here for four hours, the day before five. The gardener won't be coming, Winchester said. And Winchester walks his collie on a leash morning and night."

"How about the meter man?"

"Here last week. Won't be back for a month, I'm told. Although Winchester gets his mail at the post office, the FedEx man has come every morning."

"Okay."

"I pulled the circuit breakers for the outside lights before I left the house. We've done everything that I can think of to do."

Jake thought about that for a moment. He couldn't think of any other precautions that these few men could take, either. Moving the people in the house to another location would present two sets of problems: guarding them wherever he moved them and keeping an ambush team here. Keeping them here was the low-manpower option.

"What freq are you guys on?" Jake asked.

Harry told him. Jake turned his radio to that frequency, donned his headset, adjusted the volume and squelch and said a couple of words.

"Loud and clear," Harry said. "Nick?"

"Got him."

"We'll only use these if something goes down," Harry cautioned, not using his radio. "The less we transmit, the better. If the assholes got their shit together, they got a scanner."

"You can figure that they do."

"I suspect so."

Jake looked around, listened to the night. He could hear distant traffic, and once, from a long way off, the moan of a train whistle. After a bit he said, "If you hear shots inside the house, it'll be me shooting the protectees."

"It's that bad, huh?"

"They're at each other's throats. Already. They may bolt, and unless I lash them to a bed or lock them in the basement, there isn't much I can do about it. We'll sit tight even if they run off. The villains may not know that they left, so something might happen anyway."

"What about telephone communication?"

"We're monitoring the landline. If they call someone they shouldn't, like the police to come and rescue them, we'll kill the circuit. We're also monitoring their cell phone calls, but I can't turn those off."

"Okay."

"Good luck, Harry."

"Thank you, sir," Longworth said. He watched Jake Grafton walk back to the house.

By a few minutes after 5:00 p.m. the light had faded from the sky. Normally, of course, the grounds of the estate would be lit by decorator and security lights, but thanks to Longworth, those were off. The high, thin overcast blocked out the stars, leaving the night beyond the windows totally black. In the distance the glow of a town could be seen on the horizon, but that was about it. The big black windows in the main room looked ominous, so immediately after dinner, which Grafton and Isolde Petrou prepared, the male protectees scurried off to their bedrooms, where they all drew the blinds and drapes.

Marisa stayed to help with the dishes.

When Jake had the dishwasher humming, she lingered, looking at the kitchen utensils, examining the hanging pots, scrutinizing the paintings on the wall. Grafton leaned back against the dishwasher and crossed his arms. When she again looked his way, a startled look crossed her face.

"Want to tell me about it?" he asked.

"About what?"

"I don't know. You look as if you might have something to tell me."

"No." Marisa shook her head. "No," she said, more definitely.

Grafton nodded, and she wandered out of the room.

He called his home, talked to Callie for a moment and asked to speak to Tommy.

When Carmellini got on the line, Grafton listed all the precautions that had been taken. "In light of all that, how would you get in?" he asked.

"If I suspected infrared detectors, I'd enter the grounds at night wearing a black thermal suit and take out the guards. Once they were out of the way, you people would be toast. Are the guys outside wearing thermal suits?"

"No. But they're in holes."

"Well . . . Your worst threat may already be in the house."

"Marisa? I gathered the impression last night that you thought she was a nice package."

"I meet the nicest people in my work," Carmellini said. "That's why I'm never going to retire."

Jake went to the door of the kitchen, looked to ensure no one was eavesdropping, then said, "Did you search her luggage last night while she was asleep, like I asked you?"

"Yeah. Found that cell phone the customs people told you about. She had it stuffed inside a shoe in your closet."

"You called in the number?"

"Right after you left."

Jake grunted, then forced himself to say good-bye.

He wandered through the hallways, listening to the muffled television audio coming from each room.

And he waited.

Dinner at the Graftons' was a somber affair. Good food, but the conversation dragged. Everyone was waiting for the bomb to blow or the gun to fire.

After dinner, I insisted on cleaning the kitchen. I was bored silly with sitting. Callie retired to her bedroom to read. As I packed the dishwasher and washed the pots and pans, I got to listen to Amy tell Robin Cloyd all about her boyfriend.

I couldn't find a clean dish towel and was wiping my hands on my trousers when Robin spoke up. "What on earth are you doing, Tommy?"

"Going crazy," I snarled.

Do the French still have the Foreign Legion? What's the upper age limit, anyway?

CHAPTER TWENTY

A shotgun is a bit of metal and a couple of pieces of wood, and not much else. The two Grafton left also had slings attached, so they could be carried by hanging them over a shoulder.

The eighteen-inch barrels had once been a bright, polished blue and were now pitted, scratched and, in the one I was holding on my lap, a bit rusty in three places. The receiver was shiny, with only traces of the original bluing. All in all, the Remington Model 870 Police shotgun in my lap looked like what it was, a utilitarian weapon that was lucky to get a wipe-down occasionally and an annual look from the agency armorer.

The raw winter day outside the window was overcast, breezy and promised rain. When I talked to Willie on our radio net early this morning, he was doing okay, he said. "Gettin' a taste of how the other half lives," he told me. "More people oughta give this a try."

"My next vacation," I said.

The radio earpiece was a tiny thing, about the size of an earplug. It fit completely inside the ear channel, so was invisible from any angle but directly abeam. Most people who saw it would assume it was a hearing aid. Mine fit fairly well, so after a while I forgot it was in there.

The three women spent the morning watching chick flicks in the den, and I spent it walking around the living room, sitting in a chair with my shotgun on my lap or lying on the couch with the darn thing on the floor beside me. The other shotgun — Robin's — was on the dining room table. She pumped all the shells out onto the carpet, pulled the trigger, made sure the safety worked, then loaded it again and left it there. Out in the living room I could hear the three of them laughing occasionally above the sound track.

Ah, me.

I couldn't get Marisa out of my mind. She appeared to be a victim of an evil man — and I could go either way on this — a daughter whom he loved, sort of, and wanted to use to help with the family crimes, or an innocent child that he had made a psychic prisoner with a lifetime of abuse so that he could use her someday, someway, for his own perverted ends.

On the other hand, she might be Qasim's loyal lieutenant, following orders, playing a role for us suckers. What if everything she told me, and presumably Grafton, was a lie?

She could have killed her husband. That would have been relatively easy.

It would have been more difficult, but she could have done Alexander Surkov. At Qasim's order, perhaps.

Why did she try to distract me in the Zetsche castle when I was whanging away at a fleeing villain? The villain turned out to be her mother-in-law's chauffeur, but *she didn't know that.* Or did she?

Why didn't I ask her when I had the chance?

Was I worried about the answer I might get?

And that knife in Zetsche — conceivably she could have put it there. Probably not, but perhaps.

I walked around Grafton's living room, peeked out the crack in the drapes occasionally and worried all these beads again and again.

When I got hungry I raided the fridge, made myself a sandwich and ate it at the dining room table. Washed it down with a bottle of water. Thought about Marisa as I ate.

If something didn't happen, and soon, I was going to lose it big-time. My future would be a straitjacket and a padded room.

Jake Grafton went to Huntington Winchester's private office and locked the door, then called his boss, William Wilkins, on his portable encrypted satellite telephone.

"Eighteen cell phone calls from that house in the last three days," Wilkins said with a sigh. "They're worse than a pack of teenage girls. No incoming calls. Apparently they keep their phones off when they aren't calling someone so that they can fool you. They do get a string of messages when they turn their phones on. All pretty innocuous, so far. If they have cell phones we don't know about, they may have made and received a few more calls. Got a pencil?"

"Yes, sir."

"Jerry Hay Smith made eight calls. He called four different women, if you can believe it — that ugly little runt. And he called his editor four times, told him he was being held prisoner by the CIA. Those were interesting conversations."

"The editor going to run it?"

"Not today or tomorrow. Smith told him to sit on it, but the editor is curious as hell."

"I'll bet."

"Cairnes talked to his wife once, his kids twice and his bank associates three times. Winchester called his company headquarters twice and his divorce lawyer once."

Jake was making notes. He added the numbers. "That's seventeen."

"Yeah. Saving the best for last, ol' Marisa called someone in Brooklyn, a male. Gave him your home address in Rosslyn and told him where you and she and Winchester and Isolde and all the rest are."

"Uh-huh," Jake said, making a little meaningless doodle on his notepad.

"The bitch sold you out, Jake."

"Looks that way."

"You knew she was going to do it, didn't you?"

"Kinda had a hunch. Didn't you?"

"We have the number and location of that cell phone she called, and a voiceprint of the man she talked to. The account is in the name of some guy who isn't in our database, an Iranian immigrant, we believe."

"Don't go after him," Jake said. "Qasim probably isn't there, and if he is, he'll boogie before you can spring the trap."

"The FBI is chomping at the bit. We're

flat running out of time. I've talked to Molina three times today, and he wants me to pull the rabbit out of the hat *now.* I'll keep you advised."

"Okay."

Jake hung up and continued to make designs on the notepad in front of him. Finally he tired of it and tore the top five sheets of paper off the pad, wadded them up and burned them in the fireplace. Then he went downstairs.

The whole crowd was seated around the fireplace in the living room. Conversation stopped when he appeared at the head of the stairs, and three or four of them glanced at him as he came down.

Looks like they're planning a mutiny, he thought. He headed for the kitchen to talk to the FBI agent who was doing the cooking.

"Tommy, we got a watcher."

Willie Varner's voice in my ear brought me wide awake. I had been dozing in a living room recliner. The women were in the kitchen going through cookbooks and hunting through the cupboard, so we were going to eat well during our incarceration. I looked at my watch. Five thirty in the evening.

"Tell me about him," I said to Willie as I got out of my chair and laid the shotgun on the couch.

"He's in an old Saturn, kinda dark blue or maybe black — hard to tell in this light. Been sittin' there for a half hour or so. He's alone in the car, parked across the street, just sittin' there watchin' the building and the street."

"What's he look like?"

"Can't tell. I'm in a doorway about fifty yards behind him. Can't see nothin' but the back of his head. Don't want to move. Don't want him to pick up on me."

"Just sit," I told him. "Watch for other people. There'll be somebody else along after a while. You got something to eat?"

"Oh, yeah. Had a pit stop a while back and got a sandwich. I'm fine."

"Thanks, Willie."

I went into the kitchen and watched the women plot their culinary triumph. When Robin glanced my way, I motioned toward the living room. She followed me.

When we were there I told her about the watcher. "I suspect there will be other folks along sooner or later, and when they come, I'll go down, sorta check them out. You sit in here with a shotgun."

"Why don't you let me go out and you

stay here?" She asked that innocently, with big eyes.

I knew the ice was thin. Charges of sexism were lurking nearby, but I didn't care. "Because I'm in charge," I said roughly.

"The admiral didn't tell me that."

"Call him and ask."

"No need to bother him," she replied coolly, and went back to the kitchen.

I looked at my watch again. Five thirty-six. I was clean out of patience; didn't have a scrap left. I went to the door and peered through the security viewer, just in case. The hallway was empty.

Okay, Willie. Keep your eyes peeled.

I got down on the floor and started doing push-ups.

An hour passed, then two. We finished dinner and were cleaning the dishes when Willie's voice sounded in my ear. "Car just went by, dropped off two guys."

"Uh-huh." Everyone in the kitchen looked at me as if I'd made an audible social faux pas. I tossed the dish towel on the counter and walked into the living room.

"They're medium-sized dudes," Willie said. "Wearin' jeans, dark hip-length coats, dark wool pullover hats. Skinny. They looked around casual-like, spotted the

Saturn. Both of them looked at it, even though they drove right by it when the car came up to drop 'em. Now they're walkin' down the alley behind the buildin'."

"Let me know if the Saturn guy moves."

I motioned to Robin, who was still in the kitchen but looking at me. She came into the living room.

"We're on," I said to her. I tossed on my coat, checked that my pistol was riding where I wanted it and told her, "Lock the door behind me."

She nodded.

If they came into the building through one of the basement doors, I wanted to be there before they went higher. The fewer people around if they started shooting, the better. On the other hand, they were going to have to do something seriously illegal before I started shooting. I didn't want to kill two local teenagers who were dabbling in burglary; after all, I'd done a little of that myself, way back when.

I checked the lights above the elevators. One was on the ninth floor and one was coming up, passing four. The two dudes couldn't be in the up elevator — not enough time. I jabbed the down button and waited.

The elevator ascending went by my floor, and the one above came down. The door opened. I stepped in and pushed the button for the lobby, the door closed, and down I went.

There was an old lady in the lobby, checking her mailbox. She was the only person there, besides me. Beyond the glass doors the street contained the usual traffic and the endless stream of pedestrians going to and from the Metro stop down the street. Every parking place on the street was full. The parking garage across the street and down about fifty yards was probably also approaching capacity. Although the sun had been down for an hour or two, the streetlights, car headlights and lit signs made a good deal of light out there.

I glanced at the floor lights above the elevators. There were only three ways up from the basement: the two elevators and the stairs. If the two men out back got into the building, they had to come up this way. I opened the door to the stairwell and stood listening. I felt sure I would hear the basement door open, if . . .

Although I had thought through about a dozen scenarios in the last twenty-four hours, I was playing this tune by ear. Stay loose and keep thinking, my instructors had said. Great advice but difficult to pull off.

"They're coming out of the alley," Willie

said into my earpiece. I clicked the button on my belt transmitter twice.

I saw them through the front windows of the lobby. They walked up to the entrance, looked in — I was busy trying to find a key on my ring that would fit a mailbox — and gave the keypad that unlocked the exterior door and intercom the once-over. After another glance into the lobby at me, they strolled away to my right, off toward the Metro stop. And the waiting car. And Willie.

"They're coming at you," I said into my mike.

"Got 'em. The guy in the Saturn just started his car . . . Yeah, looks like they're going to get in with him . . . Yep . . . That's what they did. Car coming your way."

An elevator door opened beside me. A man got out and walked toward the exit without bothering to acknowledge me. I ducked into the empty lift, out of sight of cars passing on the street.

"They're gone," Willie said.

"They'll be back. Midnight or later."

"I figure you're right," Willie said pleasantly. "They're just workin' up to something mean."

So how would they do it? They looked at the entrances, decided the police weren't waiting . . . Where should Robin and I be?

The elevator started beeping at me, so I punched the button for the eighth floor.

I went upstairs to brief the Graftons and my partner in crime, Robin Cloyd. I explained that an inspection of the premises before committing a crime aged quickly. The people who had looked this building over would be back fairly soon, or not at all. We needed to be ready. Callie nodded. Amy looked brave . . . and pensive.

Robin removed her pistol from her purse and checked it as I talked. When I fell silent she asked, "Are they suiciders?"

"I don't know."

I handed her a headset. "Hopefully Willie will see them and give us a minute or so warning. I want you to stay in the corridor outside. I'm going to be downstairs. I'll disable the elevators. The only way up will be the stairwell. If you hear shots, you'll know they're bad guys. I'm going to wedge the stairwell door shut, so they'll have to blow it or do some serious pounding to get it open. Be lying here by the Graftons' door. If anyone comes out of the stairwell, use the shotgun on them. We want them dead or incapacitated quickly, just in case they're bombers."

"Okay."

I looked at Mrs. Grafton. "If you hear shots, call the police on the landline."

She nodded.

I looked at Amy. "If the phone goes out, be ready to call the police on your cell phone."

She bobbed her head once, vigorously.

I looked straight into Amy's eyes and said, "You could leave right now, you know. There really isn't any reason for you to stay. This is Robin's and my job. *This* is what *we* do — you teach elementary school."

"What about the other people in the building?" Amy asked.

"We can't knock on doors and ask them to leave. The object is to catch or kill terrorists. If the building is dark and empty, they won't come."

"I'll stay," Amy said.

Callie put her arm around her. They were Graftons, all right.

I told Robin, "Give Callie your pistol. You'll have the shotgun and extra shells. Keep shooting until they don't even twitch."

"Okay." Matter-of-fact. No sweat.

Say what you will about her hair and ditzy manner, Robin was kind of a class act. I was finding I liked her.

"This terrorist, Abu Qasim — tell me about

him," Huntington Winchester said to Jake Grafton. They were seated at the bar in the main room, and they were alone. Winchester was nursing a glass of old Scotch, and Grafton was working on a beer.

"Not much to tell," Jake said. "Most of what we know is hearsay, picked up on the streets in dribs and drabs."

"Maybe he's a myth."

"He's real, all right. Real as a heart attack." Grafton sipped at his beer. "The world is a far different place than it was on Labor Day 2001. Security is a lot tighter, more assets are devoted to it, everyone in law enforcement and intelligence takes it seriously, so it's not as easy to be a terrorist these days as it was then. Sure, screwball amateurs can always pull off a spectacular atrocity, murder some innocent people and die doing it. But there are only a few terrorists competent and capable enough, with the necessary network, to really do something that would hurt Western civilization. Abu Qasim is one of them. He's a damned dangerous man."

"There aren't many men, good or bad, who can make a difference," Winchester mused.

"That's not really true," Grafton said. "I was just getting started in the Navy when I learned that every single person who makes a stand makes a difference. How you live, what you believe, what you do — it all matters. Results are important, too, but the critical factor, the most important thing, is making a stand, which is why we have to fight the Abu Qasims."

"You see, when I weigh my life," Winchester said, "and my son Owen's, his was the more important. I've built a company, made a lot of money, but if I hadn't made oil field equipment someone else would have. Owen, on the other hand, set forth to save lives. He gave all he had doing it."

"Don't be so hard on yourself," Jake Grafton said. "You raised a fine son, which is more than many of us manage. And you took a stand when you signed on to this goat rope. With a little luck, your stand will pay off."

"Umm." Winchester sipped at his drink. "How will you know which one of these guys you think is coming is Qasim?"

"I'll know."

"How?"

"Marisa will tell me."

"How will she know?"

Jake's cell phone, which was lying on the bar, rang. He glanced at the number. "Ask her," he said to Winchester, then answered the phone.

"Hello, Tommy."

When I had finished briefing Grafton, he said, "I want the guy in the Saturn, too. Alive, if possible. In fact, get him first."

I took a deep breath. "There are no parking places on the street, as you well know. He'll probably pull up and the bad guys will pile out. If they're suiciders, he'll just drive away, leaving them."

"I understand," Grafton murmured.

"I can't just shoot him right then. These may not be bad guys. And if they are and I gun him, I'm going to be in a shoot-out with three or four armed men right on the street. I can't get 'em all before they get me."

"Use your best judgment."

"I'll try."

"After you pop him, or when he drives away, have Willie call 911."

"Yes, sir."

"Call me when it's over."

"Yes, sir."

We hung up then, and fifteen seconds later, I heard Callie's cell phone in the kitchen ring. It was undoubtedly her husband.

I tested my radio with Willie and Robin, then grabbed four wedges and my hammer and headed for the stairwell. Robin went out into the hallway, and Amy bolted the door behind her.

In the stairwell I hammered home four wedges under the door to the eighth floor, then two in the gap between the top of the door and the upper jamb. There wasn't room in the little vertical gap for a wedge. I figured they would blow the lock with some kind of explosive, unless they were willing to take the time to break the lock, pick it or remove the door from its hinges. Even if they blew the lock off with a charge of plastique, the door wasn't going to open with the wedges jamming it. I hoped. When and if they did get through, Robin was going to be in the hall with the 12-gauge. Meanwhile I was going to be coming up the stairs behind them.

I climbed a flight of stairs and left the hammer there.

I had thought about wedging every door in the stairwell shut, but the risk was too great. If these guys were bombers and a fire started, everyone in the building would be trapped.

I was trotting down the stairs with my shotgun in hand when the fourth-floor door opened and an elderly gentleman poked an old revolver at me. "Who the hell are you?"

he demanded.

"Uh, Tommy Carmellini, sir. I'm staying with Jake Grafton on the eighth floor. You probably know him — a retired admiral? And who are you?"

He was suspicious, but I looked clean-cut and wholesome. "Fred Colucci. I heard someone pounding and came to see. Don't want no trouble. What you got that gun for?"

"I heard the pounding and came to investigate. Would you please stop pointing that pistol at me?"

He lowered the revolver. Slowly, waiting for me to do something dumb.

"Thanks," I said and trotted on down the stairs.

"Four-B," Colucci called. "Stop by and tell me what that pounding was. I'm gonna call the Homeowners. Too much damn noise in this building."

"Okay," I called, and kept going.

I paused at the bottom of the stairwell and stuck the shotgun under my coat. Got my pistol out and put it in my right trouser pocket where I could get at it easily. The spare magazine was already in my left trouser pocket.

I stepped out onto the ground level, the basement. The elevator control box was mounted right there on the wall beside the garbage cans. It was locked, but I managed to open it with a pick in approximately thirty seconds. The elevator power switches were big and obvious.

"Hey, Willie, can you hear me?"

He answered in about four seconds. "Yeah."

"I need to know the instant you see them."

"They'll probably drive by a few times, man, before they pull the trigger. No parking places out here."

"Keep me advised."

"Okay."

"Robin?"

"Yes, Tommy."

"They blow that door to get onto your floor, have your mouth open and ears covered."

"I'll manage, Carmellini. You handle your end."

Willie chuckled into his mike.

The super had a little folding chair at his desk. I put the shotgun on the desk and parked my heinie in his chair. I waited.

"I'm leaving, Grafton," Simon Cairnes said to the admiral. "I've called for my car."

"Okay."

Cairnes was standing by the bar, leaning ever so slightly on his cane. He looked a little startled at Jake's answer. "What?" he said. "No comment about it's my funeral?"

Jake shrugged. "I'll send flowers. See you on the other side."

"You nervy son of a bitch," Cairnes growled and turned to go. He shot a glance at Winchester, who was descending the stairs. "Don't ever call me again, Hunt. Not for any reason under the sun."

Then he was gone along the hallway toward the front door.

Winchester came the rest of the way down the stairs and parked himself on a bar stool beside Grafton.

"She's Qasim's daughter."

"Maybe."

"Damnation, Grafton! He'll come here to get her."

"No," Jake said with a sigh. "If he comes, he'll be coming to get you."

"And you, I figure."

"More than likely," Grafton muttered and keyed the radio on his belt. "Car will be coming to pick up Cairnes."

He received two mike clicks in reply.

It was a quarter past eleven in the evening when Willie's voice sounded in my ear. "It's the Saturn. He's slowin', drivin' by, four in the car maybe . . . maybe five. On past and down the hill toward the subway stop."

"Got it," I said. I grabbed the shotgun and strode for the elevator power box. Fortunately neither elevator was moving just then, so no one was going to be trapped between floors when I killed the power. One was on the lobby level, the other on nine. I hit the switches to turn off the power, closed the door to the box, then turned off the basement lights and ran up the stairs to the lobby.

"Here they come again, comin' slowly." Willie was excited. For that matter, so was I.

I shot out the main.door and threw myself on my back behind a bush, holding the shotgun in front of me.

This position was terrible, and I was a fool to be here — but Grafton wanted the wheelman, and I had to be outside to get him.

"Still rollin' . . . rollin' . . . goin' on by."

I was so keyed up that I almost collapsed when he said that. I lay there frozen, looking up at the side of the building, the little balconies sticking out, the lit windows . . . Just then I had the oddest thought, wondered what someone up there would do if he or she saw me lying here.

"He's acceleratin', goin' on up the street. Be right back, I figure. And Tommy, there's five heads in there."

"Got it."

"Robin copies."

I got up, took off my coat and wrapped it around the shotgun, then crossed the street. There was an office building entrance there right off the sidewalk, two steps up to the door. The sign out front said the thing was full of doctors' offices. They were all gone for the night — not a light showed.

I sat on the steps and leaned sideways, as if I were about to pass out, with the shotgun on my lap.

The waiting was getting more and more difficult. I kept watching the street toward the subway stop to my left. They would come from that direction, I suspected; just turn around and come straight back. On the other hand, maybe they would go around the block. I forced myself to look in the other direction, too.

No pedestrians this time of night. The good folks were all home in bed.

When I looked at my watch I was surprised to find that only three minutes had passed.

Here came a set of headlights, up from the subway stop. The driver was moving right along.

"It's them," Willie said.

The driver turned into the alley that ran behind Grafton's building, and four men piled out. They ran off down the alley. The car's backup lights illuminated. They were suiciders. Oh, Lord!

I tore the coat off the gun, sprinted toward the car. The driver never saw me coming. He backed into the street and stopped. As he shifted gears I jerked open the passenger door and dove into the car. He put it in motion. I reached for the keys, turned off the ignition. Couldn't get the keys out one-handed, so I didn't try.

He decided I was his biggest problem, so he hit me. Hit me with surprising force, considering that he was seated and belted in. He was scared, pumped with adrenaline. So was I.

I got my knees under me and elbowed him in the face as hard as I could. He was still struggling, so I did it again and again and again. Until he went limp.

I patted him down as fast as I could. No weapon. I jammed the transmission into park and removed the keys from the ignition. Took the keys with me.

Ran into the building and listened at the stairwell door. Maybe a minute had passed since the four guys ran down the alley.

"You want me to call the cops, Tommy?"

That was Willie.

"Not yet. First shot."

I figured they would just use a pipe wrench on that personnel door, so was surprised when I heard a muffled thud. The idiots had blown the knob.

If they had any sense they would ignore the elevators. If they didn't, they would try the elevators first, and when they didn't work, come up the stairs. Either way, they were using the stairs.

I waited, my ear against the door.

And heard their feet pounding on the steel stairs.

I waited, tense as a spring.

With his cell phone in his hand and his coat collar pulled up around his ears, Willie Varner was seated on a stoop beside a leafless bush about a hundred feet north of the Saturn, which sat nosed into the curb, blocking half of one lane of traffic. Not that there was much traffic. Just one car passed after Tommy ran into Grafton's building.

Willie looked around carefully. If there were any more terrorists around, his job was to tell Tommy about it. He didn't see anyone.

Now the guy behind the wheel of the Saturn stirred. Willie saw his head move.

Then the driver's door opened and he tried to get out. Ended up falling. Picked himself up slowly and leaned against the car with his head against his arm.

Willie adjusted his baseball cap and scanned up and down the street.

I heard them running in the stairwell, their feet pounding on the steel steps. They came up from the basement and charged by the lobby door and kept going up.

When the last one seemed to be above me, I eased the door open. They disappeared around the upper landing and kept climbing.

I started up two stairs at a time, as close to the outside wall as I could get, the shotgun ready and the safety off. The rumble of their feet filled the stairwell.

As we passed the third-floor door, I had closed the gap. I saw legs between the steps on the flight above me. I used the shotgun. One shot. Two. The reports were like cannon shots in that concrete box.

Two men fell, screaming. I kept climbing. One was down, lying on the stairs, so I gunned him. He took the ounce and a quarter of buck in the back. I kept going, worked the slide, and let the second one have it in the gut. Blood erupted; he crumpled and lay still.

A bullet spanged off the steel beside me.

I paused to shove more shells into the magazine.

Another shot, this time from higher up. He was still climbing, shooting to discourage me.

I stepped over the corpses and kept climbing, looking up for feet to shoot at.

The guy stopped climbing, fired off four shots. He aimed them at the walls so the bullets ricocheted. One of them kissed me on the top of the shoulder. The damn thing burned and I almost dropped the shotgun. Held on to it and aimed for the wall, gave him a load of buckshot, just to see if I could bounce some his way.

He fired again, so I adjusted my aim and gave him another ounce and a quarter of lead.

Someone was screaming in my ears. ". . . are coming!"

I kept going, got a glimpse of a foot and shot at it. Hit it, too. A shout, and a groan. He emptied his pistol into the wall, trying to hit me with a ricochet.

While all this was going on, I shoved the last of my shells into the Remington. I had lost count of how many were in there, and my pocket was empty.

This guy must have fired seven or eight shots into the walls. I figured he had one of those thirteen-shot magazines. When the shooting stopped, I heard him sob, so I ran upward. He was lying on the landing against the concrete wall, the stump of his foot covered with blood, blood on his face, trying to get another magazine into his pistol.

I took careful aim and shot him square in the face. That close, his head exploded.

Working the slide, I eased up the stairs to the fifth-floor landing.

Keeping against the wall as much as possible, I kept going, carefully. You won't believe how careful I went up.

Heard an explosion, not muffled. He had blown the lock on the eighth-floor door. Now I heard him grunting, trying to get it open.

I kept going, the shotgun up, looking for . . .

A shot, and simultaneously a bullet hit the wall right above my shoulder. Reflexively I jerked off a shot and jacked the slide.

Pounding feet. He had given up on the door and was climbing!

I went up, too.

Then three shots, trip-hammer fast. A moment later, the sound of a door swinging shut.

I ran, knowing full well he might still be in the stairwell and waiting for me.

He wasn't. He had shot the lock of the ninth-floor door until it gave, then run out.

So he was out in the hallway waiting for me . . . or trying to get into an apartment to take hostages.

I eased the action of the shotgun open until I saw brass, then looked into the magazine well. Saw the head of a shell. So I had at least two left.

I took a deep breath, jerked the door open and looked right, then left.

Empty both ways.

Stepped carefully out. Saw the open elevator door. Oh, yes, one of them was here when I killed the power. Heard noises.

Eased my head around to see as slowly as humanly possible, every nerve ready to go.

He had gone out the emergency door in the top. A hole gaped in the overhead.

I looked up into the black void.

He was up there somewhere, that was certain.

With the cops notified, Willie Varner watched the man by the Saturn. His head was up now, and he looked at the building. He, too, must hear the muffled shots from inside the building, as if they were fired from a long distance away.

He got behind the wheel of his car and groped for the key. Willie knew what he was doing even though he couldn't really see him do it. Tommy would have taken the key, of course.

Now the man got out of the car, looked again at the building and began walking quickly this way. Now he broke into a trot.

Somewhere a siren moaned.

The man's gait became a run. He was going north, downhill toward the Metro station.

Willie timed his rush perfectly. He charged from the stoop, sprinted across the street and slammed into the running man, who apparently didn't even see him coming, or, if he did, didn't react quickly enough to change course or get out of the way.

Both men went to the sidewalk. Willie was up first, probably because he was more frightened. He thought the man might have a gun, and he knew damn well he didn't. So he grabbed the man and slammed his head into the sidewalk. The man passed out.

Lacking any better ideas, I fired the shotgun up into the emergency exit in the roof of the elevator car . . . and heard the buckshot raining down the shaft as I worked the action.

Stepped sideways and aimed for the ceiling and fired again. Blew a hole in the top, then listened to the rain of shot.

Aimed again and pulled the trigger. Click. The Remington was empty.

I dropped it, then leaped for the hole and got the edges. Pulled myself up. Got an elbow through and then my head. Kept waiting for the bullet that he would fire when light from the elevator car stopped coming through the hole.

The shot didn't come, so I knew he was below me. There had to be a ladder in the shaft.

Sure enough, when I got onto the top of the car and waited a moment for my eyes to adjust, I saw the gleam of light reflecting off the ladder rungs. The ladder was on the steel supports between the cars.

I looked over the edge as I pulled out Grafton's Colt. Dark as the pit of hell, but he was there, and I doubted if he had made it all the way down. One way to find out.

I thumbed off the safety and pointed the pistol down the ladder and let 'er rip. The flashes blinded me. Emptied the entire seven-shot magazine, then pulled back and fished the other one from my pocket as I listened to something soft smack into something hard.

Heard a soft groan, then nothing.

I stood there a moment listening to my heart gallop. Heard the wail of a police siren. Two of them.

Decided to take a chance. Got my penlight from my pocket, held it as far from my head as possible, turned it on and pointed the beam down the shaft.

Took a moment for my eyes to adjust; then I saw him. He was lying on the top of the elevator car that was on the lobby level, all sprawled out on his back.

Holding the light as steady as possible, I held the pistol at arm's length, pointed down, aimed as carefully as I could in that light and let him have another. The report was deafening. A second or two later, from far below, came the tinkle of the spent shell as it bounced off steel.

Of course, I had no idea if I'd hit him. I shot twice more because I'm a mean bastard, then gave up.

I turned off the penlight and sat down on top of the car. A little light shone up through the square emergency exit and the little round hole I had blasted. I used it to ensure the pistol's safety was engaged.

"Cops are going in the front door,"

Willie said.

I fumbled for the transmit button on the radio on my belt, found it and pushed it in. "Dudes are all dead, I think. Willie, tell the cops that the power to the elevators is off and three corpses are in the stairwell. Another one is on top of the elevator at the lobby level. Robin, tell Callie to call Jake Grafton."

CHAPTER
TWENTY-ONE

In the United States, shooting someone is a really big deal, so before very long, the building was packed with cops, FBI agents and — ten minutes after the others arrived — Secret Service agents. Some of them wore uniforms, most didn't, but they all had guns and badges and little radios and lots of questions.

Five of them ended up firing questions at me at the super's desk in the basement while someone got the elevators back in service and lab techs worked on the basement door, which had had the lock blown off.

A guy who looked like a paramedic helped me get my shirt off and slapped some disinfectant and a small bandage on top of my left shoulder. He did this while I answered questions. He even helped me get my shirt back on, then nodded at me and departed.

I kept my answers brief and to the point, explaining the how, when and where, and leaving the what and why to Jake Grafton. The five interrogators expected me to tell them more, a lot more, but I refused, which they took as a professional insult. Too bad. Finally, I was putting my Stanford legal education to good use.

An hour into this my Big Boss, William Wilkins, showed up. "Enough," he said. It would have been interesting to see if indeed Wilkins could single-handedly stop the train, but he didn't have to. The FBI director showed up, and my interrogation was indeed over.

With the brass watching, I reached over and picked up Grafton's 1911 Colt and put it in my pocket. Picked up the agency shotgun, too, even though I had no more shells for it. Robin had some for hers, so maybe we could share. The police captain thought he would say something, then decided he wouldn't.

Leaving the big bananas to confer with the police, I climbed the stairs to the lobby and strolled to the door of the building. A media circus was going on outside. A couple of television crews had set up shop, complete with lights and trucks, and helicopters with spotlights circled overhead. Spectators crowded the sidewalks and stood upstairs on balconies to watch as the police carried out the bodies one by one and sent them off to the morgue in ambulances.

Of course, I was interested in the guy who drove the Saturn. Some cop told me Willie had laid him out and was sitting on him when the police showed up. He was downtown being booked for felony murder, conspiracy and driving a stolen car, among other things. They dusted the Saturn for fingerprints, scraped mud from the fender wells and finally hauled it away to the FBI lab for a real going-over.

Squinting against the lights, I could see someone — it looked like Fred Colucci — talking to a television reporter. Not wanting to suffer through fifteen minutes of fame, I went upstairs to the Graftons' condo. I rode up in the elevator with the holes in the ceiling. The other one was still out of service as they photographed and bagged the guy on top of it.

Willie was sitting on the couch telling Callie, Robin and Amy about his exploits while some female reporter on television gave them the hot scoop from the sidewalk in front of the building. The whole scene was more than a little weird. I waved to them on my way to the kitchen, where I poured myself a very healthy drink of Wild Turkey from Grafton's liquor cabinet. I added an ice cube, then began sipping on it.

Callie came in, took the drink from my hand and kissed me on the cheek. Then she handed me back the drink, looked me in the eyes and said, "Thank you, Tommy."

I nodded, trying to hold back the tears.

My cell phone rang. It was Jake Grafton.

"Maybe I'd better talk to him in the bathroom," I said, and I went, taking my drink with me.

"It didn't go well," Khadr remarked to Abu Qasim, quite unnecessarily. They were watching CNN Headline News in Qasim's hotel room in Greenwich, Connecticut. Khadr had a room on the floor below. "I didn't know he was going to deliver the warriors," Khadr added.

"Neither did I." Qasim took a deep breath and let it out through his nose as he watched the camera pan across Grafton's building. "It was always a long shot," he murmured. "Jake Grafton is competent."

"As is Carmellini," Khadr admitted. "Al-Irani less so. Will he break under interrogation?"

"He knows nothing important." Qasim

529

used the remote to turn off the television. He had advised al-Irani to blow up Grafton's building, but the Iranian objected. He lacked sufficient explosives, there was not enough glory in such a deed, and, finally, the real reason, the warriors wanted to enter Paradise with the blood of infidels on their hands. They wished to attack, to kill face-to-face. Qasim saw that he could not persuade al-Irani, so he stopped trying. "We all must serve Allah as we see best," he admitted, which satisfied the Iranian.

Tonight he tried to forget what might have been. "Tomorrow we will drive to Winchester's estate and look it over," he said to Khadr. "It will be guarded by professionals every bit as good as Carmellini. They may have sensors deployed, and dogs. I want Winchester and Grafton."

Khadr stood and adjusted his trousers. "We will see," he said noncommittally.

Qasim made eye contact. Khadr had no intention of trying the impossible; Qasim liked that. He wanted success, not glorious futile attempts.

"Indeed," Qasim said. He nodded.

When he finally got off the telephone after talking to Callie, Tommy, his various bosses and Sal Molina, Jake Grafton went downstairs. Winchester, Smith, Marisa and Isolde were watching a television news show, which was airing an interview with a "terrorism expert." The FBI had labeled the deceased and the lone survivor as armed terrorists making an attack on the family of a high-ranking government employee, whom they refused to identify. The reporters were frantic; even though it was two hours past midnight, they obtained a list of the building's residents from someone, who of course refused to be identified. The "expert" on camera was consulting the list and making guesses.

Winchester used the remote to lower the volume as Jake went behind the bar to fix himself a drink.

"My telephone doesn't work, Grafton," Jerry Hay Smith said aggressively. "Neither does the landline or anyone else's cell. Want to tell us about it?"

"About what?"

"About why you turned off the telephones."

"I intend to get some sleep tonight and didn't want to be interrupted by people reading me transcripts or playing recordings of your conversations. I know I could tell them to wait until tomorrow to call me, but I thought, if Smith makes his calls tomorrow, maybe they can all go home tonight and get a decent night's sleep."

"You bastard!"

"You want to go home and make your calls, you know where the door is. We'll lock it behind you."

"When this is over . . ." Smith whined, trying to sound ominous. It was a lost cause.

"I know," Grafton muttered.

Jake brought his drink around and sat down beside Isolde. "How is Callie?" she asked, as if Jerry Hay Smith weren't even there.

"Doing as well as can be expected, under the circumstances. She and Amy are coming tomorrow to visit with us for a few days."

"They didn't get Abu Qasim, did they?" Winchester asked.

Grafton shook his head no.

"He might be here tomorrow, too."

"Or tonight. Or never."

"Or he might be over at Cairnes' house butchering him slowly," Jerry Hay Smith said.

"Good point," Grafton said cheerfully. "Or he might have finished up with Mr. Cairnes and be waiting at your house for you to come home. One never knows."

Smith stomped off, climbed the stairs and

headed down the hall toward his bedroom.

"I think it's time for me to retire also," Isolde announced. She smiled at Jake and Winchester, glanced at Marisa and followed Smith.

Winchester finished his drink, then followed the others.

When only Jake and Marisa were left, Jake said, "Will he come here?"

"I don't know," she said thoughtfully. "I suspect he'll send Khadr."

"Still think he'll try to kill the president?"

"Him, you, these others. The movement needs victories."

"And martyrs," Jake said, frowning into his drink.

"Those, too," she said harshly. "The blood of martyrs is like perfume to Allah. It pleases and delights Him almost as much as the blood of infidels." She rose and ascended the stairs.

"If you love me, die for me," Jake muttered.

By nine the next morning we were rolling north up the interstate in Grafton's SUV. I drove, and the women gabbled around me. Last night, before he went home, Willie and I had a few minutes alone. I thanked him for everything, including taking down the

Saturn driver.

"Some cop tol' me he's an Iranian from Brooklyn," Willie said. "I was hopin' it was that Qasim dude, then I'd be a hero and get famous and meet hot women."

"Next time."

"You always say that, but there'd better not be a next time, Tommy. I'm too cold and too old, and that wine made me 'bout half sick. Had to nip at it, you understand, just to keep up appearances."

"Right."

After the women wound down and toddled off to bed about three, I tried to sleep on Grafton's couch. The forensic guys were going to be working downstairs all night, but just in case, I had loaded my shotgun with Robin's spare shells.

I had just gotten arranged on the couch when Grafton's phone rang. I picked it up. Some enterprising television producer had obtained Grafton's unlisted number. I rudely hung up on her, and then went into the kitchen and took the phone there off the hook. That way the beeping wouldn't disturb me.

Back on the couch, I finally wound down and drifted off about four in the morning. Robin was up making coffee at five, waking me.

"Hey," she said. "Didn't mean to wake you."

"That's all right."

"Want some coffee?"

"Please. Black."

She brought me a cup. I sat up to drink it. "Thanks."

She settled into the nearest chair and sipped at her cup of joe. Her hair was sticking out in every direction. I also noticed that she had a nice set of legs. "This isn't going to become a regular thing," she informed me as she tightened her robe around her.

"You mean coffee in bed in the morning?"

"Don't want you to have any unrealistic expectations."

"I'll try to keep myself under control."

I don't think Robin had slept a wink, because she went to sleep in the back of the SUV as we rolled through New Jersey. Rain began falling from a featureless slate sky. At first it was just a sprinkle; then it became steady. When she woke up, I pulled over and we ran around the car, dashing through the drops, changing places. She hadn't even gotten up to highway speed before I was asleep.

They were sitting in a rental car on a

highway pull-off, a half mile from Winchester's mansion. Just across the fence, horses grazed on hay strewn about a pasture. Khadr studied the mansion and barn with binoculars. A gentle rain was falling. The windshield wipers worked in slow rhythm.

"You can assume that there are armed guards," Abu Qasim said.

Khadr did not reply. He was studying the trees that surrounded the house, which obscured most of it. He could see a few windows and the roofline, but little else.

"And the weather?"

"A storm is coming. The weather forecasters predict that the rain will get heavier, the wind will rise significantly, and about 3:00 a.m. the rain will turn to snow."

"Once the snow begins, the guards will relax."

"What do you know of snow?"

Khadr pondered his answer but didn't lower the binoculars. Telling clients about past hits was foolish; the information was a weapon they could use to try to save themselves if they were ever arrested and interrogated. Not Abu Qasim, though; saving himself wasn't on his agenda. Khadr said, "I once did a job in Russia. It was winter."

After another minute he lowered the

binoculars. "We have sat here long enough," he said.

Abu Qasim started the car and steered it back onto the highway.

"So what do you think?"

"I think there is a place on the next hill with another view of the house. Drive over there."

Qasim pressed. "Can it be done?"

"The risk is great. One must assume armed guards, an unknown number, and infrared and motion detectors. Some of the guards will be outside, some inside. Once I evade the outside guards, I must somehow enter the house, remain undetected, make my kills, then escape. It is a great undertaking."

"That it is."

"Your friends would undertake it for the glory. I will not."

"Twice your usual fee?"

Khadr glanced at Qasim.

"This is the last job I need you to do," Qasim said.

Khadr still said nothing. He was watching the road and looking over Winchester's estate as the car rolled along.

"You are worried, perhaps," Qasim mused, "that I will kill you instead of paying you."

"Not really," the killer replied.

"A payment in advance, perhaps? Wired to your bank in Switzerland."

"There is not enough time. It must be done tonight during the storm or not at all."

"What do you suggest?"

"I am safe from my clients only because they know that I will not blackmail them, nor will I demand more than the agreed fee; and should they fail to pay the agreed fee once it has been earned, I will kill them. I have had little monetary disputes with several clients in the past after I have done the job I was hired for, and those clients are now resting on Allah's bosom. Or the Devil's. Whichever makes you comfortable. In your case, however, the usual safeguards are unnecessary. You don't care if I get caught and tell everything. If I told everything to the press it would only add to your legend and standing with the jihadists. You will pay for results and accept no excuses. If I try to blackmail you, you will laugh."

Qasim remained silent.

"I kill because I am paid for it," Khadir said. "A crime, a sin, whatever, I do it for money, like a whore. You buy murder because you hate. I leave it to your Allah to judge between us as to who is the evil man."

When I awoke, Robin had a weather report

on the radio from a New York City station. A big nor'easter was moving in. Going to be lots of rain and wind and maybe even snow. She must have seen me stir, because she glanced over her shoulder at me. "You want to drive?"

"I can drive," Callie said.

"Let Mrs. Grafton do the honors," I said. Truthfully, I was awake but very tired.

It only took another hour for us to get to Winchester's estate. Fortunately I remembered how to get there and gave directions from the back seat.

Someone came out and held an umbrella as we got the car unloaded.

Jake Grafton was there. He escorted the women inside. I stayed on the porch, which wasn't large, watching the rain. The porch was sort of out of the wind, which was about fifteen miles per hour, I estimated, gusting higher. The rain was steady, but not too heavy as yet. I leaned the shotgun against the wall within easy reach.

When Grafton came back outside to talk about the mess in Rosslyn, I went over it shot by shot, then told him about the interrogation, everything important that I could recall.

"You did well, Tommy," he said.

I didn't feel very pumped. There were

bodies scattered all over Europe because I hadn't been quick enough.

Grafton briefed me on the security, told me where the holes were and who was in them, and gave me an extra radio earpiece, so I could listen to any transmissions he or the guys outside made.

"I've still got your Colt," I told him. "Robin has the other shotgun."

He nodded.

"You didn't tell me she was a former Marine."

He gave me a little grin and said, "There's liquor at the bar, and beer, if you want it. Dinner in about an hour." Then he went back inside. I stayed on the porch watching the rivulets on the pavement, thinking about things.

Actually I was thinking about Marisa. She was inside, of course, and I wanted to see her, yet I didn't. So I started going over it again, everything, trying to figure out who she was and what she believed. After a while I gave up. The truth was beyond me.

The night got awfully dark, and the rain kept falling. After a while Robin came out, handed me a drink and said dinner was on.

Marisa glanced at me when I came into the dining room. The dog was lying beside

Winchester's chair and stayed there. I had ditched my coat and shotgun on a chair in the living room. I seated myself across the table from her and down a seat. I looked around, found out who was there and who wasn't and nodded at the two FBI agents who were cooking and standing inside guard duty when Grafton pronounced names. It must have been a nice break for them from chasing bank robbers and doing security investigations.

Winchester was at the head of the table, talking about his son, Owen, who I knew had been killed in Iraq. Grafton sat on one side of him and Isolde Petrou on the other. Isolde and Winchester were soon in deep conversation about what else needed to be done by banks, business and industry to help governments fight terrorism.

When I looked at Marisa, I found she was looking at me. She maintained eye contact, and only looked away when Amy asked her a question. She looked like the calmest person at the table. Of course, I wondered why. The possibility that she knew what was going to happen next reared its ugly head.

Grafton looked pretty calm, cool and collected, too, I noticed, but then, he always did. If they announced World War III and told him to lead the charge, he would still look exactly the same, still the Jake Grafton you always knew. Knowing him as I did, I thought he had a good idea what Qasim's next move might be — maybe he had even played for it — but of course he couldn't *know*.

Me? — I knew the bastard had murder on his mind. I was absolutely certain of that. The only thing I didn't know was where and when and how.

Gonna find out, though. Sure as shootin'.

And I wasn't calm. My stomach was doing flips; eating was the very last thing I thought I could handle. I poured some more of Winchester's whiskey down there to settle things a little, but my appetite didn't improve. I played with the salad, stirred it around, munched a piece of tomato. When I looked up, there was Marisa, watching me with those big brown eyes.

I looked at Robin Cloyd and found she was looking at me with a curious expression on her face. I didn't have time to figure that out — Marisa was watching Grafton now. I tried to read her face and failed. It was like trying to decipher the Mona Lisa.

I gave up and went into the kitchen to see if the feds needed any help with the veggies or squashed potatoes or roast beast. Plates needed to be carried, they said. I began shuttling them to the table.

"Really getting nasty out there," one of them said when I came back for the last two plates. I had almost forgotten. I looked at the rain hammering the window. Lord, it had turned to sleet! No wonder it was so loud.

"Glad I'm inside and not out in one of those holes," the other guy said.

I took the plates in, set them down, then came back to the kitchen. The agents were settling down on stools at the counter with their own plates. I joined them and grunted at appropriate points in the conversation. Mainly, though, I listened to the wind and the sleet rattling on the glass.

I played with the food a while — I really wasn't hungry — and pushed the plate back. Grafton came in shortly thereafter. "Great dinner, gents," he said to the agents, who were still working on theirs.

He stood at the window looking at the sleet striking the outside windowpane, then came over to where I sat.

"If you were Khadr . . . ?"

"Tonight," I said.

"I think so, too," he murmured, then paused to listen carefully as a gust pounded the sleet against the window. The sleet was basically soft hail.

After nodding to the other guys and saying something else nice about the grub, he went back to the dining room.

CHAPTER
TWENTY-TWO

When I had hidden in the kitchen for as long as my conscience, and good sense, would allow, I went back into the dining room. Everyone was gone. I got busy bussing the table, and the FBI types helped. As they worked, they talked shop gossip; I tried not to pay attention but found myself listening anyway. I was reminded that everyone has problems. They also weren't happy that they were at Winchester's doing what they thought was manual labor when they were highly trained, professional crime solvers.

When that job was done they made themselves coffee and got deeper into FBI internal politics. It was a few minutes after nine o'clock.

I checked that my earpiece was in tight and my belt radio was on, then wandered into the living room. Everyone was there except Marisa. Jake Grafton, Huntington Winchester, Isolde Petrou and Robin Cloyd were into the war on terror, while Jerry Hay Smith sat silently, probably secretly recording their remarks for a future column. Callie and Amy were huddled by the piano with their heads close together, probably talking mother-daughter stuff. After all, Amy had that boyfriend in Baltimore . . .

I inspected every window and door in the lower story, ensuring they were locked as the wind whispered against the windows. The wind was howling outside, but the house was of quality construction and tight. Goes to show what real money can do.

Went to the basement and looked around down there. One door went out. That Khadr — if he came alone — this basement door would attract him like a moth to a flame.

Still, underestimating him could be fatal for someone.

Would he come alone?

All the possibilities leapt to mind, everything from an assault by a dozen or two fired-up locals intent on earning their way into Paradise to a bomb against the building or a rocket into the house.

Clearly, there was no way to do more than we had done. We had four guys outside, and me, Grafton, Robin and the two pistol-packing pro crime solvers in. I wondered if either of the federal cops had ever been in a gunfight. Or if Robin had. That was our team unless Grafton had cavalry standing by somewhere that I didn't know about. Even if he did, it was doubtful that they could get here in time to do much good. Whatever happened, if it happened, would happen damn quick.

Ahh . . . nothing will happen.

I decided I was jumpy, working myself into a state because I was a little scared. The memory of the adventure in the stairwell was still fresh as newly spilled blood. My ears still buzzed from the gunshots in that concrete sounding chamber. My shoulder still ached from the bullet in London and hurt from the crease last night.

My worst problem was my adrenaline hangover. That and congenital paranoia.

When I finished the basement, I climbed the stairs to the top floor and began familiarizing myself with the layout, doors, light switches, closets, storage rooms, bathrooms, places to hide, furniture in odd places . . . all the things I would need to know if the power went off. Room by room, I looked at everything. This joint only had a half dozen bedrooms up here — it was really a small hotel.

One of the bedroom doors was closed. Marisa's, I figured. I stood there for several seconds breathing in and out before I knocked.

Maybe half a minute passed before the door opened. She was wearing an ankle-length nightie. She walked away from me, and I closed the door. The only light came from the little reading lamp beside the bed.

She turned to face me.

"Tommy . . ."

I don't know exactly how it happened, but we wound up in a tight embrace, kissing. Her hunger was a tangible thing; her warmth and sensuality swept over me.

Afterward we lay together between the sheets in the darkness holding each other tightly. She had her head against my chest, as if she were listening to my heart.

I still had the bandage over the drain the doctor had installed in London, plus my new bandage on my souvenir shoulder crease. She ignored them both.

"Sometimes I wish," she said, "that I were a different person, a normal person, with a normal family and normal problems."

"Normal problems . . ." I echoed. "Don't we all wish?"

"But I'm not."

A blast of wind struck the house and rattled the window, which was cracked open about an inch. Cold air blew gently into the room through that crack. The sleet had stopped and now was just rain — a lot of rain, I could tell by the sound.

Somewhere a tree limb was rubbing against the house. The gutter, it sounded like. It was a random, scraping sound, whenever the wind blew hardest.

"You aren't, either," she said.

My earpiece and radio were on the floor someplace. I thought about putting it back on, yet I didn't want to move to find it.

"I'm frightened," she whispered.

"Khadr?"

"Qasim."

"One is as bad as the other," I said, trying to sound normal.

She didn't hesitate. "With our luck, we'll get them both," she said bitterly.

I kissed her one last time, as warmly and tenderly as I could, then got out of bed and dressed in the darkness as the wind moaned and rain hammered the glass.

Using the fence line and a little draw, Khadr crawled into the back of the barn. The journey from the fence to the barn, a distance of about a hundred yards, had taken him an hour. He was wet to the skin and cold, but he ignored both sensations.

Khadr was dressed all in black, with a

black ski mask over his head and face, with holes only for his eyes, and black gloves on his hands. He killed swiftly, ruthlessly and without remorse, and he was very good at it. Tonight he was armed with a silenced pistol, a knife, a garroting wire and hard experience gained through fifty-five paid kills and six that weren't. The pistol he carried in a black synthetic holster with the bottom cut out to make room for the silencer. The knife hung in a black sheath on his left side.

The large double door was closed and barred from the inside. Khadr pulled gently on the handle, then moved to the personnel door. It was unlocked. He slipped through into the barn, closed the door behind him and ensured it had latched, then moved sideways into a dark corner and stood waiting with the silenced pistol in his hand. Waiting and listening, alert with every sense attuned.

The horses knew he was there, of course, and shifted nervously in their stalls. No doubt they were looking his way, and they could probably see him, although he couldn't see them. They didn't whinny, however. These were tame horses, used to man's presence. He heard the horses' shuffle above the noise of the wind and rain, both of which came in driving gusts.

The only light in the barn was from the exit signs above the doors at either end. Khadr's eyes adjusted quickly, and he saw the layout, the stalls and the dark shapes that hung above the doors, the horses, watching him, looking around.

He waited until the horses turned away, one by one, back to their feed bags or standing asleep or lolling in their stalls. He heard one horse lie down. Ten minutes passed with only the sounds of the storm; then he heard a gentle plop of a horse exercising its bowels.

He started down the passageway that led to the front entrance . . . and froze. Something . . . A man snoring. The sound was above him.

He searched the overhead, saw the platforms and the end of the hay bales stored there — and saw the areas where they weren't.

From a pocket he removed a small infrared detector that looked like a telescope. Holding it up to his right eye, he scanned the overhead. Two heat sources . . .

Like a shadow he moved to the ladder against the wall, by a tack room, and stood at the bottom of the ladder looking upward. Listening. The snoring was closer. One man . . . no, two — definitely two — above him.

He climbed the ladder, a lithe, agile black shadow, moving slowly and steadily. No one can move absolutely soundlessly, not even Khadr, but the sounds of the nor'easter on the uninsulated roof covered the tiny noises of the rungs taking his weight, the rubber soles of his shoes scraping on the wood.

He paused at the top, his pistol in his hand, every sense on full alert. Slowly, ever so slowly he raised his head, which was still covered with the black ski mask. In the dim, almost nonexistent light they were black lumps sleeping on mats, their feet at least ten feet from him. They appeared motionless, snoring gently. Over his head the roof reverberated.

Khadr forced himself to look around, to ensure that these were the only two men in the loft. The corners of this empty area of the loft were totally black, impenetrable. He used the infrared scanner. Empty.

At any moment one of the men could awaken or someone could enter the barn down below. He could afford to wait no longer.

He holstered the pistol and, using both hands, completed his climb, then stepped onto the loft floor.

Neither of the men stirred. Now he pulled the pistol again, automatically thumbing the safety to ensure it was on. Stepping carefully, feeling the floor with each foot before placing his weight on that spot, he moved toward them. They were in sleeping bags, three feet or so between them.

He moved so he was adjacent to their waists. He thumbed off the safety. Swiftly he bent down, placed the muzzle of the pistol inches from the head of the man on his left and pulled the trigger. A soft plop. A second later he put a bullet into the head of the man on his right.

He was about to holster the gun when the first man he shot sat up, groaning, one hand on his head. Khadr placed the muzzle of the silencer against the side of the man's head and fired again. The victim tumbled over and lay still.

Now the killer holstered the gun and removed a penlight from his pocket. The beam was a tiny spot. Quickly he looked for the radios that he knew must be here.

He found them. The first man he shot had an earpiece in his ear. The wireless transceiver was lying near his head. Khadr inspected the transceiver, ensured it was on, then clipped it to his belt. The earpiece he inserted in his own ear.

He adjusted the squelch until he got static, then turned it down until the static faded into silence.

Guns lay on the floor nearby. M-16s and 1911-style automatics. He picked up one of the pistols, checked that it was loaded, cocked and locked, and shoved it into his waistband, just in case. If he had to use it, he would be in deep trouble, perhaps fatal trouble. For him. Still . . .

He went to the window and looked through the rain-smeared glass down into the yard. It was empty, but he knew there were people out there, waiting. Waiting for him. Shielding the penlight carefully, he looked at his watch. Only ten thirty. Lights were still on in the house. Four cars were parked near the small porch.

He would wait, Khadr decided. He had all night.

Standing silently, motionless, he took out his infrared scanner and began searching the area.

Behind him the leg of the first man he had shot moved, then stiffened, then finally relaxed and moved no more.

When I got downstairs, the party around the fireplace was breaking up. Callie and Amy were already upstairs, apparently,

554

although I hadn't heard them pass Marisa's door. Smith made himself one last toddy, then carried it by me up the stairs. He refused to meet my eyes.

Winchester called his dog, who followed him into the hallway that led to the dining room and kitchen. Grafton trailed along after the collie. Robin was sitting with her shotgun across her lap in front of the fireplace. She watched me descend the stairs and follow the two into the hallway.

I found Grafton talking to the two FBI agents. "Tommy and Robin will take the first watch," he said. "I want you to go upstairs and get some sleep. Tommy will wake you at three and you can relieve them."

He glanced at me, and I nodded. From a backpack he extracted two night vision headsets. He explained how they worked to the FBI agents, who had never used them before. Showed them the on-off switch, the switch to cycle between infrared and starlight, and showed them the gain and contrast knobs. The federal cops looked dubious.

"If you've never used these before, you might be better off without them," I suggested.

They both nodded.

Grafton handed me a set.

"Since we have more people than we've had the last few nights, I'm going to try to get a full night's sleep," Grafton continued, talking to the agents. "Same drill as in the past — I'll have the radio on so I'll hear anything anyone says on the net. I'm the reinforcements. If anyone sees anything, hears anything, suspects anything, say so on the net. Got it?"

He looked from face to face, then at me. We all nodded our understanding.

"Admiral," one of the agents said, the taller of the two. "Realistically, what are we facing?"

"I honestly don't know. We could be assaulted by a gang, bombed or attacked by stealth by one man. I don't know. Last night at my place in Virginia four men tried to gain entrance to the building."

The FBI types looked at each other. The shorter one, who I knew was married from his comments during dinner, unconsciously felt the pistol in his holster to reassure himself. When he saw me watching he lowered his hand.

Winchester went to the coatrack by the kitchen door and began donning a coat and slicker. The dog sat looking up at him expectantly.

"Hunt, why don't you let Tommy take the

dog for a walk?"

Winchester looked at me.

"Sure, Mr. Winchester," I said with false enthusiasm. "I need to stretch my legs."

"Okay." Winchester took off the coat and held it out to me.

"Thanks," Grafton murmured. He slapped me on the shoulder, my bad one, and headed for the living room to give the other set of goggles to Robin.

The dog looked at me as if I were its best pal.

"Her name is Molly," Winchester said as he took the leash off the hook. Molly stood up and turned around excitedly and fanned the air with her tail. "She has to walk and sniff a while before she decides to go."

I got dressed, arranged the slicker flap over my head and accepted the leash and Winchester's flashlight. It was one of those black aircraft-aluminum jobs, with three or four D-cell batteries. I almost said no, then thought, why not? The rain wouldn't do the night vision goggles any good at all, and I might need them later. I left them on a coat hook. After saying something polite, I opened the door, and the dog dragged me out into the night.

And a damned miserable night it was. Not yet freezing, but with the wet wind howling

557

at least thirty knots, and gusting higher, and driving the raindrops into my face and legs like pellets, it felt like the arctic. The wind chill must have been near zero. Tree branches writhed and whipped in the wind, and low evergreens bent over from the blasts. Why the Pilgrims and other strait-laced religious types from Merry Old England ever wanted to take this place away from the Indians, I don't know.

The dog liked it, though. She tugged me right along on her usual walk, I suppose. We went into the grass and along the hedges as she sniffed at everything. She found a couple of old dog-poop piles and inspected those carefully, but I got tired of that and pulled her on. She then charged to the end of the leash. Considering all the times she must have done this, you'd think she would have been leash-trained, but no.

I flashed the light around, just looking, shining it everywhere, in case there was a watcher. The guy in the hole by the corner of the barn could close his eyes or duck down; he didn't need me giving away his position. Mostly, however, I watched the dog. Having had a little canine experience myself, I knew the dog would detect an intruder before I did. Molly certainly wouldn't smell him in this hurricane, but she would sense him. Khadr. If he was out here. Or any other holy warrior waiting for a sucker infidel.

After a few minutes of this I led Molly on around the house. Might as well check out the whole area.

As I walked, bent down to protect myself against the wind, struggling to hold on to the pooch, I thought about my recent tryst with Marisa. Now there was a woman! But was she the real deal, or only acting a part?

The unanswered questions were right there, just beneath the surface. My paranoia was so ingrained by this time that I went over every look, word, touch, gesture — even her body language and the way she held herself — trying to find a false note. Ran the scenes over and over in my memory, looking . . .

The problem, I decided, is really me. I find it impossible to not turn over the rock to see what's underneath.

Oh, God, Tommy, you idiot, what a way to live!

From the barn window, Khadr watched Tommy trudge through the wind and rain with the dog lunging on her leash until he disappeared around the house. He didn't know who the man with the dog was — the infrared didn't allow that kind of definition. Now that Tommy was gone, he used the infrared scanner again, although he realized he was only looking at this side of the house, and the areas to his left and right were obscured by his vantage point. There must be people out here! Getting as close to the glass as possible, he used the scanner to look down to the right and left.

There he was, a man, below, almost against the corner of the barn, to Khadr's left. One man, in a hole, perhaps.

Khadr continued to look, scanning, trying to determine if this was the only man. He was still looking when Tommy Carmellini and the dog came back around the house. They entered at the door they had come out of.

A few minutes later some of the upstairs lights went dark. The people inside were going to bed.

So how was he going to get past the man in the hole and get inside?

Khadr began turning that problem over in his mind. In truth, he had no plan. He was looking for an opportunity, and if one developed, or he saw a way to make one, well and good. If not, he could always leave the way he had come in. He had a cell phone in his pocket to call Qasim to meet him.

After all, Qasim wanted to create terror, and the discovery of two dead men in the barn would certainly create it. And another opportunity might present itself tomorrow night, or the night after.

When I got back into the house, Winchester was waiting with a towel to dry the dog, who proceeded to shower us both anyway.

"You take real good care of that dog," I commented.

"She belonged to Owen," he said.

When he had the dog reasonably dry, he took her upstairs. Grafton was standing in the main living room with Robin watching the Weather Channel. The nor'easter was the storm of the day in America, apparently. Three reporters were on station to bring us the latest and greatest. They posed outside, of course, getting hammered by wind and rain as they gave their breathless reports.

All three talked about snow. When the radar picture came up, we could see it coming our way.

"Six inches by morning in this area," Grafton murmured. "Power lines are already down in Massachusetts and Rhode Island."

When the weather gurus went to a commercial, he used the remote to kill the sound of the savage beast. He left the picture on.

The admiral glanced at me and Robin. "Tonight may be the night. If you see, hear or smell anything, anything at all out of the ordinary, call me on the radio. I'll have it on and the earpiece in my ear."

"Sweet dreams," Robin said brightly. She smiled. I decided that there is nothing like the smile of a lady holding a shotgun to jar your preconceptions.

Grafton ascended the stair and we were alone.

"So how do you want to do this?" Robin asked.

"Why don't you settle in here behind something solid so no one can drill you through a window, and I'll circulate? I suggest you also turn off the downstairs lights."

"After a while we trade off."

"Okay."

She laid her shotgun on the bar and moved a chair behind it, then sat and put the weapon on her lap. The night vision goggles were within reach on the bar. I turned off the lights in the room, then, carrying my own scattergun, wandered back to the kitchen. I hadn't managed much dinner and decided to inspect the refrigerator, just in case. While I was in there I shoved Winchester's flashlight into my hip pocket. It threw a lot more light than my little penlight.

Jake Grafton found his wife just finishing her shower. She dressed in a long nightie as he washed his face and brushed his teeth.

"No shower?" she said.

"I'm sleeping in my clothes."

She didn't have any response to that. He had an M-16 lying on the chair beside the bed. When she was under the covers and he was beside her with a blanket arranged over him, she turned off the light.

"I saw you talking to Isolde," she said.

After Marisa went upstairs, Grafton had taken the banker to a corner of the living room for a private conversation.

"She thinks Qasim is a monster and Marisa is a victim," he said.

"So who killed Jean Petrou?"

"I don't know. Marisa thought he was selling information to Qasim, and he might have been. She followed him and saw them together once. She told Isolde about it. Either of them could have poisoned him. Both had access to Isolde's prescription digitalis. Isolde says she didn't and she doesn't think Marisa did."

"What do you think?"

"Marisa."

A long silence followed that remark. Finally Callie said, "Tommy is pretty taken with her."

"He's a big boy."

"Oh, come *on!*"

"Listen to me. Marisa called Qasim while she was here, gave him our address in Rosslyn. She told him we were here, and she told him we were going to the political dinner on Thursday."

"Does Tommy know that?"

"Not that. He knows Marisa may have killed her husband, and he knows she knocked him down when he was set to shoot the fleeing intruders at the Zetsche estate. Heck, she may have poisoned Alexander Surkov — that's a long shot, but it's a possibility. Tommy's been around the mountain a time or two, and he's trying to figure her out, same as me."

She thought about that for a moment. "You wanted her to make that call, didn't you?"

"I was sorta hoping she would."

"So Qasim intends to assassinate the president?"

"I think he wants Marisa there to see him do it. That's my best guess. He has been playing us like chessmen, forcing us to do what he wanted. Thursday night. That's his payoff, I think. Maybe."

"Oh, my God," she whispered.

Grafton lay there in the darkness listening to the rain and wind, trying to relax. After a while his wife went to sleep — he could tell by her breathing.

What if he had figured this all wrong and Marisa was an assassin? She was inside. What if she killed Winchester and Smith tonight? Or opened a door or window for Khadr?

After about half an hour, he got out of bed as quietly as possible, picked up the assault rifle and slipped out of the room. He closed the door behind him and made his way to the end of the hallway, which was lit with small night-lights at ankle height. There was a little straight-back chair there, along with a tiny table containing a dried flower arrangement, so he sat and tilted the chair back slightly against the wall. The rifle he kept on his lap.

From this vantage point he could see all the bedroom doors except Winchester's, which was on the ground floor. Over his head was a small window. He sat listening to the rain/sleet mix patter against it and the rising sound of the wind. The gusts were worse now as the heart of the storm came down upon them.

I was watching the snow line march toward us on the television when the power went out. The picture dimmed, brightened, then went black. I glanced at the stairs and saw that the glow of the night-lights was gone. It was a few minutes after twelve.

"Uh-oh," I said to Robin.

I put on my night vision goggles and fired them up. When I looked at Robin, I saw that she already had hers on.

I switched to infrared and went to a window to look out. Between the rain-smeared glass and all the water in the air outside, I couldn't see much. I tried the ambient light setting and saw even less. Terrific!

I opened the door to the cabana and went out there. The pool was a sheet of black. The howl of the wind was breathtaking here in this unprotected area. Everything was wet; I could feel the water soaking into my shoes. It was miserably cold, too, whipping through my clothes. I didn't stay out there long. I went back inside and locked the door.

Then I went downstairs and checked all the windows and doors. The place was gloomy, even with the flashlight. The basement door was locked tight, but . . . I leaned a rake and shovel against it so they would fall over if the door was opened. Who knows, I might even hear one of them fall. I left the door at the top of the stairs open, on the off chance.

After I checked the main-floor windows, the front door, the main rear entrance and the kitchen door, I strolled around, waiting.

Seems that waiting is the way I spend half my life. One of these days I need to get a real job.

The wind was shaking the main barn doors and blowing through tiny openings here and there. Khadr waited for about thirty minutes after the power failure to give everyone a chance to settle down, then made his way by feel to the ladder and descended to the main floor of the barn.

The horses were restless. He opened their stall doors and let them wander out into the walkway of the barn. They immediately bunched up. The noise he and they made was lost in the storm.

Then he went to the door that led to the area between the barn and the house and unlatched the door. The doors quivered. They would blow open any second.

He walked back behind the horses, trying not to spook them.

Sure enough, within half a minute one of the now unlatched doors blew open and crashed against the barn with a bang. The startled horses whinnied and pranced. Khadr slapped the nearest one on the rump. That was enough to set them off. They charged for the open door and galloped through it.

He followed them to the doorway and molded his body to the wall, his pistol in his hand.

"What was that noise?" A male voice on my headset. "Harry?"

"The barn door blew open and the damn horses are out milling around. Uh-oh, they're coming around the house toward you."

"Oh, man, the main gate is open. They'll go out into the road."

"Let them go, Nick. I'll check out the barn."

I heard someone coming down the stairs. Saw him in infrared, carrying a rifle. Grafton!

"Tommy?" he said aloud.

"I'm over here by the cabana door."

"Robin?"

"Behind the bar."

"Stay there."

"Admiral, the best place for you is the basement," I said. "If it's Khadr, that's probably the most likely entrance."

"Okay," he said. His penlight flashed on, and he headed for the kitchen and the stairs down.

"Stay where you are," I told Robin.

"I can't shoot with these damn goggles on," she said disgustedly. "I can't see the sights."

"Just point the thing and pull the trigger."

The lenses on Harry Longworth's goggles were wet, which reduced their effectiveness by a large percentage. He wiped at the water with his fingers, then adjusted the gain and contrast. Standing outside the barn looking through the doorway — one door was open and the other was waving back and forth — he couldn't see anything. A wet door, wet lens . . .

"Shit," he said softly. He took off the goggles and let them dangle on his chest. He pulled his flashlight from his hip pocket and, shielding his body against the door, held the light in his left hand at arm's length and shined it around the interior. The stall doors were open. He saw nothing.

He pulled the light back and used his left hand to key the mike button on the belt-mounted transceiver. "Hey, upstairs!"

Don't tell me they slept through that bang when the door blew open!

Caution shrieked at him.

Well, he was going to have to go in there, one way or another.

He threw himself through the door and did a belly flop on the floor, his rifle out in front of him.

Khadr's first bullet caught him in the neck. Before he could react, he felt rather than saw movement on his right. As he tried to swing his weapon to his right, another bullet hit him, this time ricocheting off his forehead, laying open a two-inch gash clear to the bone and stunning him. The third slug hit him above the ear and penetrated into his brain. He never felt the fourth and fifth bullets, both of which were fired point-blank into his skull.

Khadr took the time to change magazines in his pistol, then ran as fast as he could go toward the dark, silent house.

"Harry, the horses are going out the gate into the road." I recognized Nick's voice. He was in front of the house.

Harry didn't answer, which was ominous.

Squatting, I opened the door to the cabana area and scanned it with the night vision goggles in infrared, then switched to ambient light. The sleet was forming a crust on everything. Even though I was crouched in the door, the wind buffeted me.

Something was happening over at the barn — that much seemed obvious. A distraction? I thought so, so I didn't move. If Harry and the two guys asleep in the barn couldn't handle it, one more guy wouldn't help. My best choice was to stay put.

Yet I couldn't really see much here in the doorway. I steadied myself with my left hand and moved outside, staying low, alongside the outside bar. From here I could see the pool, the outdoor sauna and toilet building and the hedge that surrounded the whole area. The hedge and trees were waving madly in the wind. I tried to ignore them and searched with the goggles for human movement.

I slipped down to the end of the outdoor bar so I could see around it.

One step, two . . . and something walloped me in the head and I went out cold.

Khadr didn't look again at Carmellini, who lay sprawled on his face where he had been shot.

He used his infrared scanner to examine the interior of the house, then moved to the door and looked in.

He saw no one. But he did see the stairs leading up to the bedrooms above. That was where Grafton and Winchester would be.

Pistol in hand, he rose and trotted across the room toward the stairs.

Robin Cloyd poked her head above the bar in time to see the man running for the stairs. In infrared, he was quite plain.

"Tommy?" she asked loudly, above the noise coming through the open door.

The answer was a bullet that slammed into the bar with an audible whack, just inches from her shoulder. She didn't hesitate. Robin pointed the shotgun and pulled the trigger.

The report was muffled somewhat by her headset and the adrenaline coursing through her, but she didn't notice. What she did notice was that the muzzle flash had overwhelmed her goggles. Blind, she pumped the slide and fired again toward where she thought the running man might be. Did it again and again, then dropped down and began shoving shells into the bottom of the gun. She paused and keyed her mike. "Tommy?"

She heard a thumping from the staircase.

With two more shells in the gun, all she had, she flipped the goggles to ambient light and ran to the bottom of the stairwell. She saw something moving at the top of the stairs, so pointed the gun and fired upward.

After she worked the slide she saw no more movement.

I heard Robin's voice in my ears. That's when I realized that I had also heard her shotgun hammering.

I tore off the goggles and tried to rise. Later I found out that a bullet had hit the goggles, a bullet that would have killed me if I hadn't been wearing them. I fell again. Worked at it and got up. I still had the shotgun.

I found the flashlight, fumbled with the switch, got it on and headed back inside, shouting Robin's name.

I saw her in the light at the bottom of the stairs, saw her shoot once up the stairwell. She lowered the gun and started up, but I grabbed her arm.

"No." I gave her my shotgun and pulled out the Colt .45.

With the flashlight in my left hand and the pistol in my right, I went up the stairs. Saw the blood all over the carpet. So she got lead into the son of a bitch. Good!

At the top of the stairs, I paused and used the light to scan the hallway, which was to my right. Empty. No, a door was opening. A head came out, looking toward the flashlight. I recognized the face: Jerry Hay Smith.

"Get back in there, you son of a bitch," I roared.

The head disappeared.

The second door was open. A blood trail led that way.

I trotted toward it, looked in, using the flashlight.

A figure in black was standing there. He was holding Callie Grafton with his left arm and had a pistol against the side of her head. Even with the flashlight I could see the blood on his leg. And the ghastly white of her face.

"Drop the weapon or I'll kill her," he said roughly.

The distance between us was maybe twelve feet. He couldn't see me, I knew, because the flashlight must be blinding him — that wasn't a conscious thought, just something I knew. I don't even remember thumbing off the safety. I lifted the Colt and aimed as best I could and shot him. He went over backward. Callie fell away to his left, my right, pulled down by his grasp.

I walked over, watching his right hand, which still held the pistol.

Blood was pumping out his neck below the black balaclava. He had taken the bullet in the jugular vein and was bleeding to death.

I didn't wait. I could see the whites of his eyes through the opening in the black cloth when I emptied the pistol into him. When the gun wouldn't shoot anymore, I reached down and jerked the black hood off his head.

Someone was there beside me. Marisa.

"It's Khadr," she said.

I shoved her out of the way and shined the light on Callie. She was conscious, with no bullet wounds. Relief flooded over me. I helped her up. She sat on the bed, didn't even look at the corpse.

I popped the magazine out of the Colt and replaced it with the one in my pocket, then started out of the room. I met Jake Grafton coming in.

"Check on your wife," I said, trying to keep my voice under control. "I'm going to see if there're any more of them."

In the hallway I met Smith and Winchester. "Who was it?" Winchester asked.

"A man who came to kill you," I said as I shouldered past.

Robin gave me my shotgun, and I headed for the barn, using every bit of cover there was. The sleet had turned to snow. I hid, ran, hid, and ran again.

Harry Longworth's feet were visible just inside the entrance to the barn. The howling wind was whipping the big doors open and shut, causing impacts that rocked the building. I dashed between the swinging doors and, after I had swept the flashlight around, briefly examined Harry. He was obviously dead.

I'm going to end up like that one of these days.

Taking my time, I inspected the whole place. I found the two dead men upstairs, and had just finished giving the bad news to Grafton on the radio when I heard the wail of the first police siren.

I sat down beside the dead men in the loft and cried. Maybe I was crying for them or maybe I was crying for me — I couldn't tell.

CHAPTER
TWENTY-THREE

When Abu Qasim heard the moan of the police siren over the wind, he put the car in gear and got it rolling along the road, heading away from Winchester's estate. The siren told him that Khadr was in trouble; even now he might be running for the highway, trying to make the pickup point. Or he might be trapped, wounded or dead.

In any event, what Khadr wasn't doing was calling Qasim, and that was telling.

So Abu Qasim left Khadr to his fate, whatever it might be. He felt no remorse, no loyalty or sorrow, nor, he knew, would Khadr feel any if he were here and Qasim were there. Khadr fought for money and Qasim fought for Allah, whose will would be done in the case of both men, regardless.

Qasim had the windshield defrosters and wipers going, and between them, they were staying ahead of the snow. He drove westward carefully, taking every precaution. He

577

didn't plan on stopping for the night, just driving out of the storm. If it got too bad to drive, he would find a place to sit it out.

As he drove he went over the preparations for the week ahead. In the past month he had won some battles and lost some. He didn't waste energy savoring the triumphs or rehashing the losses. He had one last great battle before him, and he intended to do everything in his power to win it. Still, the only thing that really mattered was winning the war. That was the only victory that would please Allah.

"You saved my life," Callie Grafton said in the wee hours of the morning after the ambulance crews had carried out the bodies and the police had departed.

"We were just lucky he didn't squeeze that trigger when the bullet hit him," I said. "Pure luck."

"You saved my life," she said again. Then she hugged her husband, and together they went up the stairs, holding tightly to each other.

The truth, as I was keenly aware, was that if Khadr had killed her, I would have had to live with it. Not that I had a lot of choice, but still . . . No one can say that I don't have my share of shithouse luck.

I got into Winchester's liquor pretty hard. Four cops stayed behind, sitting in patrol cars in the parking area, just in case. I looked out a window at the cars being covered with snow and thought savagely that Khadr could have killed them all in fifteen seconds.

Blood, murder, butchery. For the greater glory of Allah.

After three drinks I lay down on the couch and went to sleep. When I awoke the power was back on, the sun was somewhere above the overcast, the wind had died, six inches of snow covered the ground and I had a raging headache. I felt as if I had been scalped. The police cars were still in the parking area.

I had a Bloody Mary for breakfast.

Sooner or later, I was going to have to get a real life.

Sooner or later.

Three uneventful days later we flew to New York on a government executive jet. Police escorted us to the airport for the short flight. Since the attack on Winchester's estate, I had avoided Marisa and she had avoided me, but somehow we ended up side by side on the jet. At one point she murmured, "I'm sorry, Tommy."

I pretended I didn't hear.

From outward appearances, Callie had recovered from her ordeal. I knew that getting that close to the abyss at the hands of an assassin or maniac leaves wounds that only time can heal, but I didn't speak to her about it. I figured she had Jake Grafton, and who better? What could I possibly say other than a few meaningless, trite phrases?

Callie sat with her daughter, Amy, on the plane, and they held hands. Maybe Amy understood.

The Walden Hotel on Fifth Avenue was really hopping when we arrived. Secret Service agents were as thick as fleas on a camel. Everywhere you looked you saw guys and gals with strange bulges in their clothing talking into their lapels.

They took us to rooms on the fifteenth floor. I gave the bellboy a five-spot for putting my bag in the room, then adjusted the Colt on my hip and headed downstairs to check things out. Grafton had already beaten me to the lobby. He gave me a pass on a chain, which I was supposed to dangle around my neck. He already had his on.

"All the cool people are wearing these this year," he said, which startled me. Grafton doesn't often try a funny, and when he does it is so unexpected that it jolts you. I managed a smile.

Standing there in the cavernous lobby of the Walden, surrounded by people bustling about, he looked me in the eyes. "You did the right thing in Connecticut," he said. "Just wanted you to know that I know that."

"Could have come out differently."

"It could have come out a dozen different ways, all of them bad and all because Khadr was there to do murder. You used your best judgment, you acted when others might have hesitated, so Khadr's dead and Callie's alive. Thanks." He reached for my hand and pumped it while he gave me one of those Grafton grins.

I was embarrassed — he could see that — so we left it there.

From his hip pocket he produced a program. "This is how this thing is supposed to go. There will be precisely one thousand thirty-nine people in attendance tonight, including you and me. The staff has been vetted; the place will be brimming with law. Everyone will be seated and the doors will be closed when the president and other politicos make their entrance. They'll go directly to the dais, and Senator Isner will make the welcoming remarks, which will last no more than two minutes. Then the staff will begin serving the meals. The president is scheduled to speak after dinner."

"So none of the diners will get a chance to get close to the man?"

"Oh, no. They all will. Sal Molina tells me that the president will mix and mingle during dinner, pressing the flesh. He will visit every table and shake every hand. These people paid ten grand a chair for the right to say hi to the president and be photographed doing it, so he's going to give them their money's worth."

My eyebrows started dancing.

"I know, I know. Everyone on the attendance list is a big political donor, a spouse or kid or friend of a donor. The list was finalized weeks ago, and the FBI and Secret Service have worked their heinies off vetting these people. To get in, everyone has to go through a metal detector and produce a photo ID. Absolutely no one will be admitted who isn't on the list or whose ID doesn't match his face."

"Okay."

"The feds have gone over this hotel with a fine-tooth comb. They've vetted the kitchen staff, there will be agents in the kitchen watching the food prep and the kitchen staff has to sample every dish before it comes out into the dining room. There will be at least twenty agents in the dining hall."

"What's on the menu?"

"Chicken Cordon Bleu."

"That's chicken with cheese in it, right?"

"I think so."

"I hate that stuff."

"When the president finishes speaking, he'll leave first, escorted out by a squad of agents, go by motorcade to the airport and leave for Washington on Air Force One. The motorcade into and out of the city is in the hands of the NYPD and Secret Service. They tell me it will be tight as a tick. They've even had men in the storm drains on the streets the motorcade will use, checking for bombs. The motorcade is out of our hands."

"If Abu Qasim is going to do it, it'll be here," I said. "With Marisa watching."

"I think so, too," Grafton murmured. He took a deep breath and continued. "The organizers are filming everything for use in campaign ads. So, yeah, it'll be here, so afterward the networks will broadcast it and the faithful all over the planet can see the power of al-Qaeda and Allah."

"Got any ideas how he'll do it?"

"I was hoping you might have."

I shrugged. "Gas, bomb or bullet. Or polonium."

"Geiger counters in the kitchen and at the entrances to the room. Anyone radioactive will get a bum's rush to an isolation room."

"Maybe nothing will happen," I said hopefully.

"Maybe," Grafton said, but I could see he didn't believe it. I didn't, either.

"I want you to escort Marisa. Stick to her like glue."

"Okay."

"Use your best judgment."

I thought about that for a moment before I said, "Okay, boss."

About that time a Secret Service type walked up, a chiseled hard-body who could have made a nice living on Madison Avenue posing for ads, and spoke to Grafton. "Your call from Russia is waiting in the command center."

Grafton slapped me on the arm and went off with the agent. I wondered what that was all about. A million possibilities leapt to mind, too many to process.

I went into the dining room — my pass worked like a charm — looked at all the tables and the raised podium where the guests of honor were going to sit, even peeped under the table where the president was going to sit while three Secret Service agents watched. Didn't see anything, felt like an idiot, so I wandered out and let the pros have it.

Since it was getting on toward lunch, I put my pass in my pocket, left the hotel and went walking. Ended up heading for a pool room I knew on Seventh Avenue, where I had two hot dogs with mustard and sauerkraut, washed it down with beer and played some pool with a guy who tried to hustle me. My heart wasn't in it. I could feel the minutes ticking away, couldn't get my mind off Qasim and Marisa. I lost twenty-two dollars, told the guy he was too good for me and left.

I strolled the streets, thoughts tumbling over themselves in no particular order. I still hadn't figured out Qasim and Marisa's relationship, and I knew that I was flat running out of time.

Maybe I should go back to the hotel and have a real heart-to-heart with Marisa. But what could I say to break through her defenses and get to that place she really lived?

The possibility that she was the one who was supposed to kill the president kept cropping up. Suppose she was the assassin and all this craziness and murder had been just an elaborate setup?

What if Abu Qasim managed to kill the

president? That would be the ultimate terror strike, a blow at America that would have profound, unpredictable, seismic implications. The stakes were enormous, beyond calculation. Qasim knew that . . . and so did Grafton, and the president, and Sal Molina and Wilkins and Goldman and all the rest.

I hoped Grafton had this figured out, because I certainly didn't.

I walked and walked, waiting, watching the hands of my watch sweep ever so slowly and relentlessly around the dial, ticking off the minutes toward Armageddon.

Abu Qasim worked carefully on his makeup before the mirror, taking his time, inspecting himself frequently. The goatee was glued firmly in place. He put wads of cotton between his teeth and cheeks to fill them out, altering the appearance of his face.

When he finished, he inspected his handiwork and compared that to the photo on his New York driver's license. Yes, he was once again Samuel Israel Rohtstein.

He put on his tux, dressed carefully, inspected every button and zipper. When he was finished, he scrutinized himself in his full-length mirror. Satisfactory.

He checked his watch. He had plenty of

time. The hired car would pick him up in an hour. He had used this car service before, so they knew his address and knew him. He didn't want to be early, but he also didn't want to be late. Entering the hotel ballroom with the main stream of people was the best way to minimize the scrutiny he would receive at the security checkpoints.

The enormity of the undertaking before him left him with a clarity of mind he found startling. All the extraneous thoughts, cares and concerns were as if they had never been. He wasn't hungry, wasn't thirsty, wasn't nervous.

He was *ready.*

About five o'clock I got back to the hotel. Grafton hadn't called on my cell phone, and when I got to the room, I found he had left no message. So I was just supposed to go. With Marisa as my date.

I showered and shaved, then dressed in my rented tux that the agency had flown up from Washington. There was a rental place near my apartment where I always rented a monkey suit when I needed one, so the guy had all my sizes. He even got the right size of patent leather shoes, although they weren't very comfortable.

I checked the Colt — loaded, cocked and

locked — and put it in my waistband in the small of my back. The strap of the cumberbund helped hold it in place.

At six o'clock sharp I knocked on the door to the Petrou suite. Isolde opened it. She was dressed to the nines, but Marisa was still in her slip dabbing makeup. Her slip plunged almost to her navel, leaving very little to the imagination. Of course she wasn't wearing a bra. She barely acknowledged my presence.

I could tell by looking at each woman that neither had a concealed weapon under her clothes. Just to be sure, I helped myself to their purses and stirred through them as Isolde watched with narrowed eyes.

"You are very forward, young man."

"I'm aging quickly," I replied. "At this rate I'll probably be old enough for Social Security next year." I handed her back her purse. I could see that Isolde didn't like my attitude. "They behave better in France, don't they?" I said.

I could see Marisa glancing at me in the mirror as she put on lipstick. I met her gaze. There was something going on there, but damned if I knew what.

Isolde went into the other bedroom, leaving us alone.

Marisa went into the walk-in closet to

dress. She came out in a full-skirted gown that above her waist barely covered the slip, and a set of three-inch high heels. Just looking at her made my heart go pitty pat.

She needed help putting on her necklace. I stood behind her and did the clasp. "Tommy . . ." Marisa began, watching me in the mirror.

I didn't say anything.

"I meant what I said the other night, about wishing it were different."

"I wish it were, too."

We left it there.

Jake Grafton was dressed and waiting on his wife when the telephone rang. It was Sal Molina. "He wants to see you." Sal gave him the room number.

"I'll meet you downstairs," Jake told Callie and kissed her.

She seized him by both arms and looked into his eyes. "You've done the best you could, you know."

"I do know."

"However this works out is how it works out."

"I know that, but still . . . I don't want the president dead. Not on my watch."

"Jake!"

"Hey. Being your husband has been an

adventure, lady. I just want you to know that." He kissed her gently on the forehead.

She bit her lip and watched him leave the room, pull the door closed behind him.

She knew that Jake Grafton was perfectly capable of stepping in front of the president to stop a bullet meant for him. And he had just said good-bye.

Wilkins was in the presidential bedroom with the Secret Service's Goldman, the secretary of Homeland Security, the director of the FBI and Sal Molina. They were standing around with their hands in their pockets, looking glum, when Grafton was ushered in by a Secret Service agent. The president was sitting in an easy chair. The first lady was in the bathroom, still dressing.

Grafton took a letter from his coat pocket and passed it to Wilkins. "Just in case," he said.

Wilkins knew what it was — Grafton's letter of resignation — and pocketed it with a nod.

Goldman was arguing that the president shouldn't appear this evening. He glanced at Grafton, then summed up. "This whole thing is an unnecessary risk. We'll announce that you are indisposed, and Molina here can make his first public appearance since his high school graduation. He can shake hands, tell lies, pretend he is somebody, and we'll catch this son of a bitch Qasim."

"If he shows up," the director of the FBI added. "I'm betting that he won't. This whole thing is a half-baked, half-assed, cockamamie load of bullshit, if you ask me."

The president looked from face to face. This argument had obviously been going on for a while before Grafton arrived, and these were the final love pats.

"Admiral?" the president said.

"If we knew what he looked like, we could go down there and drag him out, but we don't know."

"That Petrou woman knows," Wilkins said sourly.

"She should be able to recognize him, regardless of how he is disguised," Goldman said. "Grafton says she thinks she can, and I certainly hope so. If he's in that room, we've got him. That's the logical, safe way to do this."

They all fell silent. Everyone had had his say. The president got out of his chair so that he could look everyone in the eyes. "I don't want another 9/11. I don't want any more spectacular terrorist attacks on American soil, and our allies don't want any on their soil. Abu Qasim is the most capable terrorist alive — I believe he could pull off something like that."

"If the bastard kills the president of the United States," Goldman shot back, "that would be the biggest coup of all."

"Enough," the president said. "We've got soldiers who go in harm's way every single day, and I'm the guy who sent them there. I'll be damned if I'm going to run and hide. We are going to do this just the way it's planned."

He reached for Grafton's hand, shook it, then shook the hand of everyone in the room and shooed them out.

Isolde Petrou, Marisa and I took the elevator to the lobby and walked past a phalanx of police to the ballroom entrance. As Grafton said, the women had to pass through a metal detector. My pass got me a detour around it. I wondered if Abu Qasim had a nifty pass like mine. I didn't see the Geiger counters, but I had no doubt they were there.

Inside, the maître d' checked the master list, then a uniformed helper wearing a different-colored pass escorted us to our table, which was on one side of the room about five rows back. Jack Yocke was already sitting there, and he had a date.

"Hey, Yocke. I didn't know you gave money to politicians."

In answer, he lifted his pass, which was also on a chain around his neck, so that I got a good look. It was a different color than mine. "Working press," he said, then introduced his lady to the Petrous and me — a different woman than the lady he brought to dinner at the Graftons'. She, too, had a press pass dangling from her neck.

I looked at the name tags on the table and maneuvered the women so we were all in the right seats. Isolde was on my left, sort of facing the head table, and Marisa was on my right. Marisa and I had our backs to the wall and were facing the bulk of the room.

It took a while for the room to fill, what with the security at the door and the seating protocol. A half-dozen Secret Service agents were stationed behind the speaker's table, and two knots of three in front. Another dozen or so were scattered throughout the room, standing and moving around in small areas. New York cops in uniform were at every entrance and fire exit.

I listened to Isolde and Marisa make small talk with the two reporters and another couple that arrived toward the end, a car dealer and his wife from Indiana. The car dealer was full of enthusiasm for meeting the president. "One of my heroes," he said frankly.

I decided the guy was an idiot and dismissed him. Jake Grafton was my hero, not some politician. Not any politician.

I kept the eyes moving. Saw Winchester and Simon Cairnes come in with Jerry Hay Smith, who looked to be wearing a typical guest pass. Guess his press credentials were getting rusty. I recognized some prominent industrialists, some actors, more politicians and a couple of high-powered lawyers. Most of the people were, of course, strangers to me.

The seater led Winchester and his pals to a table where the two Grafton women were seated. The table was at least fifty feet from ours. There was an empty seat at that table, and I supposed it was for the admiral, who was nowhere in sight.

I glanced at Marisa to see if she was watching all this. She wasn't. She was listening intently to Isolde, almost as if . . . as if she were her daughter.

That thought jolted me. Where had it come from? More important, where had it been?

My eyes kept searching for Grafton. I wondered if he had had that thought. Probably, I decided. He was always miles ahead of me, which is why he was the boss.

I glanced at the car dealer and saw that he was looking me over. "Got any openings for salesmen at your dealership?" I asked.

"Dealerships. We have four."

"Always nice to meet a successful capitalist."

"We can always use another good man. In car sales, the sky is the limit." He tossed that off without thought, then he engaged the brain. "What does the color of your pass mean?"

"I'm a licensed killer."

That comment jolted him. "You mean like Double-O Seven?"

"Oh, yeah. Me and James Bond. Same deal."

Yocke chuckled and told the guy, "Tommy's with the government. Housing, I think."

"Bureaucrat," I said. "I'm bored to tears. Been thinking about a job change."

Abu Qasim couldn't believe how many people were there, and how many security men and women, in and out of uniform. They weren't running low profile, either. They stood beside the doors, manned the metal detector, and scrutinized driver's licenses and invitations.

This was the hurdle that Qasim had worried about and planned for four years to get over. He had his hand in his pocket on his driver's license, which was genuine. He concentrated on controlling his breathing. If he didn't hyperventilate, he wouldn't overperspire or look flushed, both of which would be signals for the security people.

The man in front of Qasim couldn't find his invitation. While he searched his pockets and his wife looked embarrassed, the officer beside him motioned to Qasim.

He stepped around and passed him the invitation and his driver's license.

"Mr. Rohtstein?"

"Yes."

"What is your birthday, Mr. Rohtstein?"

"July 8, 1958."

After matching Qasim's face to the photo on the license, the officer handed him back the invitation and license and motioned toward the metal detector.

Beside him, the man without the invitation was trying to talk his way in. "You people must have a list, and I know I'm on it. Why don't you look?"

Qasim handed his cell phone, watch, keys and digital camera to the officer with a basket beside the detector and walked on through. Nothing beeped. The officer put his things under a fluoroscope, examined them, then handed them back to him.

He was *in*.

"Right this way, sir," one of the ushers said and checked his invitation against a list. "Follow me, please."

Everyone was seated and the ballroom doors were closed, only twenty minutes behind schedule, when the president and other party heavies came marching in to the strains of "Hail to the Chief" over the PA system, cutting off the banter. Spotlights came on, illuminating the president and official party. There were two television cameras mounted on platforms in the rear of the room, and the big spotlights hung from the ceiling. The rest of the room was well lit, however; the Secret Service had insisted upon it.

Jake Grafton was two people back from the Big Kahuna, all decked out in a tux, but he sort of hung back, a bit out of the way. We all got to our feet and applauded. The Petrous and the reporters and I applauded politely, but the car dealer and his wife really slammed hands. The dealer started to climb on his chair, then thought better of it. Someday this guy was going to be the deputy assistant secretary of something or other.

When everyone was finally seated and the popping flashbulbs slowed to something reasonable, the master of ceremonies welcomed us, then someone — I don't know who — led us in the Pledge of Allegiance. I glanced around to see if anyone nearby was faking it. Apparently not. A prominent local preacher then offered up a prayer, pretty much a generic prayer, acceptable to all religions, inoffensive and tepid. When that was over, the designated senator started in on a fire-eating speech. This party and this president were good for the country, and deserved the support of every true American, and so on. You or I could have written it. Overwrought and theatrical, it was artificially passionate and uninspiring. Apparently no one cared.

"You taking notes?" I asked Yocke, who wasn't. He ignored me.

Marisa had finally taken an interest in who else was in attendance. She was looking around, not ostentatiously, but looking. I found myself watching her.

When the senator finished, the master of ceremonies made a few more remarks and said, "Enjoy your dinner."

That was the signal for an army of waiters

to come marching out of the kitchen area bearing salads and wine bottles. They left a bottle of white and a bottle of red at each table. At our table the car dealer took it upon himself to do the pouring. Since I thought it possible I might need a wit or two at some point, I stuck with water. Marisa and Isolde took a glass of white. Isolde sipped and made a face. California wine, apparently.

I was watching the head table. I figured if I kept my eyes on the president, I would see whatever was coming. If anything. He was on his feet now, shaking hands up and down the head table. Two Secret Service types who looked as if they could place in a Mr. America contest stood immediately behind him. Grafton was beside them, his hands at his sides, scrutinizing faces in the crowd.

I wondered what the admiral was thinking. If the president got popped here tonight . . . Just the thought gave me goose bumps. I had read books and watched television shows about the Kennedy assassination from the time I was old enough to toddle; if the president went down tonight, Jake Grafton and I were going to be cussed, discussed and dissected by the press and conspiracy theorists until the coming of the next ice age. It was not a pleasant prospect.

When the president finished pumping hands at the head table, he went around the near end of the table into the crowd and began shaking hands and greeting people at each table. The spotlights stayed on him. The two Secret Service types and Jake Grafton accompanied him, just a little behind. Meanwhile the waiters were completing the salad and wine service and accumulating plates on side tables, preparing to serve them to the seated multitude.

I eyed those tables. Of course, no one knew who was getting which plate. Then I saw that the head table was being served directly out of the kitchen by guys and gals who looked suspiciously like Secret Service. They were leaving nothing to chance.

The president's progress was slow. It seemed that he knew a lot of these folks, or pretended he did. He took his time at each table, and someone was always standing up to take a picture or two. Grip, smile sincerely, pose, say a few polite words, then do it all over again. Obviously this was going to take a while.

He was finished with the first row and starting on the second when the waiters began serving the main course. He was going to shake hands all through dinner. I guess he didn't like Chicken Cordon Bleu any more than I did.

I slurped water and watched the crowd and the president, trying to take it all in.

Soon, Qasim thought, and tried to concentrate on what the lady on his left was saying. Something about her daughter who was attending Smith College. "These young ladies at Smith . . . they talk about a 'third sex,' and wear tails sticking out of their clothes, date each other and just do what all. Of course, *my* daughter would *never* do such nonsense."

Qasim didn't know what to say. He glanced at the president, who was shaking hands twenty-five feet away.

He was rescued by the woman on his right, who leaned around and spoke to the Smith mother. "They didn't behave like that when *I* attended Smith," she declared. "So much bad behavior, nowadays. These young women — what can they be thinking?"

"An excellent question," Qasim murmured, but the ladies paid no attention.

A half hour or so into this production, I was aware that Marisa, seated on my right, had stiffened. She was staring.

I glanced at her face, which was a mask of concentration. Her attention was focused on a table in the middle of the room.

I looked that way. There were a dozen tables that she might be looking at.

"Marisa," I whispered, to get her attention. "What do you see?"

She didn't take her eyes off whatever she was looking at, nor did she answer me. My stomach tried to turn over. My instincts said *this is it,* yet I saw nothing out of the ordinary. People, just a sea of people . . .

She pushed back her chair and stood, walked behind my chair and started for the middle of the room. "Excuse me," she said mechanically to the folks around us and started off.

I got a glimpse of a pistol butt in her right hand, partially concealed in the folds of her dress. Holy damn! *Where had that come from?* Adrenaline whacked me in the heart. I uncoiled from my chair and started after her.

The Secret Service agents standing here and there gave us a glance. One or two shifted nervously, but then they saw the red tag dangling from my neck and relaxed. They were really focused on the president and the people around him; they were still fifty feet away to our right.

Marisa crossed into the center of the room, threading her way between tables.

Me — I was so damn worried I almost peed my pants. If she pointed that shooter at the president, I was going to break her neck before she pulled the trigger.

I was surveying the tables ahead as she walked. Of course, just when I was near panic, she turned ninety degrees to the right and headed for a table beside the one the president was standing at.

"When I shake hands with the president," Qasim asked the Smith mother, "would you take my picture?"

"Of course," she said, looking at the camera. "Is it on?"

"Oh, yes. Just aim and push that button right there."

"My daughter has a camera like this. I can manage."

Satisfied, Qasim took another look at the president at the next table, then glanced around, one last time. To his horror, he saw Marisa walking toward him. Tommy Carmellini was right behind her.

Jake Grafton caught my eye. I mouthed the words "She's got a gun," and he nodded, once. His expression didn't change. My gaze left him, and I tried to scrutinize faces at the tables we were approaching.

Then I saw that someone was watching us, one of the men seated at the next table the president would visit. When he saw Marisa coming toward him, he couldn't look away. He looked maybe fifty or fifty-five, with salt-and-pepper hair and a Vandyke goatee. Wearing a tux and red cumberbund. Trim, middle-sized, with a roundish face, and sitting down.

Now the president shook the last hand and turned toward the seated man's table. Marisa ignored him. Her focus was on the man with the Vandyke, and she was walking quickly, right into the glare of the spotlights.

She walked up to the table so she was on his right, maybe three feet from him. He was turned, looking right at her, when she raised the pistol and shot him in the chest.

The report was like a cannon shot. Women screamed and men dove for cover. Abu Qasim lunged for her and grabbed at the pistol. He got her left arm instead, but she ignored his grasp and, with the gun against his chest, shot him three more times as fast as she could pull the trigger. The slugs literally hammered him out of the chair onto the floor.

Marisa would have shot him a couple more times, I think, but I reached around her, pushed her sideways and grabbed the gun out of her hand. Had to, or the Secret Service agent ten feet in front of me who was in the process of drawing his pistol would have shot her dead.

So she went to the floor beside Qasim while half the people in the place screamed or shouted and everyone scrambled for cover. It was the damnedest scene I have ever witnessed.

I put the pistol in my trouser pocket and bent down. Qasim was dead as a mackerel, glassy eyes staring at nothing. Not even much blood around the bullet holes. He had died within a few heartbeats after the first bullet hit him, right in the pump, it looked like. How he managed to grab her, I don't know.

Marisa was ashen, holding her arm, which was bleeding from a long scratch.

What on earth?

I seized her arm, looked at the wound, then opened Qasim's right hand. He was wearing a ring with a sharp point on it.

Grafton materialized at my elbow. He, too, saw the ring with the sticker.

Marisa was gasping. "My arm . . ." she managed. "It's on fire."

"The bastard poisoned her," I said. "Like he was going to do to the president."

Grafton stood and shouted. "Get back,

give us room. We need a medical team and stretcher, right now!" When Grafton shouts, you can hear it in the next county, even over all that noise.

Two teams of paramedics came running. Secret Service agents with drawn pistols had surrounded the president, who was trying to force his way through them toward Marisa, Grafton and me. The agents weren't letting him pass.

The place was pandemonium, with screams, a million shouted conversations, Secret Service agents with guns shouting orders and the master of ceremonies at the podium bellowing into the loudspeaker microphone.

Over all this hubbub I heard someone ask Grafton, "Who'd she shoot?"

And I heard his answer. "Abu Qasim."

I glanced up and saw that Jack Yocke had forced his way through the knot of people. He had asked the question. He had a camera in his hand. Before anyone could do or say anything, he snapped a couple of photos of Qasim and Marisa while the docs were injecting Marisa with something in a hypodermic needle.

Secret Service agents began pushing people away from us. Some of them had submachine guns in their hands, I saw, and they were herding people out of the room.

In five minutes, while the medics worked on Marisa, they cleared the room of everyone except law and the president, who was standing nearby having it out with his bodyguards.

Marisa ignored the paramedics. She was looking only at Jake Grafton, talking to him. "I had to help him," she said. "He threatened to kill Isolde if I didn't."

"I thought it was something like that," he said.

"She's the only . . . the only . . ." She went into convulsions, her muscles contracting spasmodically. Her back arched off the floor.

When she was able, she managed, "It's better like this. I'm tired of living."

She was having great difficulty breathing and couldn't control the contractions of her facial muscles. Whatever the poison was, it was really horrible stuff.

"Who killed Jean Petrou?" Grafton asked.

"I did."

"Why?"

"Jean met with Qasim. I saw him. He sold us out. Made a deal with the Devil himself . . . for money. He was that kind of man. Immature, self-indulgent, without scruples. Yes, *I* killed him, and *I'm glad I did.*"

"We've got to get her to the hospital, right

now," one of the medics said. Without further ado they lifted Marisa onto a stretcher.

I elbowed the doctor out of the way, bent down and grabbed a hand. She latched on to me as if I were a life ring. "Oh, Tommy, I —"

She gagged . . . her tongue protruded, then she tried to breathe and couldn't. The medics hustled her out. I was going to go with her, but Grafton stopped me with a hand on my arm. "There's nothing you can do, Tommy."

The president came over and stood looking down at the body of Abu Qasim, the open mouth and the lifeless, staring eyes.

He put a hand on Grafton's shoulder, almost as if to steady himself, then passed a sleeve across his brow and turned away.

Huntington Winchester was standing there, being restrained by an agent. The president reached for him and draped his arm around his shoulder, and the two of them walked away, leaning on each other.

CHAPTER
TWENTY-FOUR

We were still in the middle of the ballroom watching the paramedics put Qasim's body on a stretcher when two agents brought Jerry Hay Smith in. The spotlights were off, and presumably so were the television cameras.

Grafton faced him. "The *Washington Post* is going to run a story in the morning about the CIA operation that resulted in the death of Abu Qasim. You're a part of it. If you deny a single word or try to give a different version, I'll have you prosecuted for revealing classified CIA operations. Do you understand?"

"You can't shut me up like that!"

"Want to try me?"

"You son of a bitch!"

Grafton merely looked at Smith and spoke coldly. "Don't fuck with me, little man. I don't have the patience or stomach for it. You've been warned."

Grafton jerked his head at the agents, and they led Smith out.

"Where'd she get that gun?" I asked Grafton. I kept my voice low.

His answer gave me my second biggest shock of the evening. "I left it for her," he said softly, "taped to the underside of the table."

"You what?"

"You heard me."

I was skeptical. "The Secret Service didn't find it?"

"I told them it was there so they would leave it undisturbed."

I gaped.

"Had to clear it with the brass, who said hell no, but the president said to do it." Grafton shook his head. "He isn't the wisest man who ever sat in the Oval Office, but he's got his share of guts."

"But *why* did you do it?"

"That was her price for spotting Qasim here tonight. She wanted to kill him. Didn't want to watch someone else do it — she wanted to kill him herself."

"Just like she killed her husband," I muttered, still reeling.

Grafton shot me one of those looks, as if I were slow on the uptake. "You didn't buy that fake confession, did you? Isolde Petrou poisoned her son. Marisa told her what he'd done, proved it to her, so Isolde sprinkled digitalis on his food."

"But —"

"You were there. When Marisa saw Isolde about to pour the stuff on Jean's food, Marisa pretended to recognize someone in the kitchen. That was a diversion, so you wouldn't notice what Isolde was doing."

"Isolde," I said, trying to process it.

"Pretty fast thinking on Marisa's part," Grafton said with a hint of admiration.

"But why cover up for the mother who murdered her son?"

He gave me another of those looks. I was really earning them today. "She's dying — what did you expect her to say? She loves Isolde as a daughter loves her mother. And she knew what Jean was. She was probably thinking of killing him herself; then her mother-in-law beat her to it."

I was in the Secret Service command center with Jake Grafton when the reports began coming in. Robin Cloyd was manning the desk. She hadn't gone to the dinner but had been stationed here at the nerve center as Grafton's ears.

Abu Qasim had come to the fund-raiser under the name of Samuel Israel Rohtstein, from Brooklyn. He had a driver's license in that name in his wallet, along with credit cards. In the hours that followed, investigators visited the address and showed photocopies of the license to his neighbors, all of whom identified Samuel Israel Rohtstein. But as the hours passed, the investigators discovered that Mr. Rohtstein only went back a couple of years. Where he had lived before he moved to the flat in Brooklyn, no one knew.

"So he was planning this for two years?" I asked Grafton.

"Probably more than that," Grafton said thoughtfully. "Setting up a false identity, giving to political candidates . . . I suspect we'll find he devoted a great deal of time and expense building an identity in preparation for the day in the distant future when he might get a chance to assassinate the president."

"Where do you think he got the poison?"

"From Surkov, of course. Surkov had contacts in Russian intelligence and was selling passports and identity papers. He could also have supplied the poison. Since he then knew far too much, Qasim killed him. Dead tongues don't wag."

The reports dribbled in. I got out of the way. Grafton and the police, Secret Service and FBI honchos huddled and conferred and did their thing. Someone mentioned that the Secret Service had taken possession of the television videos, which weren't going to be released to the media.

Grafton came over at one point, and I said, "Why not do a DNA test on Qasim and Marisa, see if they really are father and daughter?"

"Would it matter?" he asked.

Seeing the look on my face, he smiled gently and said, "Go home. You're done. Take Callie and Amy back to Washington. I'll be home in a few days."

I nodded, got up, shook his hand and turned to go.

"Thanks, Tommy," he said.

"Yeah."

I left the hotel via a side door. Outside on the sidewalk I could look straight up between the buildings at a crisp, clear winter's night. I stood there sucking in air and thinking about things while the media held a three-ring circus complete with lights, cameras and talking heads in front of the Walden. Abu Qasim had made the news worldwide, although not in the way he intended. Sometimes life goes like that.

The next morning Callie, Amy and I caught the train to Washington at Penn Station. I bought a copy of the morning *Washington Post* at a newsstand before I boarded. Sure enough, Jack Yocke had the whole front page. Photos of Qasim and Marisa on the floor covered half the page. I scanned the story. Some of it was true, most of it wasn't, which I guess is about par for any news story. Neither Grafton's nor my name was mentioned. After all, we hadn't been there.

Across the aisle the women conferred, about what I don't know. This mother-daughter thing is pretty powerful stuff. I stirred through the rest of the newspaper, then gave up on it and sat looking out the window.

Having had last night and that morning to think about it, I realized that Grafton didn't know any more about who killed Jean Petrou than I did. What he had told me last night was just a plausible story. It could have easily been Marisa who sprinkled the digitalis.

Perhaps it didn't really matter who killed him. For all I knew, they both did it.

Grafton probably knew that, too.

In the weeks that followed, Jerry Hay Smith wrote reams about his adventure and did a few talk shows, yet he never breathed a word different from what Jack Yocke printed. I don't think he felt threatened by Grafton, although maybe he did, but Yocke made him out to be a hero, and I suspect Jerry Hay sorta liked that. He played it for all it was worth.

Huntington Winchester and Simon Cairnes patched up their differences, apparently. I saw an article in a magazine a few months later about how they had both endowed a scholarship for medical students in Owen Winchester's name.

Amy Carol got engaged to her stockbroker. The wedding was set for July.

All that was yet to come. Six days after the Walden Hotel affair, Jake Grafton got back to town and called me into his office.

"Hey," he said as I walked in. He gestured to a chair. I sat.

Then I saw what was in a glass ashtray on his desk. It was Abu Qasim's ring, complete with pointy sticker.

He saw me looking at it and said, "Go ahead. They cleaned all the poison off."

I picked it up. The sticker could be flipped out from the body of the ring. When it was lying on the ring, it was almost invisible.

I laid it back in the ashtray. "Marisa?" I asked.

Grafton shook his head. He started to say something, then changed his mind.

I just sat there feeling glum.

After a while he said, "One of the television networks got a cassette from Qasim on Friday morning. He apparently made it weeks or months before, then mailed it Thursday afternoon. They decided not to run it. Want to watch it?"

"No."

Grafton shrugged. "It's a real piece of work, full of rantings about religion and jihad and the duty of the faithful and how rotten civilization is."

"And he was going to fix civilization and glorify God with murder?"

"That's about the size of it. By the way, the Secret Service is going to release some of the TV footage. They have digitally suppressed your image — you aren't in it."

"Well, I really wasn't there, according to the *Post.*"

"So tell me, why didn't you tackle Marisa and take the pistol away from her?"

"Is this for a report or my evaluation or something?"

"Nope. Just curious."

I sat there for a bit, trying to remember just how it was. "You told me to use my best judgment," I said. Then disgust washed over me. "Hell, you knew I wouldn't do that or you would have told me about the gun."

Grafton's eyebrows wagged. "I wanted you to play it by ear, process everything you were seeing. You are amazingly good at that."

He was lying, of course, probably to make me feel better. So I explained: "I could see her staring at someone and, of course, I figured it was ol' Abu. Then she popped up and marched off, and I saw the butt of the pistol in her hand. I followed right along. Figured I could break her neck if she aimed it at anyone I liked."

He thought about that for a while, then said, "You really liked her, didn't you?"

I nodded.

He eyed me critically. "So how you doing, Tommy?"

"Okay, I guess."

"Right! Well, I fixed you up on a blind date. Tonight at" — he named the restaurant, a popular place right on the Potomac in Georgetown. "You know it?"

"Sure."

"She'll meet you there at seven."

"Oh, man, you didn't need to do this to me!"

"Tommy, this woman has been hot to have a date with you. I have no idea why. Callie asked me to do this for her. Smile. Eat too much. Enjoy some feminine companionship, charm her and take her home. Or whatever."

I didn't know what to say.

"How do I get out of this?" I finally asked.

"You don't. Be there at seven — that's an order. Wear a smile. Now get out of my office."

I got to the joint five minutes late. I was trying to be right on the dot, but parking in Georgetown was a mess. I had to walk four blocks. If he hadn't said Callie asked me to do this, I would have refused. I figured I owed Callie.

When I got there, I gave my name to the girl on the reservation desk. She checked her list, then said, "Right this way, Mr. Carmellini," and led off. I trailed along.

The lady at the table was facing the other way. I recognized the dark brown hair, swept over one ear. I froze. Naw, it couldn't be . . .

"Marisa?"

She saw me and smiled. When I bent over for a kiss I saw the bandage on her arm.

I squatted down, my eyes inches from hers. People were staring curiously, but I didn't care. "I thought you were dead."

"I asked Grafton not to tell you. I knew you'd come visit, and I didn't want you to see me like that."

"I thought that stuff was fatal, which was why Qasim was out to scratch the president with it."

"It would have been fatal," she admitted, "but Grafton had the antidote in his pocket. The emergency people gave me an injection within thirty seconds."

"Grafton . . ."

"The admiral thought it would be poison — that was the only practical possibility — and he thought Qasim had probably gotten it from Surkov. He called a man he knew in Russian intelligence, and they had a long chat. Then he went out that afternoon and had a druggist make up the antidote."

I kissed her cheek gently.

She smiled again. She had a hell of a nice smile.

"So what's good here?" I asked, seating myself across the table from her and picking up my menu.

"Oh, everything, I imagine," she replied, "if you're alive and with someone you care about."

"Well, by golly, we'll find out," I said cheerfully.

It was a great evening.

ABOUT THE AUTHOR

Stephen Coonts is the author of fourteen *New York Times* bestselling novels, the first of which was the classic flying tale, *Flight of the Intruder*, which spent more than six months at the top of *The New York Times* bestseller list. His novels have been published around the world and translated into more than a dozen languages. He and his wife, Deborah, live in Colorado.